HER COWBOY PRINCE

COWBOY PRINCES #2

MADELINE ASH

Cover design: Dominic Brown

ISBN-13: 978-0-6485809-7-3

COWBOY PRINCES

Her Cowboy King

Her Cowboy Prince

The King's Cowboy

Mum
For before, now and always.

BEFORE

"He's dead. All three of them are dead."

The phone crackled in Frankie Cowan's ear as the words knifed between her ribs. Stunned, her breath gave a little *hic* and she halted on the dirt track that led to her friends' ranch on the outskirts of Sage Haven. *Dead?*

"Philip." Dread shut her eyes and she almost lost her balance. "What are you talking about?"

Her boss didn't answer. His soft crying fed her panic.

All three.

Dead.

No. The three cowboy brothers she'd spent years watching over couldn't be—not while she'd been out of town—

The ground pitched beneath her and she buckled, landing on her knees with a hand braced in front of her. This was a mistake. They weren't gone.

Kris isn't gone.

"Don't make me guess, Philip," she said, fear harsh in her voice. "Report."

"It collapsed." He spoke through his tears. "The balcony. While they were banqueting. King Vinci. Prince Aron. And— and . . ." He made a noise of muffled grief, unable to finish, and she knew he meant the king's middle brother, Prince Noel.

1

She sank back on her shins in relief. Philip's call wasn't about the brothers she'd come to know in this quiet paradise in southern Montana, but their extended family in a kingdom halfway across the world.

The king, his son, and his brother. The royal family of Kiraly.

Except. If the royal family were dead, that meant—

Her chest squeezed so tightly her ribs threatened to snap. "No," she breathed.

"Yes." Philip's own whisper was thin with pain.

"What—" She broke off as her attention settled on the brothers' ranch ahead. *Oh, boys.* Did they know yet? Were they inside with their father discussing it right now? "What's going to happen?"

The answer was obvious. Her heart raged against it.

"Prince Erik is unwell," she made herself say, and pinched the bridge of her nose. Erik was the cowboys' father, youngest brother to the deceased king—and sudden heir to the Kiralian throne. "Too unwell. He can't do it."

"Then you know the answer, Frankie."

She knew.

It was going to destroy her life.

"Your reports show Prince Markus is a good man," Philip said, voice wavering. "A decent man."

Her guilt flared at Philip's mention of her reports and she tightened her grip on the phone, pushing herself to her feet. She staggered a little as she moved off the walking track that ran between the road and the long front fence of the brothers' property.

"Mark's steady," she said about the kindhearted firstborn cowboy as she braced a shoulder against one of the many trees that lined the path. "But you can't separate them. They're triplets, for God's sake—they can't survive apart. It won't work like this."

"They won't be separated."

"Then how do you—"

The answer kicked her in the chest.

He wanted Kris and Tommy to leave Montana. Leave their *ranch*. No way. She could imagine Mark stepping up to his duty no matter how it tore him apart. But his brothers belonged here, in this small town dwarfed by the Rockies. The only home they'd known in their twenty-five years. It had shaped them, defined them—taught them to live with humility and decency and an unflinching passion for honest work.

She'd kill to have been shaped by something so pure.

"Philip—"

"You've been promoted within the royal guard." His words silenced her. "You're now head of personal security to the new royal family."

Her heart stopped.

She was *what*?

"Congratulations." The well-wishes fell like a deadweight on her shoulders.

"No." Of all things holy, no. "That's your role—"

"Not anymore. I must focus my attention on training and advising Markus. He's never even visited Kiraly." Philip paused as if that fact was only just sinking in. He made a faint sound of distress. "I don't know if I can handle this."

"You can." She offered him the confidence she lacked as she turned to press her shoulder blades against the tree trunk. "But you'll need support, and that means replacing head of personal security with someone more experienced than me. Which, and you should be nodding along here, is basically everyone."

It had been four years since she'd traveled to Montana to prove herself capable of security. To get her foot in the door—not end up running the show. Had he lost his mind?

"Give me something small," she said. "Guard duty in the

tourist precinct. Night shift at the gate." People like her didn't get put in charge. "I haven't worked in the palace before. Promote someone else."

"No."

His snap of authority made her cold.

"You alone know these untrained princes, Frankie. You've spent time with them. You know the security they need. How they'll respond to it—how to prevent trouble. I'll train you, of course, but the job is yours and you won't disappoint me."

"But—"

"I'm sure your close friendship with Kristof will be advantageous."

Hardly. Her panic rose at the thought of Kris learning the truth. None of the brothers knew she was from Kiraly. That she'd deceived them. Monitored them. Reported their routines, plans and personalities back to Philip. They didn't realize she knew that beneath their cowboy swagger, their hard-muscled bodies coursed with royal blood.

She swallowed down a dry throat and said, "But we can't stay friends."

Not once Kris became an active Prince of Kiraly.

"Things will change." Philip's voice betrayed his exhaustion. "You'll return here immediately. I'm organizing a private plane. You have two hours to get to the airport."

"Cut me a break. I just got back to town," she said as her alarm swelled. "From a job *you* sent me on."

"Yes. I assumed that was why I've been unable to reach you."

She froze. She closed her eyes against a wave of dismay. "How long ago did it happen?"

"Yesterday." Loss hung in his long pause. "Erik has already informed us of his intention to abdicate. Markus will bring the official letter. The boys are coming, Frankie. Together. They leave Montana tomorrow morning."

Thudding her head back against the trunk, she squinted at the spring sky. Spinning. The world was spinning so fast it was going to haul her guts up. "This is insane."

"I've thought that myself."

It was the thread of outrage in his unsteady response that finally wove her back to the start of their conversation. Horror met her there. "Philip," she said. "Which balcony?"

"Second floor, west wing."

"But . . . that was new, wasn't it? Part of the renovations?"

"Yes."

Her blood chilled as she breathed, "That shouldn't have collapsed."

"No, it shouldn't have," he answered just as softly.

"Shit." She pushed away from the tree, but didn't know whether to continue to the ranch or double back into town. This was too much. "What the hell happened?"

"If only I knew." Grief made him sound older than his sixty-five years. "I don't have the resilience to find out. I can't bear it. The authorities have already declared it a tragic accident—the result of construction shortcuts taken to meet the tight schedule and remain within budget. In a sense, I want that to be true, but . . . could you look into it?"

Dazed, she lowered the phone, shaking her head. Could she?

The ranch in the distance had become the closest thing to a home she'd ever known. The log and stone homestead, the surrounding meadows and mountains, and the three young men who'd ushered her into their midst. Identical, yet as comparable as three glasses of amber alcohol—each packing a wildly different experience. Mark was a reliable farmhouse ale, Kris a searing Fireball whiskey, and Tommy—well, he was a lone ranger's drink —undeterminable, but with a potency that could strip the enamel off unwary teeth.

Frankie had scarcely admitted it to herself, but recently,

she'd toyed with the idea of staying for good. Leaving Philip's employ and living out her life in Sage Haven—allowing herself to accept the dream it offered.

Now that dream was impossible. Due to a tragic architectural failing or something more sinister, she couldn't begin to guess. But having her first real shot at happiness go crashing down along with the balcony?

That pissed her off enough that she wanted to know who to blame.

Balling her free hand, she raised the phone to her ear. "We'll keep this quiet," she said, and set off along the track toward Sage Haven. "Mourn it as an accident and hope that's exactly what it was."

And if it wasn't?

Protectiveness hit her bloodstream, pumping purpose through her body. If it wasn't, then the murder of a royal family should be all the motivation she needed to track down the person responsible. But honestly—no one would escape punishment for messing up the lives of her boys.

"What will you tell the princes?" Philip asked.

Finally, she was thinking fast. "Nothing. They've got enough to worry about."

"But for their safety—"

"They'll get their own guards." No one would touch them. Not on her watch. "Two each, at all times. More if they leave the grounds."

"Guards are already stationed throughout the palace." Philip sounded unsure. "It's never been protocol to shadow our royal family down every hall."

She glanced back at the ranch and its inherent safety. "These princes don't know that."

There was a beat of silence. "I take it you've accepted the promotion?"

Had she really been given a choice? Picking up her pace, she swallowed her doubt. It was time. To go back to Kiraly—to do what she'd once dared herself to do. Prove her worth. Find her value. If she focused on that, she might be able to ignore the bleakness rippling like an oil spill inside her at the thought of returning home.

If only she'd gone back years ago. She'd achieved what she'd set out to do the moment she found the princes hidden in this mountain-ringed valley. She shouldn't have agreed to Philip's suggestion that she stay and keep watch on them—she shouldn't have allowed herself to get attached.

But she hadn't planned on volatile, sexy-as-hell Kris.

No. Not Kris. Not anymore.

Prince Kristof.

She hadn't braced for his tameless charm, wicked grin, and fast friendship. For her untrained heart to open for him. A truth she'd never told him—just as he'd never trusted her enough to share his royal heritage. For years she'd pretended she didn't know. She'd waited, desperate for that sign she meant more to him than the rest of the clueless people in this town—more than the women he charmed into his bed. For years, Frankie had waited to share her own identity in return.

Trust me, her heart begged whenever his blue eyes darkened with the desire he'd never quite acted on. *Tell me.*

Now it was too late.

If he told her today, it wouldn't be out of trust. The situation had him cornered. It would pry the secret out of his big, rough hands with little care of what it meant to her.

Shame bled into her hurt. Her secrets would air with his, though he'd call them by a dirtier name.

Lies.

She couldn't handle that pain. Not today. Breaking into a run, she hurled that future confrontation from her mind.

7

"I accept," she answered. Because despite the unbearable strain it would cause between her and Kris, despite her fear and guilt and shortcomings, there was one thing the past four years had taught her. "I'll protect these men with my life."

Kris Jaroka should have seen it coming.

No lie lasts forever.

He rolled his farm truck to a halt in front of Rose's Diner and pulled the keys, twirling them around his index finger as he stepped out. A casual act to fool his gut into relaxing and his heart into slowing down, because he'd spent all morning fixating on this moment and had yet to imagine how it could end well.

Didn't matter.

He was going to ask her anyway.

Frankie. She was back in town. When not away on an investigative case, she lived in the main street of Sage Haven, renting a hidey-hole above the worst coffee-brewer in Montana. She didn't seem to care that her apartment wallpaper puckered and tore or that the bathroom tiles were stained with he-didn't-want-to-know-what. As long as there was coffee and food within reach, irrespective of quality, all was good for Frankie.

He strode into the diner and nodded to the man behind the counter. A curtain blocked a staircase to the left of the register, and Kris slipped around it, taking the steps three at a time. Only two apartments were up here—the diner owner's and Frankie's—and naturally, hers was the one with scuff marks on the door, an apple sticker on the knob, and an old piece of paper taped beside it, reading: *Not the restroom. Turn around, asshole.*

Nerves thundered through him. He slid a hand into the back pocket of his jeans, taking in his last breath as the cowboy she'd believed him to be.

He knocked.

"I'm busy!" Frankie snapped from inside.

From her, that was close enough to permission to enter.

He stepped into the tiny studio apartment, which was nothing more than a cramped living space with a double bed down the far end. An empty takeout box sat open on the kitchen counter, a scrunched napkin beside it.

"Morning," he said, kicking the door closed with his boot heel.

She didn't look up from where she stood side-on at the foot of the bed, stuffing a jewel-bright jacket into her backpack. A small blessing, because all it took was the sight of her to nudge his lust awake like a toe prodding a dozing beast. Stirring, it focused lazily on her—then stretched wide with feral intent.

Blood hot, Kris moved in and set his keys down, leaning a hip casually against the counter.

It was getting worse. Harder to pretend their friendship was innocent, because desire had him craving her in every way imaginable. Ways he had *yet* to imagine. It was a mutual attraction he couldn't act on. He recognized the lust in her eyes—had felt it hum and crackle between them for so long, the anticipation was daily torture—but she refused to outwardly acknowledge it and he wasn't stupid enough to ruin their friendship by making a move she'd regret.

But it was building. A mounting surge of chemistry toward an end point, a moment that wouldn't be denied, a truth they were going to have to face head-on.

Unless she was about to refuse his invitation.

"Welcome home, angel," he said, the phrase bitter in his mouth. Not home for much longer.

"See, when you call me names like angel, the issue is that I can't decide *how* to castrate you." She yanked at the zip on her bag with one hand while the other ran amok in her short hair. It was the color of rust on a barbed-wire fence and just as spikey on top, with the sides and back trimmed close. "Not that I don't want to."

"Whichever way you decide," he said, touching the brim of his hat, "it'll be a big job."

She faced him, head tilted and eyes narrowed.

He grinned.

Amusement flickered in her green eyes, but she crossed her arms. "What are you doing here?"

His grin faded as his heart pounded.

He was here to tell the truth.

Denial jammed in his throat as he removed his hat. "Firstly, to check in on my favorite girl."

"Yeah, I don't have time for you right now."

He frowned. "Have you consumed recently?"

She seemed hangry; her white skin was paler than usual.

"I'll get you something to eat downstairs," he said.

She jabbed a finger toward an empty coffee cup and paper bag, discarded on the rumpled blankets.

"So what's the matter?" He noted her passport sticking out of her back pocket, and was instantly distracted by the sweet curve of her ass. God above, he loved those jeans.

"It's complicated," she said, picking up her phone from the bed and swiping it unlocked. "And like I said, I don't have time."

"Need a hug?" he asked, far too casually.

She hardly ever touched him. No contact was Frankie's unique brand of agony. Except for her sexual energy—that touched him *everywhere*.

"If you try to hug me, I'll bite you." She cast him a small, *see-if-I'm-joking* smile as she twisted and sat on the end of the bed. Lifting a foot, she tugged hard at the laces of her chunky boots. "I'm having an epically bad day."

"Why?" Concern instantly rolled his shoulders back. "Did you get hurt?"

She stilled, and then slid a strange glance at him. She didn't answer.

"Right." He crossed the room to stand in front of her. "Let me see."

"You can't help." She huffed out a breath and muttered, "It's too late." She set back to work on her boots, yanking the laces.

"Frankie." His concern swelled into frustration, but he did his best to leash it. "Show me."

"I'm not injured." Punctuated with another hard pull of her bootlaces. "There are changes at work that are out of my control, and that hurts, okay? I'm overwhelmed and so far out of my depth, I feel like I'm already sinking."

He stared down at her, and she glared back.

"Alright. Hang on." Sighing, he dropped to one knee, his eyes on her feet. These laces were one short-tempered tug away from tearing clean off.

She fell still. She was a fighter by nature, but always retreated into motionlessness when he got too close. Her stillness came with a flush on her cheeks and hunger in her eyes.

Yeah.

Suppressed desire was having a fucking field day with them.

Her next breath was shaky.

Like two hands trapping a fly, his focus contracted—latched around the woman before him. It hit him, then. He'd never been like this. On his knees before her, one greedy movement away from filling the space between her parted legs. Victim to the thought, his gaze slid up her shins, skimmed over her thighs. Christ, he needed to—*stop looking*—needed to just—*stand the hell up*—pull himself together.

At the sound of her hard swallow, he grabbed his self-control by the scruff of its neck and shoved his attention down. He reached for her laces, ignoring how she jerked her hands away.

"You shouldn't do that," she muttered.

The pulse in his neck throbbed as he released the tension at her ankles, passing the slack down the boot. "Excuse me for saving your feet from blood loss."

"You shouldn't be—there."

Still lost in desire, he asked, "Where?"

"On your knees." She sounded breathless.

Slowly, he raised his head. It was all too easy to imagine her words as a command. One he'd willingly follow, along with every pleasure-drenched plea she made after that.

She sucked in air and raised a hand, scratching her flushed cheek as she fixed her attention out the window.

After he'd loosened the laces and knotted them, then fastened the buckles that clasped over the top, he dared to place his palms over her feet. Greed and panic fueled this reckless contact. For too long he'd let his feelings hide in the shadows of friendship. Today was all they had—the brink of their future.

"Frankie," he said, looking up. "I'm going to ask you something."

Something that was supposed to be about moving to Kiraly with him, but was probably going to come out, *Can we stop pretending now?*

She met his stare in a flash, mouth tightening before she said, "You finished?" Shifting her boots out from under his hands, she stood.

He shot to his feet in front of her, achingly close, a short swoop away from her quick-tempered lips. Attraction glinted in his blood, bright and bliss-tipped. If she said yes, her tight grey tank would peel off in seconds, but he'd take his time with her skinny-leg jeans, and those punk boots would put him back between her knees . . . *God, please let her say yes.*

"Some space, please," she said sharply.

His whole body was tense. Locked and howling for contact. "Is that what you really want?"

Startled, she scanned his face.

"Serious question," he said, voice low. "Would you rather a steady friendship or honesty?"

Alarm widened her eyes.

He practically growled, "Frankie—"

"I can't do this," she said, stepping away.

"Please." He grabbed her arm, his grip loose and breakable, but—*there*.

She halted before half-turning back, her throat moving as she swallowed. "You're touching me."

No shit. His heart thundered. It was either the worst or best time in their entire friendship to push her like this, but he brushed his thumb along her forearm and said on a rough murmur, "I've always wanted to touch you."

"Oh, God," she muttered under her breath, looking away.

"I know you feel it," he challenged, because he had nothing to lose. Not today. "And I've felt it every—"

"I *can't*, Kris." She cut him off, nudging out of his hold. After swiping up her backpack and slinging it over her shoulder, she slid her phone into her pocket and moved toward the door.

He stared after her. Panic landed hard in the chest. "Where are you going?"

She looped her other arm through the backpack. "I have another job."

"Already?"

"Yeah, it's come as a shock to me, too." She didn't meet his eye as she scanned her apartment, one hand moving to touch the passport in her back pocket.

"Wait." This wasn't part of the plan. They were supposed to order food and chat about her latest case before he shared the way his life had just shattered and the future they could rebuild together. "We need to talk."

"You might, but I need to go," she said, voice thickening as she turned away. "Time's up."

Then he'd take time she didn't have. He strode across the apartment, feeling her eyes on him as he passed her. Reaching the door, he pressed a palm to the surface and took a rallying breath.

He faced her. "I should have told you years ago—"

"Then you wasted years of opportunities," she said, "because my flight leaves in forty minutes."

"To hell with your flight." It came out as a snarl as she walked up to him, his alarm finding release in his fraying temper. No woman in his life had felt like Frankie—and his reckless libido ensured that was no small claim. He couldn't do this without her. "I'll buy you a new ticket. This can't wait."

"Years, did you say?" She stared at his chest, and his body tensed in a silent demand for her touch. "Clearly it can."

"I—" He couldn't think. Couldn't believe this was happening. She refused to let him confess his feelings while she was running out the door, yet he had so much more to say and literally no other time to tell her.

"Get out of my way, Kris."

No. He couldn't actually leave without her. "Please listen—"

"You listen to *me*," she said, the last word catching in her throat. "You have to let me go."

Body rigid in protest, he stepped aside. What else could he do? Blurt his true lineage as she marched out the door? Call his suggestion for her to move across the world with him down the stairs?

"How long will you take?" he asked, grasping at straws. He could fly back to Sage Haven to meet her after this case and explain everything. But he'd have to time it perfectly or town gossip would tell her for him and there'd be nothing worse. "When can we talk?"

He frowned at the look she cut back at him—burning with regret, wide with pain.

She didn't answer, but for one unbearably hot second, her gaze slipped down his body like she might command him to his knees for real. Then she turned away, features shuttering. "See you, Kris."

She closed the door behind her.

He waited until her footsteps faded before slamming his fist against it. As predicted, their conversation hadn't ended well.

And he hadn't told her a damned thing.

NOW

1

Kris had been king-in-training for less than two weeks and he'd already started a war.

At least, that was what Philip seemed to believe.

"You walked out!" Philip exclaimed as he burst into the royal study.

Exclusive to the monarch, the round room was positioned at the top of the palace's tallest tower. Kris had only recently started working in here since arriving in Kiraly three and a half months ago, and the curved walls and panoramic views made him uneasily aware of just how far away he was from having earth beneath his feet. A large balcony overlooked Kira City, and he stood in-line with the open glass doors—because blame it on the intense summer heat or a well-founded wariness of palace balconies, Kris wasn't keen to set foot out there.

He turned to Philip, his peace shattered, as the royal advisor strode across the room to stand before Kris's desk. Thin as a grass blade and flushed with spluttering indignation, the man said, "Your Highness, with all due respect, you can't just *walk out* of the Bergstadt Summit!"

Well. Kris returned to the desk and lounged back in his chair, propping his boots up beside his laptop. "Should've told me that before I went in."

Philip appeared to be holding back some very strong words as Mark entered the study. The look his brother shot Kris as he strode to the lushly-padded sofa against the far wall was equal parts amusement and exasperation.

"I didn't think I had to." Philip's voice rose.

Kris picked up a pen and clicked it. "I'm not psychic, Phil."

"It's Philip!"

"Kris," Mark said, sitting down with a sigh. "Give it a rest."

"Prince Kristof," Philip said, and started pacing. "This summit has been an annual tradition for Kiraly and our bordering nations for almost a century. To get up and leave—while a neighboring minister is mid-presentation—is not only a major breach in royal etiquette but could be interpreted as an act of political antagonism."

Kris looked from his advisor to his brother. He raised a shoulder. "He was talking shit."

Philip made a sound that should have accompanied great physical pain.

"It doesn't matter." Mark frowned at Kris. "You sit through it anyway."

Sit through another hour of bull? "It didn't feel right."

"It is!" Philip raised his hands in frustration. "It is right! That's what kings do. You sit there—without sprawling like a male youth at the back of a school bus, I might add—and wait until the presentation has finished."

Mark was still frowning. "You'll have to apologize."

"Sure." Kris had figured that much. "I'll find him later."

"Publicly," his brother said firmly, even as he rolled his eyes.

"I'll sort it out." Kris tensed as his irritation resurfaced. The nerve of that minister, trying to manipulate the attending nations with scare tactics and a slick slideshow. "But we're not agreeing to his proposal."

"Markus." Philip spun to him desperately. "Are you quite sure you love Princess Ava?"

Kris scoffed, clicking the pen again.

Mark stiffened despite his smile. "Very sure."

Understatement. They'd scarcely arrived in Kiraly when Mark—his older brother by a whopping forty minutes—had gone and fallen in love. Ava was the last woman Kris would've imagined stealing his brother's heart, but something about her courage and scathing wit had clearly melted him. Their relationship had come hard won and without a tidy future.

"I need you to stay with me," Mark had begged Ava when all had seemed impossible. *"We'll figure this out."*

Kris had figured it out for them.

Mark would abdicate.

And Kris would take his place as king.

He was still reeling. He hadn't suggested abdication because he craved power. It was just that anyone with a beating heart could see it was the only way the pair could be happy.

It had to work. Happiness had become too scarce since leaving their ranch. Some days, Kris felt like an animal in an enclosure built for a different species. His strides down gleaming corridors bordered on agitated prowling, and sensing his brothers trapped beside him only made him want to dig their way out. At least one of them needed to be content and it was within his power to let that be Mark.

Even if it meant jumping the triplet queue so that Tommy—middle-born and seriously socially anxious—didn't have to rule.

"Markus," Philip said. "What are your thoughts on the matter?"

"Kris has a point about not agreeing to the proposal." Mark had sat in an antechamber, privately listening in on the summit while Kris had filled his place at the table. "I was thinking the same thing."

The plan was to keep Mark's intended abdication and Kris's ascension private while Kris learned the ropes. No need to get the public in a tizzy about the royal family shuffling power like a deck of cards. Not so soon after the tragedy that had killed the late ruling family and hauled Kris and his brothers here in the first place. Mark would continue to attend meetings and appearances as himself, as would Kris, but there would be events that expected the king in attendance and would just happen to receive Kris instead. Not his fault if they couldn't tell him and his brother apart.

The only people who knew were Kris and his brothers, their personal guards, Ava, her friend Zara, and Philip. The household staff who attended Mark and Ava at their mansion believed their king had simply relocated for Ava's privacy.

His advisor sighed. "Politics is about picking your battles."

"Then I pick this one." Kris held his advisor's unimpressed gaze. "That man was trying to sell us snake oil." A minister for agriculture, trying to convince all countries in attendance to form an agreement to use new pest-resistant seeds for their farming crops. A supposed protection against pests and plant disease from spreading across borders—but when Kris had asked for information on the existence of such threats, the man had failed to produce evidence. "I'll bet mega corp lobbyists are paying him a mint to show up here and convince us all to start buying this miracle product."

Philip frowned. "The modification is designed to protect the crops, Your Highness."

"From what?" Kris dragged his feet off the desk and stood. He gestured out the tower's eastern-facing window toward the lush farmland far below, bright green in the summer sunlight. "That's some of the healthiest damn farmland I've ever seen.

Rich soil, high crop yield. No tilling, and earthworms aplenty. You know we wouldn't just be buying the seeds—it's the fertilizers to go with them, the soil blends . . . The whole thing was a sales pitch disguised as a solution to a problem we don't have."

Philip blinked. "But he said—"

"I've visited our agriculture communities. Talked to the families who've been running Kiraly's farms for generations. They're good, hardworking people." Farmers always were. "They know what's best for their crops. If they want these seeds, they're welcome to buy them. But I'll shoot myself in the foot before I sign anything that mandates where they source their supplies."

Philip breathed in loudly through his nose, running a hand down the front of his blazer. He cleared his throat. Then, tugging at the hem, he answered in a level tone, "Don't walk out next time."

Kris sat back down. "Fine."

Mark caught his eye, shaking his head with the hint of a smile.

"It seems we're finished for the day." Philip's arms came to rest by his sides, his chin level with the floor. "If you agree, Your Highness?"

Recognizing the embedded request, Kris gave him a nod. "Sure." Then he paused, and picked up a thin folder from his desk. "I've been meaning to ask—is this all the security briefing I get? This is basically an itinerary of our days and corresponding security measures."

"What are you hoping for, Your Highness?" Philip's brows rose a fraction. "Espionage?"

Kris tilted his head wryly. "Security incidents."

"The royal guard handles any incidents with precision and discretion. We don't concern our king with such matters."

"Let's change that." Kris let the folder fall onto the desk with a little *slap*.

With a small frown, Philip inclined his head and turned to leave.

"Thanks, Philip," Mark said.

"Your Majesty." The older man stopped at the door and cast a frown at Kris over his shoulder. "Speaking of security incidents—what are your plans tonight, Your Highness?"

Kris clicked his tongue, holding back a grin. *Here we go.*

"Oh, you know," he answered, stretching with a hand behind his head. "Might head into the city."

Philip's features hardened. "Do *not* slip your guards again."

He quirked a brow. "Why would I do that?"

"Kris," Mark said in warning.

"I don't slip them." Since Kris had arrived in Kiraly, he'd made a habit of getting out of the palace a few times a week. He needed the relief of being surrounded by normal people, and in a crowded bar, he could settle back into his old cowboy skin and forget the royal he'd become. Philip's problem was that very occasionally, Kris would just . . . leave the bar. "They choose not to follow me."

Philip's lips thinned. "From what I've heard, you work hard to take that choice away from them."

"I need you to try, Kris." Mark leaned forward, elbows on his knees, blue gaze steady. "If you're serious about being king, you can't mess around anymore. Respect protocol. Please."

Sobering at the plea, Kris raised his hands in surrender. Mark's future with Ava depended on Kris doing this properly—for if Kris wasn't prepared by the coronation in three months' time, Mark would put Kiraly over his own happiness and take the crown.

"Alright," he said. "I promise to do the right thing."

A clever verbal loophole even if he did say so himself.

Mark gave a nod. "Thank you."

Satisfied with that, Philip bowed to them both and left the study.

Kris blew out a breath and ran a hand along the back of his neck, fingers digging into muscle. "Summits, hey," he said, leaning back in his chair. "Do we get a lot of those?"

Mark gave a laugh. "No idea." He stood, pushing his sleeves up to his elbows. "How're you holding up?"

Honestly? His life had been upended and everything that had once brought him comfort and peace had tumbled away. Horses and back porches and big skies were all out of reach.

"Hard to know," he said.

A sturdy upbringing in Montana couldn't have prepared him for daily life as a monarch. This life was bait for all species of predatory stress.

The sharp-toothed stress that preyed on responsibility. His smallest choice could have far-reaching consequences, and that pierced deep into his conscience.

The stress of dramatic change. It was always there: a million crawling *wrongs* throughout the day. Every time he woke to find his manservant setting down his morning coffee, it stung him. Every time his guards fell into step behind him, sting; every time someone called him 'Your Highness' with a bowed head, double sting; and every time he reluctantly handed the reins to the stable master after a ride because he had somewhere else to be, he stung all over his capable cowboy body.

And dwelling in the shadows of his mind was the stress that he was in over his head. That he might not be able to pull off this king thing and would cause the end of Mark and Ava's relationship.

His only defense was to give his attention to everything Philip and Mark taught him in his daily training. It had been less than two weeks, but he was trying his best. Kira City looked breathtaking at night—he knew, because he often stayed late in this tower study, revising notes, reciting what he'd learnt, memorizing names and agreements and political relationships. He might not be a natural leader like Mark or a natural learner like Tommy, but he'd be damned if he messed this up through lack of trying.

Not that he'd tell Mark any of that. His brother needed Kris's unfazed, raffish front—needed to sigh and roll his eyes. Because if Kris started acting too seriously, it'd be a neon warning sign that he was freaking the hell out, and Mark, being Mark, would back down from his abdication.

And that was not going to happen.

"The view from up here still makes my head spin," Kris said. "But I'm getting used to it."

Mark glanced distractedly out the nearest window. "I meant how are you holding up after last night."

Oh. The engagement party? "Fine. It didn't get that wild."

He received a pained glance. "I thought it might have made you think of someone," Mark said carefully, "and how much you miss her."

Gut suddenly aching, Kris looked away.

He didn't need an engagement party to remind him of Frankie. She was an emotional shadow, clinging to the heels of his heart, always half a thought away. The last time he'd seen her . . . it haunted him. *I can't do this,* she'd told him. In the months since, he'd called, messaged, emailed—and heard nothing. At first, her silence had burned a hole in him, and restless frustration had poured out. He'd hardly been able to sit still. After a while, he'd forced himself to accept the obvious.

She'd returned to Sage Haven and heard the town gossip. The news—the extent of the secret he'd kept from her—had broken her trust in him. Without that, he wouldn't hear from her again.

His fault.

All his fault.

Sometimes he crouched on the brink of going after her. He could skip the country, fly back home, and beg for her forgiveness. Lying awake at night was the hardest. Her absence would scrape over him like a phantom touch and he'd churn up the covers knowing he couldn't keep living without her.

But he had no choice.

He was a prince of Kiraly. Soon to be the king. Slipping security in the city was one thing, but he wasn't so irresponsible as to abandon his duty.

"Yeah," was all he said to Mark, because he couldn't remember if he'd asked a question.

"You still haven't heard from her?" Mark shifted, sliding a hand in his pocket, looking uncomfortable. "At all?"

"Not so much as a snicker."

Mark shook his head, gaze down and jaw tight.

"Don't hold it against her." Frankie didn't deserve Mark's blame. "I kept all this from her. Pretty big deal."

Mark didn't answer. Jaw still locked, he headed toward the door.

"Say hey to Ava and Darius for me."

That broke the tension in his brother's shoulders. Mark relaxed as he quirked a brow over his shoulder. "In response, I'm guessing Ava will scold you for walking out of the summit."

"Not a doubt in my mind."

Grinning, Mark closed the door behind him.

Kris leaned back in his chair, mentally trailing his brother down the stone steps that spiraled through the tower like an apple peel. Once he was confident Mark had reached the floor below, he pulled out his notebook from the bottom desk drawer, flipped it open and frowned over his recent speculations.

Yes, he'd put up his hand to be king.

But there were three persisting problems with that.

Everyone was well aware of the first. He had a strained relationship with authority—including his *own* authority, which he struggled to take seriously.

The second was Frankie. Kind of hard to rule a kingdom with a gaping hole in his chest.

The third was contained within the pages of this notebook. Theories, guesswork, hunches, and clues. He wasn't a detective by a long stretch, but without knowing who he could trust—aside from Mark and Tommy, whom he refused to worry with his suspicions—he'd been left to handle this himself.

This being his deadliest source of stress: his conviction that the late royal family's deaths had not been the accident the official investigation had claimed.

They'd been murdered.

And to keep the kingdom safe, it was up to him to prove it.

"Right, who wants to tell me what we're doing here?" Frankie stood with arms crossed in the palace surveillance room, staring down a select group of her team.

Kris's security detail.

Every single one of them looked unusually wide-eyed for five-thirty in the morning. Admittedly, Frankie in a bad mood got her team out of bed faster than a flipped mattress.

The king-in-training's two main personal guards, Peter and Hanna, were positioned the closest. They'd accompanied him almost everywhere inside the palace and out since the day he'd arrived. Frankie had selected Peter, a lean-muscled man in his mid-forties, for his quiet competence and extensive military experience, while Hanna was the royal guard's youngest member. Razor-eyed and quick-minded, the twenty-three-year-old was as enthusiastic as she was disciplined. She'd transferred from the police force where she'd consistently ranked best mark. Several of the other half-dozen guards in front of Frankie watched Kris overnight and on Peter and Hanna's days off. The rest escorted the prince when he ventured beyond the palace grounds.

As he had last night.

"I imagine it has something to do with the footage you've lined up for us." This suggestion came from Hanna as she cocked her head toward the nearest screen, her long blond ponytail swaying. Her uniform was impeccable, right down to the creases in her navy trousers.

Frankie arched a brow. "Care to be more specific?"

The woman winced. "And the fact that Prince Kristof disappeared again last night."

"Bingo."

There was a mass shamed shuffling of feet.

"We can all count." Frankie's agitation was running wild. She'd hoped it wouldn't come to this, but royals were only allowed to disappear on her watch when she let them. Kris might think nothing of his own security, but it was Frankie's job to protect him and he'd finally made that impossible to do from a distance. "This has happened too many times."

Last night bumped it up to disappearance number five.

"Would we all like to find out how he does it?" No one was foolish enough to respond. "The last time he slipped you, I took the liberty of installing security cameras at his go-to hot spot." The Bearded Bunting, a bar well outside the city's nightlife district. It attracted few tourists—the bar was mostly a place for locals coming together to drink and dance and hook up. Basically, a melting pot of Kris's favorite pastimes. "Let's watch, shall we?"

Pressing play, Frankie turned her back on the screen under

the pretense of assessing the reactions of her team. In truth, she couldn't stomach watching it again.

She knew by the slight roll of Hanna's eyes that Kris was dancing up close with several women in the bar's back courtyard. Knew by Peter's growing frown that his own face was captured as Kris wove past him to get inside, gesturing to the guard that he was grabbing another drink. Next up was a camera switch, and her team looked momentarily alarmed as they struggled to find him in the crowd. Not just due to the long shot taken from the rear of the room, but the ludicrous fashion trend that had exploded throughout the city since the brothers had arrived—cowboy chic. There were plaid shirts in every color combination, blue jeans, kerchiefs and cowboy hats. Kris wasn't as easy to spot as he should have been leaning in to talk with a woman in a cute sundress, who looked delightedly shocked by whatever he'd suggested. And Frankie knew by the cringes of every single guard when Kris ducked beneath the crowd cover, removed his telltale checkered shirt and hat, and straightened in a white tank with the woman wrapped around his waist. As he wove through the crowd, she tugged a cap over his hair, wrapped her arms around his neck, and angled her head to kiss the side of his face—her long hair effectively shielding him as he ducked out the door.

Frankie lifted the remote and hit pause over her shoulder.

No one spoke.

"Comments? Questions?" she asked. "Last words?"

"They kind of looked good together." Hanna was still staring at the screen.

Frankie ignored her as she scanned her team, trying to forget that just hours ago, she'd sat balled up in front of the screen, clammy and cold over watching Kris with another woman. "Anyone else?"

"We apologize for this reoccurrence." This from one of the

guards who'd been positioned across the street from the bar's front entrance. "Now we know his tactic, it won't happen again."

"You know why it won't happen again?" She ground her teeth as she took a beat. "Because the next time he leaves these walls, I'm coming with you."

Her vision blurred with nerves. For months, she'd avoided Kris. She'd ensured her job didn't require her to interact directly with the royal family. She'd existed behind the scenes—the puppet master of the interwoven network of palace security. A role that continued to terrify her, even as she strode down the halls with the confidence of someone who fully believed she belonged.

A lesson from her father.

Convince them with your own conviction and they'll never think to look past it.

"Dismissed," she said, and turned her back.

The group filed out in silence.

When the door clicked closed, Frankie held still. She sensed the young woman's presence as keenly as she could smell whatever sweetened product kept that blond hair shining.

"Yes, Johansson?"

After a moment, Hanna appeared at her side. "Do you swim, ma'am?"

Instantly knowing where this was going, Frankie met her stare flatly. "No."

"Ski?"

"No."

Hanna clicked her fingers, looking away. "Bake?" she asked, her tone spiking doubtfully.

"Yes," Frankie said. "I bake. I also enjoy book clubs and sewing my own dresses."

"Hey." Hanna frowned. "That felt targeted."

"Stop trying to find a way to outdo me. I'm your superior. I win at everything." But Frankie flashed her a smile. Since Frankie had first taken down this guard during training, Hanna had become determined to beat her in return. At what, it didn't seem to matter, which made Frankie suspect it was less of a competition and more an attempt at bonding. Frankie was only three years older than her, after all. "Now, what are you really doing here?"

Hanna's gaze slid to the paused image of the crowded bar. "It just . . . it sounded like you were planning on personally catching the prince mid-escape next time."

Frankie redirected the motion of that thought before it could hit her. "You're admitting there'll be a next time?"

"Certainly not," she answered, pulling a *whoops* face. "But if I may be so bold, you've gone to great lengths to avoid the royal family, and this plan could change that. It makes me wonder if it's really okay with you."

Frankie braced, reaching for her coffee mug. Hanna wasn't exactly a friend. Their positions didn't allow for that. But the woman saw too much and spoke too plainly for Frankie to lie to her outright.

Okay, maybe they were kind of friends, because she decided against pulling rank just to end the conversation. Swallowing coffee, she met curious blue eyes and raised a brow.

Hanna gave a quick, delighted smile. "Why would I think you've avoided the royal family, your face is asking while your mouth is conveniently busy? Let's take the first time Prince Kristof found the staff dining hall."

Oh, groan. Stellar first example.

Frankie had been eating a late lunch at a back table, minding her own business, when she'd distractedly caught eyes with Hanna across the room. Hanna, who'd been on shift. Meaning there was no other reason for the guard to be stepping into the dining hall other than to accompany Kris.

Instinct had shoved Frankie under the long wooden table a second before a room-wide murmur announced the prince's unorthodox appearance.

"Hey, everyone, don't mind me," he'd said, and his deep, textured voice had plunged clean through her chest—a hard, sliding pressure that had almost reduced her to tears. That voice. That *man*. She'd fixed her stare on his leather boots across the floor and commanded herself not to move. Life would be better for him if he believed he'd left her behind in Montana. Better for them both. "I like to snack. So if you see me in here every now and then, just carry on as usual. No bowing or whatever."

He'd stayed. He'd snacked. And Frankie had remained under the table for ten minutes after she'd been sure he was gone.

"Another example," Hanna now continued, "is the occasional flash of a bright jacket and red hair I catch darting around corners."

"Don't know what you're talking about."

Abrupt lunges through side doors, hiding in weird royal alcoves, even one undignified bolt down a corridor—she'd done it all. And not just to avoid Kris, but Tommy, and even Mark in the early days, before necessity had forced her to reveal herself to the levelheaded firstborn.

"No?" Hanna raised a shoulder. "Then there was your instruction on day one to never mention your name, and if his Highness ever asks to speak to the head of personal security— which he has done multiple times—to never bring him—"

"Get to the point, Johansson," Frankie said tiredly, hating the measures she'd had to put in place for Kris's own good.

"He knows you." Hanna's sparkling eyes had narrowed. "They all do."

"Nothing slips past you, does it?" Just as Hanna started smiling, Frankie added with a level stare, "Except, of course, the future King of Kiraly."

Hanna's smile vanished.

"My relationship with the royal family is none of your concern," Frankie said firmly.

Hanna's shoulders settled back. "Yes, ma'am."

"Hadn't you better catch up with Peter? Pretty sure your prince likes a pre-breakfast snack right about sunrise."

Hanna's eyes bulged. "Oh my God, he *never stops eating.*" Then she straightened, gave a sharp nod, and departed.

Alone, Frankie turned back to the screen. Her guard was right. The prospect of personally confronting Kris made her want to shrivel out of existence.

Insides churning, she pressed play and set the footage to repeat.

It didn't matter how high she angled her chin or how far back she rolled her shoulders—pain had speared through her the first time she'd watched it and there was no hiding that now. Instead, she used the pain to her advantage. Every time Kris spoke in the woman's ear with his sex-soft smile, something fragile inside Frankie collapsed in on itself. Every time he hoisted the woman's legs around his waist, Frankie's arms wound tighter around her own middle, and every time the woman leaned in to place her mouth on his neck, Frankie bit down on her bottom lip so hard she tasted metal.

She'd never pretended to be over him. So she took the salt from her blinked-back tears and used it to cure her heart. Preserve it for the beating it was about to endure.

Philip had said he'd talk to Kris yet again about his behavior, but the prince couldn't be tamed. He'd do it again. When he did, Frankie would catch him.

And the explanation he'd demand would be the end of them.

Breakfast was strange without Mark.

Kris and Tommy sat in the blue parlor, overshadowed by the grand room, the gargantuan table, and the empty space their brother had left behind.

In the days since Mark had moved with Ava to the outskirts of Kira City, a disconnect had formed between Kris and Tommy. As if the knot of their bond had come loose, and like beads on a string, they were starting to separate along the cord. It was an ache at his very core to realize the absence of one brother put space between them all.

"Good night?" Tommy asked quietly, skewering into his potato hash.

"Yeah." He glanced up, but Tommy wasn't looking at him.

It was never a good sign when Tommy avoided eye contact with his own family.

"Just went to the Bearded Bunting."

"You like that place."

Kris reached for more toast. "They don't make a big deal about me being there."

Back home, he and his brothers had never made a habit of eating breakfast together, instead weaving through each other's morning routines with silent companionship. But he'd grown used to it since arriving in Kiraly. Now three had become two, and it was like the whole meal was spent waiting for Mark to arrive.

"You?" he asked.

Tommy raised a shoulder. His attention stayed on his plate. "Fine."

"Reading?"

He nodded. "I'm going through our family history."

"Cool," he said, in that way that betrayed he wouldn't personally find it cool to spend his nights like that, but appreciated that his brother did. Reading and researching was safe.

They kept eating.

Guilt niggled at him in the brittle-edged silence.

Tommy had been distant since Kris had declared he'd replace Mark as king. At first, Kris had pretended not to know why. It was a good thing, wasn't it? Mark could be with Ava and Tommy didn't have to face new, high-level social situations every day. No pressure meant no panic attacks. Really, Tommy should be thanking him.

But he knew.

Of course he knew.

"*Skip Tommy,*" he'd said to Mark that night, and Tommy had flinched beside him. "*Skip him and go straight to me.*"

Every time he thought of it, that flinch was a lash down Kris's side.

He didn't know what to do. Couldn't take it back. Would make the same call over again, just with more tact. He'd shamed his brother by disregarding his birthright as the second-born son, and the wound wasn't healing.

"Any other triplets in our family history?" he asked.

Tommy shook his head.

"Any other asshole brothers who jumped the queue to the throne without asking?"

Tommy stilled. His gaze was a mix of caution and censure when he looked up. "Yes. But their version of jumping the queue usually involved murdering the heir."

Not sure how to respond, Kris pulled a face. "Brutal. So I'm not as big of an asshole as I thought."

"Yes, you are," his brother said with quiet conviction.

And there it is. Running a hand over his mouth, Kris lowered his head.

Their silence stretched out uncomfortably, but he didn't

break it. In the tension, he could sense Tommy's internal struggle, challenging himself to speak his mind, and finally his brother murmured, "You've never made me feel useless before."

Kris snapped his head up. "You're *not* useless."

"I am." The admission held too much certainty. "I couldn't do what you're doing for Mark. I hate myself for that. But you didn't even pretend I was capable. You've always at least pretended."

Insulted, he said, "I never pretend."

Tommy angled his head almost mockingly. "Then why did you skip me?"

"Because I wasn't thinking."

"No. You were thinking so fast and clearly, that you forgot to humor me."

Goddamn it. "Tommy . . ."

He knew he was overprotective—and that Tommy resented it —but Kris couldn't bear to watch him get hurt. Not again. Being a king with severe social anxiety would hurt like hell, so instinct had been to shield his brother from the weight of the crown. And in doing so . . .

Kris had hurt him.

Round of applause for good intentions and shit execution, ladies and gentleman.

"I'm sorry." Kris leaned toward him, forearms on the tablecloth. "Do you want to swap back?"

Tommy huffed a humorless laugh as the doors to the parlor opened and Philip entered with a newspaper in his hand and a scowl on his thin face.

Kris winced. No guesses what this was about.

Actually. Come to think of it—there were a few things . . .

"Prince Kristof," the advisor said coolly, halting a respectable distance from the table. "Prince Tomas."

Tommy inclined his head, while Kris said, "Morning, Phil."

37

The man opened his mouth to continue, then hesitated with an irritated look. "Why do you do that? I've expressly asked you to call me Philip."

"Philip is so proper." Kris gestured around the room vaguely with his fork. "I don't want to be stuck in formality every second of the day, so I'm trying to make our working relationship more relaxed. You know, to differentiate it from when I meet stuffy dignitaries with poles up their asses. You *do* want me to be able to differentiate between you and—"

"Kris," Tommy murmured, face down.

"Don't you?" Kris jumped to the finish.

"Fine." Philip's sigh was long-suffering. "But training to be king doesn't mean you can do anything you want."

"Trust me," Tommy said, "his attitude has nothing to do with that."

Kris smirked.

"Regardless, it's poor form to repeatedly shirk your own guard. Particularly after repeatedly being asked *not to*."

"Again?" Tommy angled a narrowed stare at him.

"It's fine." Kris glanced at them both. "I don't need guards. I wouldn't have to shirk them if we just gave them the night off. They work hard."

Philip looked aghast.

"Why not?" Kris's heartbeat grew louder in his ears. Anticipation coiled in him as he casually eyed his advisor. "What exactly do you think might happen to me?"

He'd waited for the right moment to ask, because unless this palace was populated by ignorant fools, *someone* else must share his suspicions about the deaths of his uncles and cousin. And they were keeping it from him.

"Is there a threat we don't know about, Phil?" he asked, angling his head.

Tommy froze beside him, then looked up to watch Philip.

"Only if your head's been stuck in the hay, Your Highness," the man answered. "Royal-obsessed public. Paparazzi. The usual concerns that are no less valid just because you haven't yet learned to take them seriously."

Kris gave a hum. Tommy glanced out the window.

"Do you disrespect your team so much?" Philip gestured behind him to where Peter and Hanna were stationed just outside the closed doors.

"I don't disrespect them." He didn't *know* them. Despite his efforts, the pair rarely spoke, never smiled, and their expressions always lay somewhere between mildly disapproving and dull-minded.

"You must," Philip said, "since you risk their jobs every time you run off."

Kris turned his mouth down at the corners, impressed. "Breaking out the emotional manipulation, I see."

"This is serious."

"So is what I'm doing," he said, telling the absolute truth.

"Look, this is the last time I'll bring it up," Philip said. "But be warned, security has tightened after last night. I've been told you won't get away again."

Kris almost groaned. Tighter security. Great.

Instead, he cocked a challenging brow. "Tell them to tackle me."

"I'll do no such thing." Philip's lips thinned. Then he tossed the folded newspaper onto the table. "Care to explain this?"

Curious, Kris and Tommy both tipped their heads to see the headline. *Cowboy Prince Shouts Round at Foreign Embassy.* Beneath was a photo of Kris standing at the entrance to the embassy of the neighboring minister for agriculture, flanked by his guards, holding a six-pack of the palace's own microbrew.

"I told you I'd sort it out." Kris gestured to the newspaper with his toast. "Publicly."

Philip's face flushed. "With *beer*?"

"Why not?" He bit into the sourdough. "We shared a few drinks. I apologized for walking out of his presentation. He gave me a few pointers on political extrication, as he called it. He's an alright guy. No hard feelings."

There was a room-wide silence in which even the serving staff seemed to hold their breath for Philip's response. But he just said faintly, "I'm not built for this. I'll see you in your study in twenty minutes." With that, the advisor left, the grand double doors closing in his wake.

Twisting his lips, Kris returned his attention to Tommy.

His brother was watching him steadily. "Are we really sure Mark loves Ava?"

"Why does everyone keep asking that? I can handle this." Kris leaned back in his chair, shaking his head. "Want to come out with me tonight?"

The corner of Tommy's mouth quirked. He gestured to where Philip had been standing. "Did we just experience two different conversations?"

"I didn't say we're going to slip security."

Tommy raised a wry brow. "You know I'm not coming. And we both know what you're going to do." He paused. "And that it's a bad idea."

"I have no choice." Kris shoveled the last of his toast in his mouth. "Didn't you hear that challenge?"

His brother muttered, "Oh, dear God," as he scratched between his brows. "Just bring her back here, will you? She can even have breakfast with us."

What?

For a few seconds, Kris blinked at him. Then it hit. Tommy assumed, like everyone else, that he slipped his guards in order to get laid.

"Nah," he answered. "That'd be weird."

Tommy glanced at the huge table. "It's not as if we don't have a spare seat."

"I'll think about it."

"No, you won't." Pouring a second serve of coffee, his brother added, "But you should think about the risks of being the ascending member of our family alone on the city streets at night."

"What's that word you call me sometimes?" Kris stood, running a hand through his hair. It was getting long, but he kind of liked it. "Encourageable?"

Tommy gave a soft snort. "Incorrigible."

"Yeah." Kris picked up his cowboy hat from the corner of the table and set it on his head with a grin. "Same thing."

2

Frankie made no sound as she stuck to the shadows.

It wasn't the first time she'd tailed her best friend. Four years ago, she'd finally tracked Kristof Jaroka—living under the name Kris Jacobs—to his college campus, days before his graduation. She'd believed then, sliding into the student bar behind him, that he was the only child of the outcast Prince Erik. She'd had no reason to think otherwise—Philip certainly hadn't made her quest easier by confiding that there were three of them. Whispered gossip in Kiraly about the far-flung royal had only ever mentioned a single son, and she'd been sure Kris was it, lounging on a bar stool with rippling sexuality and wild blue eyes.

Silly, laughable past-Frankie.

"Your breathing is off." Peter spoke quietly in her earpiece. "Everything okay, Cowan?"

"Fine," she whispered, lying to avoid the treacherous cliff edge of those three words. Everything wasn't okay. Her heart was pounding viciously and nervousness made her insides itchy.

In this dark street, she was alone with Kris for the first time in months.

It was almost midnight. He'd done another quick change earlier, disguised by the crowded bar and a new woman with her arms around his neck. Frankie had watched the security stream on her phone from a block down the street, trying to ignore the reluctance yanking in her gut. She couldn't do this.

Yet all day her weakened heart had yanked back. *No more hiding. I can't bear it.*

So she'd given the guards strict instructions. Let the prince escape. Leave him to her and follow at a distance. Only close in once she had him secured.

Unexpectedly, he'd parted ways with his date within minutes. For a man whose nocturnal brain was located squarely between his legs, his behavior was a real head-scratcher.

He'd ditched his cowboy hat and checkered shirt at the bar, leaving only the black tank he'd worn beneath. Paired with his jeans and a hand in his back pocket, he looked like any other local wandering home on a warm summer night. That was, if any other local had shoulders made for carrying saddles, arms for throwing hay bales, and an ass so tight it shouldn't reasonably expect anyone to ever look away.

At the next backstreet intersection, he veered right. The road levelled out, running horizontally across the mountainside. He occasionally checked over his shoulder—a casual, just-because-he-should kind of glance. As if a threat would stick to the middle of the road behind him. Unnoticed after his fifth head check, Frankie almost fell for it. Her anger sparked. He was being careless. Foolish. This was *dangerous.* She knew the area, the direction he was headed. The bars speckled on street corners would become seedier. The alleys and side streets that ran unlit and steep off this road would start to conceal the scum of society.

Then she cursed herself.

He knew he was being followed.

The first time he'd driven her to the middle of freaking

nowhere to watch the stars from the tray of his truck, an animal had slunk out of the trees beside her. In the darkness, all she'd been able to make out was a canine form and stealthy gait. Kris hadn't noticed; he'd just lounged there, hand propped under his head, gazing up at the sky. Unwilling to overreact, she hadn't commented as it approached, until finally Kris had cast her a soft half-smile. "It's okay," he'd said. "It's just a fox."

The man had faultless peripheral vision—and he'd been using it on her every time he looked around.

"Sure you're okay?" This time the voice in her ear was Hanna.

In answer, she tapped the concealed mic at her earlobe once. It meant yes, but she hoped her perceptive little guard picked up on the order to let a woman breathe, already.

"Anytime you feel like reeling him in, Cowan," Peter said.

Yeah, yeah.

Kris halted. Frankie instantly mirrored the movement, pressing herself into the recess of a residential door front and frowning when he unfolded a piece of paper and glanced from it to the nearest street sign. Oh, he had to be kidding. He was—he was going to walk down that unlit lane, knowing he was being followed. Probably in anticipation of a confrontation.

With a final glance behind him, Kris set off into the dark.

"For the love of God," she muttered.

"Just give the word." Peter spoke quietly.

"He's an idiot," she replied as she darted across the street. "A blue-blooded idiot."

"We're at the top of Hillcrest," Hanna said. "Twenty seconds away at your order."

Frankie tapped the mic again and slipped into the lane.

She could call out and have it over with, but a scare could help him learn the risk of wandering off alone. The lane was uphill, steep like so much of this city. Her soft boots made no sound on the cobblestones. Ahead of her, Kris strolled casually, back turned like a well-disguised trap. Or an easy target. *Idiot.* The lane cut behind two rows of honey-stoned houses, so nothing but latched back gates would witness their encounter.

Dread rising, she calculated a plan. He was expecting her. He was larger, stronger—and her prince. Under no circumstances could she accidentally harm him. Dismay clutched the length of her windpipe at her obvious move.

Then she ran.

No time to lose her nerve or call in his security team to take her place. She sprinted at him, her once-best friend, and he stiffened at the light scuff of her footfalls. She sprinted even as he whipped his head around, his body spinning to face her a second later.

Surprise flashed across his face—surprise, she assumed, at registering a woman's silhouette in the filtered moonlight. She kept her chin tucked low and hands open to show she held no weapon.

He uncoiled slightly, frowning as she neared. "What exactly do you intend to—"

She tackled him.

The incline lessened the fall. He grunted as she landed on top of him, but his hands swiftly found her upper arms and he rolled with her, covering her torso with his chest, splaying a bent knee out to lock over her thighs. Not painful pressure, but not underestimating her either. He had her pinned. Her breath came hard.

There was no escaping this truth.

To her horror, she started trembling.

"That was cute." His voice was rough, the words hot on her cheek.

She closed her eyes, aching at the end-of-day smell of him, and shifted beneath his weight. He was as intense and unyielding above her as she'd always imagined. If only time would stop—let her stay in this liminal moment between friendship and condemnation where she could imagine his body was a shield from the rest of the world.

"Now why are you following me?"

She didn't answer.

With a huff, he pulled back to scowl down at her. It was everything she could do to hold still, not thrash in his arms and fight her own unmasking. Not breathing, she watched his expression slowly clear. Reset. Then his whole body jolted in shock.

"Frankie?" Her name sounded numb on his tongue.

Panic rose in her. She was powerless. Trapped.

Instinct got her out. Squirming, she used his moment of shock to her advantage and levered him onto his back until she straddled him, her palms firm on his bare shoulders. His hard, broad, otherwise untouchable shoulders. She shifted her grip, savoring the ten tiny slides of her fingertips against his skin. *God.* She did it again, quickly, her thumbs tracing a full crescent of marble-smooth skin, and locked her elbows to keep from yielding completely.

Bracing, she met his stare as his features opened in such delicate disbelief, such wonder, her heart pitched like a bird that had suddenly forgotten how to fly.

"Frankie," he said in a voice so gentle, it turned her whole body to tissue paper. One caress away from tearing. "You found me."

Guilt pierced deep. "Yes," she managed to say.

"I didn't think you'd come." His eyes were wide. 'I—I thought I'd never . . .'" And with a breathy growl, he lifted a hand to cup her face. His palm was warm on her skin, his fingers pressing into her scalp behind her ear.

She leaned into his touch, willing herself not to cry.

"I've missed you." His thumb brushed a path across her cheek.

She gave a nod and hoped he knew what it meant.

"Have you been okay?"

If it weren't for the painful lump in her throat, she might have laughed. No. She hadn't been okay. She'd been out of her mind. She had a job she didn't deserve. A secret task that was taking too long. A new home that made her skittish and uneasy. And the best friendship of her life had realigned squarely into heartache. She didn't know where the lies ended, the truth began, and if either really mattered when Kris would soon be King of Kiraly.

"Hey." Suddenly Kris was propped up on his elbow, his face way too close to hers. Or not quite close enough. His hand still held her face, and concern filled his gaze. "Are you okay?"

"Not really." And it was only going to get worse. "I . . ." Her fingers tightened around his shoulders. "I've—missed you, too."

His eyes flickered, surprised.

"More than is good for me," she admitted under her breath.

"Actually," he said as desire shadowed his features. "I get the feeling that missing each other is about to make things as good as they can get."

And just like that her blood flushed and it was all she could do not to lower herself over him. It was obvious what he meant by *things*. Hands and mouths and him moving strong and practiced inside her. In a world where she'd never lied to him, their prolonged yearning would pack one hell of a release. Even now, the temptation to surrender to him almost bested her. His lust had always commanded hers. One hazy look and her insides practically moaned.

She clung to resistance only because his embrace wasn't meant for her.

Once, when she was a girl, a new teacher had called her by

the wrong name at school. *Lola, sweetheart, could you collect the pencils?* Lola, with rows of gold stars beside her name—not Frankie, with her heavy black asterisk and the last of many final warnings. Lola had been holidaying in Dubai with her family, and despite knowing it was wrong, Frankie had felt a secret thrill to be mistaken for someone greater than herself. She'd collected the pencils. Set the classroom chairs on the desks after the bell. She'd even walked with the teacher all the way to the staff room, carrying her folders, just so she'd receive a warm smile and be told she was a good girl.

Kris was like that teacher. He held her because he didn't know who she truly was. And even though it was selfish and ugly to fool him, his appreciation lit her up like sunlight on water and she couldn't find the strength to plunge herself into the dark deep below.

She didn't move, didn't speak as his attention fixed on her mouth.

"All these months," he murmured, "I've thought you hated me."

His lust-thick voice wove need between her legs. "I could never hate you."

"Frankie." He brought himself closer, so close the warmth of her own breath returned to her in the intimate space. The coils of their attraction tightened. "I've regretted the way we parted every day since I last saw you. I'd wanted to ask—that is, it's something I've always wanted to . . ." His hand tilted her face carefully toward him and his next words blew a sweet promise against her lips. "Can I kiss you?"

Yes.

A throat cleared in her ear. She went rigid.

"Shall we move in?" Hanna asked, tone neutral. "Or give you some privacy? Either option is cool."

Oh, Jesus. Her team.

"Move in," she answered, head reeling in sudden panic.

Kris stilled. His focus lifted to her eyes, brow nudging down. "Was that a yes?"

Grief clutched beneath her breastbone as she gave a slight shake of her head.

His frown deepened when she ducked away from his hand and stood up. "You're leaving?" He sprang to his feet, looking alarmed. "I'm sorry I asked that. I didn't mean to—you found me. So, we're okay now, right? We need to talk. About everything. Please tell me you know that."

"I know." And boy, was it going to be one harrowing talk. "I'm not leaving."

"Good." He stepped toward her and grabbed her hand. She didn't allow herself to grip him back. "Come with me up to the . . ." His attention shot over her shoulder. "Hey. Nice timing."

The security cars had pulled up at the end of the lane. She stood rooted to the spot, back turned, pulse pounding in her ears. A car door clicked closed and footsteps sounded on the alley stones.

"You hurt?" Hanna asked in Frankie's earpiece. "Your posture looks weird."

"I'm fine." Apparently, she slouched when her organs collapsed from impending loss.

Kris eyed her, looking confused. "Good."

"Your Highness." Peter spoke clearly.

"Hey there," Kris answered. "Sorry about earlier. I thought you were right behind me."

Instead of accusing him of a bald-faced lie, Peter simply said, "If you're both ready now, we'll escort you back to the palace."

"Sure." He leaned in, his thumb brushing over her knuckles, and spoke just to her. "You'll hate it, but this team follows me everywhere. If you ride with us, we can talk in my rooms. Or, you know, any room of the palace you want. I'll show you around. It's stupidly big. We might get lost. But you'll love the kitchen. You'll want to live there, I swear. I'll take you there first, okay?"

Soft words, a little cautious, like he feared he was losing her. It sliced her apart, and defenseless, she hauled ass behind her emotional guard. She was going to need the distance to effectively sever their friendship at the neck.

"Your Highness," Peter said again.

"Coming," he answered, and tugged her hand lightly. "Coming?"

She wasn't Lola. She never would be.

And Kris would always be royalty.

"I can't," she said, and slid her hand out of his. She stepped back.

"Frankie." A plea spoken with desperate eyes. "Don't do this again."

"Kris." Her skin broke out in a cold sweat. For the first time since they'd met, she dropped her affected American accent in his presence. "I tackled you."

He started smiling. "Trust me, I noticed. You've never so much as touched—" He stopped. For a few sickening seconds, he stared at her, smile fading. "Why did you do that?"

The eyes of her team prickled on her back; her answer rose like bile in her throat. "Because Philip told me you requested it."

Kris blanched.

"Your Highness," she added, and inclined her head.

Silence, but for the sharp hiss of his inhale.

The world spun. The cobblestones were a blur at her feet.

Then, "What did you just say?" His question was nothing but breath.

Shrugging off her jacket, she forced her chin up and found him staring at her shirt. Palace-issued uniform, with a stiff collar, and the royal coat of arms embroidered on the breast. She'd borrowed it from Hanna. Her gun and shoulder holster were strapped over the top.

His face was blank with incomprehension.

"I understand this might come as a shock, Your Highness, but I work for the royal guard," she said, her voice as hollow as her heart. "And I have since the day we met."

Frankie's words spread through Kris like slow poison.

At first, he failed to process them. *I work for the royal guard.* The statement made so little sense that he followed her into the back of the car in blank silence. Then, as they set off and a shard of light from the street hit her stark features, her confession slipped, a little too hot, into his bloodstream.

Reaction reared painfully in his chest—crude and undeveloped—but he pushed it down.

She must be having him on.

Except she was wearing the palace security uniform—sitting with an empty space between them, hands balled on her thighs, staring straight ahead. *No.* He shook his head as something nasty punctured inside him.

"Frankie," he said.

She tensed. "Wait."

"For what?" They'd been apart for months. "Part two of this prank?"

Her throat flexed and she swallowed. "I'm not doing this here." She kept staring ahead.

The puncture ripped wider. *No.* She couldn't have been lying since the day he'd met her. It would mean too much; erase too much. He shifted, spreading his knees and turning his shoulders toward her as his reaction started to take form. Voice low, he murmured, "You're going to have to do something more than ignore me."

Her hands bunched tighter, and his focus shifted to the snagged skin of her knuckles. He reached toward her. "You're bleeding."

She yanked her hand away. "A scrape. It's nothing."

"Jesus, Frankie." He hadn't treated her with care when he'd roughed her onto her back. "Where else are you hurt?"

Her answer came a beat too late. "Nowhere."

"Then explain what's going on," he said firmly.

She hesitated before giving the tiniest shake of her head. When she next spoke, it was with the rich vowels and swift cadence of Kiralian English. "He can live without it until tomorrow."

He almost asked who she was talking to—then he caught Hanna's eyes in the rear-view mirror through the soundproof partition. A chill raced down his spine as the guard swiftly returned her attention to the road ahead.

"For God's sake," he snapped, his veins prickling. "Hurry up and tell me this is a joke."

Exhaling roughly, Frankie raised a hand to her ear, and after a moment of fiddling, set a small object on the seat between them.

A wireless earpiece.

For a second, he thought the car had crashed. His vision swam; his lungs seized as if he'd been winded, and there was the kind of violent silence that accompanied a sound too loud to process.

He gripped the door with all his might as the car glided through the palace gates.

"That is why I told you to wait," she muttered.

He couldn't respond; could no longer deny it.

Only once the car pulled up to the sweeping front entrance

to the palace did he unpeel his grip. Still he sat unmoving, stunned, until Hanna opened his door with a murmured, "Your Highness."

He stepped out into an unnerving, strange world. Frankie— his Frankie—was talking to Peter on the other side of the car.

"I'll accompany him to his suite," she said a little unsteadily. The low, throaty sound seemed to slam his lungs together, winding him for a second time. Her usual east coast accent was well and truly gone. "Station the overnight team. Tell them to ignore the shouting."

"Right away, ma'am," Peter said, nodding once.

Without a backward glance, she strode up the grand sweep of steps and disappeared into the lustrous glow of the entrance hall. The familiarity of her stride, the surety of her route had Kris pressing a palm to his chest.

She really had been here before.

Horror settling, he turned to Hanna standing straight and unobtrusive beside him. "Explain the last twenty minutes to me," he managed to say.

She hesitated, her gaze skimming his. "I wish I could, Your Highness."

Not the answer he wanted. "Is she really on your team?"

The young guard's attention darted after Frankie. "She runs our team, Your Highness."

His fingers curled. A reminder of strength as fissures cracked every part of his life wide open. "This whole time?"

She inclined her head.

He didn't move. Didn't speak as he staggered through his soul for something to get him through this. It was too late for denial, for reason, and *way* too late for assuming innocence until proven guilty. Anger beckoned—he clasped it tightly.

Inside the palace, he took his time catching up to her.

He crested the grand marble staircase on the second floor,

moving past the flickering gilt torchères that flanked it, and saw her figure retreating down the hall to the royal quarters.

Her shoulders stiffened as he drew closer. Nothing sounded quite like cowboy boots echoing off the polished floors. Her stride slowed—presumably so he could overtake her—and then faltered as she angled her head to one side and assessed him out of the corner of her eye. She stiffened further as she seemed to realize he was intentionally matching her pace.

She'd trailed him tonight. It was only fair that he returned the uncomfortable experience.

Their route passed Tommy's chambers and the guards positioned on either side of his door, but she didn't stop until she reached Kris's own rooms. She knew where he lived, where he slept, and had never come to him. Gut cramping, he moved in as she opened his door and stood back with her feet apart, hands behind her back, and gaze lowered.

Unable to process what it meant, what *anything* meant, he halted in front of her. Half a stride apart, they stood in crippling silence. Her throat flexed. His heart raged. With a scoff, he turned inside.

By the time the door clicked closed, he had a palm pressed to the summer-warmed floor-to-ceiling windows on the far side of the sitting room. The night lights of the city below had the audacity to twinkle up at him. Appalled, he turned and found her standing just inside the door, her hands concealed behind her and chin tipped down.

"At ease." His anger curled around the words like a talon.

She lifted her face. Her features were blank as she met his stare.

"Where to start, sweetheart?" A quiet challenge and unmistakable swipe. He knew exactly how much she hated being called *sweetheart*.

She didn't react.

"I hardly know what I'm feeling right now." His voice came out cold. "But none of it's good."

Nothing from her.

"Just," he said, and slowly raised a palm. "Tell me. Is this really true?"

After a moment, she inclined her head. Fierce, assertive Frankie just . . . nodded. She was acutely familiar, standing there with her spiky red hair; with her pale skin and the light freckles that he'd once complimented at his own risk. She should have been a verbal nudge away from rolling her eyes or dragging him out for late-night pizza—and it jarred that their intimacy had rapidly taken on a different shape. It was distorted and unfamiliar, as if their friendship had never been.

His teeth clenched against the pain. "Say something."

"I understand my job has upset you," she said, her tone measured.

"Your job." His brain slipped over the reality of it, and edgy, he moved behind the armchair to his right. His fingers gripped the back, squeezing the cushioning. "Your job has no power to upset me. But you do, Frankie. You just told me that you work for the royal guard." His focus stumbled as a vulnerable part of him pleaded for it not to be true. "That you have the whole time I've known you."

Her green gaze didn't waver. "Yes."

Lowering his head on a hard breath out, he sank his weight into his shoulders. His entire life had already been shattered once this year. He'd lost his ranch, his town, his community. Now he would have to rebuild all over again without the friendship he'd had with Frankie.

"Our friendship was never real," he said, the words breaking apart between them. He'd been her in; her reason to stay close to him and his family. Suppressing a noise he'd be sure to regret—too close to a wounded groan—he let go of the armchair and ran a hand firmly over his mouth. "You used me. You've always been using me."

She waited until he looked at her to answer. "Yes."

He tried not to show how deeply that cut, but his hand still ended up over his chest. "You lied to me."

"I lied to you," she said, the admission peeling a thick strip off his heart.

"Every day." His voice rose with his hurt.

Her expression didn't change. "Yes."

Another strip gone. "And it's never bothered you."

Her gaze flickered to the woven cotton rug at her feet. "I've never wanted you to know who I really am."

It hurt to breathe. Anger. He needed the lifeboat of his temper to survive this pain. He fumbled for it as he demanded, "How could you do this to me?"

"You never told me you were a prince." Her tone was neutral, but something in her gaze betrayed it as an accusation.

"I never told . . ." Suddenly his anger wasn't hard to find. "Because I was never supposed to end up here!" The truth tore ragged from his throat. "Because this isn't me, Frankie—not deep down or even halfway down, and you know it. But this—" He flicked a hand toward her uniform, her position in this place. "You *came* from this. You've lied to me since the day we met. You've tricked me." Pain rose in him, threatening to swamp his strength, but he shoved it down. She'd claimed to be a private investigator but hadn't divulged that he and his brothers were her major case. "I've spent every day I've known you thinking you were someone you're not."

And he had no idea how he was supposed to handle it.

"No," he said, and closed the distance between them, staring at her in dawning dismay. He pressed a steadying palm against the door, angling himself toward her, and fought the pull of her body. She watched him, impassive, just outside of arm's reach. "I haven't known you at all."

Her only reaction was to breathe in slowly through her nose.

"Tell me I'm wrong," he said, hating his own weakness at even asking.

Her gaze was bleak. "You don't know me."

In the silence, her previous words surfaced. His eyes narrowed. "I never told you I was a prince. Is that what you said?"

She jerked her head, shoulders back.

"That day," he said, the memory twisting like a torture tool in his mind. "You knew I wanted to tell you who I was, and you stopped me." Disgust spilled down his throat. "All these months I've been sick over that. The way you left; the way I let you go."

He'd blamed himself for not trying harder. Cursed himself as every kind of idiot for ruining the best relationship he'd ever had.

She'd had no time to talk because she'd been running late for a new job.

This job.

He growled as the pain ripped down his sternum—as if she'd dug her hands into his chest, grabbed hold of all the parts that mattered, and thrown them onto an open flame.

"I've blamed myself for not telling you, but you didn't *let* me." He hauled his palm from the door and faced her properly. His lips curled in a sneer. "Now I blame you."

Her expression didn't change. It was surreal, the things Frankie could process without an external reaction. The only movement was in her throat as she swallowed.

"I understand," she said eventually.

"Understand?" She'd known who and what he was all along. He was discovering her all at once—and it was like waking with a knife in his side. Forewarning gave her the upper hand, revealed precisely when she'd intended, and her steady stare seemed to push the blade deeper. His pride arched against it. How dare she get to watch him struggle? The unfairness of it erupted inside him. "You don't understand anything! What the hell were you even doing in Sage Haven?"

Her stance shifted very slightly. "Monitoring your safety."

"Fat load of good you were," he spat, and she recoiled as if he'd struck her. Somewhere, the confused friend in him ached in apology, because despite everything, he didn't want to hurt her. "You didn't protect Tommy." The night of his brother's brutal bashing. "And now you're head of security? What a joke."

She'd gone white.

"You should have been there to stop it from happening." He was practically snarling. He forced himself to back away, put space between them. His voice rose again. "You should have known those men were on their way!"

It wasn't fair on her—shame gummed his veins as the accusation left his mouth.

That attack had been no one's fault but Kris's.

Frankie's breathing was uneven. She broke position to tug agitatedly at the top button of her uniform—and his attention caught on her fingers. Bone white from nails to wrist. So she wasn't as calm as she'd seemed, clenching her hands to death behind her back.

"You failed Tommy." This protectiveness was familiar. He let it fill him. "And you've lied to him about it this whole time. He trusted you. Mark did, too, and you've hidden from us all."

If he hadn't been glaring right at her, he'd have missed it—the minor shift in her stance, the dart of her attention to the floor. Guilt, but not at his accusation.

Dread chilled him.

"Frankie," he said, taking a step toward her. "Tell me Mark doesn't know about you."

The first crease of distress lined her forehead.

"Frankie," he growled, stepping closer.

She swayed slightly as she refused to give ground. Her attention darted from his chin to his chest, and then stayed there. "I requested that he not tell you."

"You—" His lungs drained of air. "You asked my own brother to lie to me?"

"I asked him not to tell my secret. There's a difference."

"Not between brothers." He fisted his hair in his hands. His head pounded.

"It's not his fault."

"Don't pretend to care about him now." His hands came away shaking. "If you wanted to protect him, you should have come clean. I gave you every opportunity." He hadn't stopped trying to reach her. Like a fool, he'd hoped to draw his best friend back to his side. "I've begged you to contact me and you've been hiding under this roof from day one."

Her pulse was racing in her neck, her tendons straining. She was still staring at his chest, and he rolled a shoulder, instinctively flexing beneath her attention. She blinked, and her gaze seemed to tighten, focusing more firmly on him.

She grew perfectly still.

Desire unfolded inside him, soft and forgiving and reaching. His body had reacted to everything Frankie had revealed—and still craved her. She'd grazed her fingers against his bare shoulders earlier. He yearned for that impossible touch again—yearned to kiss her and see if it brought his friend back in a world that made sense.

See if she tasted the way he'd always imagined. The way of wildflowers and flame and the open sky.

Sweet, hot and endless.

"What the fuck, Frankie?" he breathed, because after all this, he might never find out.

Her teeth set. She returned her hands behind her back, and a second later, shot a razor-edged glare up at him. "You just said it. You're under this roof now. Nothing else matters." She paused, keeping her chin high. "Since you want me to come clean, I should tell you that nothing else has *ever* mattered."

He stilled. "What the hell does that mean?"

"Why do you think I've never touched you? Why you couldn't seem to budge our friendship into something more?" The light from the wall sconce by the door gleamed on her forehead. She was sweating. "I know what you've always wanted from me. But you were my job. I did what I needed to do to stay close. Nothing about you could have ever convinced me to do more than that."

Her words were like a blunt trauma to his solar plexus.

He didn't know where to look; how to hold his body upright.

"You asked to kiss me." Her breath was shallow. Her gaze was fixed on his chin. "My answer is no. You once said you wanted to touch me. But I don't want your hands near me."

Breathe. He needed to breathe.

"Get out," he said, because he couldn't fill his lungs with her here.

"It's easy enough to convince someone of what they want to believe," she said. "But there was nothing mutual between us."

"I said get out," he rasped, pain and fury clotting inside him. This was too real. "Go show yourself to Tommy. Don't make me tell him. I never want to see you again."

"Bad luck." She grabbed the door handle, preparing to leave. "You can't be trusted to keep yourself safe, so you've forced me to take matters into my own hands. As is my duty."

Shattered, he stared at her.

"Starting tomorrow, every time you set foot off palace grounds," she said, hauling the door open. "I'll be your bodyguard."

3

Adrenaline kept Frankie going as she knocked on Tommy's door. Her body was buzzing, humming, like she'd clung to an electric fence the entire time Kris had spoken. Her thoughts were fragmented. Jumpy and unfocused. And the lies she'd told . . . it had been agony to watch her blows land while hiding behind detachment. But she'd had no choice.

Kris had to let her go.

And she needed to get out of here—had to hold herself together a little longer.

Just a little longer.

After a time, the door opened. Tommy stood in the threshold in nothing but loose pants, his expression as rumpled as his soil-brown hair—until his curious gaze locked on her and his features tightened in shock.

There was a long, crushing silence as he processed her presence.

His attention moved from her uniform to his guards on either side of the door. They had allowed her to rouse their prince well after midnight. It betrayed her rank—few had the authority to do so. By the time his arms slid slowly across his bare chest, he was radiating a contained kind of fury.

"Why you little rat," he finally murmured.

Only Tommy could piece everything together without asking a single question.

"How nice of you to finally turn up." He spoke with all the composure Kris lacked. His quiet voice was level, his stare unwavering—she'd never been a source of his anxiety and that clearly wasn't about to change. "We've wondered about you."

"Then stop wondering," she made herself say. "I first moved to Sage Haven to monitor your safety and report back to Philip. Now I'm head of personal security and have been since you arrived."

Another silence stretched out and it all started to sink in. She felt shivery; sick.

"You've lied to my brother." His expression was hard with insult, but his eyes betrayed his pained confusion. "To us all."

She clamped her hands together behind her back. Tight, so tight, the pain kept her in line. "I did what I had to do."

"Well, in that case," he said, tone mocking. Then his gaze turned critical. "You should go. You look like you're about to pass out and I don't want to have to deal with it."

An order. Her first from this quiet, contained prince, and it clamped a band of shame around her throat. It wouldn't be the last.

She left him, needing to get out. Away from these royals and the eyes of her team. Out of the palace, off the grounds. Somewhere safe where she could wrap her arms around herself and try to keep the crumbling pieces together.

Just a little longer.

Kris hardly noticed when Tommy arrived. One moment he was pressing his forehead against the window, willing the world to stop tilting, and the next he was being led by the elbow through the palace and out into the night. Tommy didn't speak until they'd reached a white stone bench surrounded by sweet-scented shrubs and a stretch of trimmed grass.

Tommy's voice rumbled. "Sit here. I'll be back."

Kris ended up on his back in the grass, staring sightlessly at the stars.

Then there were footsteps and the sound of heavy breathing, and their old ranch dogs Buck and Bull were shoving their noses against his neck, licking his face, clambering over his chest to get to his other side. Groaning and close to smiling, he wrapped an arm around their backs, muttered, "Come here, you two," and drew them to the ground beside him. Panting, the border collies settled against him.

Tommy sat on the bench, leaning forward, watching him.

"Mark knew," Kris said numbly.

After a moment, his brother muttered, "Shit."

Throwing an arm over his face, Kris asked, "What did she tell you?"

"Not much." He paused. "I didn't exactly give her a warm welcome."

Rolling onto his side with another groan, Kris pressed his face against Buck. Why did the thought of Tommy giving Frankie the cold shoulder hurt so much?

"We'll visit Mark tomorrow." Tommy sounded wide awake. "Sort this out."

"Yeah," he mumbled, sliding a fist up between his forehead and the dog's side.

Just that morning, Tommy had been cool-mannered and brittle over Kris's ascension—but now he was backing him. He wasn't any less upset about the way Kris had treated him, but their bond could stretch and bend, not having to relinquish one fight just to offer support in another. That was the wonder of family.

He'd thought it was the same with Frankie. But as it turned out, she'd never been family.

She'd never been anything.

Later, much later, the word *bodyguard* rose in his mind like a dark shape from deep water. It loomed beneath the surface, just shy of comprehension, until the thought of her in such a high-risk position surged up and devoured him in a memory of their first argument.

Just months after moving to Sage Haven, Frankie had picked up extra work as a bouncer at the local bar. Kris hadn't handled it well. Her build was too slight; the danger to her safety too real. How did she expect to dominate an aggressive male or best a group of destructive morons? A firecracker couldn't blaze if someone snuffed out her fuse. Say, with a meaty fist.

Not that he'd protested. Instead, he'd lounged at the bar during her shifts, watching her, watching the room, ready to back her up.

One night, a group fight had broken out. Panic had jackhammered in his chest as she'd darted into the fray, and he'd been on her tail, terrified someone might break a bottle or pull a knife and mark her as their target. The fight had opened its savage arms and hauled him inside.

Less than a minute later, she'd kicked him out with the brawlers.

Confused, he'd stayed until close—when she'd burst out of the bar like a feral animal.

"How *dare* you?" she'd said, moving in so close, so fast, he'd thought she was going to shove him. Her eyes had glinted; her mouth had pinched tight with fury. "What the fuck were you thinking?"

Too shocked at how close to him she'd stopped, he hadn't responded.

"I'm furious with you right now," she'd spat, words echoing across the empty parking lot. "I'm still shaking. That's how badly I want to throttle you!"

"Hey." He'd raised his hands, his own anger spiking. "This is a bit much."

"You're not my protector!" Her seething temper had sought to repel him, but he held his ground as her gaze had darted to his throbbing cheekbone, the torn seam at his shoulder. "Back the hell down."

"Frankie," he'd said. "You need to—"

"I can handle myself," she'd cut him off, and only then had he noticed her lips were pale, her eyes too wide. "How dare you wade into my fight!"

"I was worried—"

"Quit worrying." Her breath had been hot on his chin. "If you show up here when I'm on the door again, it'll be the last night you ever see me."

He'd frowned at the unfair threat. "They could have hurt you."

She'd turned away, frustration a half-roar low in her throat. "They could have hurt *you!*"

"That's enough." He'd run the back of his hand along his jaw, still stinging from a punch. "You're reacting like no one's ever cared about you before."

She'd fallen still.

"Frankie," he'd said, in a weird form of angry begging. "You can't settle five full-grown men on your own."

"The manager said something like that when I applied."

She'd rounded on him, fists clenched by her sides. Her eyes had blazed. "Said my presence is intimidating, but that I don't possess a physique that demands respect."

"So why did he hire you?"

"I told him to come at me like he meant it. He did."

"And?"

She'd held his stare. "And I got the job."

Kris had taken a step back. "Show me."

She'd scoffed. "Get serious."

"*Show me.*"

Scowling, she'd said, "You're ordering me around now?"

"Yes."

She'd paused, almost seeming confused. "Fine."

Kris had doubled over before he knew she'd moved. His triceps throbbed and a second later, he'd been stomach-down on the concrete, his arm twisted behind him, her knee pressed against his spine.

"Again," he'd said, standing, attention raking over her body as if—now that he knew to look for it—he'd be able to see the strength and skill concealed like a blade in her lean form.

"That was the gentle version." She'd stood back without looking at him. "I refuse to hurt you to prove a point."

"I don't want you to do this," he'd said. She was still new to him, but every part of him rioted against a job that put her in danger. "Can't I prove that point?"

"No." She'd turned her back completely. "I need the money —not you doubting my ability to earn it. Don't turn up when I'm on the door. Don't join my fights. Let me do my job, because if you put yourself at risk like that again, I'm out of here. I'm not kidding."

It had driven him mad, but he'd done as she'd asked, and she'd carved herself a reputation in their town for taking down threats hard and fast. A bouncer to be reckoned with, respected.

Made sense, didn't it?

That she'd be a good fit as his bodyguard.

He'd never been more than a job to her anyway.

◯

The city lights blurred as Frankie sniffled and ran the back of her wrist under her nose. She was all decorum, hunched on the top step of one of Kira City's landmarks, falling apart at two in the morning. It was her adolescence all over again. This had been her secret spot in her younger years, mainly because her dad had never managed to find her here.

Wryly known as The Scepter, the cobbled steps ran half a dozen blocks upward from the city center toward the palace. An unforgiving climb that struck straight and true, the angle of the hill concealing an entire stretch of civilization and creating the illusion that it led right to the palace gates.

It didn't, obviously. Any straight stretch of steps that long and steep would be a public health hazard. *Tourist slips on step, falls two and a half miles.* Dropping her head between her knees, Frankie considered tipping forward and seeing how far she rolled. The pain might finally stop her from replaying everything Kris had said to her.

I haven't known you at all.

You lied to me. You used me.

I blame you.

What the fuck, Frankie?

I never want to see you again.

She tried to get a hold of herself, shoving the heels of her palms against her closed eyes.

He'd reacted so visibly. Skin pale, features torn. Pulling at his hair as if he could pull her lies out of his life. It had taken every reserve of control not to buckle and admit the truth.

He was training to be the king. Royalty had standards and she couldn't even be scraped off the bottom of the barrel.

Kris might refuse to acknowledge the expectations that came with his position, but she didn't have that luxury. Her job was to stay focused on the man he would become. Royal life would apply pressure and demand he endure it. He'd shift his weight, stance widening, and take it on until he'd reformed beneath it. Give it a year, maybe two, and the cowboy inside him would hardly exist.

He'd be shaped into a king.

With duties.

Only after Mark's official abdication and Kris's coronation would Philip raise a critical matter of business. The thought alone dampened Frankie's pillow at night, but she knew by the time that conversation took place, she couldn't be on Kris's radar. He'd need to set his sights higher and use his God-given charm and sexual appetite to replenish the royal line.

Pain crushed her and she gave a strangled sob.

Tonight, she'd started that process. She'd cut him off in every way. No friendship. No attraction. Nothing left to salvage. If he believed he'd been nothing but a job to her, he'd pull back. Block her out and move on.

Then she could focus on her overflowing priorities. Ensure Mark and Ava were effectively cocooned outside of the public eye. Continue to gently steer Tommy toward public appearances. Stop Kris from getting into trouble. Manage the security of the palace. And continue her investigation into the balcony collapse that had killed the late royal family.

Quit, a defeated part of her yearned. *This mess is too big. Just leave.*

But she couldn't.

Resolve thickened like a scab over that yearning. She'd never quit. Working for the royal guard was an opportunity she'd shaped for herself. It was her chance to live an honorable life—to prove her own decency.

And she hadn't proven it yet.

The tread of footsteps from below had her stiffening. Swiftly wiping her eyes on the sleeve of Hanna's shirt, she looked up with a scowl.

"Chill, babe. It's just me." Zara Nguyen was regarding her with grim sympathy as she climbed the final few steps and sat beside her. She wore a light dress and flip-flops. Easy summer clothes to roll into after being rudely woken in the night. She extended her hands and a pile of chocolate bars rained down on the step between Frankie's feet. "Supplies."

Frankie sniffled, cheeks heating. "I didn't ask you to come."

"Yeah, well." Leaning back on her palms, Zara gave a small smile. "Women-in-need is kind of my thing."

God, was that how Zara saw her? Frankie set her shoulders, sitting straighter.

They'd met months ago while helping with Ava's escape, and soon after, Frankie had offered to deliver weekly self-defense classes at Zara's women's shelter. In that time, she'd warmed to the woman's crass friendship—obviously more than she'd realized, since she'd messaged her earlier.

Shit hit the fan with Kris. Falling apart without class at top of Scepter. Coffee tomorrow?

And Zara had found her.

"It's the middle of the night," Frankie said, cheeks still hot as she swiped up a chocolate bar. "I shouldn't have messaged you. This is nothing. I overreacted."

"Stop making this about you." Zara knocked Frankie's arm with her elbow. "I want the goss."

Frankie eyed her and Zara gazed back, teasing yet expectant. Weird. Although being caught with a puffy face was top-tier mortification to Frankie, Zara didn't seem to be judging.

"Fine," she said, and took a steadying breath. "Kris has this little habit of slipping security sometimes when he's out in the city."

Zara snorted, then sobered swiftly at Frankie's look and said, "Bad prince."

"Reckless," Frankie said. "He's been doing it more often. Tonight, I stopped him." Her throat thickened and she bit into caramel chocolate. A waste, really, because she couldn't taste a thing. "He was so happy to see me. Like a kid bursting open a *piñata*."

"Oh, honey." Zara swiped up a bar near Frankie's foot.

"I told him the truth." Well, parts of it. "He tried to be angry, but he was devastated." His desolate glances and fraught movements had gutted her. "I'd hoped he wouldn't care too much, not after I'd kept my distance since he'd arrived in Kiraly. But he did." Her voice shook as she remembered his pained confusion, his pleas for her to tell him he was wrong. "Then I pretended our friendship had been part of the job, because I can't be in his life anymore. Not the way I used to be. This needs to be the end of it."

"Hang on a second," Zara said.

Frankie's stomach balled.

Swiveling, her friend regarded her through narrowed eyes. "This doesn't sound like the end of a friendship."

"It sure as shit isn't the happy middle."

"No." She pointed her half-eaten chocolate at Frankie. "This sounds like a breakup."

Looking away, Frankie said, "Don't devalue friendship by assuming it can't hurt like this to lose it."

Zara hummed, sounding unconvinced, but didn't push.

They sat in silence, punctuated only by the rustle of wrappers and Frankie's occasional rapid, jagged intake of breath. A dog barked in the distance. The headlights of a car broke through the buildings below and disappeared again. Moonlight made liquid silver on the surface of the lake far below.

Then Zara spoke softly. "Kris *is* pretty gorgeous."

Caught off guard, Frankie glared at her.

"Oh, put it away." Toeing off her flip-flops, Zara pressed the soles of her feet onto the stone step. "If you were just friends, you'd apologize to him, explain why you did what you did, and eventually he'd come back around."

Heart tight, Frankie turned back to stare at the city below.

"So when you said *this needs to be the end of it,*" Zara said, "I assume by *it,* you mean he thinks you're pretty gorgeous, too."

"He's wanted to get in my pants since we met," she muttered, unwilling to romanticize the sweet thrum of desire between them.

"Making you the one who got away."

"He needs to move on." Frankie didn't manage to hide the dismay from her voice.

"Because he's royalty and you're not?"

"Yes."

Zara sighed, shaking her head before lowering her forehead into her palm.

"You going to try to convince me that status doesn't matter?"

"I wish I could." Zara's voice was strangely sad. "But royalty is a world above. They're not made for us. And we're definitely not made for them."

Frankie swallowed hard.

"Honestly, what's with these Jaroka guys falling for women they can't realistically be with? I swear, next thing I know, I'm going to be sitting at a bar talking coping strategies with some woman in love with Tomas."

"Pass on my condolences," Frankie muttered, because if a woman fell for Tommy, it wouldn't end well for her.

"I guess you just avoid Kris from now on?" Zara wriggled her toes in the warm night air. "And wait for time and distance to make this all go away?"

"Not exactly." Frankie resisted covering her head with her forearms. "New protocol. Whenever he's outside palace grounds, I'm going to be his bodyguard."

"You're—what?" Her friend sounded startled. "You're not much bigger than I am."

"I could take you before you'd seen me move," she mumbled.

"While that leaves me suitably terrified, I'm not planning on harming your prince."

"I'm not a full-grown male, but I know how to subdue one." Not to mention that all members of the royal guard carried a firearm on duty.

"Alright, hang on." Zara was shaking her head. "I'm lost. Because obviously my first thought is that volunteering to be his bodyguard is the perfect way to ensure he gets over you. You know, spending lots of time together one-on-one really aids separation."

Frankie pressed her eyes shut, groaning.

"You command a security team, sweetcakes. Lock someone else by his side when he leaves the palace."

"I can't." She couldn't trust anyone else. "He can be stupid. Only I can tell what he's going to do before he does it." Only she could keep him safe.

There was a beat of silence. "Oh my God."

"What?"

Zara was shaking her head. "This is not going to work."

"It won't be forever." Just until she'd removed any lingering threat to the royal family. "After tonight, he's cut me out. I'll just be there in the background to make sure he doesn't get hurt."

"Sure, whatever you said to him tonight might be what he needs to get over you," Zara said. "But this bodyguard gig is the perfect way to make sure you never get over him."

"I'll be fine."

A lie. A bulging, splitting-at-the-seams lie, because Kris wasn't just gorgeous. He was soul-stealing. And she wanted him to have it, the soul he'd lifted right out of her being, because in all her years before she'd met him, she'd never felt whole alone inside herself. Around him, she felt unbroken.

A mighty lure to resist.

"Okay," Zara said, and then gave her a glance that was the opposite of reassuring. "But do we want to make this our regular meeting spot for when you realize you've made a huge mistake? Or do you want to come to my place next time?"

Frankie glowered at her. "I can focus on the job."

"Yeah." Zara gave a little smile and patted her on the leg again. "Let's do my place."

4

Kris strode through a palace that in no way reflected the events of the night before. The chaos Frankie had wrecked should be all around him. The pre-dawn summer air should be acrid with her betrayal. The respectful, subdued palace staff should be dashing around, harried and alarmed. The wallpaper should be slashed, antique vases smashed in the corridors and the sound of weeping floating around corners. For all the pain she'd caused, there should be a rift in the damn mountainside.

Outside, Kiraly was oblivious in the early morning shadows.

Kris took off his hat—that always found its way back to him—as he and Tommy slid into the limo that would take them to Kuria Estate, the royal mansion on the outskirts of the city. The engine started, preparing to depart along with several security cars behind them.

"At least she thought better of the bodyguard idea," Tommy said, rolling up the sleeves of his old blue and grey plaid shirt.

Kris rustled up a grunt in response, vaguely aware that no member of the royal guard sat in front with the driver.

Then he saw her.

Tearing out of the wide front entrance and down the vast sweep of steps. Something pinched in his torso as the sight of her under the golden outdoor spotlights. Her hair was a mess, her features haggard. The navy-blue security uniform from the night before was gone, replaced with her old boots, blue skinny jeans and a summer jacket the shade of a good sangria. She looked . . . like Frankie.

"Or not," Tommy murmured.

She wove around several attendants without slowing her descent, and at one point, he was certain she considered leaping over the valet rather than sidestepping him.

At the car, she pressed her forearm over the driver's window to speak to them and Kris caught sight of a shoulder holster concealed beneath her jacket. Then she was hauling the back door open and clambering in, breathing hard as she sat opposite him and Tommy. Scrubbing her face with one hand—something she did when she was beyond exhausted—she reached around to strap herself in with the other. Everything about her was uncontrolled energy, until the car glided away from the palace and she sat back and just . . . shut down. Staring at the vacant middle seat between him and Tommy, posture rigid, face impassive.

This again.

Kris shifted slowly, deliberately, knees widening so his leg interrupted her line of sight. Her gaze flickered and he sensed his movement steal her complete attention.

Tension bristled in the enclosed space.

"Morning," Tommy said quietly.

Her only acknowledgement was to incline her head.

Kris bit his tongue. He wanted to say a thousand things, but it would all spring from heartbreak and he didn't want her to look inside him with that blank stare.

Teeth clenching, he turned to stare out the window.

"I have questions," Tommy said. There was a pause in which she gave no verbal response, but he continued with, "Did you instruct my guards to show me the cabin and passageways?"

Kris almost turned to gape at his brother. *That's* what Tommy had been thinking about? The reality of her working in security? Kris was too deeply entrenched in her lies to consider anything else.

"Yes," she said.

The sound of her voice, throaty and detached, collected all the tension inside him and knotted it in the center of his chest. *Frankie,* was all he could think. *What have you done?*

"Why?" Tommy asked.

"I thought it would interest you."

"It would have interested me to know you were here," Tommy said, voice hard.

Kris pressed his eyes shut as the knot tightened.

She didn't respond.

"Were our guards randomly assigned?"

"Of course not."

There was the light sound of Tommy shifting. "Why did you assign mine?"

"Aside from being faultless at their job, I'd thought you'd be comfortable around them."

Kris frowned out the window. That clearly wasn't the reason she'd assigned Hanna and Peter to him. It was impossible to be comfortable around statues.

"Was I wrong?" she asked, tone agonizingly neutral. "I can find you different guards."

"Leave them." Tommy moved on. "What was your role in the palace before you came to Montana?"

"I—" She stopped. "I didn't work in the palace."

Kris tried not to frown; tried not to seem as if he cared enough to listen.

"Philip sent you to monitor us without appropriate experience?" Tommy sounded incredulous. "The man I've seen order staff to refold napkins because the creases weren't suitable for royal use?"

"He didn't exactly send me." Her tone was equal parts uncomfortable and exhausted, and a deep-down part of Kris wanted to tell Tommy to do this another time.

"Explain *didn't exactly*," Tommy said.

"Philip wouldn't hire me. But I got him to agree that if I could find the estranged Jaroka family, he'd give me a job." She hesitated. "So, I found you. And instead of coming back immediately to a position in the palace, I—I stayed."

Kris curled his fingers against the urge to ask why.

"You stayed to monitor us," Tommy said, "officially entering the employment of our uncle."

She hesitated again. "Something like that."

"Funny how things turn out." His words were edged with cynicism. "After years of spying and lying your way into our lives in order to secure a job, your position is now in our hands."

Kris swung a glance at his brother with a sharp, "Tom."

"I'm not firing her," Tommy murmured, gaze still on Frankie. "But I feel it's important to point out that we could."

Christ. In the corner of Kris's eye, Frankie remained stiff and unmoving, and Kris almost choked on the power imbalance.

"She's concealed herself for over three months. Our own head of personal security deliberately *hid* from us. Not to mention the real reason for her being in Sage Haven. The general trend is that she thinks it's okay to lie to us. That we don't deserve her respect. You might have known us as cowboys, Frankie, but don't forget that we're your sovereign."

"I haven't forgotten." Her features were pinched. "Your Highness."

The silence was suffocating for the rest of the journey.

Mark was waiting as they pulled up at the top of the drive, his arms crossed and expression somber in the first rays of sunlight. Kris's gut wrenched at the sight of him, his resentment feeling too close to grief. How could his own brother have kept this from him? Mark would never have lied like this back home.

This place, this life, was changing them.

Mark turned without a word and led the way across the grounds to the empty, half-timbered stables. Kris got it—the unspoken understanding that they didn't need Mark's staff looking on, listening in. This was between brothers with simple beginnings and what should be simple respect for each other.

Frankie followed at a distance with the other guards.

Inside the stables, Kris ran his tongue along his teeth, leaning against a closed stall door with Mark standing opposite him. His anger at Mark's secret-keeping hummed in the dusty air, but just as strong was their almost palpable discomfort—an instinctive resistance to bad blood between them.

The moment felt barbed, and Kris's skin felt torn already.

"Mark," Tommy said, sitting off to one side on the steps that led to the hayloft.

Mark had been avoiding eye contact. Now he looked at Kris with unwavering sincerity. "I'm sorry, Kris," he said. "I didn't want this."

Kris huffed out a bitter breath, shaking his head.

"How long have you known she was here?" Tommy asked.

Mark rubbed a hand along the back of his neck. "I found out soon after we arrived."

That kicked Kris square in the gut. Months. Mark had known about Frankie for *months*.

"What the hell, Mark?" Tommy leaned forward in disbelief. "Why didn't you tell us?"

"She asked me not to." Mark glanced at Tommy, features

pained. "I've tried to convince her to talk to Kris—so many times —but she's refused."

"You should have told me anyway." Kris spoke quietly, but his words shook.

"I—" Mark stared at him, stricken. "It was complicated."

No, it wasn't.

"You knew I'd been trying to reach her." Kris pushed off the stall door, outrage swelling in his veins. "That I was struggling without her. And you're defending yourself?"

Mark half-turned away before turning back, looking harassed. "I promised her."

"You know what she means to me!" The words seemed to cut his throat on the way out. "I'm your brother! Your first promise is to me. You know how badly I—" Kris swiftly spun around and pounded his fist against the stall.

"I wasn't supposed to find out," Mark said behind him.

"But you *did* find out." Kris spun back to him. "You found out and you didn't tell me. I've been going crazy. I'd have thought that after Ava, all these months of not being able to contact her, not knowing where she was, you'd know how it feels." The agitation; the anguish. "I've found myself literally trying to pull my hair out from missing her—and you've known she's been right here!"

The following silence was strained. Tommy shifted, running a hand over his face. Mark shot a glance toward the stable door.

"She got Ava out," he murmured.

Kris stilled. *What?*

Tommy stood slowly, frowning. "What do you mean?"

"It's why she made me promise." Mark's blue eyes were so earnest, Kris almost had to look away. "Philip doesn't know. Neither does anyone on her team. She could have lost her job. She planned the escape, coordinated it, and single-handedly erased the evidence. The only reason I found out about Frankie at all is because there were complications on the night, and she had to intervene. She got Ava out," he repeated, gesturing helplessly toward the mansion, toward his fiancée. "I owed it to Frankie to keep her secret. I've hated every second of lying to you, but that's . . . why I did it."

Kris leaned back against the stall, this time for the support. "Why?"

His brother understood. "She's head of security—she saw everything and pieced together Ava's situation. You know how messed up it was. Frankie visited Ava one morning and told her she was going to get her out so she could be with Darius. And she did."

Frankie had rescued Ava.

Frankie had risked her own back to help a visiting princess—a woman she didn't know. All the while, she'd hid from him.

Kris slid down the stall until he was sitting with his face pressed into his hands. He felt dazed. "I don't know what to think."

Tommy lowered himself onto the dirt-packed floor beside him and admitted, "This does change a few things."

Mark joined them, nudging Kris with his boot. "She's still our Frankie, you know?"

The woman Mark had just described was every bit his best friend, but the woman who'd stood hard-hearted in his room last night, and who'd sat opposite him in the car—was that still his Frankie? He wished he knew.

Frankie was positioned a respectful distance away from the stables with Hanna and Peter. They were murmuring an easy conversation behind her, results from a big football game, and Tommy's guards were taking the opportunity to catch up with a few members of Mark's security on the far side of the stables. Despite the warmth of a hot summer's day in the making, Frankie was cold clean through.

The drive here had been torture. Tommy's stony questions and Kris's hostile silence had been made worse by the truth behind this visit. Frankie had come between these brothers.

Throat thick, she turned at a movement from the mansion. Ava had emerged in a bumblebee-yellow dress and was making her way toward them across the hillside on the pebbled path. Darius, her three-year-old boy, was at her side. Black-haired and olive-skinned, they looked so alike Frankie ached.

Ava was different to when they'd first met, and it had nothing to do with that pixie haircut. Her posture was less rigid; her spine no longer a coiled spring. Her gait was smoother, her features relaxed.

Nearing, she waved to Frankie, gesturing her over, and Frankie lifted a hand in return, intentionally misunderstanding. Her goal was to blend with the guards, not expose herself beside the stunning and sophisticated Princess of Kelehar. Standing beside Ava made Frankie feel like scrawled graffiti on an otherwise unspoiled white fence.

Besides, her sense of inferiority was already off the charts today.

"Frankie," Ava called, gesturing again. "Join us."

God, okay. Striding out to meet them, Frankie tried to think of something to discuss. She'd never been a fan of small talk. The only possible purpose of asking a question when she didn't care about the answer was to establish a subject for the next time she was obliged to ask a question when she wouldn't care about the answer.

"Your Highness." Frankie bowed before sliding a hand in the back pocket of her jeans. She glanced at Darius, who was blinking up at her from where he stood slightly behind the long skirt of Ava's dress, holding a book in one hand. "Hello there," she said, clueless about how to greet a small child. "You okay?"

He smiled.

"You're not." Ava was eyeing her with a frown. "You look terrible."

Fantastic. Criticism on her appearance from a goddess. "Cheers."

Ava gave a small roll of her eyes. "I was intending to convey sympathy."

"Needs work."

The woman sighed, but there was a smile hidden in there somewhere. "I'd like to invite you to my bridal shower next week."

"Invite me to—" Frankie cut off with a baffled frown. "Why?"

"Because I'd like you there," Ava answered, studying her. Then she reached back, gently touching Darius on the shoulder and steering him forward. "He wanted to say hello. He talks about you."

Startled, Frankie deflected. "All bad things, I'm sure."

"No bad things," the princess said firmly. "He remembers you taking control that night. Remembers you sending him away with me." She paused, arching an amused brow. "He also remembers that you were eating pizza."

"Now that's the kind of memory you keep close," Frankie said, not sure what else to say. She offered the kid a grin and he returned it.

Oh, man. The trust in his smile physically hurt.

"He likes you." Ava toyed with the gold engagement ring on her finger. "Don't you, Darius?"

"Yes," he said.

"Um." Frankie gave a nod. "Awesome. Thanks."

Ava cleared her throat, tilting her head downward pointedly.

Swallowing, Frankie knelt and softened at the boy's closeness. He didn't hug her, but stepped in and rested a hand on her leg as he held up the book. "I have a new book."

"Looks slick. Where did you get it?"

"Ava gave it to me."

Frankie nodded, noting that he still didn't call Ava his mother. "Have you read it yet?"

"Yes." But he crouched on the grass beside her and opened it, clearly expecting her to read it again with him.

"Uh." Lord. Kids were about as familiar to her as a pair of loving arms. But this—how exactly did she say no to this? She cast a pleading, get-out-of-jail-free-card glance at Ava, but found the princess frowning at the stables. On her own, Frankie settled on her shins and gingerly drew the book closer. "Alright, just don't spoil the ending."

Darius leaned in as she started reading, fully resting against her thigh, and then, well, she hardly knew what happened. She wasn't used to being touched by a child—feeling welcomed by innocence, and something neglected inside her gasped at the pain of it all. The way his small finger pointed out the pictures. The way his other hand fiddled lightly, distractedly, with the buckles on her boot. The way he wriggled at exciting parts, and looked up to watch her own reaction. It was so honest—but instead of wanting to run, she wanted *more,* and the impossibility of that welled up inside her like blood beneath a bruise.

"Frankie, why have you stopped?" Darius regarded her with his impossibly wide eyes.

"Sorry." She shook her head. *Pull it together.* "I didn't get enough sleep last night."

He touched her leg. "You can nap in my bed."

Jesus. Her laugh broke a little, and Ava turned to look down at her. "I'll be okay."

Frankie kept reading through the lump in her throat. And

only once she'd finished, Darius closing the book with a grin up at her, did she pull herself together enough to realize everything around her was quiet. Her skin prickled. Cutting a swift glance over her shoulder, she found Kris standing in the doorway to the stables, one hand braced high against the doorjamb, the thumb of his other hand looped through his belt.

His attention was fixed on her.

For once, his expression was unreadable.

Nerves balled her stomach as she abruptly turned away. Her face burned hot; her cheeks pulsed. His crisp blue eyes could be startlingly disarming when he wasn't mucking around. Fighting for composure, she nudged Darius lightly with her elbow. "We good?"

"Yes. Thank you, Frankie."

"Cool." She stood on unsteady legs, the thought of Kris's scrutiny making her skin shrink several sizes—pulling tight, sealing her in. She deliberately faced Ava as she jerked a thumb down at Darius. "The manners on this kid."

"You should hear him when he's hungry." Ava's gaze was speculative as she angled herself toward Kris. "Will you quit looming like that? It's boorish."

Frankie dropped back swiftly, locking her hands behind her back and redirecting her gaze to the mansion. Her heartbeat was thick in her neck as she watched him approach from the corner of her eye.

"We're all boors to you, Ava." His voice was rough, weary, but he aimed for a brighter tone as he said, "Hey, Darry, how's your new room? All settled in?"

"Yes." Darius sounded shy. "Are you Tomas or Kristof? I've forgotten."

Fair enough, since he'd only met them three nights ago at Mark and Ava's engagement party.

"I'm Kris. Tommy's the serious one." There was a brief

silence, before he said wryly to Ava, "I get that you avoid shortening names for some weird well-bred reason, but can you at least teach him ours properly?"

Ava practically sniffed. "I happen to like your full names."

"Well, *Markus* is all yours," he said. "And don't worry. He's fine, even though he deserved a round or two after he—" He cut off and Frankie felt his attention lunge for her. "You know," he finished coolly.

Even peripherally, his attention left her breathless.

Then he was striding into her line of sight, his back to her as he aimed for the car. Within moments, Tommy appeared in his wake.

Time to go.

"See you, Darius," she said, avoiding the look on Ava's face before taking off after Kris and Tommy.

She could handle the brothers' silent treatment and being cut out of their circle of trust. She could deal with her feelings for Kris like she always had—working around the beautiful, battered ache inside her, tucked up and under where her lowest ribs met. She could keep her head down—keep Kris out of harm's way.

Zara had been weighted by middle-of-the-night pessimism when she'd declared this wouldn't work. It would take some adjustment, sure, but Zara didn't know the weight Frankie lugged around as baseline pain—the sacrifices she'd made to keep those she cared for safe.

It would hurt, but she'd honed herself to withstand far worse.

This was going to work.

5

Kris didn't leave the palace grounds for four days.

He didn't want to see Frankie. Didn't want her near him, observing him, protecting him. Yet even as her deception clawed him raw, he didn't want to request a new bodyguard. That would feel too final. As if he'd decided to cut her out of his life for good, and he couldn't even reach the end of that thought without his stomach turning.

He pounded out his frustration in the palace gym, tore laps up and down the pool, and rode hard on the mountain tracks.

It *just* took the edge off.

Predictably, Philip practically crowed with delight at the resulting lack of PR disasters. Days on end without incident! Media coverage without reference to a cowboy! Kris contemplated short-sheeting the man's bed just to wipe that smug smile off his face—and for being a player in Frankie's concealment—but figured he owed him a few days' respite.

This was hardly going to be the new normal.

Philip worked with him each day in the tower study, and with Mark's help, Kris started to wrap his brain around the nation's policies and agreements. His head swam with measures for strong national health, education, inclusion, and safe living; it grappled with strategies for environmental protection and sustainability, budgets, and taxes. Unexpectedly, it all began to make sense. The fact that his hedonistic, indolent uncle Vinci had approved such strong policies almost made Kris reassess his opinion of the man.

All was forgiven between Kris and Mark by the second day. Mark turned up for their usual Tuesday beer and poker night—which Kris insisted they play in his sitting room instead of the cabin beyond the palace grounds—and Kris felt something unstable inside him realign.

But he couldn't forgive Frankie so easily.

A brutal kind of restlessness claimed him by the third night. He hated not knowing what to do, and hated that Frankie had put him in this position. The ferocity of his frustration built, making him want to knock down a wall or dig a well with his bare hands. Instead, he tracked Tommy down in one of the private libraries and stalked the rows until his brother finally agreed to play cards between his stacks of books.

"You can't avoid her forever," Tommy said, sighing as he lost another hand. "I can't put up with you like this for that long."

"Like what?" Kris shuffled the cards as if he wanted to snap their spines.

"Like a man who's waited years for something, only to find out he can never have it." Tommy's fingers tapped against the desk. "You're dazed and incensed."

Kris raised his hands, pulling a face. "I'm just sitting here, man."

"But I'll bet the thought of tearing every book off its shelf holds appeal. Throwing them out the window. Hauling the curtains down after them."

Kris narrowed his eyes at the nearby bookshelf. That did sound pretty good.

"After that, it'd probably feel cathartic to start a fight—venting through a shouting match, and it'd probably be with me because you know I don't take any of your shit." Tommy cocked a brow, as if to ask, *am I right?* "You'd keep at it until it forced Frankie to show up and intervene for our own safety."

Frankie. Her hands on him, hauling him away from Tommy. Her face close to his as she barked at him to get it together. Furious with him. Responding to him. *Looking* at him.

"I don't want to see her," he said, almost choking on the lie.

"Holding yourself captive isn't going to help."

"I'm just sitting here," he said again, voice turning harsh.

"Feeling caged."

"Hanging out with you."

"Because you have nowhere else to go."

Aggression slapped his palms on the desk, pushing him into Tommy's space. "Are you *trying* to make me start that fight?"

"No." Tommy leaned back in his chair, gaze level. "But I'm angry with her, too, and I don't like that she's won. She's confused you by coming clean and then making herself your bodyguard—so you're avoiding her. You pose no risk of ditching security if you don't even leave these walls."

Kris pulled back, crossing his arms.

"Either sort it out," Tommy said, raising a shoulder. "Or get rid of her. You've got too much going on to dwell on it."

Kris wanted to overturn the table at how matter-of-factly Tommy said *get rid of her.*

Looked like he had to sort it out.

"I don't know what to say to her," he muttered. "Still don't know how I feel about it."

"You're never going to feel only one way. It's complicated. Now, make plans for the weekend. Out there." Not meeting his eye, Tommy gestured in the direction of Kira City. "That don't involve bothering me."

Translation: Tommy was still pissed at him over the king thing, and despite being supportive, he didn't want to have to pretend nothing was wrong whenever Kris came knocking.

"But I love bothering you," Kris said, unsettled by his brother's continued resentment.

"I don't love losing at cards."

"Then why do it so often?" Smirking at his brother's glare, Kris left him to his family history research.

By the following night, Tommy's words had grafted onto Kris's already thriving frustration, growing into a rippling outrage. He prowled his sitting room. She'd lied for years and then stunned him with the reveal, using his pain as a management strategy for keeping him in line. A wicked trick. He should reposition her within the palace, somewhere they'd never cross paths, and be done with it. Except—

The image of her with Darius. He couldn't shake it. It softened her, like seeing a woman with her hair down for the first time, but well, a thousand times *more* than that. The way her body had leaned into the boy, her arm brushing against his pile of black hair as she turned the page. Kris's heart had fallen apart right there in the stable doorway. Hard and hurt one moment, then so tender the muscle had all but flopped out of his chest the next. Unfair. She shouldn't be allowed to read to children; she shouldn't be allowed to reunite them with their mothers. It confused everything.

Fine. *Fine.* He would go out tomorrow evening and drag her along with him. He might ignore her or he might confront her. He'd find out.

For now, his irritation was making him hungry.

"Kitchen trip," he said to his night guards as he strode out into the corridor.

"Yes, Your Highness."

It was late, nearing midnight, and the wall sconces in the

corridors had been dimmed to a gentle glow. On the ground floor, he made his way to the simple passageway that led to the palace kitchen. It was narrower than the main areas—a space that functioned rather than displayed, though a large silk tapestry had appeared within hours of him first sniffing out the kitchen months ago. A hurried, *he's-not-supposed-to-come-down-here* attempt to make it fit for royal presence.

He almost sighed when Hanna emerged from an adjoining corridor and entered the kitchen ahead of him, her candy-apple red jumpsuit hinting she'd just returned from a night out. Great. There'd be no stimulating conversation from her over supper.

Kris rounded the entrance—then halted as Hanna let loose a squeal.

"*Gul!*"

She ran across the half-lit room. Not in a subduing-a-threat kind of way, but more like a girl pelting toward a puppy in a field of flowers. Glee in her stride, petals billowing around her.

Kris blinked. Gul had been Ava's old guard before she'd run away, and now worked for the Kiralian Royal Guard handling VIP guests. He was the only other person in the kitchen, standing with his back to the entrance in front of an open fridge stocked with leftovers, a loaded plate in hand. He'd stiffened at Hanna's call and swiftly set the plate down on the fridge shelf in front of him—an instant before she leapt onto his back.

Stunned, Kris stood rooted to the spot.

"Gul, I've missed you!" Hanna's arms were tight around his neck, her legs wrapped around his middle. "Where have you been? I haven't seen you for *ages*."

"It has been at least six days, you're right." Gul's low voice was warm with affection. "I've been living a half-life without you."

"You're teasing me!" But she clung on, pressing the side of her face against the back of his neck. "I've been dying to tell you about Frankie and Prince Kristof. Oh my God. There's something epic going on there. Did you hear he asked to kiss her?"

Kris flinched, and his vision blazed red. Frankie had shared that moment with her team? Then he remembered her earpiece —the way she'd told him to wait on the drive back to the palace. No. She hadn't told them. They'd overheard.

His night guards shifted uncomfortably beside him. Suspecting they intended to draw attention to themselves—and therefore to him—to stop Hanna talking, he shot them a silencing glance.

He wanted to hear this.

"Yes, and that she didn't actually say no," Gul responded, picking up his plate again and rifling through the fridge with Hanna on his back. "But I think you mean tragic, not epic. She's a commoner."

"She's also a badass."

"And while that deserves its own social status, high above us working class, the world remains unjust."

"It's not imposs—ooh." Hanna unhooked one arm from his neck to pat at his shoulder. "Blueberry pastry, blueberry pastry." He passed one up to her and she continued talking around a mouthful. "They've both been bulldozed by it. He's like a rabid animal and she hasn't slept since. Her skin is a little green, like the whole episode subbed out her heart for a kidney, but it can't clean the anguish from her blood because even her body knows that Prince Kristof is supposed to flow through her."

Kris suddenly lost the ability to breathe.

"That's visceral," Gul commented, opening a large container and piling sandwich triangles onto his plate. "And somewhat poetic. You're full of surprises."

"I'm a wordsmith who likes to shoot things. What can I say?"

Gul chuckled. "I'd say you're romanticizing this more than you should."

Kris was forced to agree. He took a step forward and said, "Hanna."

He didn't need to raise his voice for it to travel across the deserted kitchen.

Hanna and Gul froze. She dropped from his back as he spun around, the humor fleeing from their faces as they ended up side by side, spines straight and features neutral. The perfect guard façade. A moment later, they bowed in tandem.

"Gul," Kris said, attention moving between them. "Evening."

The man inclined his head, emanating formality.

Kris crossed the tiled floor, forcing himself to keep it casual. "What's happening here?"

Hanna swallowed what looked to be an overly large mouthful of blueberry pastry. Her voice was thick with it as she answered, "A snack, Your Highness. How can I assist you?"

"By bringing back the Hanna I just saw and explaining why you pretend to be someone else around me."

She kept her gaze downcast. "I'm afraid I can't do either of those things, Your Highness."

His irritation flared. "Why not?"

She hiccupped. Too much pastry in a single swallow, or perhaps too many drinks wherever she'd been that night. Gul rolled his lips together, lowering his face farther, as she said, "My orders, Your Highness."

"Your *orders*?"

The corners of her mouth turned down just a fraction, as if she regretted her words.

Well, this was insightful. He moved to the stack of clean plates at the end of the counter, set out for resident palace staff with midnight appetites. "Orders from the head of personal security, by any chance?"

There were several moments of silence—punctuated by another hiccup—that she finally broke with a muttered, "Damn it."

"I've been here for months, Hanna." In an effort to keep himself under control, he opened a second industrial-sized, stainless steel fridge. He hardly saw what he put on his plate. "You've followed me just about everywhere. Avoiding eye contact, rarely speaking, regardless of how many times I've tried to draw you out with conversation. But here you are." He gestured between her and Gul with a stuffed bagel, the beat of frustration sharp in his neck. "Proving it's all been an act. And I am *done* with being lied to by the people around me."

His head spun. This energetic and excitable woman had been ordered to disengage around him. Why? *Why* would Frankie do that to him?

Hanna didn't answer, but guilt had crept into her eyes. Then she hiccupped again.

Kris stared at her.

She did it again.

He raised a brow. "That's kind of killing the tension here, don't you think?"

There—a spark of amusement lit her features. The first sign of her true personality, directed at him, in over three months. "My apologies, Your Highness."

"I want to know why Frankie—"

Another hiccup interrupted him.

Kris ran a hand over his mouth but couldn't hold back his grin. "Get some water, for God's sake."

Hanna made a small noise—a kind of "*meep*"—and darted to fill a glass under the tap. Gul waited silently, hands behind his back and chin still angled down. Kris couldn't tell if he was uncomfortable or keeping a lid on his own amusement.

Once Hanna had drained a full glass and returned

sheepishly to Gul's side, Kris continued. "From now on, I want you to be yourself around me," he said, hating that this request was even necessary. "That goes for all of you," he added, louder, throwing a glance at his overnight security posted by the door. "Have a chat, talk to me. Laugh. Joke around. Tease me—we all know I deserve it. Please?"

"Your Highness," Hanna said, wincing. "I'm not sure—"

"Finish dishing up," he said firmly, cutting her off. "Then we're all going to sit together and have a chat. That's an order. Because your boss might be a badass, but I'm your prince."

Funny. Hanna ran out of resistance after that.

Frankie's headache was a pounder. She'd opened the window of her small room and set the fan on high, but even after a cool shower, the hammering at her temples persisted. She shouldn't be surprised. This was a lot bigger than a heat headache.

Tossing the damp towel onto the desk, she pulled on a pair of bed shorts and cotton camisole and collapsed into the only comfortable seat in the room—an old, fraying armchair that had come with the simple staff quarters. With one-hundred-and-forty-eight bedrooms in the servants' wing, the rooms were old, poky and unadorned. In other words, perfect. There was a bed with a mattress several decades older than she was, but it was a double and the palace laundry handled washing the sheets, so she couldn't complain. Then there was this armchair and the coffee table she propped her feet on. All she needed.

Other staff plugged in bar fridges or brought in their own furniture to make their room feel more like home, but Frankie had never owned furniture or a home, and she had no issues grabbing her meals from the dining hall. If she was safe, she was happy.

Sighing, she closed her eyes and slowed her breathing. Her body sagged into the cushioning.

Her mind remained adamantly awake.

If she didn't get proper rest soon, her team would strong-arm her into the emergency department with exhaustion. She'd caught the concern on Hanna's face this week, the grim assessment in Peter's glances. Frankie wasn't naïve enough to believe the pair had kept her involvement with Kris a secret, but at least the rest of her team were smart enough to act like they were none the wiser.

She groaned, clamping a hand around the back of her neck and squeezing. Her tension was stockpiling. Kris hadn't left the palace grounds. Which was good. She'd had time to work, but it also meant she spent every second of the day poised, waiting for word that he was leaving, knowing she'd have to make a run for it so as not to delay a member of the royal family.

She'd then spent each night fixating on the fact that he was avoiding her.

The later the hour, the more foolish her thoughts became.

He hated her.

He never wanted to see her again.

He was going to fire her.

He was going to make her his mistress.

He was in hate-love with her and the next time he saw her, he wouldn't ask to kiss her, he'd just do it, shoving her against the nearest wall and—

Foolish or not, she'd stick by those thoughts right to the end.

Dropping her hand to her lap, she remembered the times it had been just the two of them—when she'd been too preoccupied by what separated them to soak up the simple pleasure of being alone with him. Walking the ranch with Kris in open-skied isolation, no brothers or neighbors for miles. Half-day road trips for supplies in his farm truck, filling the time by playing conversation games or songs they thought each other would like. Camping in the craggy mountains the few times he'd convinced her to do something so reckless—she'd come dangerously close to surrendering to their attraction on those rough, lonely slopes.

Now, she imagined she had given in.

Met his too-warm gaze over the campfire and held it. Allowed their stare to slide from a question into an unwavering answer. Made room for him as he slowly stood and came over to her, warmth gone from his face, replaced by a careful seriousness. Leaned into his touch as he reached for her face, his thumb brushing over her bottom lip a moment before his mouth—

Frankie started. Tangled in the ludicrous daydream, she was sure she'd imagined the knock on her door. It was beyond late. No one would come knocking.

Then she imagined it again.

"No," she called out, just in case.

"It's Hanna. I, uh—can we talk?"

Grumbling, but with no reason not to let her in, Frankie pushed herself out of the armchair. Ruffling her damp hair, she reached the door and dragged it open with a weary, "Yeah?"

Hanna stood in the middle of the doorway, still dressed up from her night out. Make up bold, blond hair loose. Her expression was peculiar. Uncomfortably apologetic.

"Realized you have the wrong room, Johansson?" Frankie asked dryly.

"No, ma'am," she answered, standing tall.

Frankie pressed her fingers into the bridge of her nose. "Do you want to come in?"

"No, ma'am. I'm really sorry about this." Hanna's gaze swung to her left as she spoke. "I understand that it's highly unprofessional. I would never, you know, except he came in while I was chatting with Gul and overheard—"

Hanna was cut off by a large male hand that reached out from the left of the corridor and cupped over her mouth.

Frankie's pulse lurched.

She knew that hand—the coarse-haired, muscled arm attached to it.

Hanna spoke again, but the hand muffled her words. It could have been, "I'm sorry." But could just as easily have been, "Don't kill me."

Slowly, Frankie leaned her head out the door, looking to the left. Even expecting him, her stomach ended up in her throat as their gazes clashed. He lounged against the corridor wall, facing her, eyes dangerous sparks of blue, close enough that she caught the woodland smell of him. Not the Kris from her campfire fantasy. He was rigid with barely contained temper, tight in his neck, bulging at the hinge of his jaw as he bit down hard.

Even angry, he filled her with a wild, hazardous need.

"Your Highness," she made herself say. "Care to unhand my staff?"

His only response was to lift a brow. His hand remained over Hanna's mouth, who was looking for all the world like, well, like a woman who'd unwillingly led an uncontainable prince to her superior's private sleeping quarters in the dead of night.

Frankie's own anger flared to life, fanned by her fatigue. How dare he put Hanna in this position? How dare he act so inappropriately?

He's your prince, her fading traces of reason reminded her. *And your guard is watching. Don't blow your top.*

"Your Highness," she said, grinding her irritation down into a measured tone. "I don't know what you're—"

"Silencing her," he said, before removing his hand. The first words he'd spoken to her in five days and the rough texture of his voice moved like friction inside her. "Though it shouldn't bother you, since you've ordered her silence since I got here."

Oh. Shit.

Frankie flicked a glance at Hanna. The woman's answering gaze was wary. "Dismissed, Johansson."

"Yes, ma'am."

Then Hanna was gone.

"Let's sort this out then." Frankie jerked her head inside and was rewarded with a fierce stab in her temple. "Since you've clearly come here for a confrontation."

God, that was *not* the right tone for addressing a prince. Not even close.

"You ordered my guards not to talk to me." Eyes flinty, he brought himself closer to the threshold. She had to tilt her chin higher to hold his stare, and her stomach curled. He was still dressed in the jeans and shirt he'd worn that day. Lush hair all over the place—too long, too prone to his frustrated hands. And still, she wanted to jump him. "Do you know how badly I could've used a couple of friends around here? Hanna made me think she was the dullest person alive"—Frankie made a mental note to praise her guard for her efforts—"until I happened to discover she's this vibrant bouncy-ball you ordered into stillness. Why would you do that? Why the *hell* would you punish me—"

"Punish you?" She bit back, too exhausted to keep herself in check as his words struck her pride. "You think that's what this is? That I'm so useless at my job, I set orders based on personal grudges?"

He didn't seem to care that her tone was out of line. He moved even closer, rolling his lips together. "I have no idea what this is, Frankie, because you don't tell me the truth."

"Let's talk about telling the truth, then." Bad. This was bad. His temper was expanding—and hers was responding big time. "Because you seem to be under the delusion that you're innocent in all this."

"This'll be interesting." His stare bored into her. "Enlighten me."

"Inside." She pulled her head back into her room, wincing at her headache. No doubt about it. His tension and her sleep deprivation were about to collide head-on.

Kris rounded the doorway, features threatening a fight. Intent pushed him passed her into the room, but she clocked the instant he realized how little she was wearing. Probably the exact same moment she realized she'd just let this wild prince *into her bedroom*. His insatiate energy seemed to chew up all the space, drawing the walls in closer, blurring the corners and edges until she was the only thing left in his field.

Facing her, his focus snapped to her body. Anger flickered in and out of his gaze like a frequency dial that couldn't decide where to land. Outrage or lust? His throat moved on a hard swallow as he took in her bare legs; his mouth parted, bottom lip pulling between his teeth as his attention traveled over her hips and stomach. Then his jaw flexed and his fingers curled by his sides, as if he couldn't decide whether to punch the nearest wall or take hold of her camisole and tear it clean off.

Hot and refusing to be flustered, Frankie kicked the door closed behind her. "You're not here to look."

The slam brought his temper rushing back. "You're right." Standing in the short stretch of space between the foot of her bed and the coffee table, he crossed his arms. "I'm here to put an end to this."

An end.

She could have let her legs buckle; could've made the sound that broke behind her lips. Instead she let his energy latch onto her. Raging, ravishing in its intensity, it held her up.

She narrowed her eyes and answered coolly, "About time."

"Here I was," he said, shaking his head. "Doing my best to accept that you've always lied to me. That you convinced Mark to lie to me." His very presence coiled with insult. "But now I find out you've ordered my guards to pretend to be people they're not around me. It doesn't—I don't understand—" He sliced a hand into his hair, a growl in the back of his throat. "What are you playing at?"

"Playing?" Affront pushed her across the old carpet, and she stopped a few feet from him. Days ago, she'd wanted him to believe he'd only been a job to her. Tonight, wrung thin by the whole damn thing, she was offended he'd believe that so easily. "You're not a game to me."

"No?" His breath lurched furiously. "Then what am I to you, Frankie? An obligation? An inconvenience? A private joke? A sucker who never—"

"My prince!" Her words cut through the air like a solvent, stripping away her anger and leaving the grain of raw emotion in her throat.

Kris looked like she'd just landed an uppercut to his chin.

Suddenly shaky, she wrapped her arms around her middle. "You're my prince," she said again, much quieter. "You don't seem to realize that yet—that I don't exist outside of this hierarchy just because we used to be friends. You're my prince, and everything I've done has been to protect you." She paused. "Your Highness."

He took a swift, stiff step back.

"It doesn't make sense to you now." Her hands pressed harder against her sides. "You accuse me of being cruel, of punishing you, but I'm not. One day you'll understand that I'm trying to do the right thing."

His breath was sharp as he shook his head.

"You want to know why I ordered your guards to detach around you?" Damn this lump in her throat, inflamed by the scratch of her words. "Because they have a job to do. They must be prepared to make an objective, snap decision in a potentially life-threatening situation, and your tendency to befriend everyone around you could put that at risk. What could seem like a harmless conversation, a casual laugh, could make them lose focus right when they need it most."

His lips lifted into a pissed-off-and-superbly-sexy curl.

"You once threw yourself into a bar fight in fear for my safety because we were friends," she continued, remembering how she'd lost sight of him in that brawl—the prince she'd been hired to protect. Remembered how she'd turned her iced-gut fear into anger in the hours after. "It's too easy to imagine you doing the same for your guards. They'll act when your safety is threatened—and you'll put yourself in harm's way to help them."

His sneer had faded into a frown.

"And I *knew* you'd want them to be your friends," she said. "You'd want to draw them into your circle. Chat and get to know them. But they aren't your friends. They aren't *supposed* to be. They work for you. A future king can't be friends with the help."

His eyes were burning. When he spoke, his voice was so rough it seemed to catch on her skin. "Who are we really talking about here, Frankie?"

She stared him down.

They both knew she didn't have to answer that.

Cursing, he turned his face aside—and finally seemed to notice her room. His gaze tracked across her unremarkable, unmade bed to her old backpack hanging from a hook beside the closet, then jumped to his other side, where he quickly ran out of things to look at.

Nothing labeled her as lower class as markedly as a room built in a time of the invisible servant.

She supposed she owed her gratitude to the old royal family that the staff quarters weren't literally underground, but still, Hanna would have led Kris through the lower courtyard to get here, an architectural division between the grander areas of the palace and this sparse servants' wing.

His mouth pulled down at the corners as he stared at her damp towel, flung over the desk. Then he looked back at her and said, "Explain why I'm deluded to think I'm innocent."

She shouldn't have brought that up. "It's nothing."

His jaw slid. "Explain it."

"Is that an order, Your Highness?"

Her cheap attempt to throw him off almost worked. He pulled back. Swallowed. Ran his tongue along his back teeth.

Then he said with a chilled calm, "Sure."

She stiffened. "You're a hypocrite."

"Really?" He gave a weak snicker. "I wormed my way into your life with lies and hid under your nose for months on end?"

"You lied to me since the day I met you." She gestured jerkily toward the door and the better part of the palace beyond. "I waited years. Years for you to trust me enough with this secret. How important could I have been to you if you never told me you were royalty?"

His frown was slow, but serious.

"You talk about friendship and betrayal, but what trust did you show me?" She tried to raise her voice, but it just cracked. "You never let me in."

He mirrored her gesture toward the door. "None of this mattered."

"It's always mattered." A flush ran up her neck as she exposed the hurt she'd kept buried. "You're a prince. And you didn't tell me. How can that not matter?"

"I tried to tell—"

"Don't," she said, raising a hand. "Don't pretend that day was significant. You were only going to tell me because you had no other choice. You didn't want me to know. You didn't trust me to keep it secret. You can't pretend that it was meant to be special to tell me hours before the rest of the world found out. It would have meant nothing, so I didn't want to hear it."

His steady gaze was troubled by realization. "You're right."

She blinked.

"I'm sorry." He rubbed the back of his neck. "I should have told you. As a sign of trust. Because I did trust you. My lineage didn't mean anything to me, but I shouldn't have assumed it would mean nothing to you."

She pressed her lips together to stop herself from answering.

It means everything to me. It rules me as tightly as it rules you.

Then he moved.

Not to the door, as he should have, but to the armchair. For a moment, he stood in front of it, digging a hand into his back pocket—then, withdrawing a crumpled paper bag, he sat down with a sigh. Knees wide, elbows on his thighs, he unrolled it and dug his hand in.

In a subdued kind of silence, he started eating cashews.

She frowned. The palace kitchen offered any snack he could crave, and he'd chosen cashews? Whenever they'd shared mixed nuts, he always fished them out for her, because he didn't particularly like them, and he knew she—

Oh. He knew she loved them.

Frankie swallowed. "Comfortable, are you?"

He glanced at her. Cocking his brow, he held out the bag and gave it a little shake.

Woah, no. She didn't budge. "I'll escort you back to your suite."

His expression seemed to say *suit yourself* as he tucked back into the bag. "I'm not ready yet."

Exhaustion slumped down her spine, rapidly replacing the fight in her. "You should be."

"Why?"

"Because . . ." She raised a shoulder, almost helplessly. Because he'd threatened 'an end' when he'd arrived, and this wasn't it. "You're supposed to hate me."

His hand stilled, and for a few moments, he watched her. "How am I supposed to do that, Frankie?" he asked quietly. "I can't stand being angry with you. This week, I've felt . . . wrong— like the earth's rotating backward or something and just existing makes me sick. If that's anger, I can't imagine how I could possibly hate you and keep living."

Closing her eyes, she whispered, "Jesus, Kris."

And there, she'd gone and said his name.

There was the rustle of the bag shaking again and when she looked at him, his lips were twisted sadly. He said, "Sit with me."

She absolutely would not sit with her prince.

Sighing again, his gaze shifted to her pile of belongings on the table. Keys, swipe cards, phone, wallet. He frowned and leaned forward, picking up the final item and holding it up. "Still carry this around?"

Her oldest possession, those brass knuckles.

"Some people feel naked without their phones." Yet Frankie felt starkly vulnerable without the weight of those metal rings in her pocket. "I don't carry them to be used. I just . . ."

Needed the reminder. Of where she'd come from; how determined she'd been to fight her way out.

Putting the bag down, he tried sliding his fingers through the four loops. It jammed before it reached his middle knuckles.

"Man hands," she muttered.

He slanted a look at her that in a different time and place would have held a grin. "Looks like they've seen better days."

"They've seen plenty of days," she said about the scratched and nicked metal. "Not sure I'd call them better."

His attention fixed on her. "These even legal here?"

Eyes on the weapon, she gave a small shake of her head.

Brass knuckles had been illegal in Kiraly her entire life—but the law couldn't keep a young woman safe in the fierce reality of a violent moment. That, she'd had to do herself.

Kris's frown was loaded with questions.

"Laws are cultural myths." She raised a shoulder. "To work, they require enough people around you to believe in them."

Concern bloomed in his blue gaze. He drew the knuckles off his fingers and set them back on the table with a light clunk. "What was life like for you here, Frankie?"

"I—"

It was with a sudden and sharp puncture high in her heart that she feared honesty, not lies, might be the only way out of this mess.

"I might tell you one day," she muttered.

"Sit with me," he said again, more firmly.

Giving in, she moved to sit on the coffee table opposite him. If he brought his spread legs together, they'd press against the outside of her knees, trapping her inside his borders. Physical awareness of him snaked through her, a faded shadow of itself, too tired and battered to tie her in knots, but there just the same.

He extended the bag. Silently, she reached in and took a handful.

"Nice room." He spoke without taking his eyes off her. "Better than the dump over Rose's Diner."

"Hey." She piled several nuts into her mouth. Roasted and salted. Delicious. "I liked it there. The mold in the bathroom was sentient. We had conversations."

"It was disgusting."

"It was as close to you as I could afford," she said.

He frowned a little. "Don't royal guards get paid enough?"

She winced, but didn't answer.

"You can't even answer *that* honestly?" he asked in insulted disbelief.

"No, it's just—" She sighed. "King Vinci didn't want any resources spent on your dad or his family, okay? No allowance. No staff. Not even basic security or monitoring. As far as your uncle was concerned, the day Erik left Kiraly, he was on his own. Philip couldn't have me on the books as a royal guard in Sage Haven, so he found a way to pay me to gather information on political figures instead."

"That's what you did when you left on private investigations?"

She nodded. "And the bouncer work helped cover the rest."

"So." Kris was still frowning at her. "You stayed to watch over us even though you weren't properly paid for it?"

"I guess." She hesitated, skin prickling at what she'd given away. "Philip promised me a role in the palace when I got back, but I wanted some experience. And I figured if I could track you boys down, someone else could, too. So it wasn't, you know, just because of . . ."

You.

Shit.

He didn't answer. Just scanned her face, expression serious. She braced for a comment she wouldn't be able to handle.

But all he said was, "Your mascara's smudged."

"I had a shower—"

In a single, fluid movement, he'd licked his thumb and placed it beneath her right eye, the contact as gentle as it was startling.

With a delicious thrum, her body tightened.

He adjusted, leaning forward, his careful attention set just beneath her gaze. Scared to breathe, to do anything that would remind him of who she really was, she held still, her cheek tingling, aching as the rest of his hand hovered just out of range. Another moment for her collection—alone with him, but unable to enjoy the wonder of his intimacy for fear of losing her head.

"You been crying over me?" he murmured as he smoothed

the makeup away. If he intended it as a joke, his tone completely missed the mark.

Always.

His touch ruined her—for something so light, brushing against the outskirts of her body, it felt like playing out a thousand heartbreaking moments at once. It was the kind of contact that broke the sky and put a stutter in the pulse of the earth. Then with another soft swipe, put it all back together again.

He stilled the instant he collected her tear on his thumb.

"Frankie," he breathed.

She blinked, refusing to meet his shocked gaze. She was too tired to miss him this much and have him this close.

"You were lying," he said, and shifted his thumb to her left side. Used the damp of her tear to clear the stain from her skin. "When you said our friendship was never real."

Focus pinned on his knee, she nodded.

"When you said I was just your job."

Her silence didn't deny it.

"When you said you've never wanted my hands near you." His voice had lowered.

"It doesn't matter what I want." She ducked her face away from his touch, even as her attention shifted up his leg to the hard strength of his thigh.

Under her gaze, his legs moved, inching inward. Not quite trapping her but setting her thoughts racing over what she'd do if he did.

"My guards overheard me asking to kiss you." Energy hummed in the air between them.

Her face heated and she snatched up the bag of cashews, pouring some into her palm. "Good for them."

"You told me later your answer was no." It wasn't phrased as a question, but they both knew he was asking her to admit the lie.

To turn this confrontation into a stolen moment; to mend the past week with taste and touch. But a kiss would never just be a kiss with Kris. Frankie had always sensed that. Once their mouths met, they'd have no hope of parting until their bodies had blended and brought bliss itself to its knees.

"My answer isn't yes." She raised her palm to her mouth, cramming it full.

He rested his hands on his thighs, seeming to wait until he had her attention before slowly sliding his palms up and down the length of his quads. How . . . how did he *do* that? Turn a simple movement into a sex act? It was everything she could do to keep chewing she watched.

"I don't know the difference," he admitted.

"For the purposes of this exercise, there's no difference. There's nothing left between us. You can't be friends with someone like me. You can't be . . ." *More* than friends. "I work for you. I'm not high born or even adequately born—and you're literally going to be king."

He raised a shoulder. "Yeah?"

"Not *yeah*," she said, resisting the urge to cuff him around the head. "Yes. You are."

"Yes, I am," he said dutifully, coming infuriatingly close to smiling.

"For the love of God." She sat back, pressing her fingers to her temple. "This is why I didn't tell you I was here. I knew you'd do this. I knew you wouldn't get it. But *I* get it. I live in the servants' quarters—you own the palace. I work for the crown—you'll wear the crown. We're incompatibility's greatest achievement."

He looked unfazed. "All I'm hearing is antiquated classism."

Frankie grasped either side of her head. "I can't do this now. I can't think clearly enough to argue."

"Then don't." Kris leaned back, withdrawing his legs, his body. "We both need to sleep."

Groaning, she nodded.

"A full night. Deep and proper," he said, and paused before he said, "Camping."

She snapped her attention to him.

"Tomorrow night." Kris rose to his feet, dropping the paper bag on the table and brushing his hands together. "You finish those."

"Camping?" She stood and swiftly put distance between them. "That's hardly at the top of your priority list."

"I don't have a priority list. Philip does. You sleep well outdoors. You've told me. Fresh air and silence." He raised a shoulder. "It's what I'm going to do. You don't have to come."

She took in a slow, steadying breath. "Will you go beyond the palace grounds?"

"I said camping, didn't I?"

As his bodyguard, she'd have to go. And the glimmer in his eyes knew it.

"I'll walk you to your room," she muttered, pushing herself in the direction of the freestanding closet beside the bed.

"I can walk myself. It'll be a twenty-minute round trip for you."

"Gosh, Your Highness, how thoughtful of you to consider that *after* you turned up at my door uninvited in the middle of the night," she said, and gave the closet two quick jabs to get the right-hand door to unstick. "And don't insult me by suggesting that I take a nap instead of do my job."

He raised a hand, palm up.

"While I'm at it, don't ever treat Hanna like that again." Her burgundy jeans were on top of her clothes pile. She tugged them free, shoving the closet door shut before everything else could fall out.

"I won't." His gaze was on her legs. Probably wondering whether she was about to change in front of him. "I shouldn't have made her do that. I was angry."

"Is anger an excuse?"

"No," he said. "I'll apologize."

"With beer?" She snorted, holding her jeans up by the waist. "Here's the part where you turn your back like a gentleman."

Weary and wild-haired, he hesitated as his gaze grew heavy. A light furrow formed between his brows. "A what?"

"Gentleman. Honor, decency, courtesy—you've heard of it?"

He hummed, a gravelly sound, as he slowly turned away. "I'm afraid not."

God. She knew him in this mood.

She changed fast.

"Let's go," she said, swiping up her essentials from the table and jamming them in her pockets.

He cut to the door, laying his hand on the knob. "Frankie," he said quietly, half-turning his face to where she stood right behind him. "Did you really get Ava out?"

Her gut clenched—at the fact that he knew and his soft tone. "Don't tell a soul."

His eyes met hers over his shoulder. "What other secrets are you keeping?"

"If I told you, they wouldn't be secrets."

"A secret can be kept between two people."

A shiver ran between her shoulder blades. *We've proven that,* she wanted to say. *We've kept this secret between us so tightly we can't even speak it to each other.*

No, that wasn't right. She couldn't speak it—and her silence muted him.

He was watching her. "Promise not to lie to me again."

"Fine." Heart thundering, she cocked a brow and made a *get on with it* gesture for him to open the door. "Let us out."

"I'm trying to," he murmured before turning the handle.

She'd forgotten never to put Kris in charge of opening doors. That something so simple could turn into an opportunity to hold her attention. Mostly her fault—he wouldn't resort to blocking if she'd just have an open conversation with him. She'd been in Sage Haven for almost eighteen months the first time it happened. In hindsight, she should have expected it sooner. He'd waited a long time.

She remembered him driving her home from the weekly trivia night at the local pub.

"Would you rather go to jail for a year," he'd asked, playing their go-to game as he guided his truck down main street. "Or lose ten years off your life?"

"Ten years," she'd said without hesitation.

He had been incredulous. "A decade instead of one year? Come on."

"Two decades, same answer. I'm not going to jail." She'd twisted her lips, thinking. "Would you rather move to a new town every month or never leave the place you were born?"

"Easy," he'd said, pulling over in front of the diner. "Never leave. You?"

"Every month," she'd said. "No risk of seeing my prick dad ever again."

"Or your friends," he'd pointed out, his glance tipped with challenge.

"Don't get sour; I wasn't born here. If I go with the first option, I'd never have met you at all," she'd said, and quickly hurled herself out of the truck and away from his grin.

He'd held open the door to the diner for her, no harm done, until she'd passed him and he'd asked a bit too quietly, "Would you rather muck out the stables every time you see your best friend—or make out with them every Christmas?"

Yeah. Kris really didn't have his head around subtlety.

"Stables," she'd said. "Nothing wrong with getting dirty."

He'd made a swift choking sound. In denying her preference to make out with him, she'd thrown his imagination something way more suggestive.

Face flaming, she'd asked, "Would you rather never see Mark or Tommy again?"

"Hey!" He'd knocked her with his elbow as the door closed behind them. "Unfair question."

Hideously unfair, but she'd panicked. "Choose one or it's the water jug, my friend."

Their punishment for refusing to pick an option had sprung from the first time they'd played the game. Frankie had asked, "Would you rather have wet socks on your feet for a year or dry socks on your hands for a year?" They'd both opted for dry socks on hands because they truly hated wet socks—which quickly set up wet socks as the consequence for avoiding an answer.

Sighing, Kris had walked over to the diner counter, toed off his boots, and trickled water from the jug over the tops of his socks. She'd watched, pretending she didn't have a strange addiction to seeing this man down a layer, even if it was just the cowboy boots.

"Squelchy," she'd said with a smirk when he returned with boots in hand.

He'd had every right to be irritated, but his eyes had held a soft sparkle. "That was ruthless."

"Yeah, sorry," she'd said, turning toward the staircase beside the counter. "Imagine if you'd answered."

"There is no answer. I don't like talking about this," he'd said, walking up the stairs behind her. He'd always driven her home from trivia and walked her right to her door. Faultless small-town manners. "Even as a joke."

She'd fished the key out of her pocket a moment before she'd sensed him come all the way onto the small landing behind her instead of waiting several steps down. There was scarcely room for two people up here, but the broad shape of him had radiated against her back.

Her hand was unsteady as she'd tried to unlock her door. She hadn't been able to get the key in—he was *right* there—the lock had changed shape or something—was he planning on making a move?—*shit*—she couldn't think with him this close—she was trembling too much—

"Let me," he'd murmured, and reached around her. The coarse pads of his fingers brushed against hers as he'd taken the key. Dizzy with his scent, his heat, she'd barely kept her balance. With his forearm braced against the wall at her other side, his chest skimming her back and his bicep *just not* touching her arm as he'd leaned around her toward the door handle, he had her surrounded.

"How long are we going to keep this up, Frankie?" His question had been a hot, dark breath at her ear. It had made her instantly, mortifyingly, wet.

Oh, God.

He was like a firework strapped to her back, already sparking, ready to erupt and ensure she burst with him. She *wanted* that— wanted everything with him.

But he was her prince. Not Kris.

Her prince.

He'd waited for her answer, holding her key loosely between thumb and forefinger, hesitating at the lock.

"I don't like talking about this," she'd managed to say, clinging to his earlier words, but it had come out unfamiliar, throaty and thick and breathless. A fantastic time to learn she had an aroused voice.

He'd responded to it, his own dropping to a growl. "I think we should."

"I don't like it," she'd repeated. Not moving, not looking at him.

"You don't like the thought of being with me?" he'd asked, holding still, his powerful body practically thrumming around her. "Being like this?"

Her breath had caught, a faint squeak. Denial was brutal; it made her tear herself apart just to hold still.

"I don't like talking about this," she'd said, stuck on those words. They weren't lies. The less she talked, the less likely she was to give in. She couldn't surrender to him. Even if he never ascended within the royal line, this man was still a prince and she was worse than nobody. He was also a prince who didn't trust her enough to keep his secret, and she knew—*knew*—that he'd have no issues getting her into bed without sharing his heritage. Bitterness had dug into her pride.

"We don't have to talk—"

"Don't make me," she'd cut him off.

Accusing him of force, small as it was, had worked instantly. He'd withdrawn like a gasp of air, shifting as far as he could to one side. Key in the lock, door open, he'd swooped down to grab his boots and started down the stairs.

"Sorry," he'd said, his voice a different kind of quiet. Confused, shamed. "I didn't mean to—fuck," he'd cursed under his breath and was gone.

That night, she'd cried herself to sleep.

She should have chosen to never leave the place she was born.

6

Frankie spent the following afternoon working in the map room. She set up her laptop on the otherwise bare table, surrounded by world maps pasted on the walls. Old and not-so-old, the efforts of cartographers from centuries past. Hand-painted illustrations adorned the wallpaper beside the maps, and she supposed it would be interesting for people who had time to care about history—which she didn't.

She cared about the heat. The room was in a non-air-conditioned part of the palace, and would have been intolerable if it weren't for the cool air wafting out of the hole in the wall. She shifted her chair over a little, trying to catch the stale breeze. The bookcase in the corner had been moved to one side, exposing the stone staircase concealed within that connected to a network of secret passageways. It led to the palace basement and beyond, and, every so often, she looked up and frowned at it impatiently.

It was late afternoon by the time Tommy emerged.

He ducked into the room, one guard in the lead, the other bringing up the rear. Smart formation. The attention of all three shot to her, startled, and she inclined her head in Tommy's direction with a neutral, "Your Highness."

Then she jerked her head toward the door. Without turning, the guard in front extended a hand behind him and Tommy gave him the book he'd been carrying. The guards filed out.

Tommy offered Frankie no greeting in return. He stood in the center of the room, arms crossed, his hard expression far from welcoming.

"About time," she said, leaning back in the chair. "I've been waiting hours."

"I'd have made it days if I'd known you were here."

She arched a brow. "Your avoidance is somehow gratifying."

He didn't react.

The most enigmatic of the three brothers, Tommy was naturally quiet, keen-eyed, and still. Like a thought that woke her in the night and slipped away before she could catch it, leaving her unsettled, grasping warily, unsure whether it had been good or bad. He was a shadow and she had no idea what cast him.

"What are you doing here?" he asked.

"Kris spoke to me last night and despite your glowing suggestion, it doesn't seem like he's going to send me on my way."

His eyes narrowed as he processed that information, so she asked, "I want to know if it weren't for him, would you fire me? Reassign me? I lied to you as much as I lied to him. It's not only his call. I can leave now, and he can think it was my decision."

Tommy considered her. "You'd leave and pretend it was what you wanted?"

"If it's what you want." She wasn't stupid. Kris valued his brother's opinion as highly as his own. If Tommy resented her, Kris would never be settled with her in the palace.

"A friend should never do what you've done."

She inclined her head in acknowledgement.

"Lie for years about something so significant." His words were bitter, an accusation aimed at her poor excuse at friendship. Then, as she caught the hooded look in his blue eyes, it hit her in a moment of clarity that Tommy was a target for his own bitterness.

"Oh, Tommy." She ran a hand over her eyes. *Damn it.* This conversation was not going to end the way she'd planned.

He said nothing. Just stood watching her coldly.

"This is about Jonah."

He flinched at his best friend's name, raising one arm to half-cover his chest. A second later, he hurled it back to his side. "What is about him?"

"You're angry at me for hurting Kris—just like you're angry at yourself for lying to Jonah. You don't think you deserve to be forgiven, so you don't intend to forgive me either."

His fingers started tapping a fast beat against his leg. "He's got nothing to do with this."

"Haven't you been friends for like, twenty years?"

His jaw slid. His fingers kept tapping.

When she'd first moved to Sage Haven, she'd met Tommy with Jonah by his side. Kris had later explained that Jonah had moved next door as a boy and gravitated to Tommy immediately out of the three brothers. Strange, since Jonah was literally the sweetest person in existence—and Tommy had always been on the cold side of reserved. Despite their differences, the friendship went both ways.

At least, it had until recently.

"Have you contacted him?" she asked, despite knowing that he hadn't. "He'll be worried sick."

Tommy made a sound of derisive disbelief.

"He would've been worried sick within an hour of you leaving the Haven," she snapped. "Unlike me, he didn't secretly know the truth this whole time. Discovering his oldest friend is a prince won't have been easy to get his head around—but you've left him to process it on his own without even calling?"

"He doesn't want to hear from me. He told me to fuck off."

Tommy's expression was haunted. "He's never said that to anyone—despite far too many people who've deserved it."

"He was hurt and confused. That's what people say. Here's some news. In order to apologize, you have to actually talk to him."

His lip curled. "Says you."

"I actively didn't want Kris to know I was here. I still behaved like an asshole, but I did it on purpose."

"You think you know what's best for me?" His tone was scathing.

"No," she answered. "But I have some thoughts on what isn't —and from recent experience, I can tell you that blocking out a friend is never for the best."

"I'm sure he's fine."

"That's funny." Absently, she adjusted her phone on the table beside her. Slid it a little closer in Tommy's direction. "Because I know he's not."

A trap, those words, that bound his interest completely. Eyes flickering, he moved closer. "You've spoken to him."

"It's Jonah." She pulled a face. "He's an angel in a cowboy's body. When he rings, I answer."

"How often does he ring?" Tommy's voice caught.

She pretended not to notice. "Wouldn't you like to know."

He took a step closer, laying his palms flat on the table. His fingers rapped against the grain as he asked, "How is he?"

"Worried sick. I told you."

Tommy didn't move, but his presence seemed to snarl in warning. "You know what I'm asking," he said, deathly quiet.

"He's safe," she said. "Just working."

Tommy stared her down. A silent command for more without the indignity of begging.

She stared back, pulse spiking just a little.

"How often do you talk to him?" he ground out.

"He calls me every Friday morning while he makes breakfast," she said, and at the flash in his eyes, added, "Don't look at me like it's another of my secrets. It's not just me. Mark and Kris have called him. He's our friend, too."

He turned his face away. "He calls you every . . ." He trailed off, whipping back around to stare at her. "Today's Friday."

Late afternoon in Kiraly meant in Mountain Daylight Time—

Frankie's phone started to ring. Tommy recoiled as if it had breathed fire.

"Always so punctual." She gestured to it. "You want to answer?"

He ran a hand up his throat and backed toward the door.

"I'll take that as a no," she said, reaching for the phone. Then she hesitated. "Loudspeaker?"

The look he gave her would have withered a weaker spine.

"I'll take that as a yes." She answered the call and put it on loudspeaker. "Morning, Jones."

"Hey, Frankie!"

Tommy's cheeks flooded red—and an instant later, the map-room door slammed shut behind him.

Swiping up her phone, she switched off the speaker and brought it to her ear. Okay, so she'd ambushed Tommy, but he needed the support of his oldest friend and it seemed a guilt trip might be the only way to make him act. His brothers were too wary to push him. It was always *careful with Tommy* or *make sure he doesn't stress*. Well, she wasn't blinded by protectiveness. She cared about Tommy—more than she or Tommy would be comfortable with her letting on—and she could see his steel in those shadows.

She wouldn't be careful, and she'd make him stress.

Then he might remember he could protect himself.

Kris stood at the window of the small green sitting room, one hand gripping the curtain tie-back, the other in his front pocket. He'd spent the afternoon posing as Mark, maintaining positive relations with industry. He'd eaten butter-soft biscuits with a billionaire entrepreneur and discussed the future of assistive technology; he'd drunk tea with a robotics engineer and discussed the future of AI and job automation; and he'd shared a sneaky scotch with a biotechnician and discussed cellular agriculture and the future of sustainable food.

He'd squinted through most of it. The scrunched-up look of a man trying to spot something familiar in a wave of blinding light.

Now, he gazed down at Frankie in the rear courtyard and his future had never looked clearer.

Staff were bustling, stacking packs and bagged tents in a neat row, while Frankie addressed a small group of assembled guards. She appeared sharp-shouldered and in control in her purple jeans and green tank, and her team's attention on her didn't waver.

She was the woman who'd lied while protecting him—who'd denied him, then cried over him. He'd never—like, an actual Frankie tear . . . *right* on his thumb. One look at the devastation on her face and he'd known there was no going back to friendship, not from here.

His breathing grew strange as he watched her, like there was a latch in his throat that kept slipping in and out of position, nudged by something inside him that was figuring out how to get loose.

She'd suppressed her desire because he was her prince. *We're incompatibility's greatest achievement,* she'd told him. *You're literally going to be king.*

Not without her, he wasn't.

The laces on her black boots were half-undone. A typical, insignificant detail, but every time she moved, he winced a little, fearing she'd trip. It was stupid. She'd lived a carelessly laced life without him and managed to keep herself upright, but that didn't stop him wanting to march down there, kneel at her feet, and tie her into safety.

Philip appeared beside him at the window.

For several minutes, they stood in silence as the camping preparations continued below. It was excessive—needless items that just kept coming—and when Frankie rolled her eyes and turned away what appeared to be a portable hot-water heater for showers, Kris laughed and said, "Attagirl," under his breath.

Then his advisor spoke. "You be careful there, Your Highness."

Philip's tone was serious, stern, yet unlike any he'd used on Kris before. There was no thread of outrage, no quaver of indignation.

Just a hard, bleak warning.

Kris faced him with a frown, and the man's scrupulous gaze seemed to press a hand to his airway, seeking to hold that latch closed. Philip's role was to uphold the centuries-old traditions of the monarchy—to protect the legacy and respect the hierarchy that advantaged the throne.

His caution against Frankie was unmistakable.

Kris went back to watching her, figuring the older man could live without his retort.

Kris didn't do careful.

Frankie climbed the steep mountain track, her thumbs tucked around the pack straps at her shoulders to stop it from rubbing against her gun in its holster. With a soft groan, she paused in the shade of a silver fir, welcome relief from the not-quite setting sun —then kept moving at a nudge to her hand from Buck.

When Kris had claimed they were going camping, she knew this wasn't what he'd had in mind. He'd been thinking of simple nights spent up in the Rockies, just the two of them, free of the attendants and half-dozen guard escort that trailed him as he hiked across the mountain. He'd have wanted a no-fuss meal, something plain straight out of his bag, not the lavish, chef-prepared food being carried in cold-packs, and he wouldn't even have known it was possible to end up with glamping-style tents and bed rolls as thick as overgrown cotton fields.

If the master of the household had been given more lead time, he'd have packed enough furnishings for a semi-permanent mountain residence.

Perhaps that would have been better. More things for her to hide behind.

Frankie brought up the rear of the ten-strong group, well away from him, but the distance didn't ease her nerves. Buck and Bull moved up and down the line, occasionally sticking their noses into her palm, demanding a pat. That helped a little. As she scratched behind Buck's ear, breathing in the sweet, citrusy smell of coniferous trees and focusing on the bird calls and the hum of insects, she still couldn't shake her growing sense of exposure. Like she was hiking toward a fight with surgical markings around her weak points. *Just strike here, here, or here, and I'll buckle like a broken marionette.*

Kris knew her weak points now.

One swipe of his thumb and she'd collapse around him.

The thick heat of the summer evening hung heavy in her chest as they passed through a clearing of pink and yellow wildflowers. There was too much opportunity out here for her to lose her head. Kris was most dangerous in his natural environment, potent with sure-handed competence and cowboy swagger, and it made her both furious and frightened to doubt her strength to resist him if they ended up alone. Simple solution: stay among her team.

Nerves settling, she glanced up—and almost tripped to find Kris looking back at her over his shoulder. His gaze was steady, locked on her through the people and packs between them. She slid her attention away, keeping her features uninterested. God, would he stop doing that? Literally everyone could see.

As if on cue, Hanna slowed her pace, dropping back to Frankie's side.

"So, I was wondering," Hanna said, fingers curled around the straps of her overnight pack and coiled bedroll. "Could you hide behind a tree the next time he does that? I'd love to see his reaction."

"Funny," she answered.

"I'm so sure it would be."

Frankie didn't respond. Her pulse stuttered, wary of Hanna's observations.

"Last night's tension seems to have gone," the guard said, voice quieter.

"Yeah." Replaced by a different kind of tension. Frankie adjusted the tent bag on her back and slowed her pace so no one overheard. "Did he speak to you?"

"First thing this morning." Hanna's glance was speculative. "He apologized for exploiting his authority—and for putting a hand over my mouth. And he said he wouldn't override your orders again."

Frankie snorted.

"He stuck to it the whole day," Hanna said in his defense. "He ate lunch in silence."

Oh. Well that was a pathetic image.

"Be honest," Frankie forced herself to say. "Do you think I'm being too strict?"

123

"It's your job to be strict." The blond woman raised a shoulder. "But King Markus and Prince Tomas's guards don't have these rules. Could chatting now and then be so bad?"

"I don't know," she said with a frown. "Maybe I can be a bit . . ."

Hanna leaned forward to better peer at her. "Harsh? Stubborn? Uncompromising?" She paused as Frankie cut her a narrow-eyed glance. "Terrifying?"

"I was going to say cautious."

"Not even in my top-ten guesses."

With a roll of her eyes, Frankie smiled.

"I know his safety is your utmost priority." Hanna's tone became careful. "But it's mine, too. Sometimes it feels like—I mean, like maybe you don't trust me to do my job."

Stricken, Frankie's amusement vanished. "I do trust you, and Peter." Her gaze found the back of Kris's black hat at the front of the line. *I don't trust him.* "Behave however you deem appropriate. Just stay vigilant and don't, for the love of God, laugh when he thinks he's being funny."

"Little chance of that." Hanna grinned. "Race you to catch up?"

"Sure."

After a burst of speed and burning lungs, Frankie joined the line two steps ahead of her.

"Damn it," Hanna said, breathing fast. "I'm *really* fit."

"Let it go, Johansson," Frankie said, clapping her on the shoulder. "You'll never win."

"I will. One day. I can feel it."

Frankie smiled again, shaking her head.

The sun was slipping from the sky when they arrived at Kris's intended camping site. A grassy ledge that protruded from the mountainside, backed by pines with a perfect view of Kira City far below. Unease quickly took hold of Frankie as his shelter was erected first—an absurdly large lotus tent that must have been arranged by someone who genuinely didn't know that Kris had lived most of his life as a free-ranging cowboy. She wasn't sure how anyone within Kiralian borders could have missed that memo, but the proof was in the extravagant cotton-lined, lantern-strung, *here-sleeps-the-prince* pudding.

There was no room for a second tent, let alone the whole camp, so all other tents were set up on a clearing just below the outcrop. It breached protocol to separate the primary from his protection, even such a minimal distance, so after setting up her tent faster than Hanna—"You can't be human," Hanna declared, pointing a peg at her—Frankie chewed on the inside of her cheeks and approached Kris.

He'd just erected a tent for a blushing non-outdoorsy attendant, and was standing back with sleeves bunched at his elbows.

"I'm not comfortable with you sleeping up there, Your Highness."

He tensed, turning to face her, his blue gaze like a finger flick to her heart.

"There's no one to watch your back," she added.

"There should be room for at least half of us up there," he said, taking off his hat and running his fingers through his thick waves. "It's not my fault I have to sleep in a giant, posh marshmallow."

She pressed her lips together. "I'll have it moved down."

"No. Leave it." Attention on the ludicrous tent, he angled his head to one side, stretching his neck. "You're my bodyguard, right? Sleep in there with me."

Her level gaze was waiting when he looked back to her. "That would be inappropriate."

"Ask yourself why," he said, angling his head to the other side, tempting her with the bold cut of his jawline. She resolutely held his stare. "I'd be surprised if it has anything to do with doing your job properly."

She sucked in a breath—held it when she realized he was right.

"You made your bed on this one, Frankie." His grin came slowly as he slid around her. "Meet you up there."

Fuck.

She delayed as twilight turned to night, briefing her team on various eventualities and preparing them for their pre-dawn departure. By the time she collected dinner from the kitchen hand in charge of supplies, an uncomfortable truth had settled in her mind. She'd let Kris get away with that flawed logic. Assigning Peter or Hanna to stay with him overnight would still have been doing her job properly.

She *wanted* to do it.

Her plan to stay among her team had been practical, but too much like pulling a coat over a little black dress because the weather was cold outside. She'd wear the wool for a little while, avoiding a winter chill, but the moment she reached the party, she'd be all slinky fabric and skin. She wouldn't have worn the dress otherwise.

And she wouldn't have assigned herself as his bodyguard if she hadn't secretly wanted something like this to happen—even though she knew it *couldn't.*

She was so screwed.

With nerves multiplying in her belly, she walked the short incline to the bulbous tent that glowed warm and cream like the moon had eaten too much and had fallen into a food coma on the forest floor.

Cresting the slope, she resolutely ignored the shadow that was Kris sprawled on his back in the slim patch of uncovered grass. Instead, she nodded at Hanna and Peter. "Go have dinner, you two."

"Would you like us to return, ma'am?" Peter's hands stayed clasped behind his back.

"No," she said. "I've got it from here."

"Very well."

"Sweet dreams," Hanna said, and the pair retreated to the main camp. Silence filled the space they left behind, and Frankie stood holding a stack of containers, plates and napkins, wishing she knew how Kris intended this night to go.

He shifted in the muted light of the tent, propping himself up on his elbows to look at her.

Averting her eyes to the dogs lying nearby, she asked, "Where would you like to eat, Your Highness?"

He rose to his feet, running a hand absently over his ass. "You know what I realized earlier today?"

Her thoughts jammed at the sight of his powerful shoulders tapering to his hips, enhanced against the shadowed forest. Clenching her teeth, she gave a disinterested hum. She could get through this. She had years of practice being sensible. Last night she'd been too tired, too easy to disarm, and it had clearly encouraged him. But she didn't have to play into his hand after a few bare-hearted words—not again. She could wear the dress *and* the coat.

"You haven't actually said sorry," he said.

"Out here or in the tent?" She kept her voice steady. "I think it's finger food."

He moved toward her, and her skin crackled at his searching gaze. "Now why wouldn't you have apologized?" He took the containers from her, fingers brushing hers, and she snatched her hands away. "I can't figure it out."

"Does it matter?" she asked. "Your Highness."

His bristle was almost palpable, raising hairs along her arms. "That's the last time you call me that."

She splayed her palms over her hips, blaming the sweat on the heat. "You'd like to get a head start on Your Majesty?"

"No. And that tone isn't going to work on me. Not anymore." He scanned her features. "Use my name."

She turned her face aside, gaze on the first stars dotting the horizon.

"Now," he said.

"Now?" she asked, frantically trying to think herself out of this, but he stood so close and smelled like safety, and all her mind managed was the possibility he'd sleep without his shirt on.

"Say my name now." It wasn't arrogance in his voice, but a low plea, and it stripped the moment bare.

Kris, she wanted to beg. *Don't.*

"Please, Frankie."

"I don't know what you think changed last night," she said. "But we're not back where we started. You're my superior, and I'm here to protect you."

"I agree." He shifted closer. "We're never going back to where we started."

She bit her tongue.

"You said because you sleep in the servants' quarters, it doesn't matter what you want. But it matters to me."

"Don't do this," she said quietly, withdrawing a step.

His brow lowered. "What am I doing?"

"Cornering me." Accusation tinged her words.

"I'm not cornering you." He sounded insulted. "I'm trying to talk to you. Every time I ask how you feel, you accuse me of intimidation. You think I'm trapping you, but did you ever consider that's just how it feels to let yourself be vulnerable?"

She shook her head, running a hand down her throat. She didn't want conversations like this. Eventually he'd make her say too much and she'd never find her way back.

"Let's eat inside," he said roughly. "The bugs are getting bad. They'll eat you alive."

With a curt nod, she opened the flap and ducked into the tent.

The interior was ludicrous. The thick, cream canopy draped in lustrous folds of fabric and several ornate lanterns glowed through amber glass, with the largest hanging from a loop on the center pole. Rugs and embroidered cushions had been laid over the ground cover, and two double bedrolls had been spread with linen sheets and pillows, and placed a respectable distance apart.

"Yikes," she said.

"I know." Kris zipped the tent flap closed and straightened beside her. "Apparently there are spare candles in that box there. And I've got matches . . ." He dug a hand into the front pocket of his jeans, fishing out a matchbook and tossing it beside the box—a second before a small square packet hit the floor directly in front of him.

A condom.

Frankie froze, skin instantly cold.

For several seconds, the only thing that moved was the mortification hammering in her neck. Then Kris darted a look at her, and she ran a hand over her lowered face and muttered, "Jesus Christ."

There was the sound of plastic rustling as he jammed it back in his pocket. "Sorry."

"Oh, don't apologize." She dropped her hand, arm weak with an awful kind of adrenaline. "It's preferable that you're not planting heirs around the city."

He paused. "What?"

"Nothing." Moving away, she hunkered down on the less decorated bedroll, hating the reaction twisting inside her. This shouldn't matter. He slept around—he always had. But proof of his wandering attention, within a minute of him asking her to speak his name, picked up her insides like a secret letter to him and shredded it into pieces.

He hadn't moved. Denim, boots and rolled up sleeves. Strong shoulders, hard-earned muscle, and a face that only ever grew more breathtaking the longer she looked.

"I haven't been with anyone in Kiraly," he said.

Her eyes burned. She angled her face away from him. "Yeah, sure."

"I'm serious. You must know." He almost sounded desperate. "You monitor my every move."

She couldn't look at him—her head physically refused to lift. "Hard to monitor you when you slip security." With a different woman wrapped around his waist each time, practically sucking the skin off his neck.

"You think I've been sneaking off to have sex?"

"I imagine it kills the mood to ask someone to sign a nondisclosure agreement," she said, discovering that if she spoke at a regular volume, her voice didn't shake. "So much hotter to put your reputation at risk and shirk protocol entirely."

"First, that obviously sounds hotter," he said, and she stiffened. "But second, that's not why I've been slipping security."

"Sure." Damn this urge to cry. Her throat hurt; the muscles along her neck strained. "You carry condoms around for no reason."

He didn't answer immediately. He seemed to give time for the thought to occur to her; for her breath to suck in sharply and a flush to crawl up her neck. *Oh, God. I'm going to sleep with him, aren't I?* Then he murmured, "There's a reason for this one."

"No." She covered her face with her hands. They shook. "Stop right there."

"I'm not trying to scare you."

"I'm not scared." She was overwhelmed—they'd never spoken openly about sex. Not between them, not like it was a possibility worth preparing for.

There was the sound of footsteps as he crossed the tent, followed by a light clunking as he set the food containers down. "I haven't packed it for tonight. Frankie. I've carried one whenever I'm with you since we met. I get the feeling neither of us could pull back if we ever got started." He paused. "Not that I don't *hope* to use it, but I'm not here to seduce you."

"I shouldn't be in here," she said, but didn't move. "I'll ask Peter."

"Stay." The soft swish of fabric betrayed he'd sat on the bedroll opposite her. "I've wanted you for years without acting on it. I'll manage for another night."

She didn't answer; she couldn't seem to draw her hands away from her face. Her fingertips trembled against her eyebrows.

"I have scared you," he said quietly.

No—he'd tempted her. And that was far worse. Protection was literally in his pocket. One kiss, mouths clashing in a fevered rush of *fucking finally*, and there'd be no hazy-minded reason to stop. Just roll it on and slide straight in, because status and titles and futures would mean nothing against the inflamed reality of this man's body in hers.

"You can't want this with me," she made herself say.

"Yet I do and that's not changing." Frustration hardened his words. "I've sworn you've always been attracted to me. Now I *know* you have—but you've avoided it because you don't think you're good enough for a prince."

She shook her head. "I'm not."

"You damn well are."

"You're asking too much of me." Her darkest secrets—that was what it would take to convince him.

He blew out a breath and for a while, didn't speak.

"Are you shy, Frankie?" he asked, the question gentle. "About this kind of thing?"

Her cheeks were hot; her palms were sweating. "What kind of thing?"

"Sex. Attraction. Intimacy."

"The last one," she admitted, because what difference did it make? "I never—it's not something I do." Clearly, since she needed the barrier of her hands against her face to even have this conversation.

"I'd like to be intimate with you." The deep abrasion of his voice left her senses shivering. "I could show you how. I think you'd be good at it."

"I don't know what you mean," she whispered.

"I want—" He broke off and there was the sound of his hat hitting the floor. "I care about you. You're good enough for me and I want to be with you. Intimately. Sexually." He paused. "Repeatedly."

Her mind hazed at the hot loosening between her thighs.

"You don't know how to be with someone," she said. "Stay with someone."

"I know how to stay with you."

"As a friend." Shaking her head, palms still raised, she said, "In Sage Haven, you had someone different in your bed every other week."

"I—look, you confused me, okay?" His voice grew a little louder as he moved closer and his nearness rippled across her skin. "I didn't know what you wanted. One minute I'd swear it was about to happen, that I'd spend the next month buried inside you to make up for lost time, and the next minute, you'd hardly look at me. You were never willing to talk about it, and as badly as I wanted—*want*—you to be the woman in my bed, I didn't want you to think that I was waiting around expecting you to go there with me."

Tipping her face down, she forced her hands into her lap. This was too real. Her skin stung. He was directly in front of her in a kind of earnest crouch, and she wasn't sure she'd ever been asked to speak so honestly in her life.

"And let's be fair," he added, a slight edge creeping into his voice. "I wasn't the only one who left the bar with other people. You'd choose a stranger instead of me."

"Sometimes," she said. But most of the time, she hadn't invited those strangers upstairs. She'd just wanted Kris to drop the idea of her as anything more than a friend.

"I hated watching you leave with another guy."

"I know." God, the intensity of his stare across the bar on those nights. The hurt, the anger, the desire crackling in that blue gaze. "And I hated seeing you watching me leave."

"Then *why*—"

"I've told you," she snapped.

"Because I'm your prince?" The question was coarse. "That doesn't matter to me. Who the hell cares that you're not high born? I've spent my life shoveling horse shit. I want to be with you, and I'm done pretending. If status is the only reason you've got, then get over it."

"Kris." Gripping her hands together, she looked up. His temper flickered out and that cut the heart right out of her. "What are you really asking of me?"

"Everything," he said, soft and fierce.

Oh, God. She might actually die from this.

"In three months, you're going to be King of Kiraly."

"Yes." His features were severe, determined. "And when I recognized you in that laneway, you know what I thought? With you by my side, I might actually stand a chance of pulling this off."

And there it was—her weakest point.

With you by my side.

133

Everything strong inside her crumpled.

"Stop," she said, eyes pricking. "Just stop. Think. When you're king, what will be expected of you?"

Concern lined his features as he scanned her face.

"And what expectation would that put on me?" she pressed.

"I don't expect anything from you." He frowned. "You can still work for the royal guard."

"No. Kris. Please. *You need to produce heirs.*"

Born with dignity and unquestionable descent.

The blood left his face. "I need—"

"And I'm never going to be the right person to help with that," she said, words cracking.

A seal broke inside her. Sorrow flooded to her edges, then rose rapidly to swallow her heart.

"Oh," he said.

He stared at her, desolate, like a man with one second left on the clock, faced with an impossible puzzle that he'd have no hope of solving even with all the time in the world.

"Oh," he said again, quieter.

They ate dinner in excruciating silence.

Frankie pretended to sleep with her back to Kris. Her hands were sweating and she couldn't stop shaking. That had been too close. This wasn't about being common. If it was, she'd have unraveled at his reckless disregard of royal expectation.

No. Frankie Cowan was not a rags-to-riches story the people would celebrate.

Journalists knew how to dig into the past until they drew blood, and they would smear hers across headlines. How far back would they go? High school? Elementary school? Would they drain her upbringing dry until her own mother spoke out against her? Or worse. What if they found her father?

It'd be the end of her.

Queen Consort—or Queen of Cons?

Frankie had been born in the squalid corner of her father's crimes and raised to stay there. Her mother used to mutter that Frankie was just like him. Quick-minded, fiery, with a pretty face that disguised a leech's mouth.

And her father's mouth was always open, sucking at the susceptibility of strangers.

Kira City was his most loyal accomplice. For him, it attracted the global elite. It beckoned with a picturesque mountain-scape and glacial lake for swimming and boating, and shoreside parties; it gestured invitingly to high-end hotels and restaurants and boutique stores. A visiting millionaire or tycoon or socialite could enter the wealthy tourist precinct and find everything their privileged heart desired.

Come and visit, the city sweet-talked. *Play with me.*

Then her father played them.

It was twisted, really, that some of the movies Frankie had watched to master her accent were Hollywood cons. Frivolous, inane bullshit—they glorified something that had filled her entire childhood with dread. Her father was charismatic, sure, but he was also truly frightening. The way his mind worked—the howling wasteland of his conscience. He never raised a hand against Frankie or her mother—but he'd never let them believe that he wouldn't.

She'd shuddered to be likened to him, yet had followed his every instruction.

Summertime was peak con season. Her dad prowled like a cat in a field of flightless birds. At every turn, he pinned another mark with the badger game, or a dropped wallet scam, or swindled them during currency exchange. Add several long-con romance scams strategically spread across different hotels and it was a sun-drenched criminal frenzy.

Like a good con man's daughter, Frankie had perfected her roles. Every summer, they had become wealthy tourists from America, and in their tale of woe, his wife—Frankie's mother—had either died the year before or abandoned them for another man. As a result, Frankie's father had either been grieving or broken and betrayed, and could never quite believe how the single, late-forties, rich female target made his heart come alive again.

Carefully selected targets. The stories and disguises were only part of the final act—the real play had been in the setup. He had taught Frankie how to sway the reluctant hand of digital privacy; how to stalk through data encryption and wave over her shoulder to broken firewalls. He'd browse upcoming hotel bookings like a man perusing prostitute listings, short-listing women who suited his perverted needs for wealth, single relationship status, and a tendency toward philanthropy.

Her father had a suite of hotel managers in his pocket. Without ever being guests, he and Frankie had made use of the restaurants, lounges, and pools. As the cons had developed and the women fell for her father's soft, hopeful heart, he'd start to send Frankie away to the hotel's school holiday club—code for *bugger off*—and she'd go home to her mum and not know what to say. More than once Frankie had looked back to see him leading the woman to the hotel elevators, his hand already sliding over her ass. He'd con his way between their legs and into their trust, and once they'd made plans for the year ahead—discussed how it could work with Frankie's schooling and his aggressive working hours—his trap would close.

It had always been money for Frankie's top-tier private-school fees. If her mother had been dead, a lucrative but poorly-timed investment had temporarily left him in the red. If he'd had a wicked ex-wife, she'd closed his accounts and his lawyers needed a couple of days to sort it out. And those school fees had always been due the next day.

Funds transferred, the women had flown home and never heard from their gentle American lover again.

Quicker games were his bread and butter. He'd coordinate extortion on rich married men and pull holiday rental scams using luxury apartments that he'd scouted as temporarily vacant. Somehow, despite it all, they had never seemed to get any richer.

Frankie had been ten when her mother left for real. Everything had gotten worse. She had been trapped in thievery, making bad friends while he made worse enemies. He'd trained her good and proper, teaching her to read people, to play the right part, to misdirect their attention and move on.

The summer she'd turned sixteen, he arranged her first long con. She'd prepared to age up a couple of years, but none of the trust-fund teens or cashed-up college boys even asked. A lifetime of masquerading among the wealthy had equipped her with the skills to pass, so she watched her tongue, crossed her legs at the ankle, and complained that her father wouldn't top up her card until they landed in Portofino. She'd longingly pointed out designer sunglasses and handbags and soon, a mark fell for it, buying her little gifts, big gifts, and she was delighted, acting as if she wanted to kiss him but couldn't quite work up the courage.

The night before her mark was due to fly out, her father had loomed in Frankie's bedroom doorway.

"If he invites you upstairs tonight," he'd said, "you go with him."

Sick with all the things wrong with that instruction, she'd been a full hour late to her date.

The Burberry boy had invited her upstairs—and she'd gone with him. Afterward, he'd presented her with a diamond necklace and earring set in farewell and didn't ask her to stay until morning. She'd thanked him, taken it, and never set foot in her father's house again.

Quite startling, the price losing her virginity had fetched at the right jeweler.

The journalists wouldn't share the rest of the story. That Frankie had stayed at the cheapest backpackers in Kiraly while she finished high school. That she'd sat alone atop The Scepter on the night she'd graduated, staring wet-eyed and hollow at the palace, and seen the spark of a better life twinkling in those grand windows.

A position working in the palace—could that act as a pardon for her upbringing? The strict principles and integrity required to work for the royal family could reform her self-worth. She'd wanted to believe that she was capable of it, that she could become something good—and everything she'd done since that night had been working toward that goal.

No, that wouldn't interest the media. But standing at the king's side after fooling him into friendship and convincing him to make her his queen?

It would look like the greatest long con of her life.

"Would you rather sleep for twelve hours solid every night, or sleep for six hours but wake up every hour and a half?" Kris's question was quiet in the still, moonlit tent.

He knew Frankie was awake. Her breathing hadn't leveled since the lanterns had died.

No response.

Then, a slight repositioning on her bedroll. "Like, as a regular sleep cycle?"

His fingers bunched. Her voice was hoarse, as if she'd been screaming.

"Yeah," he answered. "Every night."

"How long do I wake up for in the second one?"

"Ten minutes each time." It took all his self-control to stay casual, because he hated that he hadn't known what to say earlier. Hated that he hadn't been prepared for it. Obviously, he'd be expected to produce heirs. Why hadn't he braced himself and confronted that reality? He'd allowed himself to be distracted by training and meetings and royal murders instead of wrapping his head around what he'd really be asking of the woman who stood by his side.

Heirs. Children. A family.

Once his thoughts piled on the idea of that with Frankie, he couldn't haul them off. God, the fiery-haired comets that would flare into their lives—

But she either didn't want or couldn't have kids. The crack in her voice had betrayed it wasn't a stance she held easily, but that was . . . well, it didn't matter, did it? There was nowhere to go from there.

"Ten minutes?" Frankie answered, still facing away. "Disrupted sleep can get—"

"Please note, the twelve-hour sleep is impossible to disrupt."

"No alarm?" she asked.

"No alarm."

He hated, *hated,* that it wouldn't have been a game-changer back in Sage Haven, but here, now, he literally needed a life partner who would give him children. Mark had given up his sovereignty to ensure Darius and any children he and Ava had together would not be in line for the throne. Heirs were up to Kris. Goddamn it. It felt wrong to his core that his royal obligation meant he couldn't grab hold of this woman now that she was within reach. Now that he knew she *wanted* him to hold her.

"Well, twelve hours is useless." Another shifting sound as she rolled onto her back. "I'd have to go to bed before dinner just to wake up in time for work."

He waited, sliding a hand under his head.

"Six hours," she decided. "But that was a sucky one."

He smiled. She'd cracked open earlier, empty as a hollow shell, but he could feel her resuming her form and coming back to him. "Would you rather only eat tacos or pizza?"

"What?" She half sat up, sounding outraged. "What the hell impossible questions are these?"

And she was back.

"No answer?" He feigned innocence. "Your socks are about to get acquainted with my water bottle."

"Fine. Tacos. No. Pizza. Shit. Yes—tacos."

Kris grinned and rolled onto his side to face her, propping his head up in his hand.

She did the same, without the grin, and their eyes met in the soft, silvery moonlight.

"Hello," he said.

Her gaze dropped to the space between their bedrolls. "Hey."

"I'm sorry about earlier."

"Yeah."

"I have another question. Not specific to you and me. About you in Sage Haven."

She didn't turn away, but her hand rose to sit at the base of her throat. "Go ahead."

"You monitored our safety," he said. "Was there—uh." His heart rate jumped, and he could have sworn the air in the tent got hotter. Was he capable of angling for this subtly? "Were there any incidents behind the scenes?"

Her brows dipped in a frown. "Not really. Sage Haven is a very low-key town."

"Nothing at all?"

"Hmm." She settled deeper onto her side, still wearing her jeans and a tank. He'd taken her lead and stayed fully dressed, minus his hat and boots. The only thing she'd taken off was her gun and holster, tucking them carefully beside her bedroll. "I guess there was Philip and his attempts to preserve the royal bloodline." Kris stiffened, but her voice stayed casual, as if this wasn't a critical wound between them. "He wanted your uncle Vinci to invite you boys to the palace where he could introduce you to suitable matches, curated to your tastes."

"Ew," Kris said.

Her lips slid upward. "He'd spoken to your father about the possibility, and apparently Erik had refused to put the idea to you three. I don't know what Philip expected me to do about it, but I told him that even if he wrangled that invitation from Vinci, he could stuff it up his ass. You boys had zero need for curated matches. You lived in Montana—as far as I knew at the time, you'd always live there. He shouldn't mess with your futures."

Kris smiled. "One conversation with you must take years off Philip's life."

"You can talk."

Fair point. "Poor guy."

"He's stronger than he looks," she said. "I also did a spot of door knocking when I caught wind of close-minded muttering around town." She paused. "You know, about Jones."

He sucked in a breath.

"I didn't catch them all," she said more softly.

Regret bit him at the guilt in her voice. "I shouldn't have said that the other night. That you didn't protect Tommy. That you should have stopped it from happening. It wasn't your fault."

"No, you were right." She frowned. "I wasn't paying attention. I should've known those guys were in town. Should've noticed their gay-hate and aggression, and never let them out of my sight."

"Frankie," he said, sitting up properly even as his lungs tightened. Was he really going to do this? Share the shame that had eaten him alive for three years? "You know that they came to the ranch before the attack."

Her frown shifted. "Yeah."

"I don't—" Guilt lashed him for what he'd learned that night —for what he'd done. For the silence he'd kept since, refusing to distress his brothers and not knowing who else in the palace to trust. But he could trust Frankie. "They weren't homophobes after Jonah."

The air pressure in the tent seemed to drop. Frankie didn't move, but her energy gathered, a storm rising, and his ears wanted to pop.

"What does that mean?" she asked quietly.

His throat was too dry to answer.

She pushed herself up to sitting. "What are you saying?"

"I—" He reached out and pulled her bedroll closer until it was flush against his. Voice low, he said, "I hate myself for what I'm about to tell you."

She looked startled. And close, very close. "Then spit it out."

"They didn't ask me for Jonah's address. They—" Self-loathing tried to silence him, but he barreled through it. "They had accents I didn't recognize and asked about Erik Jaroka's son."

Frankie swayed as shock hit her hard.

"I lied. They clearly didn't know Dad had triplets. I told them his name was Jonah and that he lived next door. Jonah was supposed to be working late at the bar. I thought it would give me time to call the sheriff, and get Mark from the stables and drive around there. But then—then . . ."

Then Jonah hadn't worked late—and Tommy had walked home with him. The group of men had caught up to them on the dark track between the ranch and Jonah's property and beaten them both to within an inch of their lives.

"Why didn't you tell me?" She was paler than moonlight. "Tell the sheriff?"

"What could I say? Hey, fun fact: my brothers and I are princes from yonder, and I think that attack was intended for the three of us, not our friend? Not without blowing our identities and lives apart. The sheriff was all too happy to pass it off as a hate crime. Told me we should be thankful this was the first time." Kris had wanted to throw the man's desk against the wall and his bigoted skull along with it. "He said Tommy was in the wrong place at the wrong time—with the wrong kind of friend—and that Jonah should be more careful."

"Piece of shit," she muttered, and then stilled. "But you told your family?"

Shame slid around the back of his neck like clammy fingers and shoved his head down.

"Kris." Frankie sounded appalled. "Erik could have contacted Philip. He could have ensured those men were found and charged with treason."

He'd known that, but had been too sickened to admit it was his fault. "I described them down to the damn hairs in their ears. Our authorities should have caught them."

Frankie's breath turned shallow and she stared at him without blinking. "Oh my God."

"Let me guess." Had she just had the same realization that had haunted him for months?

His voice was hushed as he said, "You're thinking two critical attacks on the royal family feels less accidental than one."

Disbelief was dark in her eyes. "They can't be related."

He leaned closer. "Why not?"

She rolled her lips, breathing a little too fast through her nose. "People who bungled an attack in small-town America could hardly go on to successfully commit royal murder inside the Kiralian palace."

"Bungled?" Shame dug its nails into him. Deep, deserved pain in the pit of his being. "I still don't know how Jonah fucking made it."

But she shook her head. "It's a stretch."

"That balcony collapse wasn't an accident." Kris was sure of it. "Plans for renovations of the west wing first started three years ago. There were delays, sure, but if someone had a grand plan involving a construction accident, they acted to remove the spare heir ahead of time."

"I—I have to call Philip." Her phone was out, unlocked, her thumb whipping across the screen.

"Don't tell Tommy." Humiliation rushed out of Kris with the words. His brother could never know it was his fault. The resentment he felt over Kris taking the throne would be nothing compared to Kris nearly getting him killed, nearly getting Jonah killed. "He'd never—*I'd* never—"

Her features were severe in the glow of the screen as her attention snapped back to him. "Don't blame yourself."

How could he not? "I should have told those men it was me. They thought Dad only had one son. Common belief here in Kiraly, apparently. I could've claimed to be it. Protected everyone else. But I panicked and sent them straight to Tommy and Jonah."

Phone falling, she shifted to her knees in front of him. "No." She bunched his shirtsleeve in her fist and gave it a hard tug. "They would've killed you. You sent them to an empty property so no one would get hurt. It was smart. You didn't know the boys would be on their way home."

"What if they'd died?" His eyes stung; everything stung. "Jonah came so close. And Tommy . . ."

"It still wouldn't have been your fault." Through the fabric, the warmth of her fingers pressed against his forearm. Then her brow creased. "But you're right. Jones was in a bad state when we got there." Careful words for unconscious, sliced up and bleeding out through a stomach wound. "I called Philip. He's the one who organized that air ambulance to fly to the best trauma doctors in Montana. Jones wouldn't have made it otherwise."

"Exactly." That was part of why it made sense. "The attackers left the scene believing he was dead. A secret, spare heir out of the running."

"But." Her eyes were glazed. "Erik was next in line. For this theory to float, they should have gone after him as well."

"Too obvious." Kris had traveled this road. "One attack could be passed off as random. But two separate murders of the royal line? Not so much. Security would never have let anyone near the royal family in Kiraly again." He raised a shoulder in sad acceptance. "And Dad's been unwell for a while. They could have presumed he'd abdicate, and if he didn't, staged an accident that could be blamed on his condition."

Frankie was shaking her head slowly.

"Look," he said. "I was confused and ashamed and didn't know how to fix things then. But I'm going to find them now. The attackers. Whoever brought that balcony down. And they're going to rue the fucking day they messed with my family."

"No, you're not—" Frankie halted as her eyes narrowed. "Oh, no. You haven't been."

Pulling his bottom lip between his teeth, he looked away.

"Bloody hell," she murmured, but she'd gone pale all over again. "You're more stupid than I thought."

That was probably true.

"This is why you've slipped security?" she demanded in a harsh whisper. "To try to find the people you believe *committed regicide*. Are you insane? Have you forgotten that you're also royalty?"

His jaw set. "I can't trust anyone else."

"You can trust me." She was still holding his sleeve and he

slid his gaze down. The tent seemed to close in around the small intimacy, a touch without touching, and instead of letting go, she tugged again. "I'm already on this. Leave it alone."

That pulled him up. "You're already on it?"

"I've been looking into it since I got here. The police officially closed the investigation as an accident, but Philip and I can't swallow it either. I've been researching the laborers who worked on the renovations. The suppliers. The staff who had access to the west wing. We know that the balcony pillars weren't sealed properly—that the wood supports were water-damaged and buckled under the weight of their banquet. Yes, the damage could be due to poor sequencing of different trades during installation. King Vinci's timeline for renovations was incredibly tight and his budget didn't exactly inspire excellence. Good, fast and cheap—when it comes to a job, you get two out of three. His Majesty unwittingly chose fast and cheap, and suffered horrifically for the lack of quality. The official findings make sense." She paused, features haunted. "But it doesn't *feel* right. The circumstances were practically begging to be used as a cover for something more sinister."

Kris's heart was pounding. "What have you found?"

"Not much." Her tone turned cutting. "It's kind of difficult to wade through hundreds of possible suspects when I've had to learn a high-pressure job on the fly that involves keeping track of a certain prince who keeps disappearing."

His hope for closure fixed on her. "I won't disappear again if you promise to update me."

"Fine," she snapped. After a beat, she said, "What have you found?"

"Not much, either. I'll show you my notes. I was on my way to visit the site manager when you found me the other night."

She cursed under her breath, shaking her head.

As she picked up her phone again, he asked, "Can we trust Philip?"

"Philip had nothing to do with the death of your family." Her hushed tone was final.

He frowned. "How can you really know?"

"I know. Now, don't talk. I need to call him."

She disappeared under her bedding, and even Kris couldn't quite make out the muffled phone conversation. When she emerged, she said, "Dawn meeting in the tower. He wants to hear this theory from you—then we'll loop in the authorities to look into a possible connection with the attack on Jones and Tommy." She sighed and her shoulders slumped as she rubbed her face. "If it's true, it changes everything."

"In my defense, I did try to meet with the head of personal security about this when I first got here."

She looked like he'd slapped her. "I assumed you wanted to convince me to remove your guards."

"That too," he said. "It doesn't matter now."

"It does. I'm not cut out for this. I shouldn't even be here."

He lay down onto his side, facing her, and offered a smile. "That makes two of us."

She hesitated, attention darting to the seam of the two bedrolls, still pulled side by side. A line etched between her brows before she slowly lay down, mirroring his pose, though her muscles were locked with tension.

Her gaze was haunted. "I'm scared for you."

"Nah, don't be scared."

But she was. Fear pulled around her mouth, glinted in her eyes. They hadn't lain this close before and his chest clamped. Her night-shadowed eyes moved over him, a slow yet erratic path, as if caught in the current of his body. Longing eddied beneath his skin, and if she dove in, she'd find the space he reserved for her ran deeper than he'd ever let on.

"You asked why I haven't said sorry." The words hid under her breath, soft and shy, and he focused on her lips to catch them properly. "It's because I'm not. I found you. Across the world, when I had nothing left inside me, I *found* you. And I know it's the middle of the night talking and I'm going to be sick about telling you this in the morning, but I know I lied—and I hid from you, and I hurt you, but you mean everything to me, and I can't imagine how this could have played out differently. So, I'm not sorry. I'll never be sorry I found you."

A sharp, searing heat split his heart.

Then she swallowed, eyes wide, and her arm moved. A bolt of reaction burst up his arm as the tips of two of her fingers grazed across his hand where it rested between them. Soft, scarcely there, but he felt it with the insistent tug of a stitch woven into his skin—and he flipped his palm, opening it carefully, heart in his throat as she threaded her fingers through his.

He clasped her tightly.

The next morning, he woke alone.

7

The walk to Zara's apartment from the women's shelter was peak Kira City torture. Frankie grumbled up streets so unforgiving, the sidewalks were literally made of stone steps. It was almost enough to overshadow her ache for Kris after going all of yesterday without seeing him. Her thighs burned and the late-afternoon sun beat relentlessly at her back as she kept pace with her friend.

"That was a good session." Zara tugged the brim of her sun hat lower over the back of her neck. "That blocking move should help."

"They've just got to get close enough to splatter his balls inside his skull."

Zara pulled a face. "Visual."

Frankie often had Sunday afternoons off work, so set aside a couple of hours to teach Zara's shelter residents self-defense. She'd outline common types of attacks men used on women on the street and in the home, and then teach basic moves for them to defend themselves. These women had complicated, fragile histories with abuse, and she did her best to respect that pain while arming them with strength. Hard to say which hurt more to see—the fierce concentration of women who knew this might literally save their lives or the women who wept even as they stacked their arms, tucked their foreheads down, and blocked their practice partners' attack. "Don't hold back, ladies," she'd tell them, walking the room. "All beasts have an underbelly, and for a man, that's his balls. Strike it like you mean it. That's his procreative future right there—his brain will protect it at all costs. Make impact and he'll pitch forward, hips hinging to pull it out of range. He might even forget to throw that punch or keep his grip on your neck, so don't be half-assed about it—keep at it until he's on the ground. Then you get the hell out of there."

Afterward, she and Zara would often go out for an early dinner, but today, they'd decided to head back to Zara's apartment for cold drinks.

"Thanks again for coming in," Zara said. "You've had a big week."

"It's fine." Frankie glanced up, irritated to find they weren't even halfway up the street. "I want to help. I'd have killed for a shelter when I was growing up."

Zara kept her head down as she climbed. Her question was quiet. "Killed who, exactly?"

Her next breath was jagged and she wished she could blame it on the climb. Abuse wasn't always physical. "My dad."

The only comfort her friend offered was a light brush of her knuckles against Frankie's forearm, but it still tied a knot in her throat.

By the time they staggered into the apartment, they were sweating, groaning, and fixated on the ice cream Zara had remembered in her freezer.

Rounding the kitchen, Frankie pulled up short at the sight of an immaculately dressed blond man by the fridge, tightening his tie. His blue eyes snapped to her, assessing, and she suddenly wished she'd paid more attention when Zara had mentioned her boyfriend. He was Mark's manservant, but she'd never had cause to interact with him at the palace. She'd looked over his staff file months ago—long-term palace employee from a reputable family within Kiraly—but could she remember his name? Of course not.

"I've mentioned Frankie?" Zara asked by way of introduction, hip-bumping him out of the way so she could open the freezer.

"Ah, yes, of the royal guard," he said, voice low and cultured. "You're head of personal security."

Frankie wiped the back of her hand across her forehead. "Yep."

"I've heard a lot about you." Tie in place, he extended his hand and offered a warm, sincere smile. "I'm Adam."

"Adam." She shook, finding his grip firmer than expected. "What kind of things?"

His smile grew. "In short, to be careful around you."

Not a bad reputation for her position. "You work for Mark, right?"

"Yes, my duties have followed His Majesty to Kuria Estate." His attention drifted to where Zara was pulling two spoons from the drawer. "Zara, I've got dinner with some old college friends tonight. Do you mind if I'm not home until late?"

"Why would I mind?" She passed Frankie a spoon and plied the lid off the family pack of chocolate-mint ice cream. "Have fun."

He hesitated, pleasant expression looking a little strained. "You know you're welcome to come?"

"Maybe next time." She bopped him on the shoulder with her spoon. "Frankie will be here."

Frankie kept her expression easy despite her friend's lie. She'd already told Zara that Kris wanted to go out tonight after cooping himself up in the palace all week, and that meant bodyguard duty.

"Next time, then." Adam's hand touched the small of Zara's back as he pressed a kiss to her temple. "Love you."

"Yeah. Thanks." She angled a too-bright smile at him. "See you later."

His answering smile came a beat too slow. "I look forward to it."

"Yay," she said, before leading Frankie into the small living room and switching on an oscillating fan. She flopped onto the couch, cheeks pink, and Frankie sat beside her, waiting until the front door closed behind Adam to raise an interrogative brow.

Zara cringed, held out the tub, and said, "Ahhh, I know. My life is super awkward right now."

Frankie scooped into the ice cream. "He loves you."

"Inexplicable, right?"

"No." She stuck the entire scoop in her mouth and spoke around the spoon. "But I'm getting that it's unrequited."

"He only told me a few weeks ago." Her friend looked stricken. "I mean, he's a great guy. Kind. Gentle. Refined. I want to love him, but I just . . ."

"Don't."

Zara shifted, tucking one leg under her bum. "Well," she said, and darted a troubled glance at Frankie. It was the look of someone with a secret trying to decide whether or not to spill.

Frankie focused on scooping more ice cream, tilting her face to catch the fan's breeze.

"It's stupid," Zara said.

"My whole life is stupid right now." Frankie raised a shoulder. "I won't judge."

"I—don't tell Ava."

Frankie placed a hand over her heart.

"It's just. Okay. Adam keeps saying he loves me, like, every day. And I could've sworn I was close to realizing that I love him, too.

Then Ava came back and I've started planning her bridal shower and helping her organize the wedding, and it's thrown me off, because it means...I mean, the wedding means...it's just that I'll—"

Frankie stared. Was this how she sounded when Kris asked her a vulnerable question?

"It means I'll see Cyrus again," Zara said in a rush, her knees bunching up against her chest as she sank into the couch cushions.

"Prince Cyrus?" Ava's older brother and the heir to Kelehar's throne?

Zara nodded with a noise of distress. "It's so stupid."

"Not really." Frankie tipped her face down for the fan to cool the top of her head. "He's magnificent."

A world-renowned heart-stopper. He was elegant, lean and gorgeous. He practically glowed with goodwill. His dark eyes shone with genuine warmth, and the waves of his raven-black hair always ran a little long, hinting that his refinement didn't hold in *every* situation. Too nice for Frankie to look twice, but the appeal was obvious.

"*So* magnificent," her friend breathed. "And not someone I have the birthright to even dream about, but it's getting worse. How can it be getting worse? I haven't seen him since Ava escaped. I have a boyfriend who loves me, but just the thought of Cyrus coming over for the wedding makes my stomach fall apart and I can't imagine ever feeling that way about Adam."

Frankie made a noise of disgust. "That stomach fall-aparty feeling is the worst."

Zara looked stricken. "Should I break up with Adam?"

"Uh." Frankie winced. "I'm not a relationship advice kind of friend. But like you said last week, royalty isn't made for us and we're not made for them. Why break up with a good guy who loves you? The wedding isn't far away. Once Cyrus leaves, you probably won't ever see him again. Then you can move on—and might realize you want to do that with Adam."

Zara eyed her with a suspicious frown. "That was good relationship advice."

"Don't get used to it."

"What about your prince situation?"

Oh, the situation that had seen her spend Friday night alone in a tent with Kris, her fingers entwined with his, and woken up to find his other hand splayed protectively over her thigh? That had seen her lie there for way longer than she should have, trying to memorize the way sleep softened his features, because it was the only chance she'd ever have? That situation?

"It could be better. He's trying to get too close," she admitted, and with a hole the shape of dread in her chest, added, "But I have a backup plan."

That night, Frankie sat next to Kris at the bar of the Bearded Bunting, braced against his short-fused mood. Her team was positioned at all the entry-exit points, including both ends of the laneway behind the venue, and casual-clothed guards had been instructed to blend into the gathering. Frankie and Philip had pounced on Kris's theory, arranging their own investigation into the attack on Tommy and Jonah, but in the meantime, Kris couldn't so much as turn his head in a public place without half a dozen guards clocking the movement.

The bar was booth-lined with a packed dance floor, while the rear courtyard was even more crowded with brightly dressed locals coming together at the end of a hard day. The whole place was loud and lively, filled with people laughing, calling out and telling stories at the tops of their lungs. No wonder Kris liked it here. The throng absorbed his status and he could sit at the bar like any other guy in a black tank, unbuttoned plaid shirt and jeans. Which, to Frankie's continued bewilderment, was a lot of them. This cowboy-chic fashion trend worked in his favor.

He'd just accepted his second drink from the bartender, and was rolling his shoulders, stretching his neck, eyeing the room like a fighter in the ring spoiling for an outlet for his surging testosterone. It was dangerous. Every time she looked at him, her temperature rose, and when he'd leaned in earlier to ask what she wanted to drink, he'd smelled so sexy that some delirious instinct wanted to rub his scent all over her naked body. The man was practically vibrating with a sinful energy.

Holding her breath, she leaned in and spoke under the noise. "You're acting volatile."

His answering grin was utterly wild.

Christ.

He got this way when he felt out of control. Attempting to balance out the scales by *being* out of control.

"Get out of predator mode," she told him firmly. "We don't need trouble."

He drew challengingly from his beer, eyes locked on her. "You could handle it."

"What?"

He slid a forearm along the counter toward her. Edgy, magnetic. "Trouble."

"Your Highness," she said, nodding at the bartender as he set a bowl of hot chips between them. "I recommend you dance this off."

He stayed close, eyes on hers, so she picked up her glass of lemonade and bit down on the straw. She wasn't sitting next to gentle Kris, who gazed into her soul and murmured words she'd never forget. She was sitting next to Kris who had stress pent up inside him like a caged beast clawing to get out. And he *wanted* to let it out, with her as the closest target.

"Your hair drives me crazy," he said, voice coarse, eyes too intense for so few drinks in.

She scarcely bothered to raise a brow. For the sake of her prince's privacy, her earpiece wasn't broadcasting this conversation to the entire security team, but for the sake of his safety, it *was* being received by Hanna and Peter. Peter lurked near the dance floor and Hanna laughed easily as she fended off unwanted attention farther up the bar counter.

"You keep it so short at the sides." Kris's attention moved across her scalp. "There's no opening for me to tuck your hair back."

"If you paid attention to the look on my face," she said, "you'd see there's no opening for you to do a damn thing."

His attention slipped to the side of her neck. "Will you dance with me?"

"No."

"Will you storm onto the dance floor and haul anyone off me who gets too close?"

Frankie scanned the room, feigning distraction. "Possibly."

"What if they put their hand on my ass?"

"Depends if it looks like you want it there."

"What if they take me back to their place?" His question was quiet, but not careful. Proof that she was another contributing factor to this mood. "What would you do then?"

"Scout their home before you go in, make them sign a nondisclosure agreement, and wait in the car out front."

Scowling, he pulled back and drained his beer dry. Not the answer he wanted. He signaled for another drink, grabbed a handful of chips, and turned to talk to the guy on his other side.

Frankie was down to the salt at the bottom of the bowl, watching the room without interest as Kris continued to chat with the guy and his friends, when someone brushed against her shoulder. She tensed, turning with a frown.

"Hey," said a man with wavy hair, dark skin, and eyelashes for days. He held cash in one hand, presumably waiting for his drink, and smiled at her as he leaned against the bar.

"Hey," she said, eyeing him over.

"I haven't seen you here before."

She wanted to say *I'm with numbnuts,* but instead said, "First time."

"You look good in those shorts."

She bit back a groan. Complimenting a woman's legs was the most generic pickup line in Kiraly—mountain living worked wonders for the thighs—but admittedly, hers were on full display in her green high-waisted cutoffs. She'd dressed to blend in. She'd matched it with a cherry summer-weight jacket to conceal the gun in her shoulder holster. Before she could answer, Kris was leaning into her space, arm stretching along the counter in front of her, and saying, "Yeah, well you should see her in a crown."

Shock slackened the man's face. "Woah. Sorry, didn't see you there, Highness," he said, and hightailed it into the crowd without waiting for his drink.

Frankie rounded on Kris, her temper snarling. "What was that?"

He relaxed, sprawled against the bar, closer to her than he should be. "What?"

"That," she snapped.

"That what?"

"You were being—" Her jaw slid as she bit the word back.

Eyes glittering, he leaned all the way into her space. Close, closer, until their breaths merged, and it was all she could do to glare him down without her eyes crossing. He challenged her in a voice sharp like drawn claws. "I was being what, Frankie?"

"Territorial," she said through clenched teeth.

"You're *my* bodyguard, aren't you?"

"Don't you dare—"

He cocked an eyebrow, as if he couldn't possibly fathom what she meant.

"—make it sound so possessive," she finished.

"Mine," he said again, daring her, and she sensed his primal thrill at saying such a thing in the middle of a crowded bar. "You're mine and he can't have you."

"Brute." She flicked another glance over his shoulder—and stopped breathing as fear detonated inside her. Hand snapping to her earpiece, she said, "Secure the baby," and launched off the barstool straight at the man who was coming up behind Kris for the fourth time in twenty minutes, withdrawing his hand from his pocket with a dark shape in his grip.

Kris landed on his front behind the bar counter. Peter crushed him and Hanna dropped into a crouch by one shoulder. His heart hammered; his muscles deadlocked.

"What the hell is going on?" he shouted over the public's startled screams. His cheek was pressed into a sticky spill on the wooden floor, and all he could see was the feet of the bar staff as they gathered at the opposite end. "Where's Frankie?" Suddenly he was struggling like a deer in a drop net. "Where the fuck is Frankie?"

"She's handling it." Hanna's thigh was pressed against the back of his head and right shoulder, her weight bearing down to help keep him pinned as she presumably watched over the top of the counter. Not that Peter needed help.

"Handling *what?*" Kris roared, pushing against the resolute weight on his back.

"The threat," she answered severely. "Now don't act like a man who thinks his wife can't carry the groceries. She's got this."

"Got what?" He could hardly process what she was saying. "What's happening?"

"A man was closing in on you." Her words were clipped. "Frankie's subduing him."

"*Still?*" Panic clawed inside his lungs, shredding his breath. "Help her, for God's sake!"

"Wait." Hanna paused. "Oh, man." Then she chuckled low in her throat. "Yeah, now he's down."

Kris struggled again. "Let me up."

"Not yet, Your Highness," Peter said firmly, leaning his weight more securely onto him. "Our team needs to conduct body searches of everyone present. Then you'll be safe to stand."

"Why?" Then it struck him, and he bucked under Peter's hold. "The prick had a weapon. Did he get her? Is she hurt? If he laid a *finger*—"

"She's fine." Hanna's hand briefly passed over his shoulder blade. "It was pepper spray and she didn't give him the chance to use it."

But it might have been a knife. A screwdriver. A gun. And Frankie had thrown herself at the man without hesitating.

Kris pounded his fist against the sticky floor. The impact acted as a release, pain to fight the panic, so he did it again. And again. Anything to stop the fear from clawing its way up the back of his throat. He was breathing too fast, hardly taking in air, and his fist stung as he pounded it repeatedly.

"Hey." Suddenly Frankie spoke from beside him, voice low and heavy with concern. For a fleeting second, her hand closed over his fist. "Calm down."

"Frankie." He made a grab for her, but she pulled away. A heartbeat later, his guards retreated, and he was on his feet, stepping closer to her, scanning her face, her body—noting that aside from mussed hair and the thundercloud of her expression, she looked unharmed. "Are you—?"

"Stay back," she muttered, and glanced behind him.

A prickle passed down his spine, and he turned to see that almost everyone in the bar was watching him. They stood quietly, talking in hushed voices, contained by his security team. A couple of guards knelt on the floor, pinning his assailant.

Kris switched on a smile. "Everyone alright?"

He received grins in return, a few whoops, and one guy said loudly, "Your guard's good, Highness."

"That she is. Sorry for the trouble."

He turned his back, jaw setting as he met Frankie's bleak stare. "Do you know what his plan was?"

Anger flickered across her face as she shared a look with Hanna. "He wouldn't stop mouthing off at me," she said, running a hand down her neck. "We have ourselves a psycho misogynist. Apparently, he didn't intend to harm you, but get close enough to prove he could—because obviously with women highly positioned within your security team, your safety was at risk."

"Mother—" Kris spun around and found Peter blocking his path.

"Pretty sure Frankie disproved his theory," Hanna said.

Hands balled by his sides, he turned back, his gaze returning to Frankie like a key sliding into its lock. His breath was still coming too fast, but it quickened further as she returned his stare, her green eyes unreadable.

"Not the weirdest we've had." Hanna tugged at her ponytail to tighten it. "I heard that in his youth, Prince Noel was pulled into a public restroom by groupies who declared he had to have a five-way with them before they'd let him out."

"I've had weirder," Peter said. "Last year, a man tried to get at Prince Aron with a syringe because he wanted to run blood tests to identify markers of the royal gene."

Frankie snorted. "There's someone who failed science class."

"Yeah," Hanna said. "Everyone knows all you need is a cheek swab."

It was an effort to diffuse the tension, a few jokes to bring their stress down, but Kris's muscles were locked tight as a bull's, his heart stamping like a charge, and he couldn't tear his eyes off Frankie.

"Your Highness," she said carefully, and the others glanced at him.

"Get me the hell out of here." His demand was roughshod, but she must have heard the crack of a man about to break, because she had him out the rear staff exit and inside the car before he even noticed the blood behind her ear.

♘

Frankie took him to the only place she knew that offered privacy and an open sky. She'd instructed Hanna and Peter to have their incident reports on her desk by tomorrow morning and set her earpiece to incoming only, because she had no trust in Kris to keep his talk professional.

"We call this The Scepter," she said, sitting on the top step without looking at him. She figured if they sat facing the city, rather than looking up over their shoulders, the palace didn't even have to exist. A public garden stretched out directly behind them and the steep descent of endless steps fell away in front. The security team had swept the garden upon arrival, and finding it empty, had taken position around the perimeter. Impassable and out of sight, so it was just her and Kris alone under the stars. Exactly what Kris needed. "I used to come here growing up," she said, sliding off her jacket. "Late at night. Just to breathe and watch the city sleep."

Without answering, he hunkered down beside her, planting

his feet two steps below, knees wide. He leaned back on his hands, tipping his head to gaze at the sky.

Then he said, "He drew blood," and the fury in his voice betrayed that his silence since the bar in no way meant he'd calmed down.

Frowning, she extended her arms in front of her, trying to find where he meant.

"Above your ear."

"Oh." She touched the tender spot with a shaking hand. "I headbutted him once I had him in a lock. I think I connected with his ear piercing."

His slow breath was unsteady. "You headbutted him."

"I wanted to Mace him with his own spray, but I'm bound by minimal damage."

"How'd you know he was there?"

"I'd been watching the room." She flicked off a bug as it landed on her thigh. "You know, doing my job. He'd walked past too many times, looking at the back of your head, and eyeing me off when he thought I wasn't watching. His stance was different that last time. He was moving with intent."

Adrenaline had barreled through her blood. She'd had to trust that Hanna and Peter would keep Kris safe, that the guy was working alone, because she'd moved with tunnel vision—the clamor of the room reduced to a dull murmur in her ears, victim to her body's chemistry in the frontline of a fight. Her breathing was still too fast; her skin buzzed.

Kris shifted, leaning forward, stiff with tension. "I was scared for you."

"I know." She'd seen how fiercely he'd beaten the floor, trapped beneath his guards, prisoner to his own status. "You'll probably bruise."

"Wish it was caused by messing up his face."

"You're not a violent guy." She bumped him with her shoulder. "Let's keep it that way."

The contact drew his attention and he swiveled inward to face her. Frowning, he asked, "You okay?"

"Adrenaline," she said, running her hands up and down her thighs. There was nothing she could do to stop the shaking, the mild nausea, not until her body had leveled out. "It'll pass."

"Question," he said, still twisted to face her. "Is my code name really *baby*?"

She snickered and made the mistake of glancing at him. The desire in his eyes reverberated through her. "Yes."

"Because I'm yours?" he asked, the false innocence of the question drowned out by the dangerous undertone. A swollen heat inside her shuddered at the thought of him using the pet name on her. *C'mere, baby,* he'd growl in her ear, his hands on her skin, *I need you to do that again.*

"Because you're the youngest," she said firmly.

"Sure," he said. "What's Tommy's?"

"Chip." For the chip in his front tooth. "Mark is Jack and Ava is Pixie."

Kris opened his mouth, but it was several seconds before he said in bafflement, "Jack?"

"Mark's totally a Jack," she said. "You know, the trustworthy hero in every action movie ever."

"That is very weird," he said. "I like mine the best."

Of course he did. With his panic easing, Frankie sensed the prickle of his earlier restlessness settling back into place. He stretched, returning his palms to the cobblestones behind him. But this time, one hand crossed over into her space and he leaned into it, bringing his shoulder so close her whole arm seemed to blush. His attention, when she darted a look at his face, was roaming over her bare legs.

Ignoring the arousal that feathered low in her abdomen, she said, "You're in a mood tonight."

He hummed, a deep resonant sound that vibrated down her spine. "Can't shake it."

She bit the inside of her mouth, praying for strength, until something he'd said a few nights ago finally registered in a gut-drop of realization.

He hadn't been with a woman since arriving in Kiraly.

This sex-fueled cowboy was brimming with lust, an overfilled bucket left under a waterfall with no one to empty it, and the last thing anyone needed was his sexual frustration gushing over into his daily life. It would distract him from his training, his duty. Make him brash and careless. Horse riding and intense gym workouts weren't enough to free this man from his primal urges.

Philip had given her this job because she alone knew these untrained princes. She knew the security they needed. *How to prevent trouble,* he'd added, and maybe that was true after all, because she knew the man beside her wasn't built for abstinence.

Well, this was going to be as fun as a bludgeon to the heart.

"I think we both know what might take the edge off," she said very quietly.

His look was flat-out incredulous.

"I can line up an NDA," she said, aiming for matter-of-fact. "We can head back to the bar. You won't be short of willing—"

"Stop talking." He swooped in, twisting his body around to crouch in front of her, planting his hands on either side of her hips, bringing his face inches from hers. His eyes were bright, burning in the soft garden lights, and his voice was rough as gravel as he said, "Never suggest I have sex with someone who isn't you."

She rolled her lips together.

"I'm going to figure this out," he said, his thrumming body so close that her own ached to open to him. "I'm made of gunpowder around you, Frankie. One look and my blood sparks and my heart flares and my whole body braces for combustion." His chest was pressed against her knee, and instinctively, she slid her leg outward to give him space, only for it to position him squarely between her spread thighs. "This restlessness, this frustration, it's all you. It's finally caught up with me. Knowing you want it too—I've got no way to calm it down. I need you. Frankie." His voice dropped to a growl. "I'm on fire for you."

She couldn't move; she didn't *want* to move beneath the heat of his breath. He smelled like morning-after sheets on a bed she'd never want to leave, and his steady gaze betrayed he had no intention of pulling away without being asked.

The silence was his question—and slowly became her answer.

Features harsh with desire, his attention slid down to her neck. Her blood beat harder at her throat, flurrying, a hand impatiently ushering him closer. She shouldn't do this—shouldn't open herself up to him like a purse with a broken latch. In one deft movement he'd take everything inside, right down to the gold coin caught in the lining. She'd have nothing left when he moved on—just emptiness and the fading memory of the way he'd brushed up against her. But she knew. Despite a friendship of caution and constant evasion, she knew.

That coin had always been his to take.

Breathless, she angled her chin up just a fraction. An invitation, an opening.

He took it, lashes dropping as he leaned in to her neck.

It was a clean touch of his lips, yet still she gasped, spine arching as if he'd bore his full weight down on her. *Kris.* He stilled, before inhaling deeply, his back expanding as he breathed her in, his nose pressed to her skin, his untamed hair at her jaw. Then his lips found her again and it was the searing heat of his open mouth, the wet thrill of his tongue against her throat. Her hand tangled in his hair, soft as flowing water, and he groaned, opening wider, tasting her, his shoulders shifting as he brought himself closer, his hands moving to grasp her hips.

"Frankie," he said on a strained whisper. Buried in her neck, he spoke her name as a question, a request, a desperate plea.

Hot and aching all over, she closed her eyes. She wanted to give in, take the step that thrummed like a rope beneath her feet, almost too taut for her to maintain her balance. He'd steady her, hold her up for just long enough to feel the weightlessness of his embrace. But then—then she'd fall, hollowed out right down to her very lining.

And his duty wouldn't permit him to catch her.

"No more," she whispered.

His body grew rigid with restraint; he didn't move.

She forced herself to speak. "You said you didn't expect anything from me."

Another moment passed before he groaned, very different than the last, and drew back out of the frame of her thighs. He dropped beside her, fist pressed to his forehead. "I don't. But I want it."

Something frail splintered inside her. "I've told you I can't."

"I'm not expecting you to bear me children," he said, practically hoarse with restraint. "I'm working on it."

She pressed her knees together, uneasy. "Working on what?"

"There must be a way."

"There isn't."

"Don't expect me not to fight for you." He crackled like a live wire beside her.

She'd failed spectacularly at calming him down.

"There are ways," he said. "We can be a modern royal family. Or Tommy, he might—"

"Do *not* put pressure on Tommy to produce heirs."

"There are *ways*," he said again, firmly.

No. Nothing could erase her upbringing; nothing would stop their children being referred to as royal juvies or the state's own delinquents. Illegitimate heirs would be preferable to those borne by a criminal. They wouldn't be trusted; their every decision would be raked over hot coals. If Kris's uncle Vinci were alive today, he would refuse the very notion in an indignant, horrified rage.

Kris would be cast out of the royal family before he'd be allowed to court a woman like Frankie.

"You don't know everything about me," she said, voice shaking.

"Then tell me."

She felt a pressure in her chest, the cold of a metal clasp snapping closed. "I can't."

He swore under his breath, grasping the side of his head.

"I feel like I can't," she said again, small and painful. "Because I'm ashamed." Her insides were ice as she said, "I—I'll explain why. Let me build up to it."

"You have no reason to be ashamed." He was so serious, believing everything and understanding nothing. "I left you behind once. I'm never doing it again."

"Kris . . ."

His jaw flexed. "I asked you to say my name—not use it as another word for no." His shoulders expanded with warning. "Don't do that. Use it to mean yes."

God. On those orders, she wouldn't speak his name at all. She rolled her lips tight on bitter acceptance. She had to do it. Resort to her backup plan—and reveal her past. She had to do it right, in a way he couldn't deny.

"Stand up," she said, and rose to her feet.

He did, his frown as puzzled as it was irritated.

"Since you won't hook up with a stranger like a good randy

prince," she said, and caught the flash of humor in his eyes. "We have limited options for working that temper out of you." Lifting to the balls of her feet, she pulsed her heels a few times. "To the base of The Scepter and back. Five reps."

She set off without waiting for his response. His bark of startled laughter echoed across the city. She heard the scuff of his takeoff, the impact of his feet on the steps, and realized too late that this was just another form of giving him chase. And even though she was faster on this wickedly steep decline, skilled at staying out of his reach, a flutter of panic rose beneath her breastbone.

She'd never wanted him to catch her so badly.

8

Kris wanted to go home.

Not forever—unless that was an option—but to clear his head. Life in Kiraly cluttered his days, his thoughts, his vision. Something always needed doing, needed thinking about. And despite the palace's endless halls and towers and grand open rooms, those high ceilings and echoing chambers felt like lungs filled with stale air, showing off its power by trapping space rather than granting it freedom.

What he wouldn't give to stare out at a vast, empty landscape for a few hours and let his mind quieten. He swore his heart beat faster here. If he were back in Montana, he'd get in his truck and drive without destination—just him and the lonesome stretches of roadway and wide eternal scenery. The only signs of civilization would be the occasional passing car or old cabin tucked in the margins of nature. That kind of full-body unwind would help him haul his restlessness into line.

The closest he could manage was spending time with his brothers.

After a morning of meetings, Kris dropped onto the sofa in the tower study and swiped an oatmeal cookie from the platter.

If he closed his eyes, he could almost imagine it had come fresh from Rose's Diner. He had to give the palace chefs credit—they sought to provide touches of Montana flavor to the otherwise fine food served to the royal family. Chewing, Kris sank deep into the cushions, fatigue from his sleepless nights weighing him down even as undirected energy continued to surge through him. Without the grounding effects of his homeland, he was living on the edge, and sooner or later, he was going to slip right off.

"You okay over there?"

He opened his eyes to find Mark watching him from where he sat opposite the grand monarch's desk, looking over paperwork.

"Philip called me King Markus in this morning's meeting," Kris answered. "Gotta tell you, it's strange to be addressed by that man without reprimand. His tone was respectful." Kris shoved the rest of the cookie into his mouth. "Gave me the creeps."

"Don't worry," Mark said. "Once he doesn't have to pretend that you're me, he'll never address you with respect again."

Kris laughed and tossed a cookie at him. Mark snatched it from the air one-handed and looked back down at the paperwork.

"You're doing well," Mark said as he flipped a page. "Philip agrees. It seems like this plan will work."

Kris's gut cramped. "Yeah?"

Mark looked up, features pained, and asked, "Are you really sure, Kris?"

Was he sure he wanted his brother to be happy? "Yes."

The study door opened and Tommy stepped in, the carpet muting the heels of his leather boots. Door shut behind him, he glanced between his brothers.

"I was summoned?" He sounded amused.

"Take a seat." Kris gestured toward his desk as he sprawled wider on the couch.

Tommy hesitated, tugging on his bunched shirtsleeve and angling his face down to the right as if he was trying to discreetly look behind him. Kris had long suspected the movement accompanied heated internal debate—which clearly ended in a win against his anxiety, because he moved to take the unoccupied monarch's chair.

Mark set the papers on his lap and shot a look at Kris. "What's up?"

"I miss you guys," he said with a sigh. "And the ranch."

The heaviness of his brothers' silence betrayed homesickness was only ever half a thought away for them, too.

"The quarter horses are due to arrive any day now," Mark said, about the horses they'd secured for the royal stables. "And I was just describing chokecherry cider to Ava last night. I'm going to get some shipped over."

Tommy quirked a brow. "We'd have to hide it from Frankie."

"She's a menace for it." Kris grinned. "I'll leave the last empty bottle somewhere for her to find."

"She'll claw you to pieces," Mark warned.

Kris's smile faded. "She'd have to get close enough."

His brothers exchanged a glance before Mark leaned back in his chair, crossing his feet at the ankle. "How are things going with her?"

Kris tried to think of an appropriate word. "Strained," he said, and after a pause, added, "As in, sexually."

Tommy picked up a pen, spinning it between his fingers as he murmured, "Story of your friendship."

"Is it—would it really be so bad if I ended up with a commoner?"

Tommy looked out the city-view window, pen still twirling. "Depends on the commoner."

"She's convinced we're incompatible. She's killing me."

Mark smiled faintly. "The opposite of her job description."

"Oh." Kris shifted, remembering, and cast them a serious look. "Something happened while I was out last night," he said, and told them about the incident at the bar. He noted Tommy's tension—the stiffening of his shoulders, the way his eyes glazed as he stopped blinking. "The guy's been charged with some offence called *lèse-majesté*."

"To do wrong to majesty," Tommy translated quietly.

"That's the end of it." Kris spread his knees, draping an arm along the back cushions of the sofa, widening his sprawl to counter his tension. "Frankie mentioned she'll assign you both with a bodyguard of your very own for when you're in public." He wouldn't tell his brothers of the possible link between Tommy and Jonah's attack and the deaths of their family. They both had enough to handle right now, and as cowardly as it was, he would avoid admitting his guilt in Tommy's attack for as long as possible. "As a precaution."

"Right." Mark was frowning. "You're okay, though?"

Kris slid his bruised hand behind his head. "Fine."

"Good." His brother gave a nod. "I spoke to Mom and Dad yesterday on a videocall and introduced them to Ava. It was awkward. We got stuck on small talk. I think we spoke about the Sage Haven bakery for about twenty minutes. None of us seemed to know how to get away from it. *And the peanut butter bars are still there . . . and the bagel melts . . . oh, and Mark, you'll be happy to know they're still baking cinnamon scrolls fresh every morning—Ava you must come and try the cinnamon scrolls . . .*" He trailed off with a grimace.

"But she must Mark," Kris said with a grin. "I sent Mom some photos from your engagement party. Apparently that made her cry."

Mark sighed. "Dad's not well enough to fly over for the

wedding, and Mom doesn't want to leave him. They're both upset about it. Ava and I will visit them afterward."

"They'll love that."

"In other news," Mark said. "Ava held the press conference this morning."

Kris nodded. It was Ava's attempt to control the story surrounding her life with Mark and Darius. Protecting her son from the media spotlight and the often damaging curiosity of the public had always been her priority—and she'd sacrificed her best chance of that in order to be with Mark. All she could hope for now was that Kiraly would find her and Darius less interesting than its cowboy royals.

Tommy leaned forward, forearms on the desk. "How did she go?"

Mark raised a shoulder, looking a little helpless. "She's stressed and upset. It was a public statement, so the journalists weren't given the opportunity to hound her with questions, but they were so stunned by her reappearance that she couldn't get a read on them. She's worried about the story morphing in the media and the impact it'll have on Darius."

'The story' she'd provided was a modified version of actual events. The world would believe that after falling in love with King Markus some months ago, Ava had confessed her illegitimate son to him, whom the royal family of Kelehar had helped her to keep safe and secret. Markus then helped her slip away to visit him and she'd brought her boy back to Kiraly where the king was continuing to court her. The public would only learn of their marriage once wedding photos were released to the press.

Still a juicy story, but nothing compared to how it had really unfolded.

"I hope she doesn't think she's made a mistake." Mark rested his head against the back of his chair and pressed his eyes shut.

"She was finally living undetected, like she'd always wanted. I've ruined that."

"Seriously?" Kris hurled another cookie at him. Mark jolted, eyes springing open as it hit him in the chest. "She came back for you, man. She climbed a mountain just to see you again. You didn't drag her here."

"It's just—" Mark hesitated, eyeing Kris. "This whole plan feels loose."

"So was calling in three cowboys to replace a royal family," Kris said, "but it's kind of working."

"Kind of," Tommy said, angling his head. "How's Darius settling in?"

Mark's smile was genuine. That was the right question to ask. "He's got a lot of his mother in him. Confident. Clever. A sweet kid, but he's got a sassy little mouth when he's comfortable."

Kris chuckled, looking forward to when the boy was comfortable around him. Three-year-old sass would be hysterical.

"He asked about my boots and said he wanted to do gardening like a real cowboy," Mark said, still smiling. "I've ordered a pair in his size."

There. That look of soft joy on his brother's face was exactly why Kris was taking over as king.

Then he pulled a face and said, "Gardening?"

"It's something he does with Ava. One step at a time. The horses will follow." Then his brows shot up. "Oh. And my bachelor party. I thought we could clear out a venue, maybe the Bearded Bunting, and just eat, drink and play cards. You guys, Adam, Philip—"

"Philip?" Kris interrupted.

"And my guards," Mark finished, ignoring him. "Small and simple."

"Sounds good." Tommy gave a nod, his hands busy tearing strips off the top sheet of a notepad on the desk. His face looked pale and tacky, and his hands leapt at the sudden knock on the door.

"Come in," Mark called.

Kris straightened up his sprawl when Frankie strode into the room. The memory of her taste was lush in his mouth, and for a moment, he was back on The Scepter—night wrapping a shadowed screen around them as he pressed his face against her neck and used his tongue to raze their past to the ground. He swallowed, taut with wanting as he watched her. She held a thin folder and didn't seem remotely surprised to find all three brothers in the room.

"Your Majesty." She bowed to Mark, then inclined her head to Tommy. "Your Highness." Lastly, she sent a sideways *watch yourself* look at Kris, said, "Your Highness," and inclined her head again.

"I told them about last night," he said, thrilled when her cheeks stained pink. The kiss was hot on her mind too. "And the bodyguards."

"There goes my prepared speech." She lowered the folder to her side. "It appears to be an isolated incident, but it pays to be safe."

"You're bruised." Tommy's attention was steady on her face.

Concern pushed Kris to his feet. "Where?"

Sighing, she faced him properly, revealing the tinge of purple on her cheek not quite concealed by her makeup. She raised a shoulder. "He must have got me."

"You must have felt it," he countered.

"Adrenaline is a great pain blocker."

Kris opened his mouth to argue, but Mark cut him off with a swift, "Frankie."

Standing, his brother drew something from his pocket. A

square of pearlescent card, with a silver ribbon woven along one edge. "Ava asked me to give this to you."

"That's pretty." She took it as if it might try to steal her fingerprints and frowned as she read it. "I still don't get why she wants me at her bridal shower."

"You're one of her heroes. It would mean a lot if you were there."

Frankie scoffed, glancing out the window, and it occurred to Kris that Frankie didn't only deny his attempts to draw her close, but that of anyone she classed as her superior. "I'm not a hero," she muttered.

"You're hers," Mark said. "You and Zara."

"Fine," she said, sounding almost annoyed. "Tell her yes."

Mark raised a brow. "I might alter the tone." He picked up his hat from the end of the desk. "I'll go and see how she's feeling."

Frankie slid a hand in the back pocket of her jeans and stepped back as Mark passed her.

"I'll leave you to it." Tommy rose and strode from the room in Mark's wake, closing the door behind him.

Kris ran a distracted hand through his hair, waiting, knowing the only reason Frankie hadn't slipped away with the others was because she had more to discuss.

After a good twenty seconds of silence—roughly the time it would take for Tommy to reach the bottom of the spiral staircase —she eyed him. "I don't suppose either of you mentioned how good Tommy looked behind that desk?"

"I thought about it." His gaze drifted back to the bruise on her cheekbone. "But then he seemed ready to puke at the idea of Mark's bachelor party down in the city and it ruined his air of authority."

She clicked her tongue, then stepped forward to hand him the folder. "We've tracked down his attackers."

His pulse lurched. Already? Throwing it open, he scanned the first page and looked up in disbelief. "They've been stuck in immigration detention?"

"Morons didn't have visas to travel to the U.S. in the first place. They worked on a cruise, jumped ship along the coast and must have made their way to Montana. Three days after the attack, they were picked up for speeding outside of Portland. Evidently, they were buzzed on having taken down an heir and got happy with the accelerator."

His skin was cold. "That sounds too stupid to be true."

"How smart did they seem knocking on your door, asking for Erik Jaroka's son, then beating the shit out of our boys right down the road?" she asked. "It sounds just stupid enough for people acting under orders of someone else. Someone smart enough to have tracked you down like I did—who believed, like I did, that there was only one of you. Whoever was in charge would have stayed in Kiraly and not given a damn when those guys were caught without papers. All they'd have cared about was whether the job was done."

"I don't know." Kris tried to think it through. "Those men wouldn't have stayed quiet. They'd have named whoever sent them, blurted out the whole plan to bring their boss down with them. It all would have unraveled, surely, and Kiralian authorities would have been alerted."

Frankie paused, eyeing him. "You think anyone listens to people in immigration detention centers? No papers, no voice. Besides, no one had linked them to the attack. Just speeding. They might be stupid, but they wouldn't admit to killing a prince."

Kris blew out a hard breath. "You're sure it's really them?"

"Turn the page."

Flipping over the paper, his blood chilled at identifying photographs of the men who'd knocked on his door three years ago—and gone on to beat his brother and neighbor to near death.

"Exactly as you described," she murmured.

Anticipation spread through him. While he couldn't forget his involvement in the attack, he wanted justice. "Can they be charged?"

"It was an act of high treason." Her frown was grim. "We'll get them."

"So, what happens now?"

"I've positioned security to monitor the local families and friends of these men. We'll investigate whether any of them assisted with the renovations of the west wing. We've already got all workers and suppliers on file. If the incidents are connected, hopefully there'll be crossover. If not, it was still a lead worth pursuing."

"Okay." Reeling, he closed the folder and handed it back.

Tucking it under her arm, she said, "Do you want to go out tonight?"

He blinked, struggling to switch gears from a murder investigation to a date. Then he stepped closer. "Yes."

"There's someone I've tracked down," she said, ignoring his advance. "You have to be discreet. This person can't know they're being observed."

Not a date, then, but a lead. And was it just him or were her lips paler than usual?

"No radiating primal energy like last night. Keep it tucked in, okay?"

Primal energy. He contained his smirk. "Okay."

"You can't wear that. I'll have clothes brought to your room. Meet you in the entrance hall at seven," she said, turning away. His gaze raked down her figure, but like a thirsty man trying to lick condensation off the wrong side of glass, the sight of her ass in those jeans only intensified his craving.

"Frankie," he said, stepping after her.

She glanced back, features guarded.

"Why don't you wear the uniform of the royal guard?"

Confusion tugged on her brows. "Would you prefer that I did?"

"I don't care how you dress," he said. "But as head of personal security, you'd wear navy blue with something extra, right? Gold stripes or piping to mark your position."

"Probably," she said, looking down and tapping at the ends of the papers that stuck out of the folder. "Why?"

"For someone so determined to remind me that you're my inferior as a member of palace staff, it seems odd that you wouldn't use the uniform as a visual reminder of our differences."

She didn't react. Just eyed him with a bland expression that seemed to ask, *your point?*

"You want to know what I think?" he asked.

"Probably not."

"You don't believe you deserve to wear it." As the words left his mouth, the full truth of the theory hit him. If she couldn't even accept her role in the palace, no wonder she fought being paired with a prince. "You don't believe you deserve to be here."

Frankie's features revealed nothing—but he'd bet her heart was beating with panic.

"When you and Tommy were talking in the car last week," he said, "you mentioned you didn't work for the royal guard before you came to Montana. Philip's thrown you in the deep end, hasn't he?"

She glanced out the window at the mountains. "So?"

"So why won't you accept that you've risen to the challenge?"

Now he was sure her lips were too pale. "Can we save this conversation until we get back tonight? I have work to do."

"Swear it," he said, waiting until she looked at him. "Swear you'll explain this."

After a moment of impossibly wide green eyes, she swallowed. Her expression hardened. "I swear."

"Thank you."

She left without another word, and he sank back onto the sofa, still wishing he was home again, but with her by his side as they drove through the wild expanse of Montana. Instead of sitting in silence or playing 'Would You Rather' as they'd done on past road trips, he would ask her questions about her life, gently nudging her open, because his current ignorance was his fault as much as hers.

He'd always respected her space, steered clear of conversations that caused her silence and stillness. He'd thought that was being a good friend—but as her friend, he should have pushed a little more, trying to understand what caused her to shut down, rather than acting as if her life had begun when she'd moved to Sage Haven.

Tonight, that would change. She was nervous about what she had to tell him, but he'd take it all. He'd finally make sense of her. The reasons she pushed and pulled. Understanding her past was the last barrier between them and his stomach balled in anticipation. Once he knew it all, he could tell her with conviction that there was nowhere else they belonged than by each other's sides.

And finally, she would believe him.

◡

Frankie stood staring at her reflection. The mirror didn't lie—it had always confided the truth behind her charades. A hollow-hearted stare beneath her fine false lashes. The pinch of scruples around her rose-painted mouth. The curl of self-loathing at her top lip. A heaviness to her head, forcing her pearl-strung collarbones to catch the weight that bore down on her neck.

She'd never posed or played a part to fool herself. Never smiled or pouted or practiced lines. Her ability to fall into character had never been something she'd wanted to watch.

At sixteen, she'd sworn she'd never do it again—dress or behave like someone else.

Yet here she was, proof that old habits could rise swift and sharp to the surface like the pair of brass knuckles her fingertips never quite left alone in her pocket.

She shouldn't be surprised.

It was in her blood, after all.

The restaurant was in an expensive part of the city that Kris hadn't visited before. It was one of the many establishments surrounding a large square, cobbled and bustling, with a sparkling fountain at its heart and the last stalls of a daily market making way for nightlife.

He and Frankie sat outdoors at an elegant patio table, overlooking the piazza with a platter of canapes and two glasses of fizzing wine. A busker played violin nearby, accompanied by a pair of contemporary dancers who moved like ribbons caught in a current. Chatter was light with laughter in the warm summer evening—sounds to suit the strings of tiny lights and flickering candles in this busy hub of fine dining. If Kris hadn't spent the past few months acclimating in a palace, he wouldn't have lasted five minutes in such a wealthy setting.

He'd assumed Frankie wouldn't last two.

Yet she perched on the front half of her chair, ankles crossed and tucked beneath her. Leaning forward with a straight back, she picked up her glass in one hand and rested the forearm of the other arm with casual elegance on the tabletop, her fingers falling just over the edge. Her expression was soft with delight as she watched the dancers.

Shock had silenced him since they'd left the palace.

He'd assumed that tonight she would make sense to him. Reveal the nature of her spikes so he'd finally understand how to hold her without hurting either of them. But instead, she'd . . . instead—

She'd become someone else.

She wore a sundress with the ease of a woman long-used to such fashionable, fitted things. Green with a cream floral pattern and a square neckline, and despite the flowy hem that sat halfway up her thighs, he hadn't noticed her tug at it once. Her hair was slicked back, gel turning it a dark brown, while a green-blue silk scarf wrapped snug around the base of her head and was tied in a bow at the front. Her makeup was different—finer and wider somehow, as if the shadows and sweeping black lines exposed the innocence in her eyes. She wore lipstick and a pearl necklace, and sipped her flute like she had a lifetime of experience in indulging her expensive tastes.

It was intensely unnerving.

He'd put on the chinos and button-up white shirt she'd sent to his room, and even jammed his hair beneath the Harvard University branded cap, but all that had done was change his clothes.

She'd changed everything.

"Stop staring," she murmured, and sipped again.

Not knowing where else to look, he picked up a crescent of flaky pastry with a salty, tangy filling. Peripherally, she didn't even scan as Frankie. Normally she held herself like a concealed yet firmly gripped cudgel: straight-bodied, tight, a small swing to her movements. Instead, her posture and body language were cultivated, polished with the gleam of high society. The discord sat uneasily inside him, and as he chewed, his gaze returned to her.

She sensed him watching. "I told you in the car, I don't want to be recognized."

"*I* don't even recognize you."

Her shoulder curled forward in a demure flirtation as she smiled at him. "At least look like you do."

She was utterly convincing. The trick in transforming herself so completely seemed to lie in changing what he'd believed was her innate behavior. Her bearing, gestures, gait, expressions. If he'd passed her on the street, he wouldn't know it unless he looked straight at her, and even then . . . Yet more disturbing was that she was behaving like the kind of person who'd be comfortable receiving the attention of a prince.

And he hated it.

He watched as she set her glass down and tightened the knot of her headscarf, looking around a little as if expecting—and privately hoping—someone was watching and admiring her.

Kris's jaw dropped. "How are you *doing* that?"

"Don't look," she said, ignoring his question as she rested her chin in her hand, elbow featherlight on the table. "But shortly, a man is going to exit the hotel across the square. Pretend you're watching the dancers. He'll be with a woman in her middle years, and he'll leave suddenly, cutting their evening short."

What? "How could you possibly know that?"

Smiling, she gestured, flicking her fingers to the twilit sky as if commenting on the temperate evening. "Just wait."

Baffled, he leaned back in the uncomfortable chair and watched the performance. Within a minute, he noted the hotel doors swing around as a couple emerged. The man had a hand on the woman's back and he absently raised his other hand to check his watch. Jolting in alarm, he drew away, and after a brief exchange, moved in to kiss his companion. Kris risked a proper look, noting the kiss turn from gentle to hungry—like the man was being torn from his beloved—before he pulled back and rushed out of the square. The woman stared after him, disappointment in every line of her perfect posture.

Kris gaped after the retreating man. "I'm so confused."

Frankie stood, tucking more than enough money to cover their meal beneath the platter. "We follow him."

Alone and on foot, because Frankie had given his guards the night off and didn't call the car around. In the twenty minutes it took to tail the man uphill to the center of Kiraly, Kris reached several conclusions.

One, Frankie must have done extensive research to believe the man was worthy of observing personally—which presumably connected him to the investigation. Adrenaline nicked Kris's pulse as they climbed a winding set of mosaic steps through the arts precinct. She was closer than he'd realized.

Two, it explained why she didn't want them to be recognized. As royal security, her presence could alert the man that he was a suspect.

And three, Kris couldn't wait for the night to be over so he could get his Frankie back. Even her walk was different, kind of pulled in, a shorter stride and quicker steps. He didn't like it. Any of it.

Less than a block away from the bar the man had entered, she paused to admire a shopfront window display of women's clothing. She raised a hand, the fingernails of her thumb and pinkie flicking against each other delicately. "Give it a minute."

"Frankie—"

She pointed at a violet sun hat wreathed in a yellow ribbon and angled her head with a questioning smile. "Don't use my name."

"What do you want me to call you?" he asked, doing his best not to frown. Frankie smiled so rarely that he wanted to bask in this moment. But it wasn't right. It was too . . . sweet. Soft and open. That wasn't how Frankie smiled. She revealed her amusement with a hard grin, quick and sharp, leaving a bite mark on his heart.

"Don't call me anything. It won't matter." She reached out, bottom lip disappearing between her teeth as she made a show of tentatively tugging the brim of his cap lower and sliding her fingertips up into his hairline, pressing escapee strands out of sight. Then she pulled back and eyed him beneath her lashes. "I listen every time you speak."

"Are you—?" He ran a hand over the back of his neck. Had that admission been part of her act? "This is so weird."

"Can you do it?" Her expression was composed, attention idly following an evening cyclist that rode past, but the question was quiet, fierce, cutting through her façade. "We're not going inside if you'll give us away."

Resolve formed a band around his chest. If she believed the hotel guy was worth all this effort, Kris wasn't going mess it up. "I can do it."

"Don't act like a prince. Don't act like a cowboy. Don't act like you've never seen me before. We're on a date. You know me. Got it?"

"Of course, sweetheart," he murmured, and reaching out, he laced his fingers through hers and drew her hand up to his mouth. Her wide, thick-lashed eyes darted to his as he slowly kissed each of her knuckles, his tongue sliding over her skin. "It'll be easy—you taste exactly like the woman I want to date."

He pretended not to notice the pain that flashed in her eyes.

She withdrew her hand to adjust her necklace as they made their way to the crowded bar. Once they were seated at a table for two against the far wall, she angled her chair to sit with her back to the room, and Kris let the shadows of this rear corner conceal his features beneath the cap. Instead of beer, he ordered a whiskey on the rocks and Frankie ordered a white wine—after she'd confirmed the region and vintage.

Once again, her posture was faultless, shoulders settled just so and her spine an elegant line. Her forward lean granted him permission to admire her breasts, an unspoken flirtation that betrayed the date was going well. Picking up her glass and smiling across at him, she said, "This is nice."

Forcibly reminding himself it was an act, he did his damnedest not to look and replied, "One word for it." His smile was slow as he leaned back, stretching one leg out so his polished black shoe was beneath her chair and his knee brushed against hers. "Where did you get that dress?"

"Hanna. She made it herself." She angled her head, patting the back of her headscarf. "And she borrowed this from Gul."

"I like that color on you. It makes the green in your eyes look darker."

Setting her wine on the table, she ran a fingertip along the glass lip. "You might have noticed that he's sitting in a booth by the window. With a different woman."

Resting his head against the wall behind him, Kris swung his gaze toward the front of the bar and took a moment to assess the man properly. Roughly in his early fifties, he was of average build but in great shape. Easily good-looking, handsome really, with a kind face and ginger hair that was greying around his temples. The man laughed, effused with warmth and affection, and then raised a hand to his chest in apparent surprise as he glanced across at his companion. Surprised to be laughing?

He should be, playing two women like a stacked deck of cards.

"Stop looking," Frankie said quietly, pressing him with her knee.

He swirled his glass, ice clinking. "Who is he?"

"The woman he's with is Isadora Moretti. Filthy rich,

widowed, and missing her daughter who recently moved out of home to attend college at Cambridge. She's a woman who can afford the penthouse suite at the most luxe lakefront hotel in Kiraly but wants to experience a taste of local life."

Hence her presence in an average bar on a Monday night.

"Okay," Kris said.

"You see how endearing he is, how genuine," she said, fingers moving in little starburst gestures, so anyone watching would see her animated conversation. Her stare, however, was focused on Kris's chin and it occurred to him that she wasn't blinking enough. "By the time she returns to Italy in another three weeks, she'll find herself short several hundred thousand dollars. I'm not sure of his sob story, and a smart woman like her will probably take a night to sleep on his request, but she'll transfer him the funds he needs. And she'll never be able to track him or the money."

His brows rose. She dug fast. "How does he connect to —everything?"

She laughed, airy and light. "The woman he was with earlier is Clare-Marie Bromley. She was a principal ballet dancer with The Australian Ballet for over ten years and is now artistic director. She will also return home to find the generosity she showed her international lover will never be repaid."

Incredulous, Kris leaned forward to rest his forearms on the table. "Wait a second." He lowered his voice. "He's a con man?"

She seemed to reel, just a little, at his words. A hand rose to toy with the scarf above her ear. "Yes."

"Is this all he does?" He swirled his whiskey as casually as he could. "Romance scams?"

"No," she said, very quietly.

"Has he ever been caught?"

"Once." Pausing, she raised her glass and sipped. Then sipped again. "About ten years ago. A minor swindle that saw him serve two months in prison. A disgrace, really, for a man of his skill to be caught like a gutter grifter."

"So he's good?"

Now he was sure she wasn't blinking enough as she stared at the brim of his hat. "Very."

"Someone like that could have easily got into the palace." It made sense. A master manipulator made an effective criminal. Why break in or sneak around when he could be invited in the front door? "If he's played the right people, he could have accessed almost anything. Anyone." A revolted kind of fascination had Kris sweeping another glance at the booth. The man was seated at the front window, shamelessly courting another woman in plain view. Or not shameless—rather, so sure of his plans and the people twisted around his finger, he knew the ballerina would not come this way. *Knew* he wouldn't get caught. "Do we know how he feels about the monarchy?"

After a beat, she nodded.

Kris blew out a rough breath. "How did you find him?"

"I'll explain when he's gone."

"Gone?" Urgency pushed him farther forward. "You're just going to let him leave?"

"I'd happily kick his ass on the way out, but yes, for now." She picked up her wine—and finished it in several long swallows. Despite her sophisticated air, her nerves were starting to show. Did she suspect how this con man fit into the investigation but lacked enough evidence? When she set her glass down, Kris swiped up her hand and found it trembling.

"You okay?" he asked, tracing a line along her wrist.

Her eyes darted over his. "No."

"I still want you to talk to me after." About why she thought she didn't deserve to be part of the royal guard, or more importantly, with him. Her pulse skittered beneath his fingertips. "Where do you want to go?"

"Oh." Her eyelashes fanned over her cheeks as she looked down to where he held her. The curve of her mouth was shy, as if discussing his advances, but her voice was thin with vulnerability. "I don't think we'll need to go anywhere."

He frowned. Was she backing out? "If you're nervous, don't be," he said. "Whatever you have to tell me, it won't matter."

"Won't matter?" A familiar expression darted across her face. Irritation. "You think my past doesn't matter? What if I said that about you? If I said stop wearing those rancher clothes—your past doesn't matter. Stop going out for rides and hikes. Stop thinking that your upbringing made you who you are—that it's an integral part of your identity. You live in Kiraly now. This is who you are and all I need you to be. Forget everything that came before. It doesn't matter."

He let go of her hand. "That's not what I meant."

"It is," she said, lowered voice crisp with the Frankie he knew, even as her expression returned to soft and serene. "You can't stand the idea that there's something insurmountable between us. You want to ignore it. Deny it. And it'll be easier to do that if you tell me it doesn't matter before you even know what it is. But the thing is . . ." She trailed off to stun him with a seductive smile, so provocative and ready that it quickened his blood, slipped over his skin, and despite knowing it wasn't real, he felt himself begin to stir. "It *does* matter." She reached out, her fingers brushing the inside of his forearm in small circles, and the maddening friction only made him harder. "You're going to need to accept that."

"Hey." He shifted, sitting straighter to conceal his arousal. "What are you doing?"

Her smile vanished as she withdrew her hand. "You'll see."

"You've never toyed with me before."

"I'm not toying with you now," she said. "I'm showing you."

Before he could ask what, exactly, that sex-hot smile had

showed him, the man in the window booth laughed. It was louder this time, and he spoke to his partner through his amusement, voice booming above the general noise of the bar. As he listened, a strange chill passed down Kris's spine, and his attention slid to the con man.

"That accent . . ."

It was American, but that was like saying Frankie's skin had just turned white. There was endless variation in color, just as there was in accents. Dialect, pronunciation, cadence. The man sounded generically West American, but with a slight flatness to the vowels. Nothing significant or unusual, especially if it was assumed the speaker had spent considerable time living elsewhere, subconsciously picking up variances, mimicking the locals—basically what Kris had always believed about Frankie's accent until very recently.

Except that she . . .

In the end, she hadn't grown up in America at all.

Her accent had been false, an act to fool him.

The world around Kris ground to a halt as the man continued talking. His blood pulsed thick in his ears. The man's accent was—it was . . .

"It's exactly like yours."

Frankie sat like he'd flicked her off at the switch, expression lifeless with dread.

Heart thumping in confusion, he scanned her features. Then he eyed the man with ginger hair that might have once been rust red. With a smile that was soft and seductive and quite possibly nothing like his true grin. With a false accent learned and practiced in a country too far from the source.

The chill settled in his gut when he realized she hadn't answered his question.

Kris curled his fingers. "Who is he?"

But he knew. He knew.

Frankie's lips were dry beneath her lipstick; her face was the grey-white of smoke. *I'm not toying with you.* The deception she'd so skillfully demonstrated for him slipped as tears gathered in her eyes. *I'm showing you.*

"He's my father."

Frankie's head spun as she relinquished her truth in three whispered words. She felt weightless in a bad way, as if someone had been holding her back all her life and they'd abruptly let her go inside her own chest. Her pulse staggered, unstable—she didn't know how to catch herself.

She forced herself to look at Kris.

He wouldn't help set her right.

His blue eyes were raging, his jaw set like iron. His hands were fisted so tightly on the tabletop, his forearms bulged. He was *furious.*

His attention was cutting between her and her father. She wanted to ask him to stop—not to give them away, but he looked one lapse away from flipping the table and her throat was too swollen from pain to speak.

Finally, he leaned forward, and in a voice so rough it sounded half-solid, he said, "He did this to you."

His anger shredded her thoughts. She could hardly piece together what he'd said; what he meant. "He taught me." Mostly breath, but still she added, "And I did it."

"He taught you," he repeated, eyes sparking with rage. "And you did it."

Kris had been raised on honesty. The value of trust. She had no defense against a man with integrity, because she'd known it was wrong. Her father hadn't brainwashed her. She'd *known,* in her gut and in her soul, until the day she'd turned her back on him, that what they did was wrong. And she hadn't resisted or rebelled or found a way to get out sooner.

"I worked with him until I was sixteen." Not once, or occasionally, or for a year or two. She'd scammed and stolen for her entire upbringing.

"A con man's daughter." He practically spat her title from his mouth.

"Yes." There was no point in trying to hide from it now. "I conned in my own right. It's—" *A part of me. In my blood.* "I was very good at it."

His disgust threatened to strike her from his life.

"This is why," she forced herself to whisper, "you can't be with me. We can't be—anything. I was never caught, but that doesn't change my criminal history. My dad *was* caught. It'd be a simple thread to tug. I can never be trusted. A farm boy's family wouldn't want me around, let alone a country protective of its king."

He didn't speak, but she felt his fury swell.

"I'll go," she said, and somehow stood despite her heart still stumbling. Turning, she caught movement at her father's booth— he was also rising to his feet. The sight sickened her. She'd scarcely been able to look at him since he'd emerged from the hotel in designer clothes and his gentlest mask. It made her skin crawl, full-body bumps despite the warm evening. But her disgust fell away beneath a flood of horror at the possibility of him recognizing her.

Fright shoved her back around to Kris. She swayed, legs almost buckling beneath her. "He can't see me."

Kris moved fast, sliding his chair to one side of the table before reaching out, grabbing her hips, and dragging her onto his lap.

Startled, her breath caught. A quick embrace wouldn't be enough. If her father had glanced over, having noticed her stand only to sit again, she couldn't afford to hold his interest by looking rigid and uncomfortable. Cursing under her breath and letting it double as a soft exhale, she relaxed, sinking down to straddle him, her ass resting back on Kris's knees. Her own knees lowered as she leaned forward, her chest not quite touching his, her back arching as if she yearned for the contact.

In the seconds of stillness that followed, she fixed her gaze on Kris's top button. His face wasn't safe, nor was the rest of him beneath her. Thighs built like steel. Chest broad and breathing deep inches from hers. Hands wide and unrelenting, his thumbs pressing into the soft join where her thigh met hip. The last thing she needed was a lust-flare, but her body didn't care about his disgust—just his tight grip and biceps beneath her palms, and his woody scent rushing in to take out every form of resistance in its path.

Her breath out shuddered, betraying her as she looked up.

Kris's eyes glittered at her beneath his cap.

"What's he doing?" she made herself ask.

Tucking his bottom lip between his teeth—sexiness in bite form—Kris lifted a hand and traced the back of his index finger down the side of her neck. He angled his head as if to admire the curve of her shoulder and was granted a clear view behind her. "Heading to the bar, wallet out."

She shivered at his touch. "He won't pay."

Kris moved his face a little closer to her neck. Memories of the night before crackled between them and she felt his desire bloom inside his anger. "He is paying," he said quietly. "He's pulled out a big note."

"Way too big for the total cost." She could practically watch the scene play out. "He'll take the change. Then hand some back, asking for smaller notes. Then he'll laugh, tell the bartender not to worry, it's too much effort, and ask for the original large note back. Then he'll hand over the bartender's own smaller money to pay for his drinks and pocket the rest."

Kris kept stroking her neck as he watched. It happened fast—the key to change-raising was not giving the cashier time to feel something was amiss. A flustered or confused mark meant they'd stop and count everything out, and that'd be the end of it.

"What—I don't even know what I just saw." Kris's attention slid back to her. "Can you do that?"

Her shame churned. "Yes."

"That good?"

She swallowed. "A bit better."

He huffed, but nothing about him felt amused.

"I know you must hate me," she murmured.

His lips curled, anger flashing in his eyes. Then his hands tightened around her, tugging her slightly higher up his lap, and he said, "I hate *him*, my love."

Her heart whimpered.

"Your scummy fuck of a father could never make me hate you." Kris's voice was uneven with temper. "When he taught you to do this shit, he taught you to hate yourself. Your morals are good, Frankie, and that's because of who you are." His attention was set behind her. "But you're trapped inside your own conscience, judging and blaming yourself for the way he made you behave."

Her guilt held firm. "I chose to do it."

Kris pulled back, searching her eyes. "He gave you a choice?"

"I could've said no, refused to—"

"You're telling me he'd have respected your decision?"

Her father had never respected anything about her. She shook her head, more in helplessness than in answer. "Has he left?"

Kris leaned in, and this time, his lips grazed her neck. Her spine tingled and her eyes grew hot. What kind of man kissed a woman minutes after finding out she'd been raised crooked? Held her tighter, closer?

My love.

"They're both leaving now," he said.

She waited, lips pressed together, staring at the wall.

"Okay, he's gone." Kris ran a hand up and down her spine, firm, reassuring. "He didn't see you."

She lowered her face, pressing her forehead against his shoulder. His hand kept moving over her back. What would her father have done if he'd noticed her? Come straight over or taken time to rehearse? He wouldn't have ignored her. It wasn't in his nature to let someone get away with besting him. And she'd trounced him when she'd run away from home, armed with knowledge of his associates, schedules, routes, and habits that he hadn't even realized were habits. She'd ensured he'd never seen her again. The one risk had been him showing up at her school, but that would've meant admitting he had no other way to find her, and in the end, the prick had been too proud.

She knew one thing. If he'd recognized her across the bar— the daughter he'd trained in the family business, the daughter who'd snipped her strings and slipped off his stage—he'd want to get even.

"Frankie."

She kept her face on his shoulder as Kris spoke. It felt safe. He'd always felt safe.

"All you've ever told me about your parents is that your mom left when you were ten and your dad's an asshole. You didn't admire him. And judging by your reaction when he almost saw you, I get the feeling he didn't give a shit whether or not you *wanted* to work with him. Hot or cold?"

She lifted her head warily as she said, "Hot."

"Then it's not a reflection of who you are." His tone was

sharp, and despite his soothing hand strokes, irritation continued to radiate from him. "And it's not a reason you can't be with me."

"It's the *definition* of—"

"I have a lot of questions." He cut her off as his hands dropped to her hips. "But this isn't the place."

"We can go." Her father wouldn't have lingered.

"Actually, can we—" He slid her a little higher up his lap. "Stay for a second?"

The sensitive skin of her inner thighs ached at the movement. If those strong hands moved her any higher, she'd be flush against his crotch.

"There really isn't room for you to do that again." Her voice was thick and throaty with arousal.

"Do what?" he asked, and tugged her again. She lost a breath as she lodged against his unmistakable hard-on, and he hummed a base note of approval, dark and hungry.

"Stop that," she muttered, if only because she should.

His grip loosened, as if to say, *if that's what you really want.*

She didn't move. Didn't dare, in case she gave in to the hot plea between her thighs and rubbed herself all over him.

"My problem is that if we leave now," he said, his gaze on her mouth, "I'll lay into him with my fists."

And she wouldn't stop him.

"Thirty seconds," she relented quietly.

He flicked her a blue-eyed glance that looked dangerously like *challenge accepted.* Then his forehead brushed against hers and she pushed into the contact, angling her head down, a bull locking horns in order to keep her mouth out of range. He gave a slanted half-smile before his hands spread across her back and his elbows tucked against her sides. His biceps tensed, caging her in, and she dug her fingers into the solid muscle—not sure if she was threatening him with resistance or preparing to hold him in place if he dared to pull away.

"I can't believe I'm this close to you right now," he said, as awareness burned beneath her skin, flashing like fireflies. "Can— can we do this again?"

"I—" *Yes.* Her whole body yearned for him. "Time to go."

He groaned, and she swore she felt the vibration low inside her.

As she pried herself off him, smoothing her dress and tugging at the knot of her headscarf, she caught herself thinking in terms of all or nothing. That had always been the shape of her denial. Surrendering to Kris's chemistry seemed like opening a door to a future they couldn't have—but perhaps it didn't need to be that absolute. He now knew the worst of her upbringing and still wanted her. It was possible for them to take the next step, without secrets or lies, and to make sure they never ventured any further. Finally, this prince would know exactly who he was taking to bed.

And then he could focus on finding a queen.

She jolted as his hand moved over her lower back. They had no future. But when his eyes clouded like that, the only future in his decision-making was the very, very immediate.

Perhaps she could handle that.

"Yes," she said.

He flashed her a startled look, wallet half out of his back pocket.

"We can be close again," she finished softly.

His smile was slow and delicious, and flared heat across her face.

Out on the sidewalk, she stood with her weight pushed onto one hip and drew out her phone to call the security car. She'd positioned them several blocks away. Philip would be livid if he discovered she'd taken Kris out by herself, but no way in hell was she going to risk anyone on her team looking twice at her father. She hated it too, but this had been the only approach to revealing her past to Kris that he would take seriously.

Although if *"it's not a reason you can't be with me,"* was any indication—he still hadn't.

He slid a hand around her wrist with a soft, "Frankie."

Lowering the phone, she found herself pulled lightly against him. "I told you not to call me that tonight," she said, her cheek brushing against his shirt.

"Show me." He spoke into her hair. "Don't stop here."

She made a questioning sound while trying to memorize his smell.

"Show me how you grew up."

It wasn't a small request, but Frankie did her best. Her upbringing stained most of her memories and the entire eastern crest of Kiraly. Unlike the luxury of the lakeside district, these streets were narrower, the houses cheaper, the shops selling only to locals because the tourists didn't come this way. The people weren't bad, just doing their best with what little they had. And when she was young, Frankie had relished in the freedom to play messy, loud games with the neighborhood kids without law enforcement keeping the streets clear and quiet for camera-ready travelers.

Until her dad had made her play *his* games.

"I grew up in that apartment," she said, pointing to a dark third-floor window with potted plants on the tiny balcony. The white glow of the nearby streetlamp cast the building in stark, ugly light, and the memories that clogged her pores were slick like fever-sweat. "It was small, and the walls were thin, but it meant my mother and I could hear when he was coming down the hall."

Kris stood, holding her hand, gazing at her old home. "What were the neighbors like?"

Of course this small-town cowboy would wonder about the community she'd grown up in. "I don't remember. They didn't like Dad, so kept to themselves."

He kept looking up. "Why didn't they like him?"

She almost rolled her eyes. That question proved the efficacy of her father's disguise this evening. Gentle and genuine, so convincing that despite the change-taking at the counter, Kris struggled to imagine him any other way.

"Just . . . imagine something bad," she said, unsure how to put her father into words. "Like a pipe filled with something disgusting. If you block the pipe for hours or even days at a time, the pressure behind that bad stuff is going to build up. Then when you unblock it, say in the comfort of the pipe's own neighborhood, it's going to come bursting out. When he was himself, he was moody and unpredictable, made worse for all the hours he'd pretended he wasn't."

"Was he violent?" Kris's question was quiet.

"Not to me or mum. But he'd bring men home, accomplices for bigger jobs, and sometimes his fists did the talking. And sometimes . . ."

Kris tightened his hold on her. "Sometimes?"

"Come on," she said, and took him to where it first happened. It looked the same, just with bigger trees around the park's edges. "I used to cut through here after dark on the way home from the lake district. One night, when I was fourteen, I was in my tidy black and whites after pretending to be a waitress on her break and doing a currency exchange scam on new tourists. Usually the worst thing in the park was a couple of teenagers putting the shadows to use." She hesitated, finding the memory still too soft to touch without bruising. The blinding pain in her ribs; the blood she hadn't known how to get out of that white blouse—not with her mother long gone.

Kris waited, his thumb stroking the back of her hand.

"That night, two guys were waiting for me. They called me *that bastard Harvey's girl.* I was so terrified I didn't even try to run as they beat me up. It was over quickly, but it felt like forever, and even though I'd never seen the men in my life, I couldn't stop imagining it was my dad doing it."

Kris looked winded as he stared at her, mouth open, hand on his abdomen.

"After, I was so disoriented, they had to shove me in the right direction to get home, suggesting I tell my dad that's what he got for skimming their cut."

She'd found her way, blind from swelling in one eye, ribs too damaged to cry.

"That night, he gave me these." With her free hand, she snapped open her purse—Hanna's purse—and fished out her brass knuckles. "They ended up coming in handy."

"Jesus," Kris muttered, hand running over his mouth.

Her father had slid them across the sticky dining table and said, *For next time.*

Not, *Are you okay?*

Not, *I'm so sorry, Frankie.*

Not, *I'll make sure this never happens again.*

"He told me to cut my hair," she continued, closing the purse again. "Said they'd use it to drag me down. And that I shouldn't let them get me on the ground, because I was old enough to know what happened next and for them to want to do it."

"Fuck. Oh, fuck." Kris's eyes were bleak. "I'm so sorry, Frankie."

She raised a shoulder, looking away. "He taught me how to fight. Street rules." Dirty moves and fast relentless strikes. "It only just helped, so I pulled extra jobs after school"—plucking wallets and short-changing cashiers—"and took every self-defense and martial arts class I could find."

She'd never taken a beating for her hateful father again.

"There's more," she said, because he needed to know everything a journalist might dig up. Based on the way he held her hand, his elbow tucked around hers to keep her close to his side, his mind was far from royal practicalities. "If you want to see."

"Everything. Show me everything."

So they kept walking. She took him to her old school, the self-defense studio where she'd got her first legal job as a trainer, and the hostel she'd lived in for the better part of two years.

"It doesn't look safe." Kris eyed the backpackers' hostel in concern. The kind of place that crawled with young tourists who'd left their decency balled up in a drawer at home.

"The owners got to know me," she said. "They looked out for me. Gave me one of the single rooms with a new lock on it. I told them I was in college, not high school, and paid every week, so they pretended to believe me. Besides, I could handle myself."

Kris stared at the building for a long time. The downstairs common room was a mess of hollers and raucous laughter, and a sudden uproar of singing petered out drunkenly when the participants seemed to realize none of them really knew the words. The crash of glass bottles being emptied into a waste container travelled from the back alley, and there were unmistakable groans escaping an open second-level window.

It wasn't the place for a sixteen-year-old runaway to put herself through school.

"Okay," he said quietly, something broken in his voice.

They kept walking. It was late now, the dull beat of music travelling along the shadowed streets, the occasional burst of laughter coming from a rear courtyard. The people of Kira City rarely slept, and never all at once. Frankie led him to a traders' hub, streetlamps illuminating a steep curving road, sidewalk benches, and a strip of stores. Some were closed for the night; others were selling ice cream and kebabs and cocktails.

"I lifted my first wallet while giving directions out the front of that bakery."

He followed her pointing finger. "How old were you?"

She thought back. "Maybe seven?"

"Seven." He gazed at the bakery as if he could picture it. A young Frankie and an older woman bending over, eyes on Frankie's pointing finger instead of the wallet being slid from her handbag. "How did you feel about it?"

"Mixed." Frankie looked down the road, remembering the route she'd taken to get out of sight before the woman realized and shouted after her. Up two shopfronts, left into the back street between the delicatessen and poultry market, and then crouched low and running behind a row of parked cars. But the shouts had never come. No one had chased her. Perhaps the woman hadn't noticed until she'd reached the end of Frankie's directions. Perhaps she'd never suspected the little girl at all. "I was scared. Disbelieving that I'd really done it. Exhilarated that I'd gotten away with it and proud to tell my dad. I remember wanting to get better at it so I wouldn't have to run."

And she had. Swallowing shame, she led Kris on.

"Growing up," she said as they walked, "my dad would ask if I had my lunch money. But he would ask *after* school, not before, and I'd hand over the money I'd shortchanged when buying my lunch on the way to class."

Then finally, they reached an innocuous street corner on the border of the eastern crest and Kira City center. The place that hurt the most.

She pressed the knuckle of her thumb into her brow, pushing outward, as if she could swipe the pain aside. "This was where I last saw my mother before she left."

There was nothing to see, but Kris looked around anyway.

"Dad was pulling an all-nighter." Also known as banging one of his marks. "It was late afternoon. I was walking home from school the long way. I can't remember why. And I stopped on this street corner, waiting for traffic, and saw that opposite me, Mum was putting a bag in the back of a taxi. She looked pale and scared. She didn't notice me, and for some reason, I didn't call out. She got in and the taxi drove away. It took forever to find a gap in traffic to cross, but then I ran home. The apartment looked the same, like maybe she'd gone to get groceries, except her favorite coat was missing and it was the middle of summer. I waited up all night."

She paused, her breath uneven, as a car swept past them. It was overloaded with teens and one waved out the window, shouting, "Drinks at mine, butterflies!"

Frankie stared, dull inside, while Kris raised a hand in return.

"Dad was so angry when he got home," she continued, shaking her head at how his fist had put new holes in the plaster walls. "I've never . . . He grilled me for days about whether I'd known about it. No joke. He asked me if I'd known my own mother was planning on running away—and what, leaving me behind? Thinking that I might have helped her, but chosen to stay with him? Likelihood of fucking zero."

"So," Kris said, and then stopped to pull off his cap and rake fingers through his hair. "She just left you with him?"

Frankie stared at the street sign where the taxi had idled. "Yes."

"But she's . . ."

"My mother? Yeah. But apparently I was too much like my dad." A truth Frankie had forced herself to swallow, and even now, it cut like fish bones in her throat. "She clearly didn't trust me to keep it secret—not to tell him in the lead up or contact him once we were gone. So she left me behind." She paused. "Put that back on."

Kris slid his cap over his head and used his hold on the brim to tip his face down.

"I did everything he told me, and I did it well. I had a temper, just like him." Frankie had had so many years to think it through, her mother's defense almost made sense. "She was scared of me."

The problem was that her mother had been scared of Frankie for longer than she'd had any cause to be—which had meant she'd always kept Frankie at a distance. There'd been no opportunity to see that beneath it all, they were as scared as each other.

"And she never came back for you?" Kris's question was hushed.

Frankie considered him. The concern in his eyes, the dismay pulling at the corners of his mouth. The hand that continued to grip hers. He'd asked for her to share everything. Why should she stop here?

"No," she answered. "So I went to her."

Frankie's focus glazed in the direction of that street sign as she told him the painful details.

She'd been twenty. After high school and working for a few years, renting her very own shithole of an apartment, she'd finally felt ready. She had her mother's last-known whereabouts—on a train destined for Paris. Frankie had noted the taxi's license plate that fateful afternoon and the driver had later accepted the crisp bill a ten-year-old Frankie had offered to tell her where his passenger had been bound.

She'd never passed on that information to her father. He could have used it to track her—Frankie could have got her mother back. But despite her abandonment, Frankie still felt like she and her mother were on the same side, and she'd wanted to protect her from him.

Ten years on, she'd finally used the lead herself.

It had taken time. Internet searches that went nowhere, deep dives that spat out nothing more than an old record, but determination had eventually led her to an upper-class home in the west of Paris. In the years that had passed, her mother had married a man who earned his wealth as honestly as a banker could, and with him, she'd had two children. Foolishly, Frankie had imagined shock upon her arrival, sobbing apologies in the warmth of her mother's arms, and long-awaited introductions to her little brother and sister.

No such fantasy had awaited her.

Her mother had physically staggered when she'd answered the bell to find Frankie on the doorstep. Frankie's jeans and best red jacket had been worlds beneath the beautiful cut and dye of her mother's hair, the form-flattering outfit, the gigantic ring on her finger.

Sick with nerves, Frankie had adjusted the backpack over her shoulder and scuffed her boot on the welcome mat.

"Hi, Mum."

"How did you find me?" Wild-eyed, the woman had scanned the street behind her. *"Is he here?"*

"No." Frankie had eased her weight back, non-threatening, heart thundering. *"I haven't seen him for years. I just—I wanted to see you."*

"Why?" Her mother's eyes had snapped to her, pupils wide. *"What do you want?"*

"I . . ." What did she want from the mother who'd left her in the care of a criminal? Far too much, she was about to discover. *"It's been ten years."*

"What does that mean? My time is up? I get ten years, and then you come for me?"

"What?" Frankie had shoved a hand in her pocket, trying not to let her alarm become defensive anger. *"No. I mean it's been a*

long time. I—I thought we could talk. Reconnect, maybe." At her mother's silence, she'd gestured vaguely to the gorgeous home. *"This is nice."*

"So that's it." Her mother had nodded too fast. *"You've finally figured out that I have something worth taking."*

Frankie had taken a step back, the accusation like a gut punch. *"No. I—no."*

She'd spent months on this search—years anticipating this very moment. Not once, in all her imaginings, had she considered that this woman had *wanted* to abandon her.

"I don't want anything." Frankie had been queasy with shame. *"I have a better life now, too. I just thought . . ."*

Her mother had stared at her from where she'd half hidden behind the front door. Conveying, without saying a word, that Frankie had thought wrong.

"Can I come in?" Frankie had asked, voice small. *"Or we could go out somewhere? Or I could come back at a better time?"*

"There is no better time. I know what you're doing. The pity angle, trying to put me off guard. Well, it won't work on me. You're even more like him now than you were back then."

"This isn't an angle." Helpless, Frankie had taken another step back. She'd never wanted to be like her father. *"You're my mum."*

The woman shook her head. *"How can I trust you?"*

"How can I trust you? You left me." Frankie's voice had trembled with a decade of pain. *"You're my mother and you left me with him."*

"Of course I left you. It was always the two of you." The woman had darted another look down the quiet suburban street. *"I don't want you here."*

"But Mum—"

The door had slammed shut.

Frankie swore she could still feel it—the impact of that rejection inches from her face.

Kris was shaking his head beside her. He hadn't said a word as she'd spoken.

"That was our big reunion." She raised a shoulder as if it didn't matter. "Bit of a letdown, am I right?"

After a long silence, Kris said, "This is all so sad," and looked off down the road.

Swallowing the lump in her throat, she tugged the scarf off her head and ruffled her hair loose. "Want me to call the car?"

He ran a hand over his eyes. "Can we walk back?"

"We've been walking for almost two hours." She glanced toward the palace as she draped the scarf around her neck. It was probably twenty minutes away from here, and all uphill. "I'm not convinced your quads have acclimated to Kira City enough for that route."

He ignored her attempts to move on from her pathetic past. "I want time to process this."

She sighed. Pulling out her phone, she called the team on standby and informed them of the prince's plans. "They'll follow us a block behind."

He nodded distractedly.

As they turned onto the avenue that led to the royal parade, she wondered how long Kris intended to keep holding her hand.

"Is this why you don't want kids?" he asked quietly.

Startled, she turned to stare at him. "What?"

His eyes were grave beneath his cap. "Your childhood."

She arched a brow as insult burrowed into her pride. "You think I'm scared that I'll raise my children as thieves? That I won't know how to love them because I've never been loved?"

Strain bracketed his mouth. "That's not what I—"

"I *do* want kids." She cut him off fiercely, even though she'd scarcely admitted that brittle truth to herself. It was an unspoken dream spun from what remained of her threadbare self-worth. "I'll raise them to be good. I'll love them with everything I am. All *this* has done is make me want my own family, because I've been without one my whole life." She had no idea how to form a loving family. But she knew how *not* to do it, and that had to count for something.

"But—" His frown was confused. "But you said—you told me that you'd never be the right person to—for us to—produce heirs."

She clenched her jaw and rallied a steady tone. "That's still true."

"You want a family," he said slowly. "But you don't want one with me."

"I want a family." She tried to slide her hand out of his, but he held fast. "But I *can't* have one with you."

"Because I'm royalty."

"God, Kris." This was not a conversation she wanted to have on a sidewalk at midnight. He clearly needed longer to process everything she'd told him. "You might believe I'm nothing like my father, but that's not enough. Not for Kiraly. Not for a king." She shook her head, fighting distress. "Royalty is the highest class of citizen. The monarchy's reputation is the cornerstone of its influence. You're already going to be a cowboy on the throne— put a criminal beside you and the entire institution will fall apart. This can't happen. *We can't happen.*"

He walked steadily beside her, silent, eyes on the road ahead.

Then he asked, "How would anyone know? You were never caught."

"My father was," she said, trying to dodge the memory of his time in prison—and his conviction that she'd see the inside of a cell for herself one day. "Journalists would pursue that and he would delight in telling them about me. I don't know how, but he'd manage not to incriminate himself in the process. He'd smear my name through mud so deep, I'd never crawl back out."

She paused, blaming her struggle for breath on the hill. "If you defended me, aligned yourself with me, your popularity would plummet. And in the twenty-first century, that might not be a passing threat. It could be a tipping point in the perception of the royal establishment and ultimately bring the end of the monarchy in this country."

Kris had cooled beside her. Temper chilled, body language contained. "Back at the bar, you said we could get close again. I had hoped that meant you might spend tonight with me."

She pressed her eyes closed. "It did," she said. "I think."

"But only tonight." His tone was cold with realization.

She hesitated. "Not forever."

"Interesting," he said under his breath, and pulled his hand out of hers.

She balled her fingers and kept walking. This was how it had to be. She wasn't being melodramatic or unreasonable. The lives of the royal family were upheld by strict codes of conduct, and the rigid set of rules brokered no deviation—or deviants.

They approached the top end of the avenue where it adjoined the tree-lined royal parade. The palace gates were closed a block to the left, guards stationed on either side.

Kris stopped just short of the deserted intersection and looked over his shoulder at the approaching security car. "I want to talk to my guards."

She frowned, turning back to him.

"Alone," he added.

Taken aback, she waited until the car drew level and Kris motioned for the driver to wind down the window. Then she said, "I'll go ahead."

She couldn't read the look he shot her in answer.

Striding across the empty intersection and onto the sidewalk that bordered the palace grounds, she glanced back, but the car was out of view behind the street corner. She clenched her teeth against the wound she'd torn open for him. Vulnerability ran from it like blood. She'd shown him everything. Her pain, shame, and struggle, and he *still* didn't get it.

She needed him to seal her closed. All he had to do was say that he understood—that he agreed. Yes, she would bring disgrace and scandal to the royal family, and heartbreaking as it was, she had no place by his side.

But he wouldn't say it. He wasn't even close to thinking it.

He was a prince who hadn't grown up in a monarchy. His parents clearly hadn't instilled in him the ideal of a royal ruler—a personification of their nation. The people needed to see the best parts of Kiraly reflected in their king. The goodness. Strength. Integrity.

Not the rabble.

The entrance gates were just up ahead. She clenched her teeth tighter. She'd request the gate opened, follow the car up the stately drive and ask the guards to escort Kris to his suite. Then she could—

"Hello, Frankie."

The voice came from behind her.

It crushed her windpipe. Turned her belly to liquid.

Breathless, she spun to where her father stood several feet away. His expression was as cunning as his silent approach, and she cursed herself for not scanning the street trees. Instinct told her to run, as it always had, but fear had a sick habit of jamming that impulse.

Frozen in place, she could do nothing more than stare at him.

"She's new." He gestured at her dress, her assumed class, her persona. "I didn't recognize you. Quite convincing."

Her pulse leapt with old fright as he shifted closer. Her rage was too slow to wake.

"I might not have noticed you at all, but your charming man kept staring at me." His smile pushed shards of reaction under her skin—alarm, dread—deep into her bones. "And he can't keep a secret off his face to save himself."

She hid her dismay.

They both turned at the crunch of tires on cobblestones. The security car was passing them on its way to the front palace gates, and through the open window, the guard gave Frankie a nod and a murmured, "Ma'am."

She jerked her head in a return nod as her stomach bottomed out.

Kris wasn't in the backseat.

Her father waited until the car was nothing but fading red taillights along the stately driveway. Then he stepped closer. "Tell me the plan."

"What plan?" The first words she'd spoken to him in ten years. "I work for the guard."

"So I've discovered." His smile was biting, and it ripped the top off her anger.

How *dare* he show his face here?

"Not just with the royal guard, but as head of personal security. I knew you were good, but this? And to think I doubted you."

His implication curdled her blood—as did the fact that across the street and just around the corner, Kris was almost definitely listening.

"This isn't a plan." Her throat was tight. "I haven't done that since you flesh-peddled me, you twisted prick. This is my job."

"Your job." His eyes gleamed. "Positioned high enough to slide your way into the heart of a prince. Ingenious. I didn't think you had the patience for such a long game."

Disgust rooted her to the spot as her lip curled.

"He's completely enamored with you. And desperate. Hell, he was practically rutting the table leg back there." His laugh was low and vicious. "I don't know how you've held out this long, but

211

using yourself like a carrot on a string is clever. My commendations."

"I'm not being clever." Her words came out hoarse with fury.

He smirked.

"I'm being professional."

"As you've ever been, Frankie." He glanced up at the palace, glowing in all its majesty. "I hadn't realized you'd set your sights on building a career out of a single con. What a grand plan. Who better to know the lies and secrets of the royal family than head of security? That kind of information is a one-way ticket to unlimited power. And on the arm of your prince? You'll have it all."

He took in a long breath, lungs swelling in pride as he looked back at her.

"No doubt you've got it all worked out," he continued, inching closer. "Does he believe you're saving yourself until marriage? The wedding must be around the corner. I doubt he could hold out much longer. Then you'll have access to the royal account. The vaults. And if something went missing occasionally, who could possibly question you when you have their dirty laundry in a basket ready to go?"

"I'm not—" Confused, she bit down on her outrage. This didn't make sense. He couldn't honestly believe she'd planned all this. She'd run away from him. Tonight, she'd turned her back on him, desperate not to be seen. How could he possibly believe she'd—

Oh.

The conniving bastard.

He knew they weren't alone. He knew Kris was waiting around the corner and overhearing every word. Her father wasn't congratulating her on her skills or exquisite scheme. He was speaking to discredit her and get her booted from the position she'd worked so hard to achieve—to tear her from the heart of a good man.

He was shoving her into the dirt, his heel digging firmly into her back, because she'd had the nerve to run away from him.

"Fuck you," she said, voice shaking.

His brows shot up. "Watch that mouth, girl. What did I tell you about playing with powerful men? They don't like eating out of the gutter."

Shame burned her throat at how she'd once followed that advice. She'd once spoken as if her words were fresh as spring water—and the Burberry boy had practically licked her mouth clean. Then her shame became horror at the light scuff that came from behind them.

Kris had come out of hiding.

Her dad's look of surprise was masterful.

"Frankie?" Kris spoke her name quietly.

Chest tight, limbs shaking, she angled her face back at him.

Kris was expressionless as he stared at her. "What's going on here?"

In a kind of numb dread, she said, "He was waiting for me."

"I know," he said, voice hollow. "But what's he talking about?"

"Nothing." She was trembling, panic alive beneath her skin. "He's trying to—"

"I'm Kris," he said, moving to stand between them, his attention fixed on her father. "Prince Kristof."

"Your Highness." Her father's bow was smooth. "What an honor."

Kris waved off the formality, features somber. "I couldn't help but overhear."

"Oh." Her father feigned shock, shooting Frankie a swift glance and raising his palms. "I'm sure you misunderstand, Your

Highness. It was a joke about her previous line of work. It's been, oh, years since she's ever done anything like that."

Kris stared at him for several long seconds.

"You're right," he murmured.

Her father blinked. "Pardon?"

"As I said, I couldn't help but overhear." Kris shifted his stance, bringing himself beside Frankie. His elbow brushed hers as he faced her father. "We all know I'm new to this position, but it sure sounded like you were proposing that she exploit the royal family. I might not know the intricacies of treason, but extortion sounds a bit close for comfort."

Her father's features grew slack.

Frankie's pulse stuttered.

"You were suggesting that she use her position to gather sensitive information on me and my family," Kris said, shaking his head slowly. "You were practically advising her to use that information as blackmail in order to steal from us. That sounds treasonous to me."

"You misunder—"

"I know what I heard." Kris cut him off with a raised hand. "Perhaps a different witness might have their credibility doubted, but I'm a Prince of Kiraly and I unmistakably heard you plot against the royal family." He turned to Frankie, features hard with insult. "You should decide what we do with him—though I think we could delay charges and see whether he can prove to be an upstanding citizen."

Frankie and her father both stared at him, incredulous.

"For instance," Kris continued, "if anyone asks him whether he has a daughter, and whether he could tell them about her, he would prove himself upstanding by claiming to have no daughter at all." Head angling, he eyed her father up and down critically. "But if, for instance, he did talk about his daughter and the way he raised her, he would find himself charged with treason.

Because I won't ever forget what I heard here tonight. And sentences for treason aren't as fun as being caught on a little swindle. There will be press. Photos. The chance for women to recognize him from whirlwind romances gone wrong and come forward with charges of their own. And that kind of thing has a tendency to snowball."

Face bloodless, her father looked horrified at being backed so swiftly into a corner.

Frankie's breath shook with disbelief.

Kris took a step forward, getting in her father's face. "You thought I'd doubt her." His words were low with contempt. "That I'd believe she was capable of such deception. You *thought*," he spat, "that I knew her as little as you always have."

Her father, the great manipulator of her life, opened his mouth to protest.

Nothing came out.

Stepping back, Kris turned to her. "What's your professional opinion, Frankie?"

She slipped her hands behind her back, clasping them tightly. The world had gone wonky and her legs struggled to bear the weight of her body. She'd never dared to believe it was possible but—her father had just been bested.

Hauling herself together, she said, "Everyone deserves a second chance."

Kris nodded, features carefully neutral.

"I'll have him monitored," she said, holding her father's stare. "If he does anything that isn't upstanding—anything at all—we'll be forced to revisit this."

How he'd survive without his cons, they were all about to find out.

Kris glanced down absently, brushing a night bug off his arm. "Sound fair, Harvey?"

Her father's scowl faltered at the use of his name. For several seconds, he stared back at Kris. Undoubtedly running calculations behind those unlit eyes, weighing risks and odds and worst-case scenarios for the offer on the table.

Then, with visible resistance, he swallowed his pride. Such an ugly, inflated thing, she hoped he would choke on it. "Yes, Your Highness."

"Good. Now, Frankie, what was that last thing you said to him before I came over?"

She blinked, thinking back. Then she frowned.

Kris hooked his thumb in his front pocket. "I think you should say it again."

She set her attention on her father, recalling the dread of her childhood spent in his shadow—the canker in her self-worth that he'd fed like a guest at his table. His void conscience and his infidelity that had driven her mother away, that had positioned Frankie's mother against her, even now. His indifference for her safety and repugnant command over her sexuality. Her body. Her innocence.

She'd been sixteen. *Sixteen.*

And he'd turned up here with a scheme to ruin her life all over again because she'd had the nerve to leave him.

Now her rage was wide awake.

"Fuck you." Her voice was steady this time. "A cockroach wouldn't touch the scum in your soul."

Her father's lip lifted, but his attention continued to travel between her and Kris.

"Ahh." Kris grinned, sliding an arm around her shoulders, and she swayed into him, weak with disbelief. "I'm going to feast from that gutter every day of my life."

Her father was glowering with defeat.

"Hey, you heard her." Kris's brows rose. "She doesn't want you here."

Frankie braced for a final fight from the man who had

molded her childhood into the worst possible shape. She met his glance with her chin up and shoulders back, and saw in his eyes that he had no moves left. This was it—she wouldn't see him again. He wouldn't risk prison to get even with her. This was the farewell they'd never had when she'd run away. Her final chance at closure.

She leaned harder against Kris's side, telling herself to watch her father go in silence. To be the bigger person; not sink to the pettiness of having the last word.

But she couldn't help herself.

"I've always been better than you," she said.

Her father's inhale was razor-sharp. He'd stew on exactly what she meant by that for years to come. Then he was retreating, crossing the street on silent feet and slipping out of sight.

Gone.

She spun into Kris, clamping her arms around him and holding so tightly, he gave a breathless, "Oof." He returned the embrace, and her heartbeat gradually slowed as it worked out the last of her fear. She was safe in his arms, one banded across her shoulder blades, the other firm at her lower back.

"Thank you," she breathed.

"I've got you." He gave her a gentle squeeze. "He can't touch you."

For the first time in her life, the threat that stained her future lifted. The abrupt opening of possibility was disorienting, and she closed her eyes and pressed harder into him.

It just made her dizzier. Kris. He was holding her.

I've got you.

She'd hidden so much of herself since they'd met. Her identity as royal security. As a Kiralian citizen. Her nightmare of an upbringing. Now, not only did he know everything, but her father could never ruin her life again.

It was like opening every window in the house to let in a weather change—and having it gust inside all at once.

"I saw him," Kris said into her hair. "Waiting across the street back there. I didn't know how to tell you without him overhearing, and I figured he had a plan. I'm sorry I pretended, even for a second, to believe what he'd said. I figured we needed to play into his hand in order to bring him down."

Overwhelmed, Frankie just hugged him tighter.

"Is your mother likely to be a problem?" His question slipped softly across her head. "Would she tell the press about you?"

Her mother wouldn't dare put herself in a position that could catch her father's attention. "No."

"So—this can be our secret," he said, and she wanted to fall into the deep vibration of his voice. Then she realized what he meant.

With a strange sense of awe, her grip on him slackened.

"I'm almost scared to ask." He paused, and she slowly pulled back. "Do you have any other reasons we can't be together?"

Silenced by disbelief, she stared at him.

Kris. The charismatic young man she'd first found at his college bar—their chemistry immediate and intense as she'd slid onto the stool beside him and asked when the trivia was supposed to start. The blue-eyed rogue who'd offered to be her teammate when her 'friends' never showed—who had sat far too close, known far more of the answers than she'd expected, and made her laugh more than she'd ever laughed in her life. The cowboy who'd mentioned that his brother Tommy was unbeatable at trivia—stunning her with the realization that he wasn't the only child of Prince Erik Jaroka. That to prove herself to Philip, she'd need to find *all* the heirs, and had to swiftly disengage from this brother's charm. He was the new friend who had responded to her lie that she didn't know what to do with herself after college by inviting her to come home with him to

Sage Haven, since their local bar had wildly competitive trivia nights and she simply *had* to help him win.

Kris. The prince who had wanted her since they'd met, but who had never, ever pushed her—was now asking if anything else lay between them.

Stunned, she shook her head.

"Please," he murmured. "Be sure."

"I am," she whispered.

His answering smile held wonder as he leaned in to press his forehead against hers. "Frankie."

She trembled. Her name had always seemed made for his voice.

"Kris." Her skin felt worn against his brow; her heart felt unusually close to the surface beneath her breast. The night's events had left her brittle, but she'd exposed too much of herself to retreat now. On a near-silent breath, she asked, "Be good to me?"

His hold tightened. "Every second of every day."

"I don't know how to do this." But her nervousness shimmered, luminescent. It existed only because this brink was new—not because she feared what waited on the other side.

"Neither do I," he said. "All I know is that I want to be with you."

"I—" Overcome, she faltered and brushed her nose against his. His bottom lip disappeared between his teeth, even as he continued to smile. "Me too."

His smile became a grin—then a groan as he picked her up completely and buried his face against her neck. Reaction flared in her, a tingle from her scalp to the arches of her feet, and she angled her head back as he planted openmouthed kisses down to her collarbones. No protest formed on her tongue. No need to stop him. Just the electric thrill of this man's desire and the beauty of it reacting inside her.

Then her half-lidded gaze drifted down the road—to the men at the palace gates.

"The guards," she murmured, stiffening.

After cursing against her skin, Kris stepped back with his hands on her shoulders, putting himself at a distance, but not letting her go. "How do you want to do this? I mean us, going forward. I don't want to embarrass you in front of your team. Or impact your reputation."

She ran a hand down her neck. "I don't know."

Where was the line dividing her position within his security team from her place by his side? She wanted to be both equally.

"Can we figure it out as we go?" she asked.

"I'll follow your lead," he said, and his palms slid outward, cupping her shoulders as his thumbs stroked her skin. Her entire upper body tingled. "How do you want to figure it for tonight? We could go back to our own rooms. Find other ways to be alone, because my guards will always be outside my door. Or yours, if I come to you. If we spend the night together, word will get around among your team."

She clamped her hands around his wrists, holding onto him. This all felt impossible. Standing on the brink of a relationship with Kris and discussing how to navigate it through their roles of royal life. Knowing, in a held breath of hope, what this meant for their future. And even if this had happened in Montana, with no royal ramifications, surrendering herself to this darkly addictive cowboy would still have felt impossible.

"Frankie?" he said, a quiet nudge.

"Word can get around the royal guard. Most of them already know I'm mad for you." Heat flooded her cheeks; warmth crept into spaces that had only ever known cold. "I don't want to spend another night apart. I can't handle us being within the same walls and not being together. It—hurts."

His features melted. Softly, he gave another, "Oof."

Unbalanced by her admission, she ducked her face.

"It hurts me, too," he said softly. "So much about us has always hurt. But not anymore." His energy shifted along with his stance, deepening, rippling, and it didn't take a genius to know desire had settled at the front of his mind. "Would you like to come to my room tonight?"

The question unlocked something inside her that she'd always believed had no key. The possibility of something real and honest and true—and the knowledge that just maybe, she deserved to have it.

Happiness lit her up as she smiled. "Yes."

9

They didn't make it to his chambers.

Kris's blood coursed in an intensified rush as he led her up the stone steps and into the palace's grand entrance hall. They hadn't spoken since they'd passed through the gates. Too fixated on the reality of what they were doing, on the new thrill of touching each other without immediately letting go. With one hand gripping hers, he used the fingertips of his other to trace up and down the exposed skin of her forearm. When he grazed the inside of her elbow, his touch as soft as a whisper in her ear, she sucked in a sharp breath.

"That okay?" he murmured, fingers pausing.

She slanted an astonished look at him. "That feels incredible."

That. He wanted to cause her more of that startled pleasure.

Her shivers and goose bumps and shaky breaths absorbed him so completely that when her phone buzzed, he halted on the marble floor in indignation. Who would call Frankie well after midnight as they were making their way to his bed? Then he remembered that her position, like his, was around the clock.

Holding back a growl—after four years of waiting, surely the universe could slip them a quiet couple of hours—he released her. "If it's not important, they're fired."

"It's always important."

His attention strayed to her lips. "So is this."

"I'll be one second," she murmured, raising her freed hand to cup his cheek with a look of unguarded affection. Then she turned away and answered with a clipped, "Report."

He swore his torso grew several sizes from the swell of his heart.

"Are you serious?" she asked after a long silence. She scanned the great staircase in front of them distractedly as she listened, and then snapped her gaze to Kris. Still watching him, she said, "That was fast," followed by, "Hold on a second." She lowered the phone, hand over the mouthpiece. "There's been a development. I'm needed at a quick briefing. It's something I'd tell you about anyway—do you want to save time and come with me?"

The plea in her eyes was unmistakable. She didn't want to leave him.

Easiest decision of his life. "Sure thing."

Phone raised again, she said, "I want all personal guards in attendance. Prince Kristof will join us, but get the other night guards covered." She listed the names of a lucky few who were about to be woken to fill the role of standing outside his brothers' doors. "Okay, put all that in a file and I'll come and collect it. Meet in the king's study in thirty minutes," she said, before hanging up and taking his hand again. Her grip was hard. "I could punch this bad timing in the nads."

He winced. "Not what I'm keen to visualize right now."

She rolled her lips together, but her grin broke through. "I need to stop by my office on the way."

He let her lead. Ground floor, south wing, and through a door that required her fingerprint and retina scan to enter. It wasn't full-blown secret service sterility inside, but the white walls and immaculate offices that adjoined the center corridor were unlike the rest of the palace.

"Wait here," she said, and disappeared through the first door on the right. In the time it took Kris to slide a hand into his back pocket and meet the stare of a blinking surveillance camera, she'd got what she needed, emerging with a slim folder under her arm. "Alright."

Her office was deeper in the security warren behind another fingerprint-coded door, and he stepped inside as she held it open for him. Roughly a quarter of the size of his tower study, the room was in a better state of organization than he'd expected. The desk was near-empty—just the silver slimline shape of her closed laptop, a relatively neat stack of folders, and several used coffee mugs. Two chairs sat opposite the desk, and a filing cabinet was positioned beneath a high, frosted-glass window. Her wheeled chair was pushed halfway across the room, the seat facing the side wall as if she'd left in a hurry. Or, more likely, she placed the same nonexistent value on pushing her chair in as making her bed or tying up her bootlaces.

"Who else's fingerprints can open this door?" he asked as it snapped closed behind them.

She tossed the new folder on the pile before unwinding her scarf and draping it over the back of a chair. "You assume someone else is permitted in here?"

"Rephrasing," he said. "Can anyone else's prints open this door?"

She gave him an odd look. "Just yours, Mark's and Tommy's."

He huffed a not-quite amused breath as he looked around, recalling having his fingerprints taken for *security purposes* upon arriving in Kiraly. "So many things we're not told."

"Need-to-know basis, babe."

His attention shot to her.

She'd said it offhand. *Babe.* Like she might tack on *mate* or *buddy* when talking to someone whose name she couldn't remember. Except she knew his name and she'd never called him babe before. And they both knew it.

The air between them sparked; caught with a whoosh.

He took off his cap and tossed it onto her desk. Raking his fingers through his hair—intentionally dragging it off to one side in a way he'd always sensed drove her crazy—he asked, "How long will the meeting take?"

"Not sure. Half an hour, maybe?" He'd expected the reason for this office drop-in to be the folders on her desk, but instead she moved toward the filing cabinet and knelt down to open the bottom drawer. "Aha."

She tugged out purple jeans and a grey tank. Of course. She wasn't about to face her team wearing that dress. Not when one glance would reveal the flawlessness of her figure. The fabric was snug at her breasts and cut high across her thighs; all it would take was one sweep of his hands to peel it clean off her and another few tugs to cast her underwear beside it, freeing her skin to his touch, his hungry mouth, the slide of his hardening—

Aaand he was distracted.

What were they doing here again?

Clothes. Frankie wanted to change. She was kneeling with jeans and tank in hand, watching him with a raised brow.

He tried to interpret her expectant look. "Is your face asking me to assist you or be a gentleman and turn my back?"

Her attention darted to the sealed office door. Her return gaze was slower. "Assist me."

Lust flared in his veins, but he didn't cross to her. Helping her change was one thing—one sexy, bare-skinned, ultimate foreplay thing—but he knew himself. Knew the electric arc his body burned to form with hers. And holding himself back that close to her near-naked body would defy the laws of his own restraint.

Unless . . . she knew that.

"When did you say we have to be in the tower?" His question was rough.

She rose to standing, face flushed. "We've got twenty-five minutes."

He sucked in air. Shook his head. "Not enough time."

The desire bold on her face dared to argue. Her gaze openly traveled his body, undressing him, touching him, working him. His arousal spiked, pulsing hot and hard so abruptly that he hinged forward a little, his breath hitching.

Surprised, her darkened eyes flashed up to his face.

"Need more time," he managed to protest.

"You sure about that?"

His heartbeat pounded everywhere. His ears. His neck. His groin.

"I feel like it'll hardly take any time at all," she said, her voice thick with self-consciousness. "With the way I . . . need you."

"Is that what you want, Frankie?" He hadn't intended to move, but found himself in front of her.

"I want something to have changed." His body thrummed beneath the palm she ran over his chest. "After tonight . . . I need us to have changed."

"We *have* changed."

God, this woman. She'd dragged herself out of the immoral pit of her upbringing—and hadn't stopped hauling ass until she'd taken charge of the lives of the country's most esteemed family. Talk about reinventing herself.

"And I don't want to wait anymore," she said to his mouth.

"Me, neither." He took her small pile of clothes as she shoved it against him. "But for our first time? We can do better. Longer.

After this briefing, we'll go back to my room and I'll show you exactly what I mean."

If there was anything she deserved, it was time and tenderness. After the life she'd lived, the years they'd spent building up to this moment. Not rushed and panting and pressed against her work desk with their clothes bunched, her elbow knocking a coffee mug to the floor as he grasped her hips tightly, filling her again and again and—

He almost groaned as his cock strained.

No, God. *Not* that.

Why was it so damn hot in here?

"I really like the sound of your room," she said, a throaty admission.

Hauling his desire into line, he made himself nod.

"For our second time," she added.

Blood roared in his ears.

"Twenty-two minutes and counting," she whispered with a wicked little smile. "You might want to hurry."

He was hardly aware of throwing her clothes over his shoulder as he pressed her back against the nearest wall. She moved with him, making a soft noise he'd never heard from her before—a kind of hungry whimper—and it left him awed and gratified and sensually ravenous all at once. Her face was close, chin angled up, her breath a scent he was desperate to swallow. "Frankie, can I—"

"Yes," she said, and met his open mouth with hers.

Her kiss was like falling into his own heart and landing in her arms. She was there; she'd always been there. It almost knocked his knees out from under him. She was a wave crashing over him, a slide-tackle hauling him down. He slammed his palm against the wall and pushed harder into the slick sweetness of her tongue, her mouth, her need for him.

This was—*she* was—everything.

Her taste spread through him like he'd always known it would—like wildflowers and flame and an open sky—and the world levelled out around him.

With Frankie by his side, he wouldn't slip off the edge of duty and into disaster. He could lead without losing himself. He could be a cowboy royal, for she'd always known him as both and would bind those parts of him together. With her, he could handle his future.

Their future.

They kissed desperately. Wide and wet and fierce like a storm rolling in.

Her hands were tight in his hair, her body hard against his. He ran his knuckles down her side and she broke the kiss as he grazed the edge of her breast, her back arching. He nudged her thighs apart with his knee and pressed his quad firmly between her legs.

"Oh, God." Her breath hitched as she slid over him.

His bones ached with the urge to please her. "Tell me what you want."

"I told you, with the way I need you, this won't take—" Her eyes fell closed as she rolled her hips, rubbing against his thigh again. She shuddered. Hard. Heavy. Way closer than he'd expected. "Kris, please."

Frankie. His best friend. Begging for him.

Edgy with need, he ran his hands over her hips. Then he was peeling her dress up and over her head, discarding it as he flicked her bra open and drew the straps down, collecting her underpants on the way and letting both drop to the floor.

Skin. Curves. Breasts. Beauty.

It knocked the wind right out of him. He'd never pretended to be a saint—he'd imagined her like this over the years with varying degrees of physical accuracy. But no matter how his mind had played with her, shaped and embellished, nothing could compare to the reality of her before him now—lean and sculpted and every inch the most intense fantasy of his life.

So this was Frankie.

She was blinking at him.

He stilled, hesitating. "This okay?"

"No one's ever got me naked that fast."

Lust clawed low inside him as he looked her over. "Four years isn't exactly a record."

Her smile bordered on shy. "Your turn."

She helped him. Their hands tangled at his shirt buttons, fumbled at his trousers because their mouths met again and split focus was beyond him. He stopped caring when his hands found her waist and slid up to cup her breasts. *Christ.* He dragged her nipple into his mouth, sucking and reveling in her ready moan. She was perfect. That was his only clear thought.

Utterly perfect.

His breath was quick, his cock rigid. Vaguely, he was aware of her hand dipping into his front pocket for the condom before she freed him and kicked his clothes aside. Sparks flared beneath his skin at the slide of her hands on his chest.

"Goddamn," she muttered, shifting closer and brushing her lips over his pecs. "No wonder you're arrogant."

He smiled distractedly, struggling not to gather her naked body to him and show her the more pertinent reason for his arrogance. "You've seen me without a shirt before."

Her fingers drifted lower. "I've never touched you."

"I wish you—"

His mind emptied as she grasped the length of him. All that was left was the tight stroking of her hand. The slam of his palm returning to the wall. The blaze of his pleasure growing ever-hotter. The strained sound of her name on his lips. And cursing, he was almost definitely mouthing profanities in mindless reverence at her rhythm. Frankie was touching him. *Frankie* was pressed naked against his side, her mouth roaming the muscles of his arm. It was too much. Urgency surged through him and he dragged her hand away.

Then he was returning his thigh between her legs, angling it against her clit—and rubbing firmly. She moaned, shuddering, and moved with him. If her gratification lay in outer orgasms, he'd have no regrets for it to end just like this.

"Kris." Her indignance sparked through her pleasure. "I don't need a bed for our first time, but I draw the line at coming on your fucking leg."

That answered that. He laughed, darkly delighted by her crudity, and raised his head to kiss her slow and deep. Feasting from her gutter-mouth was literal bliss.

"Lift me?" she asked, fastening her arms around his neck.

He passed a hand down her stomach. "I want to touch you first."

"Next time."

"Once." His fingers found her soft curls and he went mad imagining how she must feel beneath them. "Please, just once?"

"Okay." Her green eyes were burning. "But we're on a timeline."

Jesus. Okay. Just once.

With his mouth behind her ear and eyes closed, he slid his fingers between her legs—and almost lost control at the silky, swollen feel of her. She weakened in his arms, pulling on his neck with a tremble, and he stroked her, a single two-fingered slide that went deep and wet and drew a sound of strangled pleasure from low inside her. Lost in the sensation, he dragged back the other way, harder this time, teasing, closer to where he most desperately wanted to delve.

God. He had to feel the inside of her.

"Just once," he murmured, seeking permission through his

mindless haze. He grazed against her, preparing, poised to start shallow but not making any promises to stay there.

"Cheater." She nipped his earlobe and he opened his eyes with a swift breath. "You can't start again from zero." Her voice was hoarse with wanting. "I don't want it to happen like that—not this time."

Freeing his ear with a tug, he scraped his teeth down her neck and murmured, "How do you want it?" He was pushing her. She'd claimed she could do sex and attraction, but not intimacy. And while dirty talk was all sex on the surface, peel back the lust and those confessions were intensely intimate. "Tell me."

"I want . . ." She trailed off as he circled his hands around the backs of her thighs and lifted her to his hips. He fought the urge to enter her as he pressed her back against the wall. "You inside me," she said, the quiet words seeming to blush. "Right here."

That made two of them.

"Well then." Skin on skin now, bodies hot and damp. The air was scented with sex and his entire being coursed with the primal urge to finish this inside her. He dragged his tongue up her neck to the hollow behind her ear. "Clock's ticking."

At the nape of his neck, he heard the rustle of her opening the condom.

They were really doing this.

Disbelief momentarily dizzied him as she slipped a hand between them to roll it on. Years of pretending she wasn't his greatest desire—years of aching and hoping and holding himself in check—finally over. In all that time, he'd never imagined it happening like this.

Sheathed, he positioned himself at the apex of her thighs—and slowly pushed inside her.

"Kris." Frankie's fingers dug hard into his shoulders as he eased further in. "I—I need you—"

And then she was kissing him, sweet shadows and searing light, and it was all he could do to keep the pace slow to let her pleasure build. She moved with him, skin slick and sweaty, working toward release even as her body adjusted to his size. Barely keeping his head at her hot clasp, he filled her more with each push until finally he was fully seated inside her.

Then he took their timeline very seriously.

The sounds she made at his thrusts went straight to the dark, dirty stores of his mind, and he almost burst from that alone. Blood raging with sensation, he filled her again and again, until the promise of release shimmered down his spine. He was trembling, hands shaking over her body. His chest felt tight and huge at the same time, like something was growing beneath his solar plexus and his ribs had fastened tight to contain it.

He knew what it was.

Knew that even now, fully surrendered to him, she wasn't ready to hear it.

"Kris," she said, spine stretching to take him deeper. Her breath was shallow, heightened. Close. So very close. "Kris. Please."

Tightening his hold, he caught the edge in her glazed stare. It stunned him; thrilled him. The look in her eyes wasn't simple desire. It was core-deep, an endless reserve.

God above, she was all in.

"Hold onto me," he said, and felt her tighten—felt his nerve endings fraying as he neared ecstasy. Then she clenched around him with a cry that fell beneath the roaring in his ears as his own orgasm beat its way out of him, brutal and blinding and boundless.

More.

Before he'd even found his breath, he wanted more. Frankie was sinking in his arms, shaking, her grip growing slack around his neck. He kept his hold tight, unwilling to let her go so soon, and lifted his face from her shoulder to find her watching him, her eyes heavy-lidded yet somehow more open than they'd ever been.

"You okay?" He pressed her a little harder against the wall as his muscles relaxed.

Her smile was like a love-nip of her teeth straight to his heart. "Yes."

The base of his sternum ballooned with feeling, but before he could put it into words, she was pushing at his shoulders, saying, "Let's move."

Grudgingly, he eased out of her and set her on her feet. As he dealt with the condom, he asked, "Are we late?"

She picked up her phone from the desk and cursed. "We have seven minutes."

They dressed fast. He tugged his trousers on and fixed her hair, trying to give it a generic end-of-a-long-night look and less thoroughly-wall-banged. Then she tucked his shirt in and he almost ruined her hair all over again.

"Best not to touch me below the waist," he cautioned, letting her palm restrain him.

"Noted." Her cheeks were flushed. "Ready?"

He grinned. "For anything."

She rolled her eyes, swiped up all the folders on her desk and strode to the door.

"Frankie," he said, reaching around her to cover the door handle. The sideways look she cast him was both irritated and amused. He kissed her between the eyebrows and said softly, "You're everything."

She waited a beat before arching a brow. "You stopped me for that?"

"Yes," he said, trying to alleviate the pressure in his chest. He didn't want to return to a reality where he had to be discreet about touching her, kissing her, betraying the way he felt about her. "I might be the king of a country, but you'll always be my world. And I'll do anything—"

"What's happening here?" A shadow passed over her face. "We're running late and you think we have time for a sonnet?"

"I was just trying to—"

Ah. This was too intimate.

"Enough." She slapped his hand aside and hauled the door open. Then she stopped, hesitated, and pushed it closed again so the latch rested against the frame. "Oh. Except. It turns out that condom was a good idea."

He grinned. "You think?"

"Yes." Her green gaze was heavy as she looked back at him. "I know we'll be spending nights together, but just thinking out loud here, there are a lot of secret rooms and secluded nooks in this oversized display of wealth you call home." She patted the front pocket of his trousers, swiping her hand rather firmly across his crotch as she pulled away. "You might want to replace it."

He almost growled as she strode into the corridor.

Utterly perfect.

10

They ran from one end of the palace to the other, bolting up too many flights of stairs, and still reached the base of the tower five minutes late. Breathing hard with a hand on his side, Kris flatly refused to run up this final staircase. So Frankie strode into the tower study ahead of him, her core temperature high, her heartbeat a post-orgasm mess, and forced herself to concentrate on Philip and the twelve guards in attendance as their attention shifted to her.

These were the personal guards of the Jaroka brothers—four assigned per family member—two for the day shift, two for the night. She had selected each of them personally and entrusted them with the safety of the royal family. Some were sitting on the study couches and chairs, others were leaning against the curved walls or standing by the windows. All in uniform, clear-eyed despite the late hour and connected by grim tension.

"Ma'am," several greeted her.

She gave a nod, hoping to God they couldn't see the past half-hour on her face. "Thanks for coming."

Mark's night guards looked understandably harried, having raced across town from Kuria Estate. And Philip, bless his straitlaced cotton socks, sat in one of the chairs opposite the monarch's desk with spectacularly wild bed hair and the telltale piping of a pajama top askew beneath his shirt.

Her cadre all snapped to attention when Kris entered the room behind her. They were the only royal employees who knew he would soon be their king, and every one of them bowed low.

Taking advantage of the moment of privacy, Kris grazed a hand over her back and slanted a soft-eyed glance at her mouth as he passed her.

"Tell me."

His demand had been hard as granite; his fingers had been equally unyielding at her core.

"Tell me how you want it."

She flushed, having not even known to want it like that.

As the guards straightened, Kris said, "Don't mind me," and crossed the room to drop into a languid sprawl behind his desk.

"We'll make this snappy." Frankie closed the door with her heel, adjusting her grip on the folders. "But before we start, who made the best joke on Philip's hair?"

A pause as everyone looked pointedly at Hanna.

"It's just," the guard said, "it looks like it was subjected to an incredibly isolated extreme weather event."

Frankie snorted, Kris said, "Ha," and Philip grumbled as he patted his head.

Then Frankie caught Hanna eyeing off *her* hair and swiftly moved things along.

"Right," she said. "The authorities have confidentially reopened the case regarding the late royal family's deaths. This is following Prince Kristof's testimony about the violent attack on Prince Tomas and his friend Jonah Wood in Montana three years ago, which we covered at yesterday morning's briefing." She tapped the folders against her palm. "The detectives' search—and ours—has shown that four of Prince Tomas's attackers have contacts in Kiraly who worked on the renovations of the west wing. This could be coincidence. Or it could be an indication that whoever orchestrated Tomas's attack is also behind the balcony collapse. These people might all be from the same network."

Unease blew through the room, shifting feet and stiffening shoulders.

In a casual movement, Frankie stepped back to lean against the door. She opened the top folder and flipped through its contents. She saw none of it. Dread was too busy squeezing her throat closed, robbing her of focus.

Holy hell. This was real.

Somehow, she'd managed to disconnect from it. To treat the threat like an abstract problem to be solved, but if the incidents were truly connected—

Someone wanted Kris and his brothers dead.

And weren't afraid to act on it.

A feverish rush made her skin too hot and too cold at once.

Kris was watching her. She flicked over another page, refusing to look up. He'd see the panic in her eyes—would ask about it later. And she didn't want to voice this fear. It was poised like a tipping point inside her, a confession that would unbalance her control and drag a landslide of vulnerability down with it.

I'm scared for you.

I don't want to lose you.

I can't live without you.

Reality whipped down her spine. Her fears shied away. What the hell was she doing?

She'd wanted to be with him since they'd met, and now she couldn't muster the courage to be honest with him? His life was in danger—and she was too chicken to be emotionally intimate.

You're everything, he'd told her, like the sweetest secret, and she'd batted it away without a thought.

Stupid. So unbelievably stupid.

She plucked the top photograph from the folder.

"This morning," she said, her voice miraculously level, "guards were assigned to discreetly monitor these contacts. And tonight, we got lucky. All subjects converged at a pub called the Bull's Quest at ten-thirty this evening. Photographs show that upon arrival, each of them wore an identical pin, indicating it's some kind of club."

Hand not quite steady, she held up the top photograph. A close-up of a circular silver pin on a shirt collar, hollowed out with a capital '*A*' in the center.

"Anyone recognize the symbol?" she asked.

"Anarchism." This from Zoltan, one of Tommy's guards.

"Spot on." She kept her back against the door, maintaining a pose of late-night weariness to cover her previous overwhelm. After the night she'd had, it wasn't hard to feign. "It's possible we've got ourselves some violent anti-authoritarian rebels."

Kris frowned behind the desk. "These people want chaos?"

"Anarchy is more complex than chaos, Your Highness," Zoltan said, turning to face Kris with an air of respectful neutrality. "That's reductionist and a common misinterpretation of the movement. Many anarchists believe in a highly organized society, but don't feel they can entrust the management of their lives to kings or other rulers, and seek to build a democratic society from the bottom up, instead of the top down."

Kris blinked. "Right."

"That said, we do seem to have a group of extremists on our hands," the guard finished.

Did they ever.

Frankie cleared her throat. "I'll find out if they accept new people into the group. If they do, I'll join them the next time they meet."

In the corner of her eye, she noted Kris sit forward slowly. "What if they recognize you?" he asked, and even though his voice was admirably calm, none of the guards turned to look at him. In fact, he was the only person looking at *her* in a room of fifteen people. The privacy was discreetly granted, the guards looking at their shoes or out the windows, but it betrayed they all knew Kris's concern sprung from affection and that this particular exchange wasn't any of their business. "It could be dangerous."

She held his stare. "They won't recognize me."

His forearms were on the desk, hands clasped together. "You've been seen in public as my bodyguard."

Shame slid down her sternum. "I won't be going as myself."

With a nod, he ran his tongue along his back teeth and looked away.

"Right." Her tone hauled everyone's attention back to her. "Do not share this information or investigation with anyone outside this tower. Do not share the possible connection between the attacks with your primaries." She glanced at Hanna, Peter, and Kris's night team. "Clearly you're the exception."

Lazlo, a mid-forties guard with a shaved head and oversized shoulders, raised a polite hand. "Markus is still officially king." He pointed out. "Should the king not be made aware of such critical news? If not of the possible connection between the attacks, then at least the possibility that the late royal family's deaths weren't an accident?"

Frankie glanced at Kris. "Your Highness?"

He frowned back. "I don't like the idea of telling Mark and not Tommy."

"So we inform them both?"

Stricken, he shook his head. "I don't want to cause Tommy

additional anxiety. The threads are still too loose. Can we wait until we have something concrete to tell them?"

Frankie and Lazlo both gave a nod.

"Any other questions?" she asked.

They all shook their heads.

Blowing out a hard breath, she extended the bottom folder to one of Tommy's night guards standing closest to her. "This is everyone who attended the anarchist meeting this evening. I'll email you the image files shortly. You spot any of them near your primary, you send out an alert and take immediate evasive action. We don't know whether they have a new plan, so expect the worst."

Her team passed around the folder, taking long looks at the profiles. Once the folder returned to her, she braced herself—and made a move completely against her nature.

"One last thing," she said.

The room fell silent. Everyone looked at her. Panic prickled down her spine, and she fought the urge to turn and flee down the spiral staircase.

Her hands curled into fists. "It's—not related."

Curiosity flickered across their faces.

"I just wanted you all to know that Prince Kristof and I are . . ." Alarm fuzzed her brain. They were what? What the hell was the end of that sentence? No longer in denial? Still shaky from sex in her office? Boyfriend and girlfriend? *Shit.* She forbade herself from shifting or swallowing nervously as she met Kris's widening stare.

His blue gaze hung onto hers, intense, waiting.

She could do this. *Just spit it out.* They all damn well knew anyway.

Running a hand over her face, she muttered, "Together."

Kris actually laughed. A sound of disbelieving wonder that

made her want to bury her face in his chest so she wouldn't have to look at anyone.

Her team exchanged grins and offered a round of congratulations.

"Thanks." Her cheeks flamed as she opened the door and positioned herself to one side. "But it's not common news, so if I catch any of you gossiping about it, you're going to wish genital regeneration was a thing." That didn't dim their grins, though Philip had turned away. "Alright, alright, get back to your posts and beds, and stay vigilant."

"Ma'am, yes, ma'am," came the single answer from a dozen mouths.

She stood firm as they departed, accepting waggling brows and whacks on the arm with reluctant good humor. Hanna lingered in front of a mountain-view window with the look of someone who wanted to talk privately. So once the study had otherwise emptied out, Frankie pressed the folders against her forehead, closed her eyes, and willed her embarrassment to back the eff off.

Then she crossed to where Philip was standing, patting down his hair to no effect.

"Hey," she said, prodding him lightly in the ribs. "Thanks for getting out of bed."

"Thank you for singling me out," he said with mild indignation. "I'll have you know Peter wasn't wearing any shoes."

"Snitch. Peter was smart enough to stand behind the armchair so I couldn't see." She reached out and tweaked the curved collar of his pajama top, aware of Kris watching and waiting behind the desk. "And it made you feel like part of the group. Don't deny it."

Philip sniffed, but she caught his smile.

She angled her back to Kris and whispered, "Are you upset with me?"

The advisor regarded her steadily for a few beats. "No."

She tilted her head, not buying it. While Kris's opinion of her mattered more than anything, the thought of Philip disapproving of her relationship turned her stomach. "He's going to be king and you know my background. You can't possibly approve."

"Actually, I don't know your background." His brow furrowed. "You don't have a digital footprint from before you were sixteen."

Her gut churned as she murmured, "That tells you enough."

"I'm not upset with you." His quiet words were firm. "I want to see you happy."

God. It was weird how much she liked this stuffy, stiff-spined man. "And I want to give you closure," she said. "We're going to get to the bottom of this."

The balcony collapse. The royal deaths.

"Yes." He cast her a look of suppressed grief. "Call me if you get an update? No matter the time?"

"You'll be the first person I call. Promise."

"Good." His chest filled on a swift breath in. Then he flicked nonexistent dust from his jacket sleeve and strode from the study.

And then there were three.

"Johansson." Stifling a yawn, she turned her attention to where Hanna still waited by the window. This was the night that never ended and weariness was closing in on her fast. "To what pleasure do we owe your loitering?"

Hanna grinned. "Friendly chat?"

"That's funny." Frankie looked to the ceiling with a frown. "I know both those words, but they make no sense together."

Kris gave a soft laugh behind her.

"How did the dress go?" Hanna raised a pointed brow. "Get any . . . compliments?"

"I didn't wear it for compliments."

"Yet I gave them to her anyway," Kris murmured. "You can really sew, Hanna. I'm sure you can imagine how sexy she looked."

"I don't find anyone sexy, Your Highness," she answered. "But I'm sure she looked gorgeous."

Kris paused, and Frankie and Hanna met eyes as if to say, *here we go.*

Three, two, one . . .

"What do you mean, you don't find anyone sexy?" he asked.

Hanna's features tightened, but she kept her gaze level. "I'm asexual, Your Highness," she said. "I know you're highly charged —but not feeling sexual attraction is as much a part of me as desire is a part of you. I find people aesthetically beautiful, sure, but I don't think *wow, they're hot, I want to bang them,* you know?"

Frankie eyed Kris over her shoulder. No. He didn't know. He was frowning at Hanna like she'd told him her grandmother had died.

"Stop looking at her like that," Frankie muttered sharply.

"Sorry." His features leapt from concern to confusion. "I've just—never met someone who's asexual before. Or, uh, ever heard of it."

"You've probably heard us called other names." Hanna cleared her throat, running her hand over her collarbones. "Frigid. Unfuckable. Being ace is often viewed as a failing, instead of an orientation. Which kind of sucks."

"Yeah." He paused, frown deepening. "Jesus, sorry. I kind of just did exactly that." Then he offered her a smile. "Thanks for telling me."

Hanna raised a shoulder. "It's not a secret."

"I've known next to nothing about you for over three months," he said. "Everything about you is a secret."

"Hey, I kind of like that." She moved her shoulders a little, as if trying on the title of *woman of mystery*. "Speaking of secrets . . ." Her attention shifted to Frankie. "It's late, and your eyes are glazing over, but tomorrow, I'm going to charm you into giving me details of your night out. You borrowed my dress. It's my price."

Frankie rolled her eyes, but didn't argue as the guard turned to leave.

Then an uncomfortable fear lurched up her throat.

"Hanna," she said abruptly. The woman turned back to her, smiling curiously at the use of her first name. "Do you think the others will stop respecting me?"

Hanna looked baffled. Then she arched a brow at Kris. "You offended by that question, Your Highness?"

"The implication that being in a relationship with me makes her less respectable?" Kris sounded amused. "Not particularly."

"That's not what I meant." Frankie eyed them both in exasperation. "Will they think I only got this position because of my relationship with Kris? Everyone's figured out that we knew each other in Montana—that there's been something going on between us. Will they cry favoritism?"

"Ma'am," Hanna said, quite frankly. "You're intimidating—flat-out terrifying if we have to deal with you before breakfast—and the closest any of us will ever get to an actual badass. Your time up and down The Scepter thrashes anyone on the team, I can't beat you at *anything* and you took down that psycho misogynist like a boss. Everyone's seen the footage. You deserve your position. Favoritism will never cross anyone's mind."

"Oh." Frankie looked down, twisting the pearl necklace that she'd forgotten to take off. "Good."

"It's criminal how fast she takes those steps," Kris said.

"I know, right?" Hanna answered in mock scandal. "And the way she elbows you as she passes you on her way back up?"

Kris's chuckle tingled down Frankie's spine as he walked around the desk to lounge against it beside her. "I think she thinks it's cute."

Frankie barely held back a laugh. Then she yawned. "Sounds like me."

Hanna grinned. "See you tomorrow, sleepyhead."

Frankie offered a small wave as she yawned again and the guard closed the study door behind her.

Then Kris's hand was sliding around her waist, drawing her in, and she turned to press her cheek against his chest. She shivered at the feel of him even as exhaustion dragged her eyelids closed. She could do this now—lean against him, bury into his strength. Marveling, she buried harder.

"She knows what we did, doesn't she?" Kris kissed the top of her head, his hand slipping to the rear of her jeans.

"One hundred percent." Frankie pressed her ass into his palm, a challenge he accepted when he shoved back, pushing her firmly against him. Her lips parted on a light, hot breath, before her mind played a distracted game of hopscotch.

Hanna—friends with Gul—would talk to Gul about her and Kris, assuming he'd have heard about it from Ava—except Ava couldn't tell Gul because she didn't know—*because Mark didn't know—*

"Oh, God." Horrified, she drew back and scrubbed a hand over her face. "I told the guards before you'd told Mark and Tommy."

Kris raised a shoulder, unfazed, his eyes on her mouth. "I'll tell them in the morning."

"They're your brothers. You're not upset?"

"Upset that you announced our relationship to a room full of people? Are you kidding me?"

Well, when he put it like *that*.

Blushing, she leaned her forehead against his chin. "I missed touching you."

"When?" That clever hand of his was getting lower. Sliding over and down her ass, following the center seam of her jeans like a beeline to her core. "During the meeting?"

"Yeah," she breathed, shifting so he could reach more easily. Eyes closing, she sank against him—more completely than she'd intended. He was just *so* comfortable . . .

"You're crashing." He withdrew his hand, running it softly up her spine, and spoke the words she'd spent years yearning to hear. "I'm taking you to bed."

Frankie didn't get a good look at his royal suite. She'd only visited these rooms once before, but she'd been too distracted by Kris's hurt to take it in. Now, the lights in the wall sconces were dimmed, a barely-there amber glow that cast most of the sitting room into shadow, and as Kris led her through the open double doors to his bedroom, she could hardly make her eyes focus. Not that she needed to see to sense the understated wealth of the bedroom furnishings and the enduring stately luxury weighted in these four walls. She'd have been more comfortable in his old room at the homestead in Sage Haven, with his clothes strewn over the chair and his hat on the side table. But then again, so would he. And they were here now.

By the bed, Kris let go of her hand and faced her with a frown. "Unless you'd prefer your room?"

"Obviously," she murmured. "The ceiling fan makes a really cool clicking noise and the pillow stuffing has separated into independent states."

"Great, let's go there," he said, and undressed her in smooth movements. Top over her head, bra off and over his shoulder, and then his hands were at her jeans, knuckles pressing low on her stomach as he unbuttoned her. Her body started to tighten and ache despite her exhaustion, and as he knelt to peel the jeans down her legs, she swept her fingers into his hair and star-fished her palm over the crown of his head. She pushed back with a murmur of protest when he tried to rise.

She heard him smile. "As badly as I want to stay on my knees, I intend to be thorough when I get my mouth on you, and you're not in a position to withstand that right now."

Hey.

Wait. She'd meant to say that out loud. Hmm. Brain lag. Then she realized she was standing with her eyes closed, swaying between the real world and a thick, hazy dream-state, and had to concede his point. She slid her hand off his head.

"We'll get back to it," he said, rising and brushing his lips over hers. Still aching for him, she opened her mouth to catch him in a kiss, but he drew back, murmuring, "Later." He gave her a gentle push. "Sleep."

Too tired to be intimidated by the oceanic bed, she crawled beneath the water-soft green covers and collapsed onto her side. "Your bed's nice," she spoke against the sheet, dully noting it held his woodland scent.

He slid in close beside her. His body was warm—stripped as bare as hers. "It's nicer now."

Hardly knowing what she intended, she reached out and ended up with her hand on his face. After a moment, she felt his cheek lift under her palm and he said, "This is slightly less nice," and peeled it off, lacing his fingers through hers.

"Night." She managed to say that one out loud.

"Frankie," he said quietly, tugging at her drifting mind. "Would you give me your brass knuckles?"

The question sank in slowly. Confused, she cracked an eye open. "What?"

He was watching her, lashes heavy in the dark.

"Why?" she asked.

"Not to use on anyone." He lifted his other hand, brushing it softly over her forehead and into her hair. Lulled, she closed her eyes.

Not to use. To dispose of, then. If she was truly to stand by his side, she couldn't be tied to her past. *This can be our secret.* And the best-kept secrets left no evidence behind, symbolic or otherwise.

Smart man. Asking when she was too exhausted to suffer the full impact of his request. It wasn't just loss at having to hand over the only keepsake of her childhood—it was the indignity and identity-deep humiliation of having to shed her upbringing in order to be worthy of a life with him. Her truth literally wasn't good enough. Most of the time, she wanted nothing to do with her past, yet something inside her gave a significant tug of resistance, resenting that he was doing what had to be done. *No.* That part of her almost refused. *Those knuckles saved me.*

Then he ran his fingers over her scalp and sleep reached out, curling around her like a sun-warmed cat, and she found herself surrendering with a fuzzy, "Sure," into the new, tender space between them.

She'd miss the reminder of what she'd overcome.

But she preferred where she was going.

11

The next morning, she woke to Kris whispering her name. Gentle, like the stroke of his calloused hand down her back; disorientating, like waking up in her best friend's bed and not needing to freak out about it. Her lungs filled on a large breath, and with her eyes still closed, she stretched out on her stomach in the cool linen sheets. One leg straightened sideways, aiming to stick over the far side, but her toes moved through nothing but deliciously soft bedding.

Frowning, she pulled her head out from under the pillow and blinked at Kris. "You on the edge?"

He was propped up on an elbow facing her, watching her, his hair a mess. Shirtless, with the sheets pushed low over his hips, he was a sight of muscles and radiant sexual potency.

She shivered as he continued stroking her back.

"The edge of something," he said, with a slow half-smile. "Not the bed."

"Huh." She looked around. The mattress was endless. "Bigger than a king."

"Palatial?"

"Huh." She settled down again with a groan. The drapes

were still closed, but a pale predawn light was seeping around the edges. "What's time?"

"Five-thirty." His fingertips reached the small of her back and started tracing circles, casual and tender. "I didn't know what time you had to be up."

"Usually briefing six o'clock." She wasn't awake enough for full sentences. "Don't today because last night."

"So, what you're saying is," he said, his low voice seeming to caress between her thighs. "We have time."

Insides twisting, she nestled deeper onto her front. "Maybe."

Those lashes dipped to her body, then back up. He looked surprised. "Are you hiding from me?"

"Maybe," she said again, tucking her chin down to rest on her shoulder. She hadn't exactly concealed her modesty the night before, but that had been a heated moment. "It's just . . . this is new."

"Then let's make it familiar." He raked his hair off his forehead, elbow at the perfect angle to show off his rounded bicep. "Would you rather go back to sleep before breakfast," he said, "or work up an appetite together?"

Biting her lip, her gaze drifted down.

He was hard, straining against the sheet. A significant early-morning proposition.

"Yours if you want it," he murmured, and her body melted like the thick wax of a candle.

She hummed, pretending to consider.

"Last night." The sheets rustled as he shifted. "I'll never forget."

She let her gaze continue drifting over him. "You mean the part where I was raised as a con artist, the part where you got rid of my father, the part where anarchists probably want you dead, or the part against the wall in my office?"

"As far as memories go, the office wall has the most staying power."

Her lips quirked.

"You can go back to sleep, if you want," he said, and despite being rock hard and ready down there, he sounded like he meant it.

"You're not fussed either way?"

His voice dropped. "That's not what I said."

She pretended not to hear. "You could take me or leave me?"

"Take you." The words were rough. "Ask me to take you."

Lust ran a finger over her abdomen and she shivered. "Kris?"

He inched closer and practically growled, "Yes?"

"Will you take me," she said, and as desire curved like an arched spine across his lips, she finished, "to breakfast?"

He made a noise of pain, but his eyes were sparkling. "Not yet."

Her muscles loosened, aroused, as something flitted from her chest to her belly and back again. Light, an airborne sensation that darted and tumbled, wingtips grazing her sides and gliding up her sternum. No barriers in its flight path this morning, nothing to knock it out of her skies, and it swooped low in her tummy when Kris held her stare and arrowed up to nest in her heart when he smiled just for her.

So, this was happiness.

"Not yet?" She grinned at him. "What are we waiting for?"

"This game to end, so I can make you come ten times harder than last night."

Her breath caught. Last night had been the best sex of her life. What did he plan on doing, growing a third hand? Curious, she stopped teasing him and asked, "You still on fire for me?"

"Ravaged by flame," he said. "Day and night."

"What else?" She hardly knew what she meant, but still wanted to hear his answer.

His gaze was unwavering in the dull light. "I've woken up next to my best friend. And I can't believe it's really happened—that you're here, looking sleepy and sexy, and the same but somehow so different in my bed without clothes on. I can't believe I'm going to wake up next to you every morning. That I'm going to learn more about you—little things, amazing things, like that sound you made right before you woke up or how hot you take your showers." He paused, voice dropping to a rumble. "Or the feel of your release when I've had you for longer than a few minutes."

Her skin flushed, and emboldened, she rolled onto her side to face him. His attention leapt to her breasts, hungry, yet holding back.

"Want to learn that one now?" she asked.

"God, yes." She felt his answer in the pit of her stomach. "Yes."

Then his hands were on her, drawing her to him as his lips found hers. Slow and lavish, his tongue took her straight back to the night before. *That's right*, her mouth remembered, *that's his taste*. His naked skin sparked against hers, waking her in a rush before he pressed her onto her back with the hard length of his body.

She tensed, and he drew back in silent question.

"I—don't generally like missionary," she admitted, curling a hand around his shoulder, somehow seeking his protection against the threat of his own position.

"Doesn't feel good?" A line appeared between his brows. "Or something else?"

She swallowed at the old memory of the Burberry boy—at how she'd felt powerless and scared and trapped within his braced forearms. "Something else."

He scanned her face, serious. "You want to sit up? Turn over? Choose a wall, any wall? Table, chair, windowsill?"

She rolled her lips together a moment before she laughed. "All of the above."

"Anywhere except on top—not yet," he said, kissing outward along her left cheekbone. His breath was a soft shock in the shell of her ear. "I get to do things to you first."

She heated at his wicked promise, and found herself relaxing, loosening back onto the bed. On her back, with him above her. "I think this might be fine."

She *wanted* it to be. For her—for them.

He grinned back. "It's going to be more than fine."

Then he kissed her again, banishing thoughts of her past while his hand moved down to the waistband of her underwear, toying with the elastic, his fingers dipping beneath as far as his first knuckle and running across her stomach from one hip to the other. The touch teased her, flared heat between her legs in calling. *Down here.* His fingers ran back the other way and she lifted her hips a little with a gasp. *Come all the way down.*

"Just once, wasn't it?" he murmured against her mouth.

"I'll kill you," she said.

Chuckling, he slid down her body, tugging her underwear off over her feet. Settling at her hips, his erection snug against her outer thigh, he pressed an openmouthed kiss to the sensitive skin below her belly button—at the same time as his fingers pressed between her legs. Her body arched, she moved her hips against him, and he made a deep noise of satisfaction as he started to circle her.

Time passed, measured in his strokes.

Not that she had the mind to count.

Heat bloomed beneath his fingers. She gripped his shoulder tighter and tighter, almost embarrassed at how quickly her pleasure built. She'd hardly held on the night before, blamed it on years of anticipation and the thrill of finally being with Kris, but already, the heat at her core was threatening to spill beneath his touch.

On a moan, she stole a glance at where he lounged beside her, one arm draped over her waist, the other busy, so busy.

His gaze flicked up, and he smiled, his eyes glinting. "So ready."

"Maybe I like you," she said on a gasp.

"It's going to make this next bit a little harder," he said, ignoring her frown as he moved to settle between her thighs. His broad shoulders brushed against her skin, and something about all his strength and rough-hewn intensity serving her pleasure sent shivers right to her toes. *God above, there's a cowboy between my legs.* And his tongue was about to swagger all the way inside her. He held her stare, giving her time to call off what he had planned, then said, "Tell me when you're close," and bent to her core.

She'd thought she'd known heat. But as his tongue—as it slid over—*mother of*—as it slid *inside*—

It was a lick of fresh fire.

Her hands found the pillows, squeezing as she cried out. His puff of hot-breathed laughter only drove her higher. A mindless, *oh-yes-yes* stretch of bliss later, her face was pressed into her knuckles and tension was twisting tighter and hotter inside her, and she distantly found the focus to say, "Close."

With one hand on her stomach, he kept up the rhythm, building her higher, mouth and fingers working her with masterful precision, until—

He stopped.

Literally, just—stopped. He gently lifted his mouth from her and eased his fingers out.

Any thoughts that he was going to crawl up her body and shatter her from the inside flickered out when he stayed put. Stunned and teetering on the precipice, she released the pillows in trembling, half-numb hands. He gave a low growl, as if *he'd* been pulled from his peak, and bit her thigh with scraping teeth. Sensitivity heightened, she gasped—and gasped again when he cupped one hand between her legs, moving very lightly, and pressed a firm path down her thigh with the other.

"Um." Disbelieving, she forced herself to her elbows. "You lost my orgasm."

"I didn't lose anything." His voice was hoarse with desire and he swept a line of wet kisses along her inner thigh.

She throbbed in response.

"We're going to catch it on the way back up."

She stared. Body thrumming, aching, roaring for what he'd withheld.

"Frankie." He hovered between her legs, his cupped hand continuing to rub and his touch continuing to roam, enchanting her skin, sending sparks and jolts of delight racing back to her core. Sexual potential rolled off him in tidal waves—neither of them was done here. "I'm planning on edging you into another universe."

"What?" The excitement inside her was slipping, and an unfulfilled restlessness took its place. It was both agonizing and blissful, and she moved herself against his palm, trying to rebuild what he'd broken.

"You haven't been denied before?" It was his turn for disbelief. His free hand was running down her thigh, over her knee, down to her foot. Farther and farther from where she wanted him, but not breaking his touch or releasing his command of her body. "Just—trust me, okay?"

She surrendered to a whole-body shiver as his fingertips found the arch of her foot. "You meant to let that one go?"

He drew his bottom lip into his mouth, heavy-lidded gaze on her body stretched out before him. "M-hm."

"And you plan to do that again?"

His eyes locked on hers. "M-hmmm."

She lifted a leg, nudging him in the shoulder with her foot. "Get up here."

Eyes dark, he slid up her body until he covered her, and for a moment, she stopped breathing, caught by the reality of being naked in his arms. His torso seemed wider, safer, stronger now that she was underneath it. She ran a hand over the taut plane of his chest, aware of his heart thundering beneath. When her hand dipped, aiming south, he dropped his stomach on hers to block her path, and she gasped at the sensation of their bare bellies together.

Swallowing, she managed to say, "Spoilsport."

"Denial isn't easy for me either." He grazed his teeth lightly along her jaw, and as webs of pleasure spun down her spine, she rolled her hips to feel him hard and full against her. "And *that's* not helping."

"Not trying to help." She wrapped a leg around the back of his thigh and rolled again.

Groaning, he slipped a hand under his pillow and came back with a little packet. "Anticipation is good, too, you know."

"Uh-huh. Sure."

He was playing at exasperation, but she sensed his dark delight at her greed. After sheathing himself, he settled over her. His gaze seemed to sink into her heart. "You're really okay with this position?"

"Yes."

He spread his fingers into her hair. "Then let's find your next one," he murmured, and pushed inside her.

Oh, God. He was—this was—oh, *God.*

"You'll have to tell me again." He spoke against her neck and slid in deeper.

Eyes closed, head tilted back, she whispered, "Don't want to."

She never spoke during sex. Rarely made eye contact. She'd always tried to pretend her bedpartner wasn't really there, and when the soft somersault of release tumbled through her, she'd be straight back into her clothes and angling them out the door. She definitely had no experience with morning afters, but she was pretty sure they didn't usually go like this.

This . . . this felt like a proper first time.

The way she should have parted with her innocence all those years ago. On her own terms. In the embrace and care of a man who adored her. At ease enough to talk to him, tease him, look deep into his eyes as he pushed ever-deeper inside her.

It was different to last night. Frantic coupling in a work environment hardly lent itself to romance. But this bed cushioned her back against the impact of his thrusts, and with the drapes drawn and bed never-ending around her, she could almost believe they were the only people in existence.

"Frankie," he said, a sound of unfiltered worship.

As he worked a hand under the small of her back and tilted her hips—as he kissed her with such sincerity, her eyes welled—she slipped so far over a line she'd never crossed, she knew she'd finally done it.

Finally fallen.

Her childhood had made her guarded and distrustful of the world. She'd banished any hope from her mind of being treated better, leaving that wish to tunnel into her heart instead. She felt it sometimes—a hollow clamor for affection, a frail longing—but knowing the impossibility of such a thing, she'd done her best to ignore it. Now, she could feel Kris beneath her breastbone. Inside that hollow space. Not as hope, but certainty. He would treat her better than she'd ever been treated—better than she'd ever treated herself. He'd do what no one had ever done in her entire life.

He would love her.

Her whole body flushed with sensation. The pressure inside her was building, more intense than before, and her breathing grew so hard, so loud, she used it to carry his name from the edges of ecstasy. "*Kris.*"

"Fuck, sorry about this," he murmured in her hair, and pulled out so swiftly, she had no chance at stopping him. She clenched as if she could leap from the precipice without him, but hovered several thrusts away from flying as he shifted and wedged his thigh hard between her legs. While a part of her marvelled at his self-control, the rest of her was taking none of it.

"I warned you." Even though her body was humming—singing in suspense, alive with anticipation—she pushed herself up and started crawling across the bed. "I'm getting my knuckles and I'm going to kill you."

He caught her around the waist and dragged her back, drawing her into his lap and touching her all over as he murmured, "Trust me, trust me," and she said, "I'll make it quick, you could learn something," and he said, "No, you won't, just trust me," and she surrendered to his mouth when it came hot and urgent for hers.

She wriggled, more for the game this had become than any effort to escape him, and he twisted her, pinning her front-down on the bed. He was heavy against her back, erection nestled against her ass, his mouth instantly pulling on the sensitive spot where her shoulder swept up into her neck. Heat flooded her. Her muscles throbbed, ever-tightening. She was moaning, pleasure-drenched, wetter than she'd ever been.

Okay. Maybe he was onto something.

He reached down and slid a finger inside her. Not enough to finish her—just enough to torment, to make her buck against him. Practically vibrating with need, she angled her head and nipped none-too-gently at his forearm.

"The thanks I get," he muttered in her ear, and even that light brush of air rocketed through her blood.

Denial pushed her beyond thought—hypersensitive to every tiny pleasure, wordless with euphoria.

He resisted, and rubbed against her until her blood fizzed, and then kept on resisting. She shuddered as his hands praised her—caressed her sides and massaged her ass and swept across her breasts. It was only when she angled her hips and managed to get his tip inside her that she finally found his line.

On a strangled groan, he flipped her onto her back—and drove hard inside her.

Buried all the way in, he fell still, taut as a bowstring. One second, two . . . then he pulled back and started slow all over again, building her up until her tension was a tight tangle and her edges stretched and strained as her pleasure mounted higher. She'd never seen this mountain before, never known she could approach such a peak, but with his hand on her back again, angling her hips to receive his thrusts just right, he guided her two steps as a time, three, urging her to climb ever-higher.

On each stroke, friction dug in and *heaved* her pleasure with him. Layers and layers of it, like dense fabric, like silken fire, gathering and dragging and burning inside her on every thrust. Crazed with readiness, she pulled his bottom lip into her mouth and begged him to take more, more, *more.*

Finally, a swelling rush built inside her.

"Don't stop this time," she pleaded, clutching him against her.

"I won't." He rocked higher into her. "This is it."

And then, the pleasure he'd taken from her body, one gasp and moan and tremble at a time—all that tingling and bursting and surging—

He gave it *all* back.

It converged like the center of a storm, and then blew,

thundering outward, tackling her beneath an endless rolling beat. The strongest orgasm of her life.

Lungs empty and body wrecked, she was vaguely aware of Kris shuddering through his own ending. When he relaxed over her, she wound her legs around his hips, warm and glowing and too satisfied to speak.

It was a while before he asked, "Still want to kill me?" against her neck.

She smiled, moving her hips gently. "No. You win."

"You're telling me," he said, and raised his head and kissed her. Opening to him, she sensed an aching impatience gathering low in her chest, demanding to connect with him beyond what was possible. Even now, with him buried inside her and his tongue deep in her mouth, he was still too far away, and she longed to haul him through her rib cage and right into her beating heart.

Or was it less that he was too far away—but still too unknowable?

She'd spent years of friendship skirting around his edges. Holding back questions, keeping her distance. Well. Now she'd have to wait. Months, years even, because what she really wanted from her best friend was to *know* him, as utterly as she knew herself, and only time could offer such truth. Mornings wrapped in each other's arms; evenings deep in conversation; moments that tested and punished and rewarded them. Time would grant her the power to decode him one piece at a time until she understood the man he was, in all his complexity, and could fit seamlessly against him.

That was why she ached—for an intimate relationship.

And he would give it to her.

Eventually, he pulled back and said, "You're so perfect, I never want to move."

"But however will we eat?"

He grinned and her happiness soared. She raised a hand to the side of his face, stroking her thumb over his bottom lip, scarcely believing she was allowed to spend her life with him.

"Say it," he murmured. "Say what I can see in your eyes."

She blinked, startled, and focused on his chin. "I—"

Had never said it. Never heard it. She hardly knew how it was supposed to sound.

Panic kicked up her pulse and he made a soft sound of reassurance as his fingers circled her shoulder.

"I'll help," he said. "This is all you do. Just say . . ." And he paused, waiting until she looked up, right into his eyes. Her heart stuttered, like the pair of trembling hands she longed to hide behind, too shy to look his emotion in the face. But she did, kept her attention fixed on the affection raw and tender in his gaze as he said, "I love you."

It sounded like the gentle brush of his lashes against her heart as he saw all the way inside her; sounded like an extended palm, held out, waiting for her to take hold.

Her breath was fast, and she couldn't look away.

"Frankie," he said, whispering this time. "I love you."

As the silence stretched out, a tear slid down her cheek. Not because she was scared of his love or her own for him. Rather because she had a lifetime of fear inside her and his confession had just nudged some of it out.

"It's okay." He brushed the tear aside with his nose and murmured, "I know you do."

She wanted to confirm it, speak the words out loud, but as much as the past twelve hours seemed to disagree, she couldn't change her entire life overnight, and that included her emotional limits.

She looked back and hoped he could still see it in her eyes.

"Okay." Kris pushed higher onto his elbows, features growing serious. "You raised something significant earlier and I think it's time we finally did something about it."

Oh, hell. Her heart fluttered as she struggled to remember. What had she said? And what did he mean by earlier? They'd recently spoken about spending their lives together—God, surely he wasn't about to propose? Too soon, way too soon. Tension locked her jaw and she was halfway through planning her escape route before she got a hold of herself. Because this might be about her continuing to work for the royal guard—he'd mentioned that night in the tent that she could keep her position. Had he been advised otherwise? She should expect it. The partner of a king should be compassionate and virtuous—not combative and violent. Her gut churned as she remembered that just last night, walking the streets of Kiraly, she'd confessed to wanting a family of her own. Did he think now was as good a time as any to discuss producing heirs? Because it wasn't. He should at least let her go for a run first, and chase that with several hard drinks.

Her alarm flared at the intensity of his stare, until she demanded, "What?"

He grinned. "Breakfast."

Frankie emerged from his bathroom and suspected she finally understood why people went to day spas. She was used to handsy shower curtains and a vanity mirror that refused to show her head and torso at the same time, but Kris's vast, cream-tiled bathroom offered every luxury. The showerhead had the circumference of a patio table, a silver lever had brought water cascading down a glass wall in a gushing waterfall and a small sweep of tiled steps descended to a pool the size of his palatial bed. She'd run her toes over the surface, vowing to put it to good use later, and dried herself with a towel as soft as powdered sugar. Lush indoor plants grew green in large pots and dripped from high tiled ledges, while the lighting was the holy grail of illumination, displaying her skin at its healthiest in the full-length mirror. There were no bags or blemishes in sight, and she decided she was happy to be fooled by such clever visual trickery.

Kris waited for her beside the bed, dressed in jeans and a green plaid shirt.

She froze at what he was holding.

"For you." He quirked a brow and held the folded clothes out to her.

She didn't move. "What's that?"

"Your uniform."

"Interesting." She defaulted to an easy defense even though he'd see right through it. "Is it kink or a power trip to make me exhibit my lower status now that you've dominated me?"

Features tightening, he said, "Don't even try it."

She crossed her arms against the alarm pounding in her chest.

"You've never thought much of yourself, Frankie," he said. "After everything you told me last night, I understand why. But it's time to move on. You're worthy of your title. You grew up scamming the streets, sure, but you earned this position. You're head of personal security to my family and it's time you accepted that. This uniform won't push you further beneath me. It'll bring you closer." He extended it toward her again. "Wear it."

The folded navy trousers and shirt had gold-edged seams. It would mark her as an official employee of the crown—signal her status above her team and most other palace staff. It would prove that she'd done what she'd dreamed of after graduating high school. Found a better life—become something good.

"It's not part of a con," Kris said. "It's not a costume. You won't be deceiving anyone. It's *you*."

She rolled her lips together and hated that she couldn't stop staring at the neatly folded clothes. She wanted them so badly.

"You deserve to be here." He didn't move closer, but she sensed he wanted to. "Not just with me, or because of me. You deserve this in your own right. If we'd never met, you'd still deserve to work here, doing what you do."

It was a nice blue. Bold and respectable. A dignified blue.

"I trust you," he said. "Now you need to trust me."

Her pulse skipped. This prince trusted her to protect him.

"Take them, for God's sake," he said. "I'm hungry."

It was the prompt she needed. Avoiding his stare, she snatched the pile from him, not sure how else to handle the significance of finally possessing her worth.

"Good," he said quietly.

The fabric was cool, sturdy. Her finger moved along the bottom fold of the trousers, out of sight, stroking the weave in both caution and disbelief.

Then Kris held out an empty palm.

Her gut fell. This uniform would lead her forward—and he was making sure no one could look back the way she'd come.

With her uniform pressed to her chest, she found her bag from the night before. Returned to his side.

And handed him her brass knuckles.

His fingers closed over the cut of metal and the spiked tips seemed to cut into her lungs.

"You won't regret this," he murmured.

Throat tight, she nodded.

"Get changed." His gaze was soft with understanding. "Let's see who you really are."

12

Kris settled on a satisfied grin when Frankie stepped into his sitting room, tugging self-consciously at her top shirt button. Better to not make a big deal about how she was made for that uniform. The cut of the trousers, the crisp-edged collar, the status symbol of the gold thread. When she stopped fiddling, it would tap into her air of command and send it skyrocketing.

"That's just how top buttons feel," he said, and stood. "Ready?"

Hand lowering, she glanced around. "Where's this breakfast you promised?"

"In the blue parlor," he said. "Where I eat breakfast every morning."

Unease flashed in her eyes. "I thought we'd eat here together."

"No. We'll eat there together."

She swallowed. "In front of people?"

"You're the one who told the guards about us." He gestured for her to lead the way out, mainly to ensure she didn't try to hide under the bed. "I won't touch you outside of this room. To anyone who doesn't know, I'm just a prince walking with a member of the royal guard. Nothing suspicious about that."

She looked wary, but jerked her chin up and strode across the room. He followed, and as she reached for the door handle, it hit him that this was their first day as a couple. Him and Frankie. When they went their separate ways after breakfast, they'd still be together. His heart swelled so big that he reached around her to hold the door shut, sliding his other arm around her stomach, stealing one last moment of contact.

She shot a look up at him over her shoulder and muttered, "I really should expect this by now. What?"

"I love you."

He was allowed to say it—allowed to watch the words seep into her like sunlight.

Every trace of strain left her face and she smiled, cheeks pink, and gave a little nod. Unable to stop himself, he angled his head and kissed her, and for a while, all he knew was her taste.

"Alright, I get it," she said, pushing him off and looking flustered.

Laughing, he drew back so she could open the door. The first awkward moment—for Frankie—happened immediately, when she emerged to find Peter and Hanna standing guard. The pair bowed as Kris stepped out behind her, pretending not to notice that their superior had spent the night with their prince.

"Good morning, Your Highness," Peter greeted, straightening. "Ma'am."

"Morning," he said. "We're off to breakfast."

Frankie's face was bright red. She looked mortified and ready to bolt.

"I've heard it's pancakes this morning," Hanna said politely.

"Great." His stomach rumbled. "Frankie loves pancakes. Don't you?"

She flung a desperate *I-don't-know-if-I-can-do-this* glance at him.

He casually slid his thumb into his front pocket and waited.

"Yes," she said through clenched teeth.

He smiled. There—she'd contributed to the conversation. The first step toward a future where she'd walk out his door and greet his guards in her stride.

Kris briefly caught Hanna's eye. The woman raised a hand to the collar of her own uniform, and mouthed, *Wow.*

He raised a brow as if to answer, *I know, right?*

Then he said, "Let's go," and Frankie fell into step beside him, his guards following behind. As they rounded a corner, he asked, "Was that so bad?"

"I don't know." Her cheeks were still pink. "It's just—a whole new dynamic to figure out between me and my team. I'm not just their boss anymore. I'm your—"

He eyed her, gratified that he could suggest, "Girlfriend?"

She almost looked shy. "Yeah?"

"Yes," he said firmly. "And I get it. But the two aren't mutually exclusive. Stepping out my door shouldn't be a changeover from one to the other. You can be both."

"I'll work on it." She tugged at the top of her uniform again. "I've never been a girlfriend before."

"And I've never had one."

It should have bothered him. That his life with Frankie would be set on a public stage, their status exposing them to endless demands and intrusions of privacy, expectation that would surely strain the bond of the most seasoned long-term couple—and neither of them had even been in a relationship. And he'd heard relationships weren't easy. It would be like learning to swim together in the middle of the ocean, and being told, *also, there are sharks.* They would get things wrong—panic, make bad decisions, communicate poorly, and all within the stretched-thin, rigorous confines of palace life.

Oh, and with a target on his back.

Actually. *That* did bother him.

Entering the blue parlor resulted in Frankie's second awkward moment when she caught sight of their breakfast companions. Tommy, obviously, was there with a mug of black coffee in his hand and a closed book beside him, but thanks to Kris's dawn text message, Mark and Ava sat on the nearest side of the table, Darius sitting between them.

Frankie halted in the doorway and spoke under her breath. "You didn't tell me they'd be here."

His family had looked around at their entrance. Mark was pretending not to smile, while Ava wore an expression of subdued delight. Tommy's gaze cut between them once before he returned to his coffee. Darius sat up straight, his eyes bright and latched onto Frankie.

"You've kind of met them before," Kris muttered dryly, wishing he hadn't promised not to touch her. She was starting to splash in this new ocean and his hand on her back would be helpful to them both right now. "And I told you I was going to tell them this morning."

"I didn't know you meant *with me*." And then she darted into the corridor and dragged in a bewildered Hanna, ushering her into position on the inside of the door. "I need someone else normal in here."

"You belong with us," was all he said, and moved to sit down, keeping a seat empty between him and Tommy. None of the brothers used the chair at the head of the table. "Morning, everyone."

"Good morning, Kristof," Ava greeted smoothly. "Thank you for inviting us."

"Thanks for coming. Let's start." He reached for a platter of blueberry, banana, and butter pancakes. The serving staff had long since learned that this royal family dished up for themselves, and he took two of each flavor, intently aware that Frankie still stood rigid across the room.

"Hey, Darry," he said, pouring maple syrup over the stack. "What do you think of the palace?"

He was only half-aware of Darius turning to look up at him. Kris was asking a lot of Frankie—pushing her into self-acceptance at a dizzying rate. She could do it. If she was going to spend her life with royalty, she had to be capable of pivoting fast, mentally and emotionally, and that meant kicking self-doubt to the curb. They'd have too many other challenges.

Darius's eyes were wide. "It's so big. And beautiful."

Ava ran a hand lightly over his hair, her lips pinching. "We've promised to show him the stables before we leave."

"Good timing," Kris replied. "The quarter horses have been settled in."

Mark grinned. "I know."

"They're magnificent," Tommy said, dishing up four butter pancakes. He hesitated, jaw tightening, before topping off the stack with a blueberry one, reminding Kris that Jonah used to make epic batches of blueberry pancakes for breakfast during foaling season. He'd come around to their ranch bright and early, and they'd all wake exhausted from the accumulation of long, hard days to the smell of sweet cooking batter and pan-warmed syrup. In recent years, Frankie had joined them, often halfway through the first batch by the time they'd shuffled out into the kitchen.

Under the table, Kris toed the leg of her chair, pushing it out a little.

Her attention snapped to him.

Then Tommy spoke without looking at her. "It's getting cold, Frankie."

"Yeah, Franks." Mark was setting another pancake on Ava's plate. "Come and try this chocolate maple topping. Just don't drink it all."

"I want to talk to you about my bridal shower," Ava said, turning to eye Frankie over her shoulder. "And I'd prefer not to shout."

Darius half-twisted out of his chair to follow his mother's glance and worked up the courage to say, "Hi, Frankie!"

After a pause, Hanna reached out and nudged her encouragingly in the back.

"Okay, okay." The strain eased around Frankie's mouth as she added, "Hey, Darius," and moved to take her seat.

"I have some news." Kris caught her eye as she pushed in beside him, and accidentally-on-purpose brushed her hand as he reached for the coffee pot. "Frankie's my girlfriend."

She flushed and held her mug out to him, silently demanding fuel.

"About time," Tommy said, but gifted them with a rare smile.

"Congratulations." Mark smiled, absently running a hand across Ava's back. "I would say welcome to the family, Frankie, but you've been a part of us for years."

Face down, Frankie mumbled her thanks. Not because she didn't care—but because they were the only real family she'd ever known and Mark's acknowledgement that it ran both ways was probably too much for her to process openly.

"You can be my second bridesmaid." Ava leaned forward excitedly. "How do you feel about emerald green? Zara has already chosen it for her dress."

"She looks incredible in green." Kris lifted the pancake platter for Frankie to dish up. "They're all good," he added to her as she hesitated. "Try them all."

"Perfect." Ava sounded thrilled. "Green it is."

Frankie selected one of each, not looking at the princess as she said, "Has Prince Cyrus decided when he's arriving yet?"

"He'd like to stay for two weeks," Ava said. "One before the wedding and one after."

"I'll be assigning Gul to him." Frankie accepted the chocolate maple syrup from Mark. "What exactly does a prince get up to on a holiday in Kiraly?"

"Oh. I don't know." Ava poured Darius more juice. "I was hoping Zara might take him around town. They know each other."

"Great idea," Frankie said, tone a little higher than usual.

"Yes. So, the bridal shower is this Friday," Ava said.

And as she explained that it was three days away, and it would be in a feminine-chic cocktail lounge in the city, and that she would only have a handful of guests, and that the bachelor party would meet up with them later in the night for a traditional Keleharian ceremony, Kris sat back and exchanged glances with his brothers. They all seemed tuned into the fact that their family was shifting. They had partners at the table, and a child. And after twenty-five years of being an unbreakable trio, letting others in didn't unknot their bond as he'd first suspected, but rather shifted their position on the cord to fit the extra beads. They were family. They might not always exist shoulder to shoulder, but they'd always be on the same string.

Then Tommy looked at his untouched pancakes, features strained, and the moment turned bitter in Kris's mouth.

When Ava concluded with, "And wear something bright, please," Kris leaned back to look at Tommy around Frankie.

"You still looking into our family history, Tom?"

"Yes," he said, and at Mark's frown, explained, "There's a lot to learn from looking back. I want to understand the relationship we've had with our people throughout our rule. The good and the bad. And the interesting."

"Give us an interesting one, then," Mark said.

"Okay." Tommy paused, eyes narrowing. "Did you know that about six generations back, we had a succession dispute? The third prince in line for the throne went to war and never returned. His two older brothers died, leaving behind no male heirs, so the crown went to the son of the fourth brother, who'd also died. Almost twenty years later, a young man came to court claiming to be the son of the third prince, who had survived war, but been too ashamed by Kiraly's loss in battle to return home."

Ava leaned forward, curious. "Was the claimant deemed the rightful heir?"

"No." Tommy shook his head slightly. "His father supposedly died during the trial, so couldn't be brought home as conclusive proof. The royal family offered the man a place at court and an annual allowance to let the dispute rest, and he grudgingly accepted."

"That is interesting," Kris said, hiding his unease behind a lazy stretch.

He hadn't meant to bring the conversation so close to succession disputes. Was this how Tommy thought of himself? A royal inconvenience to be placated? Granted a home within the palace, but treated like a risk to be managed? No. That kind of thinking would grow like a noxious root in his brother's silences. Yet Tommy *did* resent Kris for leapfrogging his way onto the throne. In taking the choice of ascension from him, Kris had rendered Tommy a token figure—royalty in name only. For what use was a prince without a role in succession?

Damn it all. Kris couldn't go back and change the moment he'd demeaned his brother; he couldn't step aside and let Tommy take a crown he didn't want. But Tommy's animosity was like silt in their shared waterskin, a slight off taste every time he drank, discoloring their exchanges until the day Kris would tip his head back and have to swallow the lot without objection.

He needed to face this head-on. Clean up the mess he'd made, and quickly.

The parlor doors swung open as Philip entered, tall and thin and impeccable, halting in the center of the room like an erect jousting stick, ready to poke holes in Kris's approach to pretty much anything. He bowed low. "Good morning, Your Majesty. Your Highnesses." Straightening, his attention moved around the table. "Darius. Frankie."

Darius mumbled his hello, clearly not sure who Philip was, while Frankie swallowed her mouthful and said, "Hair looks good today."

Hanna snickered from her position inside the doors. When Philip shot a glare at her, she lowered her face to stare intently at her shirt buttons.

"I must say how delightful it is to see you all together." Philip gave a surprisingly genuine smile—until his attention landed on Kris and something hard glinted in his eyes. "Princess Ava, it's heartening that your statement to the press has been received so positively. I understand you've been concerned about your brief return to the spotlight, but might I reassure you that while understandably curious, none of the public's speculation about Darius runs negative. They're thrilled that Markus is courting you. In fact, our public relations officer has informed me that you two now have the most fictional works out of any Kiralian Royal Family pairing, which is a positive sign. The nation is rooting for you."

"Wait, what?" Kris raised a hand, baffled. "What do you mean *fictional works?*"

"Kristof." Philip exchanged an amused glance with Frankie. "People like to write stories about you. They've been at it since you three strode out of your ranch and into these halls."

"But . . . we're real."

"Real royalty," his advisor answered. "And therefore, a perfect fantasy."

Kris looked sideways at Frankie. "You knew?"

She tapped the emblem on her uniform. "We scan any content related to the royal family."

Intrigued, he leaned closer. "Who have I been paired with?"

"That is beside the point," Philip said, as Frankie rolled her eyes. "Now, a matter of business. There is an annual pride parade coming up next month. Prince Noel always made an appearance to support the festivities, and it would be an appreciated gesture if one of you three could attend. That is, if you support the—"

"Of course we do." Kris cut him off. "I'll go."

Hanna made a coughing, scoffing sound, and Philip turned to her, his eyes wide with affront.

"Problem, Hanna?" Kris asked.

"No, Your Highness." She inclined her head in apology. "It's just—you're literally the straightest person I've ever met."

He cocked a brow. "That doesn't mean I think everyone should be."

Her mouth turned down at the corners, conceding his point. "If you go, would you require me to work that day? Because I signed up to walk with the ace procession."

Philip actually spluttered.

"It's fine, Phil. I want my guards to talk to me." He returned his attention to Hanna. "And no, that sounds important."

"Agreed, Johansson," Frankie said, pouring more syrup over her breakfast. "You go. I'll reassign his security for the day."

Kris raised a shoulder. "Or I don't have to go? Maybe . . ." Very carefully and as nonchalantly as he was able, he turned to his brother. "Tommy? You want to do it?"

Tommy's jaw clenched and he took a long swallow of coffee. His hands were still, but a tremble of the tablecloth betrayed his legs were jiggling. Eventually, he set his mug down and murmured, "The crowds."

"Fair enough." Kris's gaze skimmed over Mark's in a split-second exchange of disappointment. "We'll run through the details later, Philip."

"Thank you, Your Highness. Enjoy your day, everyone." Philip bowed again. When he straightened, he looked Kris dead in the eye. "I'll meet you in the tower shortly."

Anger tightened Kris's bearing as his advisor swept from the room. No guesses how that encounter was going to play out. Philip would make his disapproval of his relationship with Frankie clear—and Kris wouldn't tolerate a second of it.

Fun morning ahead.

Before long, Mark and Ava excused themselves to take Darius to the stables, and as the doors closed in their wake, Frankie's phone chimed from her pocket.

She slid it out and then shot to her feet. "Shit. I've got to run." Jamming her phone back, she looked alarmed as a waiter appeared and drew out her chair. "Oh, ah, thanks." She stepped away from the table. "Some jackass scaled the palace wall and took the fast route down on the other side. He's mangled both his arm and the topiary, and the head gardener is pissed." She then seemed to experience her third and final awkward moment of the morning, hesitating with her gaze on Kris's mouth, a goodbye kiss in her eyes. She turned away, gave him a light slap on the shoulder and said, "I'll find you tonight."

"Stay safe." He leaned back in his chair, hands clasped behind his head and elbows wide, ready to take this chance to talk to Tommy alone.

But Tommy stood abruptly. Without a word—without so much as a parting glance—he swiped up his book and strode across the parlor in Frankie's wake, leaving his breakfast uneaten.

Confused, Kris rose to his feet. "Tom—"

"Don't." Tommy spun around, his voice hard like a staff cracked against the marble floor between them. His features were a mess of pain, uncertainty, and command. *"Don't follow me."*

Startled, Kris dropped back into his chair and stared after him.

It wasn't that Tommy had hardly ever spoken to him like that, or that Kris had screwed up worse than he'd imagined, or that hurting his brother so deeply was like taking a sledgehammer to the walls of his own heart.

Tommy had never sounded more like a king.

Philip marched into the tower study as the morning sun reached the far edge of Kris's desk. His hands were balled, elbows bent slightly by his sides, but instead of staring Kris down in preparation for the usual battle of *experience in royal life* versus *actual royal person*, his gaze flicked around the room like he couldn't bear to make eye contact.

An odd approach to the argument Kris knew was coming.

"Lost something, Phil?" he asked, leaning back in his chair.

His advisor stopped in front of the desk. Sunlight exposed the grooves beneath his eyes, the lines around his mouth. Did he always look so tired? He didn't move, just stared at the back of Kris's laptop with the air of someone daring themselves to speak their mind, but teetering on the brink of backing out.

Intrigued, Kris waited.

"Sometimes, Your Highness," the man finally said, "your charm and complete disregard for other people reminds me of Prince Noel."

The accusation struck Kris like a close-range arrow. *Complete disregard for other people.* That was how he'd treated

Tommy, wasn't it? Blithely shoved him aside without consultation or consideration. He was an asshole and a poor excuse for a brother, and as disgust raided his pride, he rallied sarcasm as a defense. "Loved him as much as you love me?"

Philip paused. A peculiar look tugged across his face as he finally met Kris's gaze. Then it was another long wait, suspended in Philip's sad silence, before the man said quietly, "I loved him considerably more than you."

Oh.

Oh.

"Oh," Kris said, blindsided, and thought, *Why the hell didn't I know this?*

Probably because of his complete disregard for other people.

"And he loved me," Philip said, his shoulders settling beneath that truth. "But unlike Markus's actions for Ava, Noel never dreamed of defying his position for me. We were lovers for fifteen years—and almost no one knew. Just King Vinci, Prince Aron, and a few members of the household. I kept my own room in the servants' quarters to avoid suspicion." He looked down, fidgeting with the silver signet ring Kris had never thought to notice until now. "He was comfortably out, if you didn't already know, so he didn't hide our relationship because he feared a homophobic scandal. Not that Kiraly would cause one." Philip took in a large breath, his brow a wavering line of pain. "He hid me because I was common."

Stunned and stricken, Kris had no idea what to say.

"I sat at the love of my life's funeral and no one knew to say how sorry they were for my loss."

"Philip . . ." Kris blinked back the sudden heat behind his eyes.

Philip focused on him, his gaze fierce. "Except Frankie. She found me in the crowd—risked you seeing her—to squeeze my hand and pass me more tissues."

God, that woman.

Philip raised a finger. "Don't you *dare* treat her the same way."

Don't—*what?* Kris sat forward with a lurch. "But you . . ." He gestured in bewilderment. "You told me that she wasn't good enough. You warned me *against* her."

Philip pulled back, insulted. "I did no such thing."

"Yes, you did." And it had made seamless sense with his previous behavior. Months ago, Philip had tried to push Mark into that strategic engagement with Ava in an effort to cultivate the royal line. "That day in the sitting room when we were watching Frankie in the courtyard. You warned me to be careful."

"I was warning you to be careful *with her,*" Philip said, indignant. "Warning you not to hurt her."

Disbelief hung from Kris's jaw. So . . . *so,* that meant Philip hadn't angled for the strategic engagement out of heartlessness—but because personal experience had taught him that marrying within one's station was a nonnegotiable royal rule?

And he'd since decided that was absurd.

"What the hell, man?" Kris ran a hand over his forehead. "A little less ambiguity next time."

"Right." Philip's knees unlocked and he sagged slightly. "Sorry."

Kris gestured to one of the chairs opposite his desk. "Sit down."

The man dropped into it. "Thank you."

"I would never hide Frankie." Kris didn't have to consider what he said next. "But you and Noel were together for fifteen years. Living in this palace together. That's effectively a common-law marriage. That's pretty significant." He paused, and Philip's frown betrayed he had no idea where this was going. "I'd like to honor your place in the Jaroka family. Move you out

278

of the servant's quarters and into a royal family suite where you belong. I assume we have more of those. And I'd like you to eat with us, sometimes. I won't be a jerk. We'll do Sunday night dinners or something."

Philip had gone pale; his bottom lip trembled.

"Please," Kris said, sure he'd never said the word with more conviction.

The man's next breath was a gulp. The one after that shuddered, and then he turned his face away, covering his eyes to hide his tears.

A yes, then.

Careful not to rush him, Kris pressed his fist to his mouth and turned his gaze out the nearest window. Well. He hadn't seen this coming. When his shock subsided, Philip rested both hands on the arms of his chair and blinked up at the ceiling. His foot tapped lightly against the carpet, betraying his grasp on control was tenuous.

"Hey, I just realized," Kris said, aiming to distract him. "If you'd married Noel, you'd be my uncle right now."

Philip's attention snapped to him, and after staring in apparent consternation, he made a show of recoiling. "Ghastly thought."

Kris pulled a face. "Yeah."

But perhaps not quite as ghastly as either of them pretended.

"Okay." Philip withdrew a handkerchief from his breast pocket and dabbed at his face. "Shall we move on to the issues of the day?"

An hour later, they wrapped up their most harmonious meeting yet, and Philip bowed before moving to see himself out.

"Philip," Kris said.

His advisor turned at the door. Their gazes connected.

Kris rose, swallowing the ache that returned to his throat. For fifteen years, this man had been concealed by his lover like a dirty, common-bred secret. He'd loved Prince Noel; he had been loved but not respected in return. He'd been head of personal security before Frankie took over the role, which meant he'd have been in charge of keeping his own relationship a royal family secret. For all that suppressed humiliation, Philip had still lost his life partner and hadn't been free to openly grieve. He'd thrown himself into the task of training cowboys—who'd arrived clueless to fill the position of the man he'd lost.

If Kris had been wearing his hat, he'd have taken it off and held it to his chest.

Instead, he placed a hand over his heart.

"I'm so sorry for your loss."

13

The investigation sucked Frankie into a time-lapse of interviews, research, and theorizing. She kept the folder of Tommy's attackers on her desk, dragging it open every time she had a spare second. In between organizing security for Ava's bridal shower and Mark's bachelor party, she visited the Bull's Quest pub where the anarchists had met—showing photos of the men in question to the proprietor, and learning they'd been meeting with a group in the rear function room for years.

"Twice a month, without fail," the man said. Sweat clung to the roots of his thinning brown hair, either from the summer heat thick in his office or the presence of a senior member of the royal guard who'd declined his offer to sit down.

"What's the group?" Frankie asked.

His brow buckled nervously. "What?"

"Chess? Goat yoga? Cuddle parties?" She arched a brow. "What do they do in there?"

He looked as if he didn't know whether to laugh or beg her not to hurt his family. "I don't know."

"You don't know?"

"Disclosing their activities isn't a requirement of booking, ma'am."

"Huh." She narrowed her eyes. "You're not avoiding telling a royal guard that you host anarchists in your fine establishment, are you?"

He sank into the chair with a cringe. "All they do is talk. And, you know, drink a hell of a lot."

"How lucrative," she said. "Do new people join or has it always been the same members?"

"Uh. The group used to be bigger years ago, but about half the members just stopped turning up. Sometimes I notice new faces, so they must take on new members."

Good. "How about you introduce me at the next meeting? I can be a Bull's Quest patron with views that you've recently learned align with theirs."

"Of course." His nod was eager. "Actually. There's a jeweler in Ledge Square that sells those silver pins. If you wanted to seem enthusiastic, you could get one made ahead of time."

"Thanks." She'd do that. "When's their next booking?"

"Uh." He typed on his laptop, pressing backspace more than any other key. "Next Sunday night."

"Call me if that changes." She stepped forward and wrote her number in the margin of an invoice on his desk. Then she showed him photographs of Tommy and Jonah's attackers. "Did these men ever attend? Years ago?"

He considered each face carefully, and when he looked up, his frown was wary. "Is there a problem, ma'am?"

Would she be here if there wasn't? "Answer my question, please."

"Yes, I think so. But they were alright. And the men who still meet here—they seem like decent people."

Jeez. Her father would string this guy up like a paper chain and shake the money from his pockets. Probably already had.

"Yeah." She turned to leave. "That's where they get you."

On Wednesday morning after breakfast with Kris, she received confirmation that the men under surveillance had not just worked on the west wing renovations, but more relevantly, on the balcony construction. *Closer.* As she dug into progress reports, time logs, and purchase orders, searching for red flags, she couldn't shake the feeling these men were soldier ants. If they really had contributed to the balcony's shitty structural integrity, who had planned it? Who'd been so sure the royal family would dine up there at all?

And did they have new plans now? Instructions to harm Kris or Mark or Tommy?

Or all three at once?

Focused to the point of fixation, it wasn't until midafternoon on Thursday that she read the memo from housekeeping informing her that Philip Varga was being relocated from the servants' quarters to a royal family suite at the order of Prince Kristof.

She was out of her office in seconds.

"Johansson," she said, a hand over her ear. The door to the security suite sealed shut behind her as she raced toward the nearest staircase. Her skin prickled; her head felt too light. "Report your primary's location."

"Summer drawing room," came the woman's reply. "Third floor."

"Alone?" Frankie's shoulder protested as she swung hard around the bottom post of the bannister. She launched toward the first floor, her boots taking every second step.

"Meeting with several members of parliament. Another half an hour at least."

"Get him out."

Hanna's voice turned hushed with concern. "Is he in danger?"

"No." Pressure spread across Frankie's chest, a metal breastplate secured too tightly under her skin. "I need ten minutes. Say he has to sign something as a matter of urgency."

"Yes, ma'am."

By the time her footsteps pounded down the arched corridor toward the third-floor drawing room, her brow was damp. Hanna slipped inside the room at her approach, and a half-minute later, emerged with a bemused Kris in tow.

"Another contract? I just signed—" He broke off with a frown when he saw Frankie waiting, hands on her waist and breathing hard. "Hey, you okay?"

"I'll bring him back," she told his guards, and then, without looking at him, she said, "Follow me."

She set off the way she'd come and Kris matched her pace in silence. After a quick call out over comms, she cut toward the portrait hall as the nearest unoccupied space, a grand room of blushing pale pink wallpaper and gold-framed portraits.

The sound of the door closing echoed among his immortalized ancestors.

"What's going on?" His voice was low behind her as his hands rested on her shoulders. "You're upset."

"You." She spun to face him, gratitude thick in her throat. "Acknowledged Philip."

Comprehension slid across his face in a one-sided smile as his hands resettled on her shoulders. "Turns out he's family."

Her muscles were stiff under his palms. "You didn't think to mention this last night? The night before?"

"I figured you'd already been told."

Technically, she had. The memo had been sent to her on

Tuesday. "But you've always spoken to him like—like you don't even . . ."

"Like him?" he asked wryly.

She nodded, biting her bottom lip, scarcely understanding what Kris had done.

"He warned me not to hurt you." A shadow flickered in his eyes and he stepped into her, his touch drifting down her arms and sliding around her hands. "Not to keep you a secret, like Noel did to him. Obviously that's never been an option for me, but I respect his intentions." The pads of his fingers brushed over her knuckles—rough skin and reassurance. "Not only is he the closest thing I have to a living uncle, but I got the impression you two are pretty special to each other. So that makes him family in an entirely different way."

Frankie ducked her face. Philip had softened toward her over the years she'd reported from Sage Haven. He'd learned to understand her; to say the right thing, as best he could, when guilt left her struggling to maintain her cover. In turn, she'd discovered his stuffy chest pumped with a loyal heart that cared more keenly for the royal family than his duty alone required.

"Am I wrong?" His question was quiet.

Eyes stinging, she shook her head.

"Hey," he said, and she looked up at his strange tone. "You know how your father taught you his line of work? Teaching you to embody the con as if you were born for it? Yet here you are, trained for this role by a different man, wearing the same regalia that he once wore." He pressed a kiss to her forehead. "Can you see where I'm going with this comparison?"

Commanding security was Philip's own kind of legacy—and he'd trained her and passed the position on to her like a daughter. Sniffling, she said, "Stop it."

Kris's smile was gentle—a barefooted approach through the mess her father had left inside her.

How could he be so intuitive? He came from a strictly traditional family: mother and father, and brothers forged in blood and birth. His royal ancestral line was neat, perfectly traceable where it wanted to be, all unbroken unions and children within marriage.

Philip wouldn't appear on either of their family trees—unconnected by marriage or descent—yet Kris had written him in without hesitation.

On an unintelligible murmur that only her heart understood, she kissed him.

His mouth opened on a sigh, tasting of sweetened coffee, and his hand slid to cradle her head as his tongue blended with hers. Slow and soft, his kiss was like a cushion that remembered the shape of her, giving and guiding as she sank into him. She pulled him closer, sensing him start to swell and stretch as their bodies locked together, but he didn't rise to take control. He didn't act like he wanted to; he leashed his desire so far down, he was nothing but a warm, receptive lover on the surface. This kiss was hers.

He was hers.

She gripped his arm at the wobble in her chest—the sensation of losing her balance on a path she'd walked her entire life.

He held steady as stone beneath her palm.

"Frankie," he murmured when she drew back. Lashes low, breath heavy. "Don't stop."

She almost caved to his plea. "We both have work to do."

He released her with a groan.

She fought the urge to chase his touch. Work. She had work to—

"Oh no," she said, gaze skimming the portraits on the wall over Kris's shoulder. There was a reason the memo had been sent to her in the first place. A bubble of pained amusement rose up

286

her sternum. Was it funny? It wasn't funny. "Philip's going to hate this."

Kris frowned at her, his eyes kiss-dark and distracted. "What? Why?"

"You've essentially named him part of the family. Presented him with a royal suite. His own manservant. An ongoing invitation to dinner at your table."

"*Our* table," he corrected her in a low voice, shifting closer.

"Word will spread within the palace."

"That's okay, though." He ran the backs of his fingers down her neck, and shivering, she curled her fingers around his wrist, holding him still. "It's his decision whether or not to explain his relationship with Noel. The point is that the palace staff will know we consider him family and will treat him like it."

"That's exactly *my* point."

Finally, he met her gaze in question.

"His status has shifted. He's not an heir, but he's valuable. Possible leverage. I have no choice." She saw comprehension dawn with a glint in his eyes. "He used to monitor the security team's every move—now they'll have to monitor his."

Naturally, Frankie's softness about the way Kris had treated Philip didn't flow over into any other matter. Like, say, where he could find Tommy. For days, she'd refused to tell him, and as she escorted him from the portrait hall back to the summer drawing room, she held firm.

"Can you at least give me a hint?" he said, tasting grit in his mouth.

Kris had tried calling him—a lot—and Tommy had finally answered and asked him for space. Tommy's distance felt like the bottom falling out of Kris's world.

"That's his prerogative." Frankie cast him an exasperated glance. "Stop trying to exploit my position. This is between you two."

Frustration surged beneath his civility for the remainder of his meeting. Tommy hadn't come to breakfast the past few mornings, and Kris had worked until late. Instead of hunting his brother down after-hours, prowling the palace for the kind of sheltered spaces Tommy preferred, he'd been obliged to play nice and dine with visiting dignitaries. Important in its own way, but he'd be led like a horse in a harness from one critical matter to the next if he didn't plant his feet.

Tonight, his only duty was to his brother.

"A ride before the drinks reception, Your Highness?" Peter asked as Kris thrust himself from the drawing room. His guards bracketed the door, features composed in the face of his unconcealed temper.

"No." The rider in him winced, longing to be on horseback at a gallop. Wind loud in his ears, eyes watering, lungs working like bellows. "No ride. No drinks reception. Just Tommy. Tell me where he is and don't suggest I find him myself."

Peter cleared his throat lightly. "He's in the stables, Your Highness."

"He's—" Kris blinked, and softened fractionally. "You're sure?"

"Totally sure," Hanna said with a nod.

"Then let's go."

At the royal stables, Kris burst through the entrance in a glowering temper, and within moments, every groom and stable hand swiftly and silently exited through the rear doors. He'd never seen a mass exodus look so knowing.

Tommy was definitely here.

In the time it took Kris to swallow his impatience, Tommy had noted the quiet and poked his head out of a stall halfway up the stable. His hair was ruffled with work; the top few buttons of his plaid shirt were undone. His features shuttered when he saw Kris.

"Oh," he said, and pulled back inside the stall.

Yeah. *Oh.* Hands balling, Kris strode up the aisle, scarcely noticing the horses in their loose boxes. The stable was huge and perfectly presented with a white high ceiling and pristine stalls. Large enough for the horses to stand or lie down, each stall was fitted with partitions that allowed them to see their companions but not engage through the white vertical bars of the stall guard. The sound of a latch snicked the silence and Kris lunged forward just in time to stop the sliding stall door from opening.

"Kris," Tommy said, his crisp tone adding *get out of my way.*

"Tomas," he said, his own tone adding *not fucking likely.*

The door was just below shoulder-height, the stall guard bars on top halting at their chins. They stood precisely at eye level, and Kris stared back at a face he'd never recognized as a reflection of his own. It didn't matter that they were identical. Tommy used his features so differently that Kris hardly understood how people could mistake them. Tommy wore his sharp: his eyes razor-cut from all the books he'd read, his jaw and cheekbones honed by self-control, and his mouth perpetually hard, as if the hand of his own mind clamped over it.

"Mark isn't here to handle this for us." Kris's voice was as unrelenting as the concrete underfoot. "We have to do it ourselves, and that means you need to listen to me."

"Go on." Tommy's attention slid darkly to where Kris barred his retreat. "Since you've sweet-talked me into cooperating."

Kris's fingers tightened around the bars. "I'm sorry."

Tommy held his stare without reaction. A sleek, sorrel quarter horse watched on curiously behind him.

"I am." Regret was like a broken rib inside him—it throbbed with every movement. "I'm so sorry."

Tommy swallowed, glancing to one side. "For what?"

"Assuming you weren't capable," he said, pain bright in his chest. "Making you feel useless. Not noticing sooner that it'd pushed you away." He inched closer, the toes of his boots coming up against the door rail. "I'm sorry this life is the last thing you wanted, and that I haven't been around to help you to adjust."

Bitterness curled around Tommy's top lip.

"I get that I messed up when I took this role from Mark," Kris continued, and imagined Mark standing beside them, nodding encouragingly at his attempt at peace. "I should never have said it like that. Like you didn't count. Like you didn't deserve to be a part of that decision. But I did and I can't change it. I'm sorry. I never meant to hurt you. I—I don't think I ever *could* mean to hurt you."

After a moment, Tommy's jaw softened as if he'd unclenched his teeth.

"If it helps," Kris said, "my stupid heroics have left me training to replace Mark as the damned king, and it's endless and thankless and I'm terrified."

His brother's brow dipped. "You have Frankie to support you."

"I know." Kris had believed that with Frankie by his side, he'd be capable of shouldering a king's burden—but he'd meant in addition to his brothers. Not as a replacement. "But you and Mark are my baseline support. I was made with you guys. I don't know this life without you. I'm not *supposed* to." A tree couldn't stand without its roots. "And you're not supposed to get by without us, either, Tom."

At that, his brother turned his back. The horse shifted forward, lowering its head, and Tommy ran a hand gently down its nose.

"It's not you," Tommy said quietly.

Kris wanted to slide the door open and stand beside his

brother until Tommy looked at him, like he'd always done as a boy, because then, shoving into Tommy's personal space had been the only way to make him talk. But Tommy was safely isolated. Kris wouldn't enter the stall of a horse that didn't know him.

"What do you mean?" Kris didn't understand. "Why avoid me if it isn't about me?"

Tommy didn't answer, his posture strained.

Kris held down his frustration. "I need you around," he said. "That's what I'm trying to say. Don't hide from me. Please? This king thing is too big for me to manage without you. I can't do it. Not like this."

Tommy froze. The horse snorted and he carefully resumed patting.

Kris wished his stare could grab the back of his brother's shirt and haul him closer. "Tell me how I can make this better."

"You can't." Tommy's strong shoulders were rigid. "It's not you."

A different kind of regret panged in Kris's chest and he lowered his voice. "I thought you were doing okay."

Tommy lowered his head. "I wanted you to be wrong. About skipping me. I wanted to prove that I could cope." He scoffed in disgust. "I tried going into the city a few weeks ago. I asked my guards to find a quiet bar with pool tables. Halfway there, I had a panic attack. We were in a grocery-store parking lot for thirty-five minutes before I could breathe properly."

Kris muttered a curse.

"I took it out on you." Tommy angled his head to one side. Not looking at Kris, but no longer blocking him out. "I've been feeling like shit and envying how easily you move through life. You can be around people. Talk to them. Make them like you. You forgave Frankie." He paused, and Kris saw his throat move on a hard swallow. "And here I am, freaking out at the thought of being in a half-empty bar holding a fucking pool cue."

"Well, you've always sucked at pool, so the thought *should* scare you."

Tommy huffed out a breath, shooting Kris a wry glance over his shoulder. Then he sobered. "Sorry."

"Yeah." Kris lowered his forehead to the bars as relief unwound him. "Can we hang out?"

"Don't you have a drinks reception in half an hour?"

"Who, me?" He straightened, pulling a face. "Nah."

"Oh, God." But there was a shadow of pleasure in the corner of his brother's mouth.

Kris jerked his head at the magnificent stallion behind Tommy. "Tell me what's been going on in here."

"I spoke to one of our saddlers earlier about him and the other quarter horses." Tommy gestured to the neighboring stalls where the newly arrived horses had been homed. "They're about to start the leatherwork for new saddles and bridles."

"They'll be faultless."

"Without a doubt." With a parting pat, Tommy crossed to the door and this time, Kris let him out. "Did you know that many monarchies have mews instead of stables?" Tommy slid the door closed behind him and latched it shut. "But Kira City is too steep for carriages. Until cars, our family only ever kept horses. Even for ceremonial occasions."

Kris started to smile. "You're telling me we come from a long line of horse riders?"

Tommy's head tilt confirmed it.

"That's the best," he said, shaking his head with a grin.

Then Tommy asked him to explain more about being terrified, so Kris spoke about policies and dignitaries and the looming pressure to produce heirs. All the while, they redid chores that had already been done, because it felt good to move, to breathe in the familiar stable smell of hay and wood shavings, leather and manure, and the warm fragrance of clean horses.

Working and moving, they chatted until the sun went down.

It was almost like being home.

"And *I* said I don't need my own security!"

Philip stood in the middle of his new sitting room, flushed in equal parts indignation and embarrassment. It was a plush suite, tasteful in olive green and cream tones, and he still held the embroidered throw pillow he'd been admiring when Frankie had first walked in.

"And I said you do," Frankie said, crossing her arms.

"It's wildly unnecessary," he said, and set the cushion back on the armchair. "And frankly, it will look like a foolish waste of palace resources for a pair of guards to shadow a mere royal advisor down every hall. I'm not a Jaroka. My life is hardly at risk."

"Yeah, yeah." Frankie's attention swept the room critically. "Just let me know when you have plans to leave the palace and I'll arrange the proper security escort."

"I'm not important enough to—"

"Wrong." Her voice hardened and he caught her eye with a start. "My job is to protect this family. And now that includes you. No, stop—stop arguing."

"Fine." Philip held her stare before sighing. "I wish that tone would work on Kristof. He's lucky Markus was able to step in for the drinks reception tonight."

"Never doubt they've got each other's backs." She gave a final glance around his new suite. "Get someone to clean those windows or you'll miss the way the lake sparkles at sunrise."

He grumbled, but his brows rose interestedly as he turned to his sweeping second-story windows.

Adding Philip to her list of primaries threatened to jailbreak Frankie's panic, but she locked it down as best she could. She could handle this. Her team had secured the royals since day one. The situation had not worsened—she was just getting closer to the black heart at its core.

And she was going to take down whoever she found lurking there.

By Friday morning, she was wrung out. Her mind wouldn't stop chewing on the investigation—cud she refused to spit or swallow, not even to sleep. Kris had done his best to distract her the night before, but the intimacy had put an ache in her heart.

Obviously being with Kris would come with a catch. These first nights in each other's arms should be wondrous and tender— and she was finding it harder and harder to forget that some group of psychos wanted him dead.

"I'll be okay," he'd murmured afterward as they lay facing each other. "I will."

"I know," she'd replied, clinging to his hand.

Because it was up to her to ensure it.

Too torn up, she'd left Kris sleeping and spent the night working at her desk. Of all the ways to dispose of a royal family, why a weakened balcony? The main advantage was clear. Many hands contributed to its construction, making it difficult to pinpoint sabotage, and as an unlikely murder strategy, the deaths seemed far more tragic than suspicious. They'd been smart on that score. But she couldn't work out how a group of laborers could know that the entire family would dine there together. The plan was absurdly improbable without someone to encourage the family onto the balcony.

Frankie was in the staff dining hall for breakfast, grabbing a slice of juniper jam toast and coffee when the question hit her.

Whose idea *had* it been to dine there that night?

It was common knowledge that Prince Aron had enjoyed a riotously popular social media presence, and had cajoled his father and uncle into a banquet on the un-rendered balcony. The final post before his death had been a staged selfie taken with King Vinci and Prince Noel, revealing the extravagant banquet laid out on a slab of chipboard behind them, flower arrangements bursting out of old paint tins, and the Kiralian mountains towering beyond, complete with the hashtags #royallife #royalsofinsta #kingviews #verygranddesigns.

Frankie had assumed the balcony banquet had been Aron's idea. Shallow displays of frivolity were very much in character—but had the suggestion come from someone else?

Picking up the thread, she scheduled a meeting with Prince Aron's old manservant for later that morning. She'd spoken to him soon after she'd arrived and he'd been so genuinely distressed that she'd discounted him as having any malicious involvement. But the prince would have spoken freely to his discreet, ever-present manservant and just might have mentioned something useful while dressing for his last meal.

Halfway through her second coffee, Frankie received a delivery from the jeweler. The silver anarchist pin that would help get her into the next meeting. It was a perfect match for the pin in the photographs and her blood buzzed in anticipation of working her way into the group.

She was in her office planning a watertight cover when Zara texted.

Hey, honey. Can we meet for like twenty minutes? I'm in freak-out mode about tonight and just want to be told I haven't forgotten anything.

Tonight? Frankie blinked at her closed office door. Oh, no. The bridal shower.

She texted back: *You haven't forgotten anything,* and slid her phone aside.

It buzzed again. *Ha. Nope. Still a-freaking.*

Frankie groaned. Zara had crawled out of bed in the middle of the night just to bring her chocolate on the top of The Scepter. The least Frankie could do was give her twenty minutes of reassurance in return. *Okay. Come to palace at ten-thirty. Ask for me at the gates. They'll show you in.*

It felt like no time at all before Frankie was marching herself into a small ground-floor sitting room reserved for hosting informal visits.

"Hi." Zara stood from a firmly-padded floral armchair and gestured at Frankie's uniform. "Swish. Now help me."

"Sure." Serving staff had laid out tea and sweets on the coffee table, and Frankie swiped up a lemon tartlet as she dropped into the armchair opposite her friend. "Go."

With a flustered sigh, Zara sat again, hands sliding between her knees. Her ponytail lay flopped to one side and wispy bits fell frazzled around her face. "Okay. Thanks for organizing the royal guard to secure the venue. So, we'll arrive at seven."

As Zara went through the details, right down to the love-song playlist and color theme of the petit fours, Frankie distractedly toyed with the pin in her pocket. Her concentration was blurry, like this conversation was a lake and she'd only waded in up to her knees. The anarchist meeting wasn't until next Sunday—nine days away. She'd need that time to work on her cover story, but nervous anticipation would eat her hollow by then. It was possible that Aron's manservant might remember a crucial detail, but it was a long shot. She needed more—the balcony only made sense as a murder strategy if they had someone on the inside.

"And that's when Mark and the guys will get there," Zara said, gaze unfocused across the room as she ran through her checklist.

Mark. When should Frankie explain all of this to him and Tommy? It was feeling less and less like a theory based on a gut feeling and more like a legitimate investigation. This weekend so they could enjoy the bridal shower and bachelor party without worry? Or by that logic, should she wait until after Mark and Ava's wedding in a few weeks' time?

"Hey." Zara paused, and her odd tone pulled at Frankie's attention as she pointed at Frankie's hand. "Why do you have Adam's pin?"

Why do—

In a rush, Frankie tasted bile.

The room tilted. Pressure pulsed inside her skull as if her brain was trying to shove the question back out her ears.

In her distraction, Frankie had pulled the pin out of her pocket. It was perched between her fingers.

The capital 'A' encircled in silver.

Adam's pin.

"Frankie?" Zara prompted, confused.

"This?" Frankie acted on old instincts, casually tossing it in the air and catching it in the bloodless fingers of her other hand. When she uncurled her grip, the pin stuck to the sweat of her palm, facedown. "I found it in the dining hall."

Adam was an anarchist.

Adam. Mark's manservant. One of the most trusted roles in the palace. Positioned closest to their monarch. Could he—*no.*

But why would an anarchist choose to work for a royal family?

Her marrow soured; her body shuddered. It was the feeling of scraping against something repulsive and not realizing it until much later—the sickening spike of comprehension, the crawling awareness that it was all over her.

Adam. It was Adam.

You're head of personal security. I've heard a lot about you.

His grip around hers had been firm. Too firm, as she'd asked what exactly he'd heard. *To be careful around you.*

Oh, Jesus.

"That's weird," Zara said with a frown. "He works at Ava and Mark's mansion now."

"That's right." Tucked away out of sight in the private residence of the king. Pulse lurching, Frankie kept her gaze on the pin as she tossed it again. Never before had she been grateful for her ability to slip into an act. "He was here yesterday visiting staff he used to work with."

"Oh." Zara relaxed, smiling a little. "That's nice. I hadn't considered that it must be hard for him to move away from his team."

Frankie nodded, tension a vise around her neck. This was wrong—she was wrong. Adam was Zara's boyfriend. Subdued, gentle. Living with her, sleeping with her. *Oh, God.* She swallowed the revulsion that rose in her throat. No, she was wrong. Running on sleep fumes and obsession. Seeing connections that weren't there.

She held the pin up with a cocked brow. "You sure it's his?"

"'*A*' for Adam," Zara intoned, picking up a tartlet and biting into it. "It's definitely his. I see it every couple of weeks—he wears it when he goes out for drinks with his cousins. His great-grandfather gave it to him for his sixth birthday. I'm sure he's noticed it's missing."

Shit.

"I'm sure he has," she lied.

Zara held her palm out across the coffee table as she continued to eat. "I'll give it back to him."

Alarmed, Frankie said, "Actually, I'm heading to Mark's place later to touch base with my team about tonight's events. I'll find Adam while I'm there."

Her friend raised a shoulder. "Okay."

Okay. Damn it. Zara might even mention this to Adam when Ava and Mark's parties met up later that night. Which meant Frankie had to pursue this fast. If Adam wasn't a part of the anarchist group, he could chuckle about the improbability of Frankie finding a pin so similar to his. But if he was . . .

Frankie eyed her friend, dread in her heart.

If he'd played a role in the balcony collapse—then they'd *all* been fooled.

"Do you have anything else you need to organize before tonight?" Frankie pocketed the pin and mentally added, *because I sure as hell do.*

Zara slumped back in the armchair and blew a breath up her face, shifting a wispy hair away from her eyes. "I think that's it."

"Then let's finish these." Frankie grabbed another tartlet and let out a sigh. The silence of the sitting room was ringing in her ears. "Thanks for coming. It's good to have an excuse to sit still for a second."

"Tell me about it."

"So, Adam." How was this for subtle? "How are things going with him, anyway?"

Zara blinked. "Oh." Her surprise swept into a small smile. "Good, I guess."

"I don't remember your hook-up story." Frankie quirked a vaguely amused brow. "How did you meet the man who personally serves our king?"

Blushing, Zara said, "It's not very exciting. I advertised a room for rent like six months ago to help pay off my mortgage, and he seemed the most respectable of the applicants."

"The handsome part had nothing to do with it, obviously."

Her friend grinned.

"It worked out well for you both that he didn't take up residence at the palace when he became Mark's manservant."

Which, now that Frankie thought about it, was an odd logistical choice.

"He prefers having his own space. More privacy."

Frankie bet he did. "And you hit it off once he moved in?"

"Well. I know it's weird, but for the first few months he was hardly ever around. When he was home, he was polite, but distant. I found it pretty mysterious and got this huge crush." Zara shook her head at herself, reaching forward for more tea. "It wasn't until Ava's visit that things changed."

Frankie's dread expanded at the suspicious timing.

"Yeah?" she asked, extending her own cup. Zara poured for her and they both leaned back again. "He finally noticed how freaking awesome you are?"

"Supposedly he'd already noticed." Her friend laughed, cheeks still pink. "But he was so subtle, I couldn't tell. Anyway, I'd seen his bags packed inside his bedroom door one morning. I assumed he—"

"Sorry, when was this?"

Zara blinked. "Uh. Like, Ava's visit. So, around the royal funeral and stuff? I assumed he'd wanted to leave because he'd figured out that I was into him and he wasn't interested."

Frankie nodded. Having his bags packed so soon after the balcony collapse screamed *quick getaway*.

"I got in first," Zara continued. "I bumped into him randomly at the palace after I'd called on Ava and told him that he should move out—it would be better for both of us. He looked so shocked."

Frankie shoved the rest of the tartlet into her mouth so she wouldn't have to think of a response. Yeah, it must have been quite the shock to discover his flat-mate was friends with the very princess who was getting close to his king. Zara would have gleamed like a gold tap of information—but he had to get close before her words would flow freely.

"Instead of agreeing, he asked me out. I was like, what? We met up at the Bearded Bunting—oh, you might remember that night. You probably handled security. Mark, Kris, Ava, and, uh, Cyrus were all there." Zara's voice caught a little on Cyrus's name.

"Four royals gathered in one public courtyard," Frankie said as dryly as she could manage. "Trust me, I remember."

"Adam told me he liked me, too, but he'd always thought I was too good for him." Zara rolled her eyes, but she was smiling. "Something about his position as Mark's manservant helping the privileged stay that way, but that I worked selflessly at the shelter to protect the vulnerable, which benefited the whole community."

Anarchist views. Flaming red flag.

"Anyway, we sorted it out and got together."

Frankie's heart was hammering, pounding against her ribs as if trying to catch Zara's attention. *Adam's bad,* it beat fiercely. *Adam's bad.*

"Cute story," she said instead.

Zara snorted, smiling, and drank more tea. Then she said more quietly, "I'd kind of forgotten about it. How sweet he was that night. He kept telling me that I was beautiful. Courageous." Her fingertips drummed lightly on her teacup, features soft, almost surprised. "He still says those things." She paused to cringe. "Wow, I'm so stupid. I hear stories of foul men at the shelter every day—and I have this gentle guy at home who loves me, and I've talked myself out of loving him back because I daydream about a prince. How blind can I get? I'm not a freaking cartoon. I can't do that anymore."

Sure, you can. "Oh," Frankie said.

"Do you think—" Zara pulled a face of tentative delight. "Do I love him?"

"I don't know." Frankie pulled a face in return—hoping she

looked more like a friend who was uncomfortable talking about feelings and less like a she feared Zara was falling in love with a murder suspect. "Does he know much about Ava's past? I'm just thinking about how hard it must be to keep secrets like that from him."

"Oh, yeah." Zara waved her hand distractedly. "Ava said that if I trusted him, she trusted him. I told him all about Darius and the escape."

Frankie's vision blanked. "And the king swap?"

"What? No, not that. That's between Mark and his brothers. Not my place."

A small win. "Why did he have his bags packed?"

Zara frowned at her. "What?"

Quit sounding like an interrogation. "It's a funny detail," Frankie said offhandedly. "You'd said you'd noticed his bags packed before you bumped into him at the palace."

"Oh, I think it was because I was too good for him? He thought I'd be better off sharing my apartment with someone more like me."

A simple excuse sweetened by flattery. Clever.

"Enough about us. We're old news." Zara pulsed her brows with a grin. "You've been very quiet about Prince Kristof. Tell me what you're not telling me."

It was everything Frankie could do to act casual as she shared details of the past week. Alarm held her in a trembling grip and each sip of tea tasted like time running out. She had to contact Mark's guards and instruct them to monitor Adam. She had to tell Philip. Tell her team and the involved authorities. She had to show Adam's photo to the manager of the Bull's Quest to confirm he attended those meetings. If this lead proved true, she'd have to tell the full story to Mark and Tommy and Ava.

And Zara.

"Holy mother, Kris is hot," Zara said as Frankie finished a

short yet uncut version of the past week's developments. "I'll probably combust being in the same room as you two tonight." She paused, and then groaned. "I hope it goes well. It has to be perfect for Ava."

Frankie stood. "You've put together a very thoughtful event." Her voice sounded hollow in her ears. "She'll love it."

Zara beamed as she reached for her handbag. "Thanks."

No. Not a smile. Frankie couldn't bear to return it. "Shoot, I've lost track of time," she said, and launched herself toward the door. She had to get out—before she bled dry at what this all could mean for Zara.

"Frankie!" Zara called after her. "I meant to ask what you were going to wear."

"Something bright." Frankie pulled the door open, not looking back. "Got to run."

The door swept closed behind her, and as she strode across the arch-ceilinged hall, she pulled out the pin. It shone up at her like a warm, sincere smile.

Adam.

She'd been fucking conned.

14

The rest of the day passed in a horrified flash, and before she knew it, Frankie was pulling on a canary-yellow dress and spiking her hair in Kris's bathroom mirror. She was so drained her eyes and throat were gritty, and her body felt like something she was wearing rather than controlling. Her hands trembled as she flipped open her foundation and met her own dismayed gaze in the mirror.

She'd wanted to be wrong.

She'd sped to Kuria Estate straight after her talk with Zara. She'd wanted to stand before Adam and sense in her gut that he was a good man—incapable of malice, of planned murder. Instead, she'd discovered he'd left the mansion just minutes before to organize a surprise for the bachelor party, claiming he would meet Markus and the others at seven.

Mouth dry and head aching, she'd tripled security for Darius that night. Nothing would happen to that child while his family was celebrating in the city.

She'd returned to the palace, telling herself it could still be a coincidence. The 'A' of his pin might really stand for *Adam,* and he might really be out arranging a surprise for Mark.

But Prince Aron's old manservant had confirmed it. Frankie had asked why Aron had decided to dine on the balcony that night. At first, the man couldn't remember. The conversation moved on, but then he'd circled back, and said, "Actually, I think it was suggested by one of his younger servers. Blond. Quite formal." He'd paused, remembering. "Adam."

Cream powder dusted the vanity. Cursing, Frankie clenched her teeth and wiped it onto the marble floor.

Next, she'd shown a photograph of Adam to the proprietor of the Bull's Quest. "Yes, I've seen him. He doesn't come to every meeting, but most of them."

"Can you tell me anything else about him," she'd said faintly. "Anything at all."

"He doesn't order much from the bar. Seems to like to stay clearheaded. And his brother used to attend the meetings with him, but stopped turning up about six months ago."

Brother? On edge, Frankie had ordered a shot at the bar before leaving.

This much she knew—Adam attended anarchist meetings and lied to Zara about it. Through these meetings, he was acquainted with a number of men who'd worked on the construction of the west-wing balcony. He'd personally suggested Prince Aron eat with his father and uncle on the unfinished site. He'd had bags packed in the days following their deaths. He'd been disinterested in Zara until the moment he realized she was close with the princess—who was getting close to Mark. He'd worked hard and faultlessly for the royal family for over a decade, according to the head of palace HR, and requested the opportunity to be promoted to personally serve the new king.

And he would be at the bachelor party.

All three brothers in one place.

Did Adam have a plan? She'd ordered both the bridal and

bachelor venues to be thoroughly searched for potential threats. Nothing. She'd ramped up scheduled security and organized a detection dog at the venue entrances, and if asked, would claim standard procedure for times when the entirety of the royal line was gathered in public. If Adam himself was a threat, he wouldn't go undetected. She also had the anarchists who'd worked on the construction under continued surveillance in case Adam rallied his team.

Frankie applied her base coat in determined strokes.

No one would get near her boys.

"Frankie?"

She jumped, startled at the call from Kris's sitting room. Tommy?

"In here," she called. "I'm dressed. Come in."

Pulling herself together, she dabbed her brush into a cocoa-brown eyeshadow until Tommy's reflection appeared in the bathroom behind her. He'd scrubbed up for Mark's bachelor party in a steel-grey shirt and black jeans, even had a haircut, but his blue eyes were too wide and his skin too pale.

"Hey," she said, looking back at the palette.

The steadiness of his stare bore into her in the mirror, and after an assessing silence, he asked, "What's wrong?"

"Big day." She met his gaze. Avoiding it would give her away. "Headache."

He paused. "Most people don't look that good in yellow." It was the closest she'd ever heard him get to a compliment.

"Thanks." Frowning a little, she leaned over the vanity to apply the shadow.

"You could have an attendant do that for you," he said. "Several, actually."

"Oh boy, my dreams are coming true." She kept brushing. "What's up?"

He stepped to one side and sat on an elegant stool positioned by the door. Knees wide, elbows on his thighs, hands clasped between. Head angled to regard the lush vine spilling down from a hanging pot beside him. "You're sure the bar will be empty tonight?"

"Positive," she said. "There won't be a crowd."

He nodded, but didn't leave. "And no one knows we'll be there?"

The question crawled across her throat. "The public haven't been tipped off." She shifted to shadow her other eyelid. "The car will pull into the alley behind the venue, so no one will see you go in either. Does that sound okay?"

"Yes." One of his legs started jiggling.

"Security will be tight. Only guards that you're familiar with will be positioned inside."

He gave a single nod. Then his attention skirted her phone where it sat on the vanity beside her makeup bag—and she realized it was almost five o'clock. On Friday.

He'd come for Jonah.

"Loudspeaker again," she said, digging in her bag for eyeliner, "or do you want to answer this time?"

At his silence, she turned to meet his stricken stare.

"Well?" she prodded, almost gently.

"I just—" Pain bracketed his mouth as he looked away. Tommy rarely spoke in fractures. He took the time to be articulate. Lowering his face, he fisted a hand into his hair and she recognized the tension in his grip—the charged potential to pull as hard as he damn well could. His voice was hushed and tortured as he said, "I just want to hear him."

Oh God. After the day she'd had, Frankie felt like overstuffed luggage—heavy, splitting, bordering on unzippable— and Tommy's words jammed in sympathy and frustration without even folding first. Her skin frayed a little further. These friends had been through hell together and Tommy had yet to come out the other side. And he wouldn't. Not while they lived on opposite sides of the world.

Despite her ache to agree, she said, "It's not fair to listen without him knowing. Loudspeaker means we both talk to him."

"One minute," he instantly challenged.

"There are things he might not want you to hear."

His features sharpened—she practically heard the *shink* of a blade against a whetstone. "What things?"

"Well, since you asked, I'll just break his trust and spill, shall I?"

He scowled at her sarcasm. He'd timed his visit well. Before she could talk him into answering the call, her phone started to ring.

"Would you excuse me?" She picked it up, arching a brow. "This is private."

"Loudspeaker." An order.

She hesitated. No. He couldn't abuse his authority to eavesdrop on Jonah. She crossed her arms as the ringing continued. "So, you'll talk?"

His tense-jawed silence denied it.

She sighed. "I think you should leave, Tommy."

"Please." He stood abruptly, broad and fierce, and seemed to struggle to contain his surging desperation. "Just this once." Pain crushed his features as he turned to press his forearm against the tiled wall. His next words were a murmur directed at his feet. "I'm never going back."

He was—never going back.

To Sage Haven.

Frankie almost groaned as concern crammed into the mess inside her. Kris had relayed the conversation he'd had with Tommy in the stables—that Kris had admitted he couldn't be king without Tommy's support. Was it possible that in all the time Tommy had been in Kiraly, he'd squirreled away a kernel of hope that his brothers would find their feet and offer for him to return to Sage Haven? Was it possible he'd been waiting all this time to go home—only for Kris to finally, explicitly, state he needed him here? Would *always* need him here?

Tommy would've struggled to leave his brothers at their request—but he'd never abandon them. His seed of hope had died.

He would never see Jonah again.

"Fine," she said. "One minute."

He kept his back turned as she answered the call and switched to loudspeaker.

"Hey, Jones," she said, setting it on the vanity and picking up her eyeliner.

"Hey, Frankie!" Jonah had the kind of sunshine voice that made rain-drenched fields sparkle. Positive, genuine, forever helpful. She was equal parts in awe and in love with it. "How was your day?"

"Epic. I feel like I've been trampled by a fucking gorilla."

"Oh no." Even serious, his brightness shone. "That's awful."

"All part of the job." She retraced the line beneath her eye, aiming for dark and defined. "Sorry, but I can't talk long. Mark and Ava have their events tonight."

"That's right! Send me a photo or two? I'd love to see." He fell silent, and she imagined him sitting alone at his kitchen table, house empty around him, staring past the hay sheds toward the farmstead next door in the distance. Staring toward the friendships he'd lost when his neighbors had embraced the royal heritage he'd never been told about. Then he asked, "How's Tommy?" and his voice scratched over his friend's name, as always.

Frankie drew in a heaven-calm-me breath and slid her attention to where Tommy stood with his back to her. His head was angled to one side, listening intently, and there was something coiled about him. The hissing tension of a wild animal that sensed a hand reaching toward it, and couldn't decide whether to strike or scram.

"Hiding," she answered, and suffered the slice of Tommy's cautionary glare over his shoulder. She arched a *prove me wrong* brow.

"Will he ever stop?" Jonah's concern was sad.

"Even lone wolves have to eat," she said.

Jonah hesitated. "I don't know what that means."

"It means his basic needs will drive him out eventually." She held Tommy's stare, shaking her head at him. Honestly. This was bordering on absurd. "Basic needs like, I don't know, a best friend."

"I don't think so," Jonah said.

"Maybe," she said, all false astonishment, "you both secretly want to talk to each other?"

Tommy faced her properly, his thunderous expression equal parts pleading and threatening. *"Don't,"* he mouthed at her.

"You could try calling him," she said, addressing them both.

"Yeah, right." Jonah gave a wretched laugh, and her seams tore as Tommy flinched. "It wasn't my friend who abandoned me. It was a prince. And he's left me here."

Tommy's face went white.

"Tommy's still—"

"No, he's not," Jonah cut her off. Not rude—Jonah was never rude—but measured like he'd thought about this long and hard. "My friend wouldn't have done this to me. He's different now. He has to be. He's a prince. I get it. And I get that someone like me has no business being friends with a man like him."

Frankie couldn't bring herself to look at Tommy. "That's not true. He's—"

"Please, Frankie," Jonah said in the tone equivalent to a hand over his eyes. "We both know there's nowhere to go from here."

Her throat ached. Tommy stood as motionless as a broken statue across the room.

"You've still got me, Jones," she made herself say. "I'll call you tomorrow, okay?"

"Yeah. Anytime."

Hanging up, she turned back to the mirror and blindly picked up her mascara. The bathroom air felt thin, drained. The result of the sucker-punched cowboy behind her or Adam's suffocating truth still pressed over her face like a pillow, she wasn't sure.

"I guess that's closure," she said quietly, and glanced up to find Tommy gone.

Tossing the mascara in the sink, she pressed her face into her hands. Her fingers were shaking; her blood moved through her heart like oil. It was all too much. How was she supposed to hold it together tonight? Even Tommy, distracted by an upcoming night out and Jonah's phone call, had known something wasn't right with her when he'd walked in.

She looked up at a faint scuffing sound, and jumped to find that Kris had materialized behind her. He'd done something gorgeous to his hair, and his black shirt was both elegant and effortlessly casual, betraying the royal tailor had been put to good use.

He was frowning. "You okay?"

"Fine," she said, turning to face him.

His frown dug lower into his brow. "No, you're not."

"It's been a big day." She didn't want to sound breathless; didn't want to weaken now that he was finally here. But he moved in, arms sliding around her, and she practically collapsed into his embrace. He was strong, steady, and her tension melted away, fears drifting back into shadowed corners, and for a moment, she was just a quickening heartbeat in her lover's arms.

311

Then her gut knotted and she tightened her hold around him. Her eyes squeezed shut, fingers bunching his shirt.

"You were gone when I woke this morning." He spoke softly against her hair.

"Couldn't sleep." Suddenly, she hated that she'd crept out in the night. She could never get that time back. She should have stayed beside him, her hand in his as he slept. He was under threat and she'd chosen to be apart from him. Something heaved beneath her breastbone, a panicked flutter, and she pressed even harder against him.

His breath loosened, and a low beat of energy passed between them. His hand slipped to the base of her spine. "What's going on, Frankie?"

Too much. She lifted her face. "Kiss me."

The look he gave her said *nice try*, but his mouth sank over hers anyway. Gentle, nudging toward persistence. It was a kiss for a different time, the start of a languid weekend spent between his sheets. His palm passed over her shoulder, thumb slipping easily beneath her dress strap, and her body hummed, plucked by the promise of his desire.

Then he pulled back and spoke in a tone of non-negotiation. "Now tell me what's wrong."

"It's bad," she breathed.

In a smooth motion, he turned with her in his arms and set her on the stool Tommy had filled minutes before. Kris knelt in front of her, one hand spread over her thigh and the other tangling lightly with her fingers. "I'll help if I can."

She swallowed. "You can't."

But she relayed her conversation with Zara, and Aron's old manservant, and the owner of the Bull's Quest. As Kris sat down hard on the bathroom floor, face bloodless, she told him that while the circumstantial evidence was strong enough to bring Adam in for questioning, the authorities wanted to search his apartment for something concrete and they were currently waiting on the search warrant.

"Mark," was all he said, the word absolute and terrified.

"I've tightened security at the estate and lined up extra protection measures for tonight. We'll protect him."

His attention locked on her, eyes burning with blue fear.

"I promise," she said, and her head cleared with purpose.

"It's Adam." Kris's grip on her thigh hardened and she felt a charge travel through him. Fury broke across his face. "He's in their house every day. Alone with Mark. Close to Ava and Darius. He could do anything. Why the hell aren't we moving?"

She covered his hand with hers, curling her fingers tight. "We don't believe he'll hurt them. He's waiting."

"For what?"

Dread tried to knock the wind out of her, but she did her best to wrangle it, reshape it, wear it like armor on her shoulders. *This* was why she would fight. Because she couldn't bear to lose.

"We believe he's waiting for a chance to take all three of you down at once."

Kris swore, dropping his forehead onto her knee.

"As far as most people are aware, the balcony collapse was an accident. But two separate instances of royal deaths? That would throw the collapse into retrospective suspicion. It's not what he wants. If he kills you all together, the royal line ends. You're the last of the Jaroka heirs. Once that happens, whether he gets caught or not is irrelevant."

"Where is he now?" he demanded. "This very second?"

Uncertainty flickered inside her. "We don't know."

"But he'll be there tonight."

"He should be." She locked her jaw against an icy flood of what-ifs. "It's critical you don't give us away, Kris. We need him there long enough for the warrant to come through and the authorities to search the apartment. Please?"

He rose to his feet. "You're saying I have to pretend to be happy in the same room as the man who might have ordered the attack on Tommy and Jonah? Who killed my uncles and cousin? Whose unhinged actions dragged me and my brothers from our home? The man who likely wants us all dead to culminate some crazy antiestablishment rebellion?"

"Yes."

He swore again.

"Mark and Tommy can't know. There's not enough time for them to process it." Concerned, she stood beside him. "You know that, right? Kris. You have to act normal. If he suspects we know about him, it'll put you all at risk."

"I know, but I need you to keep me updated." He ran his tongue along his back teeth, shaking his head. "I won't hold it together if I'm left in the dark."

"I will." She didn't need agitation eating him alive. "I'll give Peter permission to relay information as we get it."

He nodded once, reaction laboring inside him. His breath was fast, his shoulders straining.

"There is one other option," she said, almost carefully. "You could not go tonight."

His gaze snapped to her in outrage.

"I know." She hated suggesting it—how badly she wished he'd agree. "But if only two of you are there, it could reduce the chance of Adam acting out."

"I can't." Kris shook his head. "I get your logic, but—I can't."

She nodded and murmured, "Okay."

"Hey." Reaching out, he drew her against him and pressed his lips to her temple. His mouth was hot; his body locked with tension. "You're doing an amazing job. This is fucked, but you're doing it, and I love you."

Her breath shook over his shirt pocket. "Thank you."

"I mean it," he said, then released her and turned to leave.

"Kris," she said, and he stilled in the archway. "Promise me something."

Resistance rolled across his shoulders as he looked back at her. He seethed with an alpha-powered protectiveness. His features were feral with vengeance, body taut with volatility. A man who'd locked eyes on a threat to his brothers—and was snarling with hackles up in response.

"Don't do anything stupid," she said.

His eyes flashed. Then his gaze moved over her, softening, and he said, "I promise to try."

Kris laughed as he took everyone at the table in another round of poker. Leaning back in his chair with his hands clasped behind his head, he said to Mark, "Hey, sorry man, I should have asked if you wanted to win tonight."

Mark shook his head, grinning. He hadn't stopped smiling since they'd arrived. Good. And although Tommy's fidgeting had led him to strip the label off every beer bottle on the table, he didn't seem on the verge of a panic attack. The bar had been cleared out for them, and they'd welcomed an endless supply of food, drinks, and cards since strolling in the back entrance. Mark's personal guards sat with them, the two men playing quietly but comfortably among the royal triplets, while Philip had kept Kris on his toes with his startlingly quick poker skills.

Adam was nowhere to be seen.

Mark had sent a pair of guards to his apartment earlier to check if he was okay, but no one had been home. As Tommy collected their cards to shuffle, Kris wondered how he was supposed to judge what constituted a stupid idea. Seemed like a matter of opinion, because right now, heading over to Zara and

Adam's apartment to figure out where the fucker had gone seemed like one of his brightest.

"Last round," Tommy said, and began dealing.

Kris pushed against the roll of red temper that balled his hands and pushed him to the front of his chair. It was hell to sit here pretending nothing was wrong. But he made himself relax and flick a bottle lid at Mark with a *can't-believe-you're-getting-married* grin.

He could do this. For his brothers.

Twice now, Peter had absently run a hand over his scalp—the prearranged signal—and Kris had wandered around to the guards stationed at the exits and offered them pizza. He'd lingered as Peter and Hanna dove into the box, Hanna exclaiming her enthusiasm while Peter quietly relayed the situation under the cover of her voice.

At the bridal shower, Frankie had found out that Zara had texted Adam as soon as she'd left the palace that morning letting him know Frankie had his pin. He hadn't responded to her. Zara hadn't thought anything of it and believed he was currently sitting at this very poker table. No one knew where he'd gone. The authorities were still waiting on the search warrant. The plan was to stay on high alert and allow Mark and Ava their night of celebrations.

Tomorrow, the royal family would be informed.

Now, Kris made a final lap of the guards, wafting half-empty pizza boxes in front of them and inviting them to finish it off. At Hanna's turn, she deliberated between slices.

"Anything?" Kris asked, a model of patience as she asked him to open each of the five boxes so she could make an informed decision.

"No update, Your Highness," Peter murmured, hands behind his back. "But Frankie assures us that the moment we receive information, she'll make a move. You and your family will be protected at all costs."

Kris's blood ran cold as Hanna settled on a puttanesca slice.

He and his brothers would be protected—at the risk of Frankie's own safety.

She'd made him promise not to do anything stupid. With a wave of black nausea, he realized his mistake.

He hadn't demanded the same of her.

Frankie blew a trail of cool air across her shoulder and down her arm to her wrist. The henna was drying into an intricate stain on her skin, the final activity before Mark's party would arrive at this glam-chic cocktail lounge. Zara had nailed the decorations. An abundance of twinkle-light balloons bobbed at the ceiling, shimmering over white and silver silk bunting strung from corner to corner. Glass vases filled with tiny strings of lights were scattered around the cherry-toned carpet, while vines and candles adorned every surface. Cocktails flowed like ambrosia and world-class pastry chefs delivered an endless selection of magical, brightly colored desserts.

Ava had actually clasped her hands beneath her chin with a gasp when they'd arrived.

"It doesn't hurt to have a king's budget," Zara had said, downplaying.

"You're the best friend I've ever had, Zara Nguyen." Ava's declaration had been firm with regal finality, and Zara had flushed down to her collarbones.

Frankie didn't recall much of the evening. She'd sat through games of romantic movie quotes, and love songs, and personal questions about Mark, but had waded even more shallowly into the activities than her earlier conversation with Zara. Feet wet, she'd kicked up just enough sparkling spray to pass as present, but the rest of her was wrung dry.

Adam might be out there raising his stone and taking aim at the Jaroka brothers.

He might want her boys dead.

Panic sparked in her bloodstream. Despite rational thought assuring her that Kris was fine, some stretched-thin part of her reached for him. It had been three hours, yet she *ached* for him like he'd taken away the front half of her rib cage with a wink and a promise she'd get it back on his return. Her chest throbbed; her heartbeat felt uncontained.

Sending another breath over her inked arm, she met eyes with the royal guard positioned by the front entrance. He raised two fingers. Two minutes away. When she continued staring, he gave a subtle headshake. No news on Adam.

Her stomach churned. This was agony.

"Can you spot them, Frankie?"

She jerked around and found Zara watching her with a pointed smile. She frowned. "What?"

Zara gestured at Ava's outstretched arms. "The artist hid them well."

Frankie forced herself to focus. Ava's henna design was exquisite. Tiny flowers and leaves spread outward from her palms and wound up her forearms, the patterns curling into lace-like detail, glints of gold paint embellishing the earthy brown ink. Mark's initials had been secreted into the design and Ava was beaming with both arms extended as Zara, Yasmin and Gul tried their best to find them.

"Uh, let's see." Frankie scooted her chair closer. After scanning the ink, she said, "There," and pointed at a cursive *M.J.* at the pulse point on Ava's wrist.

Ava smiled at her like she'd completed some kind of quest.

"Wow, you can see the forest and the trees," Zara said, impressed.

Frankie's ears pricked at a sound from the rear entrance. "Sometimes."

"A bride in Kelehar always wears her groom's initials over her pulse." Ava lowered her arms, looking every part a princess in her ivory evening dress and diamond tiara. "To symbolize his place in every beat of her heart."

"Aw," Zara said in an appropriately gooey tone.

"Yasmin, Gul," Ava said, and nudged her old guard. "You both knew that."

"I wasn't going to spoil your fun, Princess." Gul grinned. "But it's on both wrists."

With a sound of astonished delight, Ava examined her other arm.

Frankie stood, shaking her arm so the damn thing would finish drying as the back doors opened and Mark's party entered.

Their arrival was like a steel-tipped arrow passing through a magnolia bloom. The feminine ambiance of the room scattered like torn petals. These men were cowboys and elite guards, masculine and hard-edged, and the bridal party fell quiet at the sudden punch of their testosterone.

Gul sat back in his chair with a murmured, "I feel faint."

Frankie couldn't tell whether he was joking.

As the royal triplets advanced across the twinkling lounge, she suspected he wasn't.

Mark strode in the lead. Pure-hearted and grounded, he was the gravity that pulled his brothers in close. As if to prove it, Kris swaggered on Mark's right, untamed and impulsive, a man who drove the people he loved up the wall but knew no greater force than loyalty. Frankie's ribs seem to fasten back in place at the sight of him. Tommy stuck to Mark's left, all ragged edges and deep waters—and that vein of authority running through his core like gold trapped in granite.

The warm shadows played over them. Broad-shouldered, sculpted, reverberatingly attractive. It wasn't a new thought for Frankie that nature itself must have sensed the genetic perfection of that face and split cells for two more on the spot. Privately, she applauded such quick thinking.

Royal. Breathtaking. Cowboys.

These brothers didn't know their own power.

Then Ava called, "Markus!" and dashed toward him.

Mark stopped abruptly. "My God," he said, looking dazed. "Look at you."

Ava's smile turned shy and she spun in a graceful circle to show off her bridal ink. "It's to bless us with a marriage of contentment and joy."

"But I'm already blessed," Mark said, and his brothers rolled their eyes with grins beside him.

As the couple embraced, Frankie glanced at Kris and found him checking her out. She was no princess. She'd paired her short yellow dress with her trusty black boots, spiked her hair as usual, and with her henna sleeve tattoo, she was infinitely more punk than pretty. When he looked up, the hunger in his eyes betrayed he was totally into that.

After an evening spent straining for him, she wanted to drag him into an unused room and let him devour her.

"Hey, where's Adam?" Zara asked.

And like that, everything hot in Frankie went cold.

Zara was scanning the men in confusion. "Did he drive separately?"

Mark pulled back from Ava, looking concerned and, though he tried to hide it, hurt. "Actually, Zara, he didn't show. He didn't say anything to you?"

"What? No." Zara's good mood died like air in a vacuum. "Where is he?"

Mark glanced at his guards, shaking his head. "We're not sure."

"Maybe his phone died?" Ava suggested, looking concerned.

"Yeah, but he wouldn't ditch your bachelor party." Zara was frowning. "Um. I could run home and check if he's there. We live on Blueridge Crest; it's like five minutes away."

Mark said, "Actually, I sent guards—"

"Don't we need to start the ceremony?" Frankie cut in, feeling like shit as she used etiquette to tie a rope around her friend's feet. She didn't want Zara out of her sight while her boyfriend was an unknown quantity. "We're already running late. He's probably had a family emergency, or has come down with something and gone to bed."

"Oh." Zara glanced around like she'd misplaced something that should have been attached to her. His absence didn't make sense. "I guess. Yeah. He's probably just sleeping off a bug. Um. I'll set up."

As Zara moved to the far side of the lounge where the Keleharian bridal ceremony would take place, Frankie turned away from the group, scrubbing a hand over her face. Guilt clamped her lungs. Jesus. She hadn't thought about Zara returning home tonight to find Adam missing. She couldn't wait until morning to tell her—she'd have to do it immediately after the bridal shower.

Frankie scrubbed her face harder as dread dropped her heart like a stone. How was that conversation supposed to go?

Hey. So, funny story. We have reason to believe your boyfriend is a murderous psychopath. Left field, right? Remember when you thought about breaking up with him, but I said to wait because he's a good guy? My bad.

This was messed up. This was so—

The back of her neck prickled and Kris murmured, "Can we talk?" from directly behind her.

She dropped her hand, but didn't turn around. "You've been told everything."

He paused. "We need to talk."

She could do with the excuse to steady herself. Possibly while wrapped around him. "Alright."

Fingers brushing his as she took the lead, she crossed the vacant dance floor and passed two guards stationed by the swinging doors to the kitchen. The chefs had departed for the night, leaving the stainless-steel space half-lit and silent. Pressing both palms to the metal table in the center of the floor, she lowered her head and let out a long breath as the doors flapped shut behind her.

"Frankie," Kris said, standing just inside the door.

"Give me a second."

"Frankie."

Slanting him a glance, she expected to see a suggestion shining in his eyes. Or, perhaps, the release of his suppressed anger at Adam's disappearance now that it was safe to show it.

Instead, his attention was on the floor in front of him.

"What?" she asked.

Lines gathered on his brow and quietly, he said, "I need you to leave."

"As soon as there's news, I'll be on him like a pile of fucking bricks."

"No." His voice was weird. He still wasn't looking at her. "You need to leave Kiraly."

The order landed like a strike to her solar plexus.

Sliding her hands off the table, she slowly faced him. "I misheard you."

"For your safety," he said, and his voice dulled into a buzz in her eardrums. Oh God. He was doing it. After all these years, he was finally shoving her behind him as he faced the fight. "Adam knows we're onto him. I don't want you hunting him down. You're a target as much as I am. He's dangerous and he knows you're close to me."

The buzzing in her ears grew louder.

"No," she said.

"Yes."

She should have expected this. Seen it coming ever since he'd waded into a barfight for her in Sage Haven. Since he'd pounded his fist into a black bruise on the bar floor of the Bearded Bunting. For years, he'd burned to protect her and had never been allowed.

Now, it terrified her to realize that he was done taking no for an answer.

Her pulse hurt—throbbing in her chest, her neck. "I don't understand."

"Yes, you do," he said, and looked up at her.

"No." She gave a single shake of her head. "I'm not leaving you."

"I didn't protect Tommy." Pain etched around his mouth. "I sent those men *to* him. I can't send you to Adam. I can't do it."

"It's not your decision." Her alarm spiked. "Think about what you're saying."

"I know I can be impulsive—"

"Then be sensible—"

"But being near me automatically puts you at risk and I can't have you here." His voice was level, alarmingly rational. "Not now. Not until this is over. You're my future, Frankie."

"And you're mine!" She fed her anger with the entitlement of his argument—the infuriating assumption that his desire to protect her trumped *her* desire to protect *him*. "I have as much right to be in danger as you. And if you've forgotten, it's *my job* to protect you."

He pressed his eyes close and said, "Not anymore."

Shock shoved her back a step. Those words nocked an arrow in her bones. This would break her. To build enough tension to successfully shoot her to safety, he was going to end up snapping her apart.

Her voice shook as she said, "I'm going to pretend you didn't say that."

"Pretend all you like."

"Don't." She turned away so abruptly her knee twinged. Her face felt oddly hot from loss of blood. "Don't be calm when I'm angry."

She knew that tactic. She'd used it on him the night she'd tackled him. It was the only way he could stay in control and walk away with what he wanted.

And he couldn't have this.

"Calm is the last thing I'm feeling." His low voice wavered.

"So, what is this exactly?" It was like he'd lit a match and set her lungs burning. She faced him again. "You're firing me?"

"Temporarily relocating you." Regret was heavy on his face, but she tried not to see it. Actions counted. Regret meant nothing. "You used to collect information in the United States for Philip. You'll do that again until it's safe to come back."

"No." She shook her head as heat gathered in her eyes.

Apology gleamed in his earnest gaze. "I need you to be safe."

"But you gave me the uniform. I thought—that meant you trusted me with this position."

That you trusted me with your life.

"I do trust you." He shoved his sleeves to his elbows. Finally, some agitation. "I don't trust *him*. You don't deserve to play chicken with a murderer. Not for me. Not for my brothers."

"This job is my worth," she whispered.

Who would she be without it? A woman with too many regrets and not enough purpose to stem the flow. Drowning in her own past. Kris might think he was saving her, but he'd be the hand that held her under.

His gaze was desolate. "It's not."

Yes, it *was*.

"I fought for this job because I wanted to prove to myself that I'm not screwed up. That I can do the right thing for good people. And I struggled for so long to believe that I deserve to be here, but you—you convinced me that it was true. I *believed* you and now you're sending me away."

His breathing was rough, coming in stops and starts. "Did you take an oath?"

Startled, she tripped over the question. "What?"

"To become a royal guard, did you take an oath?"

She froze.

Every pump, course, and flow hung motionless inside her.

"Yes," she said.

He crossed his arms and swallowed hard. "What was it?"

"Kris—"

"What was the oath, Frankie?" He took a step toward her. "What did you swear?"

Her body shook. Something huge was caving in on her and she didn't know how to shield herself. Or if she even could.

Eyes stinging, she forced herself to recite the pledge.

"*I, Francesca Grace Cowan, do swear that I will faithfully obey and bear true allegiance to His Majesty King Markus Jaroka, His Heirs and Successors; that I will protect and defend His Majesty, His Heirs and Successors against all enemies; and that with my life and my death, I will remain duty bound.*"

Kris stared at her. His eyes glistened.

No. "Please, Kris."

"Your death?" It was a whisper. "How do you expect me to bear that?"

"I don't know." She shook her head, distressed. "You just

have to." The same way she bore that he would always be a target. That it was possible, despite all security measures, for a threat to take aim and strike true. "You can't strip me of my position because it's easier than being scared for me. That's not fair." Her voice rose, furious and terrified at once. "You just have to be scared! That's what it means to love someone."

"Yeah, and how would you know?" he shot back, and the harshness of his voice slit her open.

The kitchen fell sickeningly quiet.

Her next inhale was tattered. Broken.

Kris stepped toward her, his features stricken. "Frankie . . ."

She shook her head, tears falling. "You're right."

"That wasn't what I—"

"It's a good question and I should—"

"No." Kris kept coming, stopping in front of her with a wildness in his eyes. He took her hands. They both trembled in each other's grasp. "Don't. I didn't mean that. Don't say anything."

"You think I don't?" Dismay bled cold in her chest. "I thought you knew—"

"I do." He kissed the back of her hand, his mouth hot and helpless against her. "I know you do. Please. I don't want to ruin the first time you say it. I didn't mean that, okay?"

She stared at him, numb from sternum to spine.

"Please don't," he murmured, shaking his head.

"I love you, Kris."

He closed his eyes as if she'd gutted him in return.

"I love you," she said, "and I'm not going anywhere."

Panic rode on his protest. "You *have* to—"

"If you make me leave, I'll never trust you again. My job has to be separate from our relationship. And our relationship has to be separate from your authority. If you pull rank to protect me right now—to make me *obey* you—I can't trust that you won't do it again."

Distress reddened his eyes. "I don't know what else to do."

"Love me enough to risk me."

A tear ran down his cheek and he used the back of her hand to swipe it aside. "I don't want to. I'm not breaking up with you. I'm keeping you safe."

Then why did it feel like the opposite? "You can't."

Those words seemed to break him. On an agonized groan, he pulled her into his arms. "Don't say that."

She let him hold her, but she couldn't find the strength to lift her arms around him.

He hadn't taken back his threat to relocate her.

A knock came from the kitchen door and Kris pulled away, running a hand over his face. "What?" he demanded.

Zara poked her head inside. "Guys?" Worry was wide in her eyes, no doubt for Adam. Guilt clamped back down on Frankie's lungs. "We're ready for the ceremony. Kris, have you got the rope?"

He cleared his throat and gestured to the bag sitting on the kitchen floor, just inside the door. "It's in there."

"Bring it out," Zara said, and slipped away.

Frankie and Kris didn't move for several beats. In the small moment of her interruption, his energy had reformed. No longer broken but seething between them, fierce and loyal and snarling.

He wasn't going to let her stay.

"Would you rather keep me safe," she said under her breath, "or keep me by your side? Because you can't have both. If you choose safety and send me away, I'll never stand by your side again."

That tore fresh torment across his perfect face.

"No wet socks on this one," she said.

Then she wiped her cheeks and walked out.

15

The others seemed to sense they'd had a fight, but aside from troubled sideways glances, no one said anything. Which was useful, because the buzzing in Frankie's ears had morphed into an underwater distortion, and when the ceremony started, she couldn't make out what anyone was saying.

It didn't matter. She positioned herself on the far side of the display, ensuring everyone else blocked Kris from view, and kept her face directed at where Mark and Ava sat on silk-cushioned stools exchanging what she assumed were words of devotion.

Under different circumstances, she would have liked to listen. It seemed like a beautiful tradition. An elaborate floor spread was laid out on a pristine white sheet with gold embroidered edges, rich with items to symbolize a happy marriage: flatbread and fresh herbs for prosperity; eggs for fertility; walnuts and almonds and hazelnuts for abundance. Coins and flowers and fruit; honey and spices and books of poetry. Candles were lit, and a large mirror was set before the couple.

You need to leave Kiraly.

It was like he'd poured concrete down her throat.

I can't have you here.

Set hard in her airways.

I need you to be safe.

Tight and heavy and impassable.

She couldn't breathe.

What about what *she* wanted?

Zara was saying something. Mark and Ava poured cardamom tea and drank it from each other's cups.

Frankie almost turned away when Kris moved up the front with Tommy to fasten Mark and Ava's hands together with rope from their old ranch. Binding their past, present and futures together.

You're my future.

Kris swung a pleading glance in her direction. She dodged it —and instead ran into the excruciating likelihood that he would choose her safety. That he would prefer to ensure she *had* a future than hope she survived to have one with him.

What would she do then?

She'd told Kris she wouldn't go. But if he ordered it as her prince, as her future king, she'd have no choice but to obey.

Except—

The oath. It became a contradiction. She'd pledged to obey him—to die protecting him. She couldn't do both if his direct command for her safety went against her vow to uphold *his* safety. She'd have to decide how to best remain faithful to the crown.

Obey his command and break the most critical part of her oath as a royal guard?

Or uphold it at the risk of insubordination?

Well.

That made it easy.

Her chest still stung. That he'd suggested it at all—

threatened to pull strings that only he could pull to reposition her—that wound wouldn't heal easily.

Then it was her turn. She kept her gaze down as she stood opposite Zara, holding a lace cloth over Mark and Ava as they shared an apple and Gul sprinkled sugar over the cloth to sweeten their union. Standing there, she couldn't even bring herself to scan for Kris peripherally. She'd struggle to stay upright if she saw his tension, his hurt over their impasse.

Light-headed, she returned to her spot and stared at the rest of the ceremony.

The instant it was over, Peter appeared beside her.

"Ma'am," he said quietly. "The search warrant's come through. The authorities are on route."

Thank God. Something to do.

"I'll meet them there," she said, ignoring her unease at leaving the boys in the protection of others. She ran a capable team—the brothers would be safe. As she turned to farewell the heartbreakingly happy couple, Tommy stepped into her path.

His attention was fixed on her face. It didn't waver as she bumped against him and he clasped a steadying hand around her arm. Then he spoke, and the panic and fear and dread that had been building in her all day finally broke free.

He said, "Where's Kris?"

Kris unbuttoned the navy-blue guard's shirt as he strode down the cobbled laneway and shrugged it off. He'd waited a few blocks before glancing over his shoulder, and finding no one on his tail, figured it was safe enough to shed the disguise. The warm night air gusted lightly against his bare arms, and if he'd been in any other mood, he would have smiled.

He honestly hadn't expected that to work.

After his part in the ceremony, he'd put the rope back in his bag in the kitchen and simply hadn't returned. He'd changed into the guard's uniform he'd stashed with the rope, put his phone to the side of his face as if in heavy conversation, and walked right out the rear kitchen door into the alley. Frankie's extra security tonight had pulled in guards from outside the usual team—and focused on any incoming threat, Kris had gambled they wouldn't think to keep watch for a prince dressed in uniform slipping out into the night.

The guard wedged between the door and the dumpster hadn't even shifted position.

Kris quickened his pace, shoving the shirt back in his bag. The royal tailor had sewn it for him when Kris had claimed he wanted to prank his brothers and needed a uniform of the royal guard. Almost a month ago now. He'd actually intended to use it to shake his personal security team once they clued in to his woman-around-the-waist tactic, but then Frankie had shown up and the uniform had gone unused.

Until tonight.

Until Frankie had told him about Adam, and he'd packed it without a second thought.

Until he'd bungled his attempt to get Frankie off Adam's radar. Dismay had dismantled her trust in him right before his eyes, and he'd realized a loophole in her *would you rather* question—a shortcut that meant he didn't have to choose at all— and he'd taken it at a flying leap.

He'd find Adam himself.

He didn't have much of a plan. When did he ever? He'd knock at Zara and Adam's apartment. If Adam answered, he'd put the rope to good use and call the authorities. If he didn't, Kris would try the neighbors and ask if they'd seen anything. Good enough place to start.

Reaching Blueridge Crest, he headed toward Zara's four-story apartment building half a block up the hill. This was the only solution he had. If he could find Adam, he wouldn't have to get Frankie the hell away from here. This would all be over.

If he found Adam, he'd pound the guy's face in.

"Well, lookie here," a coarse voice said from behind him.

The hairs rose on the back of Kris's neck and he turned sharply.

"Jackpot, boys." A barrel-chested man was wandering toward him. He looked normal enough, casual clothes and an average face, if it weren't for the loathing glittering in his stare. A few more figures took shape behind him.

Jesus Christ. What had he walked into?

"Hey," Kris said, as a foot scuffed on the road behind him. He shot a glance toward Zara's apartment building as two shapes emerged from the shadows either side of the entrance.

They were moving in fast.

The man with loathing eyes said, "We have ourselves a Highness."

Kris adjusted his stance as panic bleated inside him. "What the hell is this?"

"Where's your pretty bodyguard?" someone asked from his left, and Kris's stomach turned, before a stringy man from behind said, "Hurry up. We won't have long."

Kris glanced around. Five—no, six of them, and for a moment, he saw in double. The brutal grins in front of him—and the cruelty in the eyes of the men who'd come to his ranch for Erik Jaroka's son. Not the same men, but the intent had endured.

So, this was how Tommy and Jonah had felt. Surrounded. Frightened. Knowing in their bones they were on the brink of violence. This was what Kris had done to them.

Now he'd done it to himself.

His skin was ice as he raised his hands. He might be

outnumbered, but he wasn't going down without a fight. "What do you want?"

"Don't you worry about that," the man said, and they set to work.

Frankie ran.

Hardly breathing, muscles tight as a bullet, the alley walls blurring beside her. Her skin smelled bitter with sweat, yet she was chilled to the marrow.

Kris had gone to Zara's apartment alone.

"Left," she snapped, and banked up a cut-through. Hanna, Peter, and Gul darted in behind her, nothing but huffs of air and swift footfalls at her back.

Turned out Kris had offered to check on Adam with Zara after the ceremony—so she'd told him her address to pass on to his ever-prepared guards.

He hadn't passed it on.

"Right." Frankie threw herself around a narrow splice between buildings and mounted the steps three at a time. Guards from the venue had set out in cars, but they'd take too long. The roads in this architecturally cluttered city were haphazard at best. Half the laneways were too tight for vehicles and many were linked through narrow steps and shortcuts.

Snakes and ladders. All uphill. Faster on foot.

At the top, she hauled ass down a residential street.

This bitch of a day needed to end.

Maybe it was the series of emotional blows it had dealt, or an intense love–fear for Kris that instinctively assumed the worst, or the simple fact that he'd slipped security to aim directly for the home of a man who wanted him dead, but back at the cocktail lounge, Frankie's composure had finally shattered.

She'd forgotten to pretend she wasn't terrified.

Her reaction had scared the others. Ava and Zara had rushed in with questions, but she'd barked at her team over their heads. Alarmed, Tommy and Mark had tried to follow her out, but their guards had barred their exit at her order.

Kris. The foolish, desperate, impossible man.

Adrenaline made a whip of her heartbeat, slashing and gouging inside her chest.

More steps. She hurdled over the gate to a community-garden laneway, sprinted out onto Blueridge Crest and struck straight up the hill.

Fixated on reaching Zara's building, on getting to her unguarded prince, she didn't immediately notice a black clot in the street's shadows. Thick with men, thrashing with movement. A fight. Too concentrated; too familiar.

Terror zapped her at high voltage.

Six against one.

Booted feet pulled back and pounded in. Fists dropped. Light grunts wafted downhill.

Her eyes grew hot; her breath ripped in her throat. And that was before she realized Kris's silhouette on the ground wasn't moving.

Her pace stumbled.

"I'll beat you," Hanna panted from right behind her, a challenge to reset Frankie's focus.

No, she thought, pulling farther out front. *I'm going to beat* them.

Silent, she sped so fast up the hill it felt like her burning muscles would shred clean off her legs. Her team were right on her tail.

They punctured the group like a spearhead.

Frankie first, slamming the blade of her hand into the biggest man's windpipe, and then the others cleaved through in her wake. There were startled shouts, filthy curses. These men weren't trained fighters. The reaction was sloppy, unskilled. One man started to run—Gul slide-tackled him. Another sped off downhill—and Hanna body-slammed him so he landed face-first and she pressed her foot to the back of his neck to keep him down. Peter delivered a single knockout blow, crackled his knuckles, and started in on the next.

Frankie couldn't stop her tears. Blind with fear and fury, she grabbed the remaining man's shirt and delivered several elbow jabs to his face. His nose broke with a crunch and a gush and she finished him with rapid shin strikes to the groin. He dropped right next to Kris.

Kris. His lively face unconscious. Skin messed up, torn open and swelling. Arm at a perverse angle, his white tank bloodied.

Still not moving.

And his shadow, it was a weird shape. No. Not a shadow. Blood. Slipping out from beneath him.

"Kris?" Her knees gave way and she pressed two numb fingers against his neck. Found a pulse. Her other hand shook his shoulder. "Wake up."

Distantly, she heard Hanna call out over comms for an ambulance.

A movement, and Frankie whipped around to see the big guy with the damaged windpipe staggering up the slope—saw the knife in his hand, and felt her soul break out in a fever.

Too much blood.

She didn't have her gun; she'd dressed as a guest, not a guard.

"Hanna," she managed, and pointed.

The man took four more steps before a gunshot echoed off the mountainside. He went down with a scream, clutching at his calf. The knife clattered beside him, the metal blade flashing red and blue light into her eyes. Gut and lungs heaving, Frankie turned back to Kris and vaguely noted the rest of her team pull up, tires screeching, at the same time as the authorities. They'd arrived with a search warrant and found a crime scene.

"Kris." Her shoulders heaved in panic as she bent over him. "It's me."

His head sagged to one side. He was bloodied, bruising, almost definitely broken. *I don't know what else to do,* he'd said to her. Not this. She pushed his hair off his forehead and found it clumped, warm with blood. She swallowed a helpless cry. Never this.

It was her fault. She'd given him an impossible choice. Risk her or give her up. Stupid. She knew him too well to think he'd accept either option. This time, she couldn't blame him for being impulsive or arrogant or overprotective.

He was just a boy in love with a girl, trying to make things right.

"I'm here," she whispered, and kissed his face. "I'm sorry."

There were stern shouts. Concerned questions and curses. Attackers being hoisted to their feet and manhandled into vehicles.

The dark stain was spreading. How much had he lost? Urgency surged through her. Without an outlet, a way to help, she gave in to the scream building at the back of her throat.

"Where's the fucking ambulance?" It came out half-hysterical.

"On route." Hanna sounded dazed.

"Goddamn it." This fucking city and its fucking slapdash streets. The paramedics should get out and run. Kris was their prince. They should be here already. A siren wailed faintly, too far away. They should get out and fucking *run*—

Then, she heard a different sound that tore her heart hollow.

"Kris?" Tommy. Hoarse with horror. Racing up the hill.

"Kris!" Mark's voice broke in the way bone splinters.

They collapsed to their knees on Kris's other side. Faces

stunned; ashen. They didn't ask what happened. Didn't seem to be capable of it. Mark's chin was trembling, his hands slipping uselessly under his brother's side, and Tommy's breath was hitching too fast as he hauled his shirt over his head, balled it up and jammed it into Mark's hands. He grasped Kris's torso and pressed against Mark's efforts to staunch the flow.

Frankie stared through wet eyes. Why hadn't she done that?

"Come on, man," Mark murmured, tears on his face. "Come on."

Tommy's head was down. His breath grew more rapid as his body caved under the apparent chest pain of a panic attack—but he didn't let his brother go.

"Kris." Frankie tried to take his hand, but she couldn't feel her fingers. Why hadn't he woken up? "We're here."

Tommy's shirt was growing dark. There was too much blood and the sirens weren't getting louder. The world was spinning. He wasn't moving, he wasn't moving, he wasn't—

16

Zara didn't understand.

The police wouldn't let her into her apartment. They wouldn't even let her inside the building.

"But I live up there," she said, "and I need to get water and a blanket."

It wouldn't help Kris, but this was a crisis, and action felt more important than reason.

"No one goes in or out," the police officer said firmly.

"But . . ."

She looked around as an ambulance pulled up along the clutter of security and police cars. Shock hit her anew. Usually peaceful and calm, her street was coated in violence. Kris lay unresponsive a dozen strides away, stabbed, beaten, and she recoiled a step in a flare of panic. Why would anyone want to hurt him? Frankie and his brothers knelt powerless at his side. Ava hung behind Mark, a hand over her mouth, and Philip stood unmoving beside her.

Then the advisor glanced up at Zara's apartment windows.

Guilt squirmed in her. Did he think it was her fault? If she hadn't been so worried about Adam, Kris wouldn't have come here.

Hands shaking, she pulled out her phone. Something was wrong. Adam hadn't answered her calls or texts all day, but she stepped back as she called again, following Philip's gaze to her apartment windows as if to summon him.

A chill shot down her spine.

Her main lights were on. But—it couldn't be Adam. He only used lamplight. He called the stark LED of the overhead globe tasteless. Then her chill froze over as a figure passed close by the window.

A uniformed officer.

A memory pitched forward inside her like a drunk preparing to vomit, but she shoved it back, unwilling to project that long-ago night onto this one.

Adam's phone rang out and she spun back to the officer barring her entrance. "Is someone hurt up there?" Alarm pounded in her chest. Why were police in her apartment? Kris had been attacked on the street, but had the men been inside first? Had they broken inside on a random rampage and hurt Adam? "Why are people in my apartment?"

The man regarded her without expression.

"My boyfriend's up there!" Her distress rose in a shout. "I think he might have been home sick tonight, and now there are police with him. What the hell is going on? Is he okay?"

A small frown darted his brows, and in a low voice, he said, "No one's home, ma'am, and no one's hurt."

"What?" No one's home? "Oh."

She stepped back, disoriented. So, where was Adam?

"But," she said, "why are they in my apartment?"

The man's face set. "Please wait outside, ma'am."

Her sense of wrongness grew as she sat on the lip of the curb and stared at the scene. The paramedics had worked fast. Kris was stirring on a gurney as they slid him into the back of the ambulance. Mark and Tommy both moved forward to climb in, and Zara heard a medic state that only one of them could travel with Kris.

"We *are* one," Tommy answered with such royal fury, the woman swiftly let both brothers in the back.

In the queasy contrast of flashing lights and black shadows, Frankie stared after the ambulance as it pulled away. She ran a hand roughly over her face, exhaustion seeming to press down on her like a bad hangover, and then, looking around, she met Zara's stare.

Frankie staggered a little—and Zara knew.

It was that *look*. The same Zara had been given by the responding officer on the most traumatic night of her life. The woman's face had blanched with bloodless pity at the sight of her before flattening into a reluctant mask. Just like Frankie's.

Zara was about to receive very bad news.

Features haggard, Frankie crossed the cop-strewn street to the curb.

Zara wrapped her arms tightly around her stomach, as if that had ever been able to keep her from breaking, and said, "Just tell me."

Frankie didn't answer. Her eyes were as hollow as ghosts.

"Where's Adam?"

Kris was out of surgery by the time Frankie dragged herself into the hospital. Her adrenaline was long gone, leaving her shaky and sick, but she chugged a shitty hospital vending-machine coffee and carried several bags of corn chips through the ward toward Kris's private room.

Guards were positioned at every turn.

The police had informed her of the attackers' story before she'd left the scene. They were the remaining members of the anarchist group who hadn't been involved in palace renovations. They'd received texts from Adam earlier in the day with instructions to keep an eye on his apartment. They were to leave Zara alone, but if anyone else came snooping, they had to report back to him. Beating up a royal had not been part of the plan, but Kris had strolled unprotected within range of anarchist extremists who'd just had a member smoked out of the nest. As far as they were concerned, the universe had slid them a freebie.

The police had also informed her that although their apartment search hadn't turned up any evidence, it seemed that Adam had disappeared along with his valuable possessions. He wasn't missing—he'd gone to ground.

Ava had called while Frankie was en route to the hospital. Kris had a concussion, but the scans showed no signs of internal bleeding, in his head or elsewhere. Thankfully, the knife hadn't entered his abdominal cavity to reach his organs, though the angle of the cut meant the blade had sliced through a lot of muscle. He had stitches, two fractured ribs, a broken arm, and more bruises than clear skin.

Frankie halted in the hospital room doorway.

Her inhale was sharp and sensitive, and everyone turned to look at her. Mark and Tommy from where they sat on either side of the bed, Ava from where she reclined in a chair against the wall with Darius sleeping on her lap, and Philip from his position by the window. The brothers' features were shuttered. The air in the room was tense.

Kris was okay.

He just didn't *look* okay.

"Is he allowed to be sleeping?" Frankie didn't move inside.

She'd asked Philip to explain Adam's connection to the balcony collapse to Kris's brothers and Ava—omitting any connections to Tommy's bashing—while she'd been busy reducing Zara to the fetus position right there in the gutter.

Her lungs still felt wet with grief.

"Doctor's orders," Mark said, because he was too decent to ignore her despite the huge truth that she'd kept from them. "He was able to hold a conversation after surgery, and his pupils looked good. Sleep will help him heal."

"Okay." To stop herself passing out, Frankie opened a packet of chips and started eating.

"He asked where you were," Ava said quietly. Then after a pause, she asked, "How is Zara?"

"Destroyed."

The princess shifted, running a hand over her son's hair. "Is she alone?"

Frankie shook her head and jammed more chips into her mouth. "I had Gul take her to the palace and set her up in a guest suite for as long as she needs. He'll stay with her overnight."

"Thank you."

"I'm afraid you're going to have to do the same thing," Frankie said. "Just for now."

Mark and Ava exchanged a grim glance. Drawing the curl of Darius's sleeping body closer to her, Ava said, "We understand."

The following silence was broken by Frankie's crunching.

She was well into her second packet when Tommy spoke. "Why didn't you tell us?" He refused to look at her. His broad shoulders were stiff, torso firmly facing Kris. One hand clutched the covers on the bed beside his brother's leg.

"Until this morning, we had no idea how the threads came together," she said. "Once we identified Adam, the plan was to tell you all tomorrow. This evening was meant to be a celebration and we didn't want to taint it."

Mark's bleak glance basically said *backfire*.

"And obviously, we didn't want to cause you unnecessary stress."

Tommy's eyes squeezed shut, his lip curling. Then he was standing, gesturing to the chair, and muttering, "You sit down. I need a minute."

He strode from the room without another word, and Frankie leaned back in the doorway, watching his night guards peel off the corridor wall and follow at a distance.

"We need to discuss our communications strategy." Philip looked worn to the bone. "Rumors will fly when Kristof suddenly stops appearing in public."

"Not tonight, Philip." Mark spoke with gentle resolve. "I'll resume all of the king's duties for the next couple of days. We can talk about the rest once he's back at the palace."

"Of course," Philip said, inclining his head.

"Philip," Frankie said. "Go home. Sleep. Be wild—don't set your alarm."

As the royal advisor passed her in the doorway, she reached out and gave his hand a long squeeze.

"He's disappeared," he whispered in dismay.

She squeezed tighter. "The authorities have issued a nationwide manhunt. We'll get him."

After a moment, he squeezed back. "Thank you."

She finished the second packet of chips before daring herself to take Tommy's chair. She'd been able to disconnect a little from the doorway, but as she sat beside Kris, she couldn't ignore the injuries that made a mockery of his muscled body.

Strong or not, six against one were cruel odds.

As she took his scuffed, scabbed hand in hers—evidence he'd fought back—she resolved to a new security measure. This royal family would no longer rely exclusively on guards. She'd train them all in self-defense.

"I'm not leaving you," she murmured, and leaned forward to

press her lips to the back of his hand. The bed was soft around her face, and the next thing she knew, his fingers were wiggling a little, waking her up.

"Hey." Kris spoke on a groan.

She straightened, confused.

Tommy was sitting opposite her. Mark, Ava, and Darius were gone.

"Hey," Frankie and Tommy said together.

Kris looked between them without moving his head, his gaze groggy from the painkillers. "Good night so far?"

"Piss off," Tommy murmured with a tiny smile.

Frankie held his hand a little too hard. "Don't try to be cute."

"You look awful," he said to her.

She arched a brow. "Guess who needs a mirror?"

He started to smile, then winced with a pained hiss. His attention slid to his brother. "You okay?"

Tommy was pale. "Better than you."

Kris closed his eyes, lines gathering on his brow. "I hate that you've been through something like this. I'm sorry if this has made you relive it."

Swallowing, Tommy didn't answer.

"We can bond," Kris said. "Now I know how it feels."

Tommy ran a hand over his mouth. "I never wanted you to know how it felt."

Frankie looked down at where she held Kris's hand, a lump tightening her throat.

"Frankie." Kris's voice was little more than a rough scrape. "Are you angry with me?"

"No." She fought back a wave of emotion. "I mean, I'll beat the hell out of you later for scaring me like that. But I'm not angry."

"Sounds fair." He was quiet for a while. "My face feels twice its usual size. I don't think I can be seen for a while."

Frankie and Tommy both nodded.

"And did you hear my ribs are fractured?"

More nods.

Kris's blue gaze found hers. "You won't be able to hug me."

He'd meant it as a joke, but for some reason, it seemed like the most devastating news she'd ever received. Her eyes filled and she gasped to hold back a sob.

"Oh, hey," he murmured, blinking slowly. "Just for a few weeks."

She sniffled. "That's *ages*."

"Naaaah," he said, the vowel drawn out on a sigh. His eyelids sagged shut. "You should both go home."

She clutched his hand tighter. "Only when you can come with me."

"I'm not leaving," Tommy muttered.

He groaned in groggy protest. "You're both just going to watch me sleep?"

"Yes," they answered, and started doing exactly that when his next breath took him under.

17

Frankie hardly left his side.

Kris would wake and feel her hand in his, or hear her talking on the phone by the window, or open his eyes to find her sleeping in the armchair she'd dragged to his bedside. She ate hospital café food, showered in his patient bathroom, and climbed up the walls in agitation. Every time he told her to go, that he'd be fine, she gave him the same answer.

"I'm not leaving you. I'm never leaving you."

Despite knowing why she kept saying it, it was pretty damn nice to hear.

He hurt a lot; slept a lot. At one point he woke to Hanna exclaiming, "I beat you! Holy cow, I actually beat you!"

"It's snap, Johansson. Not hand-to-hand combat."

"Not the way you play," his guard had argued.

After three days, he was discharged under the condition of bed rest. Frankie's team secreted him out of the hospital via a staff-only route late that night, and eased him into a waiting car that drove as smoothly as water on glass to the palace entrance. To his shame, he was carried up the flights of stairs to his suite, but he forgot all about it as soon as he was lying in his soft, palatial-sized bed.

Frankie kissed him gently, and curled up close to him.

"I love you," she murmured.

"I never doubted it," he said. "Never."

It was midmorning the following day when he awoke to find his family passing time in his bedroom. Mark and Philip were going through paperwork, Tommy was reading, Ava was drawing with Darius, and Frankie was pacing like a cat in a cage.

Philip didn't waste any time once he noticed Kris was awake.

"We need to discuss our strategy," he said, and everyone stilled to listen. "Kristof's broken arm and fractured ribs will take roughly six weeks to heal, though the doctors believe he'll be able to tolerate small appearances in as little as four weeks. His face, of course, won't be suitable for public viewing for at least a fortnight and we have our Kicking It program launch announcement in two days."

"Has his face ever been suitable for public viewing?" Frankie asked.

Philip looked confused when Kris's brothers both snickered, as if wanting to say, *but you all have the same face.*

"Our issue is keeping news of the attack contained," the advisor continued with a frown. "Obviously, it would look poor on the global stage for a member of our royal family to be attacked in our streets. It could convey far greater tension between the monarchy and our people than this situation warrants. In addition to his royal appearances, my concern is Kristof's habit of socializing in Kira City. The people will notice his absence." He paused and gestured out the window. "A possible solution is to say that Kristof is abroad."

"That could work," Kris said, feeling muzzy.

Mark nodded at him, then exchanged a somber glance with Ava. "I'll resume the king's duties in the meantime."

"The other thing to consider," Philip said, "is that a six-week recovery will bring us two weeks from the coronation."

"These injuries aren't forever." Kris closed his eyes as his side throbbed. God above, this stab wound was a bastard. "I'll still do that."

Philip sounded affronted. "You'll still do what?"

"The coronation."

"One doesn't *do* a coronation—"

"About that," Tommy interrupted quietly.

The room fell silent—and Kris almost drifted back to sleep. He jolted, opening his eyes when Frankie tapped him lightly and held out a glass of water and painkillers. He nodded and started the drawn-out shift into sitting up. Putting the glass and tablets aside, she crawled across the bed to his other side and slid a pillow under his back.

"I love you," he murmured, and she smiled and kissed his bruised cheek.

"Yes, Tomas?" Philip said.

Kris returned his attention to the conversation as his brother stood.

Tommy was sweating. His jaw was tight. Kris had the fleeting fear he was about to admit that he couldn't handle royal life anymore, that he was going to return home to Sage Haven and wouldn't be here for the coronation. That was until Tommy said—

"I'd like to be king."

The words settled into a stunned silence.

No one spoke.

No one even moved, until—

"You'd what?" Philip asked faintly.

"You'd *what?*" Kris demanded, sitting up straight and catching a cry of pain behind his teeth as his stitches pulled and his ribs screamed.

Mark stood to face Tommy, concern tight in his stance. "What do you mean, Tom?"

Tommy held himself perfectly still. No jiggling, no avoiding eye contact as he stared back at Mark. "I want to do it."

"No way," Kris said, and started to say, "Over my dead—" until Frankie slid a hand over his mouth and said, "Shh."

Tommy's attention slid to him, and Kris felt pain in his chest that had nothing to do with his injuries. "I'm next in line, Kris."

With Frankie's hand firmly in place, Kris shook his head.

"I know you think it'll be too much for me." Tommy's gaze was steady, but Kris could see apprehension in his reserved gaze. "You might be right. But you have to recover. And Mark shouldn't have to step back into a role he's not ultimately going to fill. Kris, you only offered to ascend because you'd do anything for Mark and me—not because you actually want to do it."

Kris shook his head again, eyes pleading. *You don't have to do this.*

But Tommy said, "I *want* to be king."

Denial surged inside Kris, and he said a muffled, "Why?" against Frankie's hand.

Kris had been in a fight—that was all. A few injuries shouldn't cause his brother to cut himself open in an attempt to balance the scales. Tommy didn't owe him this.

"You told me you're terrified of being king," Tommy said carefully, and Mark jerked around to look at Kris. "And you were going to do it anyway."

Heartsore, Kris just shook his head again.

"The thing is," his brother continued, "I'm not terrified of being king. I'm terrified of crowds, and meeting new people, and social interactions. But not ruling."

Frankie and Philip were exchanging a long look.

"Tommy," Frankie said, removing her hand from Kris's mouth and shifting onto her knees. Kris prayed she was going to

349

talk his brother out of it. "I have to remind you about Adam. If you do this, you'll make yourself even more of a target." She stared at him—and even though he shifted his stance, he stared back. "You're smart and unreadable and no one really knows you. Mark says he's never mentioned your anxiety to Adam. You're an unknown quantity. He'll want to weigh you up, but I believe he'll try to take you down." She paused, angling her head. "Until we've caught him, it's a high-risk position, even with the guards."

"I understand," he answered.

Silence crept through the room again as everyone shared glances. Mark looked at Kris as they both seemed to realize that Kris had no power to deny Tommy's claim. His brother was the next in line. The crown was his to take.

Every one of Kris's injuries seemed to intensify in protest.

"I'll help you," Ava said softly. "Facing crowds as royalty can be like wearing a mask. Perhaps hiding behind a persona could help your anxiety."

Tommy nodded.

"Anything you need," Frankie said, "and security has got your back."

"We can attend events together," Mark said, "so that you become less of a novelty in public. Cause less fuss."

"Okay." Tommy was starting to sound breathless.

Philip spoke next. "It would be sensible to approach this with the same arrangement we had with Kristof. While he is recovering, you can take on most of the king's duties. Markus will still cover some so as not to raise suspicion. Markus, you're going to need a haircut. We will not inform anyone outside of this room except for the inner circle of the royal guard. If you find the daily interactions and public appearances too overwhelming, we will proceed with our plan for Kristof to ascend as king."

This time Tommy swallowed hard before saying, "Okay."

Then everyone looked at Kris.

"Tom," he said, and his brother's name came out strangled. "I'll be okay."

"The problem is, Kris, if I don't at least try to do this," Tommy said, forehead gleaming in sweat, "*I* won't be."

And that was it.

Every possible argument faded, because all he wanted was for his brother to be okay.

"Alright," he said in defeat.

Frankie laced her fingers through his on the covers and he clamped down tightly.

"In that case . . ." Philip looked dazed. ". . . your first appearance will be to launch the new mental health program the day after tomorrow."

Tommy hesitated for a beat. "Okay."

"Shall we go discuss the details?"

Tommy inclined his head and, with a backward glance at Kris, followed the advisor from the room.

"This isn't happening." Kris laid a hand over his eyes.

"We'll be right here with him." Mark crossed the room, and when Kris looked up again, his brother was standing by his bedside, withdrawing a rectangular object from the back waistband of his jeans, covered in navy-blue velvet. He winked as he tucked it into Kris's hand. "Now take your mind off it."

Frankie stared at the box in Kris's hands.

It was too big for a ring—but something about Mark's knowing smile and the look of adoration Kris slid her betrayed she wasn't necessarily in the clear. Her suspicion spiked when Ava hustled Mark and Darius from the bedroom as if Frankie and Kris needed privacy.

When the door closed, Frankie tugged her hand from his and crossed her arms. "What's that?"

"It's for you."

Her stomach bundled up into a nerve cluster. "Why does it look like a jewelry box?"

"Hey," he said with a grin. "Give a man a minute."

"Don't," she said, but hardly knew why. She *wanted* this—whatever it was. "Go on."

"Frankie." He paused, and the amusement faded from his wild blue eyes. "I'm sorry for hurting you the other night."

She nodded, gaze darting to the box. "It's okay."

"It's not okay. Look at me."

Complying, she found his expression serious, his gaze sincere.

"I don't know how to be in love with you," he said. "It's so early. I'm blinded by it. I don't know how to fight it yet. I'm like—" He broke off, eyes scanning the bed as if the right description was hiding in the sheets. "Like a werewolf turned for the first time. The full moon is so bright, my senses are flooded by it. My *sense* is flooded. I love you. I want to keep you safe and that's such a big feeling, it overwhelms me. I don't know how to temper it or control it. And so, I ended up saying something stupid and doing something even stupider."

"No kidding." But she uncrossed her arms.

"I never want to hurt you again," he said. "Never want to speak to you like that, because I can't forget the fear I put in your eyes when I threatened to order you to do something against your will."

"That was a bit shit," she admitted, lowering her head. "But it's not just you."

Neither of them knew how to navigate this bright, overwhelming world of fierce feelings.

"I don't know how to accept feeling protected," she said.

Heat rushed to her face and she doubted she'd ever get used to speaking intimately, but she'd flush and shrivel and do it anyway —for him. "Before you, no one had ever wanted to protect me. Accepting it makes me feel . . . vulnerable. Like I'm handing over control. Every time you've tried to do it, I've knocked you back, telling myself that it was because you were my prince and that your life was more valuable than mine."

Kris jerked a little at her words, and then lifted a hand to his ribs with a wince.

"But I didn't stay in Sage Haven because I was motivated by loyalty to the crown. I stayed because I'd fallen for you, and if anything happened to you, I honestly didn't think I could survive."

The pain cleared off his face as that won her a one-sided smile.

"I've always been driven by the urge to protect you, Kris. Every step I've taken, every decision I've made. I'd do anything for you. I swore on my life for you."

"Frankie," he said, and took her hand. "It's my turn to take an oath."

Her breath stilled.

"Ready?" His smile was nervous.

Her heartbeat was loud in her ears as she nodded.

"I, Royal Highness Prince Kristof Lucas Jaroka, do swear that I will faithfully obey and bear true devotion to my best friend, lover, and wife, Francesca Grace Cowan; that I will protect and defend her against all enemies; that I will honor, support and encourage her every day of our shared lives; and that with my life and my death, my body, heart and soul will remain only hers, forever."

Frankie didn't bother to wipe the tears from her face.

"You said wife," she said, her voice breaking.

"I said wife." And he let go of her hand to offer her the velvet-covered box.

Trembling, she opened the case.

A tiara. Not dainty or diamond-encrusted, but made bold and strong with her old brass knuckles fixed at the center. They'd been bent to curve with the tiara's base, the rings slimmed down and reshaped into ovals with an intricate filigree. Simple curls of brass had been added at the peak and tapered into a small pattern around the circular band, disguising the shape of the knuckles.

"Kris," she breathed. The entire piece was home to a cache of lustrous emeralds.

"I had it made by the royal jeweler," he said, reaching in and picking it up. "I wanted the green to match your eyes."

She didn't take it from him; wasn't sure she could. "Those emeralds must be worth a fortune."

"They are," he agreed, darting a sparkling glance at her. "And that's your future with me, Frankie. The life we'll live together. But we're not going to forget the life you've already lived. If the crown demands that we erase your past—then we'll display that past in the middle of your goddamn crown."

"Tiara," she corrected faintly.

Her breath felt heavy, so full of hope.

"No." He gestured to the band. "Tiaras are semicircle. This goes all the way around. I was very specific about my symbolism."

Shakily, she touched it with the tip of her index finger.

"Frankie. I want to spend my life with you. Raise a family with you. Will you do me the honor of wearing this crown?" She scarcely saw his bruised, battered face for the love shining in his eyes. "Will you be my best friend, my lover, and my wife?"

And she said, "Yes."

Grinning so hard she vaguely worried he'd split open his lip, he set it gently on her head. It settled with appropriate weight for all it signified, a concealed weapon adorned in jewels.

She was his best friend, lover, and wife.

His princess and protector.

"You're worth everything to me," he said, and when she kissed him, she finally believed that was true.

THE KING'S COWBOY

Tommy and Jonah's story is coming mid-2021.

Don't miss the third instalment of Cowboy Princes!

Tommy is long overdue his happily ever after—and our broken brother will get everything he needs and more in The King's Cowboy.

Visit my website madelineash.net for updates.

Madeline Ash xx

ACKNOWLEDGMENTS

I'm guilty of living in my own head much of the time. My characters feel like real people—and I'm constantly checking in on them. This results in half-present conversations, dinner table brainstorming, and middle-of-the-night notebook writing, but my partner Dom never complains and I'm eternally thankful.

Thank you to my writing group, Louise, Janis and Sandy for your critiques. Mum and Grace for your considered feedback. Special thanks to Shelagh Merlin for beta reading. Lauren Clarke and Anna Bishop, thank you for your world class edits.

To the Madeline Ash Sweeties, my advance review team, and to my readers, old and new, thank you for following this unlikely tale of three cowboy princes.

I would also like to respectfully acknowledge the Boon Wurrung people of the Kulin Nation, who have traditional connections to the land where I live and wrote this book.

One more to go . . . xx

ALSO BY MADELINE ASH

Rags to Riches series

The Playboy (#1)

Alexia needs to become sexually confident for an upcoming acting role and playboy Parker agrees to teach her. Now all they have to do is let each other go.

Her Secret Prince (#2)

2016 RITA Award finalist

As a teenager, Dee had her heart broken by Jed. Years later, he's back in her life—but will a surprising royal discovery ruin their second chance together?

You For Christmas (#3)

2016 RUBY Award finalist

Black sheep Regan arrives on Felix's doorstep to take up the debt he owes her. Will they act on their feelings this Christmas or are their pasts too painful to bear?

Breaking Good (#4)

2017 RITA Award finalist

2017 RUBY Award winner

Years after spending a night with bad boy Ethan, Stevie runs into him again. She's shocked to discover that he's alive—and she has to tell him he has a son...

Morgan Sisters series

The Wedding Obsession (#1)

2019 RUBY Award finalist

After life-changing surgery, Emmie is overwhelmed by the urge to marry. Despite his love for her, her best friend Brandon struggles to believe her proposals—until a shocking revelation changes everything.

His Billionaire Bride (#2)

Business investor Carrie is guarded for good reason, while artist Edwin —rejected by his family—will only settle for commitment. Their intense chemistry builds them so high she's blinded to the fall. And the only way out is to break both their hearts.

ABOUT MADELINE ASH

Madeline Ash is an Australian contemporary romance author and two-time RITA Award finalist. She has won Australia's Romantic Book of the Year award (RUBY). She delves deep into the hearts and minds of her characters, creating flawed and compassionate leads—who are always rewarded with a happy ending.

madelineash.net

Printed in Great Britain
by Amazon

41324635R00212